Praise for John Brady's
MATT MINOGUE series:

The Going Rate

"As always, Brady delivers an INTELLIGENT, SKILLFULLY CRAFTED NOVEL, with a wonderful, gritty urban setting. *The Going Rate* is a luxurious book, full of fascinating characters and wonderful insights into the new Ireland." – GLOBE AND MAIL

"The Celtic boom may have busted but it has left behind the crime that comes with prosperity. There are no happy endings with John Brady, no punches pulled. There is justice, and heartbreak, and the knowledge that the streets will be just as dirty and dangerous tomorrow, though tonight you can set that aside and enjoy friends." – NATIONAL POST

"*THE GOING RATE* IS JOHN BRADY'S BEST THRILLER YET . . . scenes so well composed that one is tempted to re-read them. Brady has reached new heights." – THE HALIFAX CHRONICLE-HERALD

"One of Brady's best gifts, besides fast, tight plotting, lies in dialogue that reflects not only idiom and wit, but the intricacies of relationaships." – THE LONDON FREE PRESS

Islandbridge ★ ★ GLOBE AND MAIL TOP 100 ★ ★

SHORTLISTED FOR THE 2006 DASHIELL HAMMETT AWARD

A GLOBE AND MAIL BEST BOOK OF THE YEAR

"Particularly powerful stuff . . . genius." – TORONTO STAR

Wonderland ★ ★ GLOBE AND MAIL TOP 100 ★ ★

"IF THERE ARE AUTHORS BETTER THAN JOHN BRADY at chronicling the events of modern Ireland, I HAVEN'T YET READ THEM . . . Brady's best so far." – GLOBE AND MAIL

"ANOTHER SUPERB NOVEL BY A WRITER OF INTERNATIONAL STATURE." – TORONTO STAR

"BRADY'S BEST: informed, subtle and intelligent, with Minogue revealing a hitherto unseen depth of soul, humour and emotion." – THE TIMES UK

A Carra King ★ ★ GLOBE AND MAIL TOP 100 ★ ★

"DENSE AND MULTILAYERED . . . a treasure of a crime novel." – TORONTO STAR

"Brady has a great eye for the telling detail . . . and a lovely slow pace of storytelling. There's much talk and thought about events and you can't read this book at warp speed. Instead, save it to savour." – GLOBE AND MAIL

All Souls

"As lyrical and elegantly styled as the last three . . . A FIRST-RATE STORY WITH MARVELLOUS CHARACTERS . . . Another masterful tale from a superior author." – GLOBE AND MAIL

"Nothing gets in the way of pace, narrative thrust or intricate storytelling." – IRISH TIMES

"A KNOCKOUT." – KIRKUS REVIEWS

Kaddish in Dublin

"MATT MINOGUE, THE MAGNETIC CENTRE OF THIS SUPERB SERIES . . . and Brady's tone of battered lyricism are the music which keep drawing us back to this haunting series." – NEW YORK TIMES

"Culchie Colombo with a liberal and urbane heart . . . like all the best detective stories it casts its net widely over its setting . . . [Minogue is] a character who should run and run." – IRISH TIMES

Unholy Ground

"RIVETING . . . The suspense builds to barely bearable intensity . . . crackles with pungent Irish idiom and its vignettes of the country's everyday life." – TORONTO STAR

"Excellent Sergeant Matt Minogue . . . MARVELLOUS DIALOGUE, as nearly surreal as a Magritte postcard the sergeant likes, and a twisting treacherous tale." – SUNDAY TIMES

A Stone of the Heart

"Towers above the mystery category as AN ELOQUENT, COMPELLING NOVEL . . . a tragic drama involving many characters, each so skillfully realized that one virtually sees and hears them in this extraordinary novel . . ." – PUBLISHERS WEEKLY

"A MASTERFULLY CRAFTED WORK of plot, atmosphere and especially characterization . . . Minogue, thoughtful, clear-eyed and perhaps too sensitive . . . is a full-blooded character built for the long haul of a series . . ." – MACLEAN'S

The Good Life

"Brilliant Craftsmanship." – LIBRARY JOURNAL

"Brady's dead-on ear for dialogue and his knack for creating instantly engaging characters keep the pages flipping . . . one line of prose leads inexorably, compulsively to the next . . ." – QUILL & QUIRE

"Brady, like Chandler, has a poet's eye for place . . . (he) is emerging as one of the supreme storytellers of Canadian crime fiction."
– GLOBE AND MAIL

Also by John Brady

Matt Minogue Series
The Going Rate
Islandbridge
Wonderland
A Carra King
All Souls
Kaddish in Dublin
Unholy Ground
A Stone of the Heart
The Good Life

Other Novels
Poacher's Road

www.johnbradysbooks.com
www.mcarthur-co.com

JOHN BRADY

The Coast Road

A MATT MINOGUE MYSTERY

McArthur & Company
Toronto

First published in Canada in 2010 by
McArthur & Company
322 King Street West, Suite 402
Toronto, Ontario
M5V 1J2
www.mcarthur-co.com

Library and Archives Canada Cataloguing in Publication

Brady, John, 1955–
          The coast road : a Matt Minogue mystery / John Brady.

ISBN 978-1-55278-805-9

          I. Title.

PS8553.R245H37 2010   C813'.54   C2009-904287-8

The publisher would like to acknowledge the financial support of the
Government of Canada through the Canada Book Fund and the Canada
Council for our publishing activities. The publisher further wishes to
acknowledge the financial support of the Ontario Arts Council and the
OMDC for our publishing program.

Design and composition by Szol Design
Printed in Canada by Webcom

10 9 8 7 6 5 4 3 2 1

*For Anton and Elfriede, who have
come so far and done so much.*

And as always, for Hanna

"Every day miracles dwindle and marvels go away."
–Baal Shem Tov

Dalkey – 'Isle of thorns' and a forgotten saint

"…Turning the corner in the centre the village, one enters upon a narrow road lined on both sides with high walls. But within a half statute mile, one is returned to the coast road, for before us lies the small harbour of Coliemore. As modest and snug as this harbour may present itself, this appearance is sure to deceive, for there is much to contemplate. Known in earlier times as Dalkey Harbour, this port was until the 1600s nothing less than the maritime port for the city of Dublin six miles to the north, then an estuarine settlement whose waters were choked with silt. Sitting on a cape, and providentially girded by its geology, this tiny harbour saw passing through it kings and their armies, cargo and goods of every kind, travelers and emigrants, and as the wayside poets recite, 'the pilgrim and the pirate.'

"The view across the sound is of Dalkey Island, that very place that gave the area its name from the Old Irish *Delg Inis*, 'the island of thorns.' Surveying this grassy islet, the eye is drawn to the ruin of an ancient church, and to the south of it, a Martello tower. Many centuries before Napoleon sought to make cause with the Irish against his foe, this small but strategic isle had been a redoubt from which the Vikings preyed on the coast and struck terror far and wide. It is from before these times however that this church, of which we see only the walls, was erected, dedicated to a local saint, Saint Begnet.

"Little or nothing is known of Begnet. Some contend that she cannot be separated from earlier peoples, those 'shadowy presences, faintly glimpsed at twilight' who lived here in the times of the Druids, and to whose enigmatic presence stone edifices across the area bear silent witness. The Ireland of those times was remote from Roman authority, and its many female saints attest to a native church with roots firmly in local custom. One such saint was Begnet, and born the daughter of a notable in early Christian Ireland, this young woman of great spirit and startling beauty was much sought after in marriage. Her father thus arranged a match for her with a son of the King of Norway. Yet unbeknownst to him, she had taken vows to dedicate her life to God, and thus refused marriage. Angered by this, her father took against her, only relenting when she revealed to him how her vocation had come to her as a child. She had been visited by an angel, and as proof she displayed a bracelet that the angel had given her to symbolize her fidelity.

"Taking only that bracelet with her, Begnet became one of the first who sought 'the green exile' for that divine purpose. She and her successors would usher in what would become known as Ireland's Golden Age, those centuries when its monks left in their thousands, bearing the light of learning back to a darkened continent. The only account that the author has been able to discover, sees Begnet completing her earthly duties as a renowned abbess in Britain. There are two accounts of Begnet's bracelet as a relic or an object of veneration and miracles in later times, and of its use as a proof of truthful statements."

– J.G. Sadlier, *Walking Ireland's Coasts*, 1883

Chapter 1

By midday of that soggy June Tuesday that was to turn his life upside down, Detective Garda Thomas Malone was fighting off impatience. That battle wasn't going well. He had about six minutes yet before he'd see the impossible, a man trying to fly.

Slouched next to him in the rear of the unmarked Mondeo was Keaveney, another Drugs Central veteran. Keaveney was okay company most of the time. He had a sharp, dry answer for almost everything. In the three years since Malone had moved to Central, Keaveney had become his most frequent partner.

"Christ Almighty."

It was Buckley, from the passenger seat. His words came in a rueful murmur.

"It's rounding up animals we should be doing, lads. Two by two, and all that?"

Buckley had been a Sergeant for several months now. He had been posted to the Drugs Unit office in Store Street Garda station the day of his promotion. But not even Flynn, the driver, and by far the most junior in the car, felt he should offer Buckley anything for his wit. Things were bad enough, on the job and off. And it had all been said anyway, hadn't it? Dire summer so far. The economy in meltdown. Gang crime out-of-control. Pay cuts on the way for certain.

Blah blah blah.

Malone's earpiece came to life again. It was Doyle, one of

the detectives in the runner car: Kelly and the Chinaman had hit the road again.

Buckley leaned around the headrest.

"Well, lads? Praise the *Lord*. Well worth the wait, I say."

Malone shifted and pulled his new vest to the side and down a little. Somehow he had managed to find a way to strap in his Glock so that the grip was poking him inside his upper arm. That had never happened before. What the hell had been so wrong with the vest he had used before, the one that fit?

"Kelly'll have to change his name after this," Keaveney said. Buckley eyed him in the mirror.

"Walking into this?" Keaveney explained. "'Artane Kelly' is going to be history after this. It's going to have to be 'No-Brain Kelly.'"

"He's a crackhead," said Buckley. "What do you expect?"

"My point is, Kelly was never a rocket surgeon. Was he, Tommy?"

"He'll do," Malone said. "It's him they sent."

Keaveney's sigh was a show of resignation.

"Can't argue with that. You're the resident expert on him."

Buckley cleared his throat, and pretended the mirror needed adjusting. The suspension on the Mondeo squeaked as he stretched, and then settled again. His eyes found Malone.

"No love lost there between you and Kelly," he said. "Is there, Tommy?"

Malone shrugged. He focused again on a patch of graffiti. Not a single tag here in the lane made any sense to him.

"Okay lads," Buckley said. He rubbed his hands together. "Just a reminder. We want actual entry into this lockup. We want them standing in there, a key in their hands – that's possession. And we want the both of them going in. The whole shebang – conspiracy, possession. Are we right?"

"Grand," said Keaveney, and opened his door. He followed Malone over to one of the doorways, where the shutters had buckled. He watched him open and close the Velcro on his vest.

"Mister Dramatic there."

Malone squinted at him.

"Not you," said Keaveney. He flicked a glance toward the car. "Boss-man."

Buckley's door was still open. He had more redundant instructions for Flynn.

"Kelly's a big nothing," Keaveney went on. "Cheese on the mousetrap. But Mr. Whoflungdung, mystery man, well he's going to be an interesting fish."

Malone zipped up his jacket a third of the way. He tested it then as he always did, reaching in once quickly, and then a second time. His knuckles slid down the nylon and his hand closed smoothly on the grip. His thumb found the quick-release right away.

"For sure he's Triad. Sniffing around for years, haven't they?"

Malone shrugged. Keaveney scraped something from his shoe.

"Well they're a bit late to the party then," he said. "The Tiger's passed out. In a coma. On life support? Anyway, the competition got here first. Nigerians, Ukrainians, Moldovans, Bulgarians – am I missing any?"

"Romanians. Russians. Bylorussians. Balbriggan men even, I hear."

"Ah," said Keaveney, a smile flickering around his mouth. "A man in the know. But you keep things to yourself, don't you? All the goods from your old pal there, what's his name, Mannion, over in the glamour end there."

"Minogue. Like you didn't know."

Moments passed.

"Tell you what," said Keaveney then. "Let's get ahead of the game. You ready? Fire off a few bits of Chinese at him, this Chinaman. Just to see what he does. The look on his face...? How about it?"

"Ease off, will you."

"'Ease off?' What 'ease off' are you talking about?"

Malone made a quick study of his colleague's expression. Keaveney had never said anything directly about Malone's girl-friend, Sonia, eldest of an immigrant family from Macau. The

3

nearest he came was to state his keen preference for Chinese food.

"Because it's raining, is why," Malone said. "Rain. June? Because the country's up the creek. But mainly because I have six frigging days' leave for the rest of the year. That kind of 'ease off.'"

"Just a few Chinese words. Like, I don't know – how do you say *Céad Míle Fáilte* in Chinese? No, wait. Triad – how do you say Triad? Or no, how about: *Why are you hanging around with a scumbag like Artane Kelly?*"

Malone gave him a hard look.

"And ease off because you're giving me a headache," he said.

Keaveney snorted quietly, and he looked away. Buckley stepped out of the car.

They followed him down to the mouth of the laneway. Where Kelly and Chan were supposedly heading was the third unit in a row of battered, roll-up doorways. The whole place here had been jerry-built, a decade before the Boom. Signs of neglect were plain: dark and layered oil stains, broken glass shoved against walls of fraying brickwork, weeds amongst the rubbish. Malone found a spot by an oil drum that was overflowing with rusting pieces of engine transmissions.

He paused then to catch the radio traffic. The Audi that Kelly was piloting was turning in off the road.

"A minute or so," Buckley called out.

"What's the Chinaman's name again?" Keaveney asked. "I forgot already."

"Chan."

"Charlie Chan, like?"

"Ask him when you get a chance."

"Is Chan like Smith or Murphy for the Chinese, is it?"

"How would I know?"

A minute passed. A drain was gurgling, but Malone couldn't see where it was. The hush of traffic on the M-50 hung in the air, but over it he still heard the gentle, whimsical patter the rain, one that could not be trusted. He tested his lapel mike, turning it until it hissed and then dialing it back.

"Heard the one about the Chinese fella visiting Dublin? They interview him, right? 'So what do you make of these Irish people?'"

"That's an old one," Malone said. Keaveney turned to Buckley instead.

"How long is Kelly out on parole? A month even? He's a goner here then: right back in, five to seven years. You think he knows that?"

It was Buckley who answered.

"I imagine he's aware of it. In some dim and dark recess of his mind."

"What's left of it," said Keaveney, with a snort. "What do you say, Tommy?"

"I say, let's talk about the weather. That's what I say."

The rain that was working its way down in tickling lines over Malone's forehead had gathered in his eyebrows. Malone would long remember that minute or so that he had kept his eye on the laneway. He would recall feeling Keaveney's mocking eyes on him, but also feeling a little pleased with himself that he was able to ignore Keaveney.

More than one Ombudsman investigator would ask Garda Malone his thoughts as the operation proceeded then, his feelings too. Malone would ascribe this line of questioning to Keaveney's testimony.

Did you experience anger that morning, Garda Malone? You had a history with Mr. Kelly for some time? Concerning your deceased brother? You were aware that Mr. Kelly had become heavily involved in heroin trafficking?

It was Doyle on the radio again. Kelly and Chan were approaching the junction. That was the only kiss-off point where the runner car would have to go by. Kelly and Chan would be out of sight for five seconds or more.

While he waited, Buckley waved the handset around in slow, small arcs. The glance from Keaveney made Malone wonder if Keaveney actually wanted the situation to blow up on Buckley. But then Keaveney's expression changed. Malone had heard it too: car wheels crashing through a puddle. Doyle radioed that they had put the block on.

Buckley looked relieved. He almost smiled. He began to tap his fingers on his vest. It was that accordion-playing gesture that had become so common amongst the Guards that it was a staple of wry humour. Then he stopped abruptly, stepped smartly to the car, and dropped the handset in to Flynn. He backed in to the doorway next to Malone, rattling the shutters a little as he did.

"Let's do what we're good at, lads. Right?"

Reflections of the low and formless clouds that had covered Dublin for days now slid along the Audi's windscreen. Chan was the passenger; he was on a mobile. He seemed to be having a lively enough conversation, one that had him gesturing still as he stepped out of the Audi. He stood still then for several moments, and stared at the laneway ahead. The light rain didn't seem to be registering with him.

Kelly lit a cigarette from the end of his old one, cleared his throat and spat across the laneway. He was blinking a lot. The goatee and the rings in his ears reminded Malone of a pirate in his niece's school Christmas pantomime.

"Come on," Buckley whispered. "Produce the goods here, one of youse."

Chan slid closed his phone and pocketed it. He held out a key to Kelly.

"Well well," said Buckley. "So Paddy the Irishman is just the go-for here."

Kelly palmed the key and moved it around in his hand. Then he stared at it, as though it held a secret.

"Just do it, gobshite. It's a key in your hand. Doesn't take a miracle to use it."

Buckley had his lapel mike pushed up close. His frown deepened. It seemed to cause him to slump a little. Then Kelly's hand flipped over, and he was on the move.

"Christ," said Buckley, darting upright. "He made us! Tommy, he's yours!"

Malone would later recount wanting to yell something at Buckley at this point. Something like he wasn't a moron, for Christ's sake. Like, he had actually been awake at the briefing. Like, drop this control-freak new Sergeant's thing, the one that made him think that nothing happened without him, that no-one knew anything unless he said so. Like, would he just frigging cool it, Buckley, and stop giving Keaveney any excuse to get more sour, more sarcastic, more bitter by the minute here.

Keaveney had come out fast too. He was ahead of Malone, and with his pistol displayed he was headed straight for Chan, roaring. Chan stayed frozen, his eyes locked on Keaveney. The detective slid to a stop ten feet from him, in firing stance.

But Kelly was sprinting around the bigger puddles now. Surprise collided with anger in Malone as he watched Kelly actually speed up. With every step, the new armour bit at his armpit again. Where was Doyle or the other fellas from the runner car?

A figure, then another, appeared at the head of the laneway. Kelly came to a shuddering stop, hopping and sliding over the wet cement, his arms churning the air. He glanced back at Malone, at the shuttered doorways. He seemed to see something he liked, and he bounded toward it.

Malone began swearing aloud then: somehow, Kelly was managing to rise up the wall there. This wasn't supposed to happen. Buckley had sussed the place the other day, hadn't he?

Doyle too was disbelieving. He too slowed his dash. Wild-eyed, he looked at Malone. Overhead, and just out of reach were Kelly's running shoes, the zigzag patterns of the soles flecked and glistening. It was a galvanized pipe, some kind of conduit, he was using. Bits of the brackets that held them to the wall had given way.

"Come down," Doyle growled more than shouted.

Kelly ignored him.

"You stupid bastard. Get real here, yeah? There's nowhere to go."

Wheezing, whimpering, Kelly now pulled the barbed wire back from where it had caught his jacket. With a pained grunt, he got a knee onto the lip of the roof. He pulled himself up on his elbows over a parapet.

"Jesus Christ," said Doyle. "How the hell did he do that?"

Malone saw bright spots of blood now, the track of Kelly's desperate flight up. He had to be high, to go like a monkey at that wire. Anaesthetized. Buckley's voice in his earpiece was driving him mad. He yanked it out, and began searching for a handhold on the pipe.

"Doyler, gimme a hoosh up there."

"Are you cracked? It's not worth it."

"Come on. Don't be a bollocks."

"Are you mad? Leave him, I'm telling you. He's not going anywhere."

"You don't know that, do you? So come on – give me a bunt!"

"Christ's sake, Tommy! Where can he go? Get a grip there!"

"Says you – like 'No worries, man, we have the place sussed out'?"

Doyle sighed and looked around.

"Just get me a start and I can get up. If I make a bollocks of it, it's on me. Okay?"

Doyle slowly cupped his hands, and braced his back against the wall. He grunted as he took Malone's weight.

"Tommy. This is *retarded*. Wait for him? He has to come down, man. Jaysus!"

Malone would remember Doyle's expression very clearly, his face twisted with the strain of holding him up. It would be the same Doyle who would be there when things would fall apart.

Malone pulled himself up, felt Doyle try to steady himself better beneath. Carefully he settled his feet on Doyle's shoulders, and he wedged his back against the bricks. Squinting against the raindrops, he searched the five or six feet between him and the barbed wire. There was a gap, a small one, with a long filament torn from Kelly's nylon jacket. He looked at the bricks next to his hands. Kelly had shredded some part of himself here. His knuckles probably.

Malone reached up and eased his fingers around the pipe. It was greasy with the rain. It gave out a scratchy protest when he pulled on it. He pulled harder and it began to shriek. But it held. He got what he could of the side of his shoe on the gouged face of the bricks. Then he stopped.

When did you form this intent to scale the wall there, Detective Malone?

It was the one from the London Met, the retired Super from their CID, the one with the shut-up face and the Cockney accent. Mr. Sell-you-down-the-river-while-he-smiled-at-you.

Did you hear others trying to dissuade you from this?

It had to be from Doyle's statement, for sure.

He looked up. The sky was barely overhead. The rain was more of a drizzle really. It was actually refreshing.

"Bastard's not worth it," Doyle was saying to him. "Hear me up there?"

"I'm going up. Go around the end of the lane there yourself."

Later, Garda Malone would depose that he had actually enjoyed the effort of getting himself to the rooftop. Yes, enjoyed. Why 'enjoyed'? He had always had a competitive temperament, he told them. When told he couldn't do something, that got him wanting to. He didn't care that his interviewers were almost uniformly skeptical of this. Called to expand on this, he had told them that it was more than just the satisfaction of getting Kelly. Climbing up there was hard, yes, even a bit dodgy. Kelly had left enough signs of that in his panicked clawing up on the roof himself. But if Kelly had done it... And it was more even than the kick of doing what another copper – Doyle, say – would balk at. It was the actual exertion he enjoyed, plain and simple, that burst of energy that freed him from the sour thoughts that he couldn't shake off earlier.

Malone would have plenty of time – too much in fact – in the next four months to wonder why he had uttered those words that he now did. The words, the phrases, kept coming up over and over again in the interviews.

"I'll take care of the bastard," he said. "I'll sort him out."

And then, all too easily it seemed to him, and still believing that it was Kelly's tortuous climb before him that had eased his own, Malone had his elbows on the edge of the roof himself. Kelly wasn't thirty feet away. He was bent over, holding one hand in the other. There was blood, a lot of it, on one sleeve of his jacket. His jeans were torn too. He didn't straighten up, but watched Malone sideways, his chest heaving while he grimaced, revealing crowded, greying teeth.

"You're under arrest, you fecker."

Kelly didn't seem to have heard him. Malone tugged his windbreaker open now.

"Give it up, gobshite. You know the drill. Hands on the back of your neck, nice and slow there. And knit them fingers tight."

Malone kept up his stare. He stepped around the clumps of pitch and the messy leftovers of roof repairs over the years, the odd shaped pieces of tin and metal, and pieces of bottles and faded beer and soft drink cans thrown up here. Kelly eyed him all the while, but seemed unwilling to focus on him. Kelly's arms were trembling. There were blotches and spots of blood on his neck.

He began to pace, and to retrace his steps. To Malone it looked like a dance.

"You want resisting arrest too?"

Kelly grimaced.

"You listening there at all?" he called out again to Kelly. "Get serious. Hands together, the back of your neck."

Kelly came to a stop. His eyes focused on Malone now, and he frowned.

"You," he said.

Just 'you,' Garda Malone? Mr. Kelly didn't address you by name? No name, Malone would reply. *It was sufficient, because he knew you, he remembered you? Remembered you well, would you say?* Hard to say, was the best Malone would offer on that. *Likely. How likely? He feared you, and had reason to remember you very clearly. Because of an association with your deceased brother, correct? Because you believed Mr. Kelly played a part in his overdose?* Lanigan, the Association barrister, had warned him this would come up early: 'the Ombudsman crowd goes straight for the nuts.'

But Malone had wanted his say. He replied that he had no insight into Kelly's mental processes. *Kelly feared what you might do, would you not agree?* He feared going back to jail, Malone countered. Lanigan had given him an earful after that session. If nothing else, Lanigan told him later, Malone had damaged his own career with the combative replies.

Malone heard the wet sizzle of tires in the lane below. It was Doyle's car braking to round the corner. Kelly began to blink now. It seemed to Malone that he couldn't stop blinking.

"Kelly. Are you deaf, or what? Listen to me. Play ball here and we'll see what we can do for you. All right?"

Kelly's chest was heaving less now, but he had nothing to say.

"Help us out," said Malone. "We'll get you into Coolmine. Help you kick it, see? It's never too late. You hear?"

He stopped when he heard the noise. The low moaning that he was hearing could only be Kelly. He looked down at the man's hands. The bloodied left was dangling by his side and dripping darkly. But Kelly's right was slipping into the pocket of his jeans.

"Don't," Malone said. "Don't!"

He had already stepped down and dipped into his stance, his left arm completing its sweep up to steady the pistol.

"Take your hand out of your pocket. Slow. Where I can see it. Now!"

Kelly slowly began to withdraw his hand.

"All the way," Malone yelled. "Show me! Open your hand!"

Asked what he had observed that had caused him to take out his firearm, Malone could only say that the hair had stood up on the back of his neck. *Had he concluded that Kelly had a firearm?* It was a feeling, Malone explained. A feeling, a hunch, that's all.

Kelly's eyes had slipped back out of focus. He was licking his lips.

"Open your hand, and show me, where I can see it's empty."

Kelly had flinched at the shout.

"Stop bollocking around there, I'm telling you!"

Something tripped in Malone's mind.

"Now!" was all he could think to shout.

What Malone would later call a grin – a word he stuck with through every session of interviews, adding a few qualifiers like 'weird' and 'freaked-out' and 'odd' – was settling on Kelly's face. Malone sank further into his stance, feeling his forefinger pushing too hard against the guard. He wondered if Kelly had heard him release the safety.

He didn't shout now.

"Whatever you have there, don't. Don't do it."

Kelly took a small step to his side.

"Stop," Malone said. "You're high, man. You're not thinking straight."

Kelly's eyes snapped back into focus. His smile faded. He eyed Malone as though seeing him for the first time. For several moments Malone almost believed that there were only the two of them here on this rooftop, that the city about them was deserted, that the clouds were so close and dense that you could reach up and grab a lump of them.

Detective Garda Mick Doyle was the one who first saw the figure, arms out and churning like an Olympic swimmer, plunging toward him through the air above.

Chapter 2

The evening of that same Tuesday, Rhiannon Brophy had had it. She had been here on Killiney Hill for over a half hour now. Here she was, waiting for the light to be 'right' for these last stupid photos. This project had turned into a nightmare, an absolute mess. At least it had stopped raining.

Miss Conway was a bitch. How had Rhiannon ever thought otherwise, for one second? Jesus! Miss Conway had told her to actually go out in the rain, and destroy her father's expensive camera equipment! Like, this crappy weather was Rhiannon Brophy's fault? She was being punished for the weather, or something? Bitch. Art teacher tyrant two-faced total loser Miss Helen Conway: colossal bitch. Smiley liar bitch. Frustrated, permanent PMS, no boyfriend. Old maid thirty five-ish jealous over-the-hill *stupid* bitch.

She scrolled down her calls, her thumb hovering over several. Then she snapped her mobile shut. Why should she always be the one to call Maeve, or Kate, first?

She studied the scratches and the dings on her phone. In a way, she was almost proud of them. The more scratches, the easier it'd be to justify a new one. It was a year old already. The battery was acting up, or the charger, or something. She had thought about losing it on purpose. Kate had been doing it for years. It wasn't just to get a new model, it was to piss off her father. Kate had a nasty streak to her. Everyone slagged their parents, fair enough. But was it actually possible that Katie hated hers?

The sea had gone from muddy brown to grey. A bit of weird blue too? She'd better start to write them down now before she forgot. She turned inland and began to key them in. Beyond the lights of the south Dublin suburbs, the hills were fading. A bit of colour lingered behind Two Rock Mountain. She keyed in 'lemon,' and 'mustard,' and then 'a bit orangey.' Miss Conway wouldn't go for 'orangey.' That's why she'd put it in, then.

A breeze had come up in the past few minutes, carrying with it a coolness from the sea. If Miss Conway were a real teacher, and not a bitch, she'd have told her that the whole project had been too much to take on in the first place. Maybe, in some twisted way, she wanted her to screw up. She had so wanted to impress Miss Conway with this project. And it hadn't been fake either! She had storyboarded the presentation on the projector, with Coldplay and Sloan, and the transitions and timing perfect and—

Her anger surged back: that stupid thing Maeve had said last week! She had been moaning to Maeve about the project, how it was such a pain now, and how Miss Conway was Satan and all. Well that'd teach her, was Maeve's comment. Teach her what? Teach her for getting a crush on Miss Conway, the cool Art teacher. Joke, ha-ha! Really? Not. But so totally Maeve. So totally sly. So typical. Why was Maeve her friend then?

Rhiannon eyed the lights under the mountains where the suburbs petered out. No answers there. She began to circle the tripod with slow, measured paces, her irritation curdling into resentment. There was no way around it: Maeve was a total bitch. Pretending to be her friend, but setting her up. Like to Kate, who was her friend first. Sabotage, that was Maeve's thing. No way was she going to put up with that two-faced—

It was only the toe of her shoe that caught the tripod leg. It was enough to move the camera. Rhiannon lunged for it, and she resettled the leg carefully in the beaten earth. Jesus, it was close. She made sure the view in the finder was close to what she had before. She stepped back, and eyed the set-up.

It was just one more thing to worry about, one more thing to go wrong. For all his annoying culchie ways, it was actually decent of her father to let her use his stuff. There was about fifteen hundred euro worth of camera stuff here. And he was very territorial about his gadgets, fussing over them, big-time. But that was his job. She had seen a lot of wicked-cool gear on visits to his office in the State Lab. It was the forensic side she was most interested in. He never liked talking about stuff to do with that.

A gust found its way under her jacket. This was June, for Christ's sakes? Not much longer, she thought. Never again, for sure. Even the title of the project annoyed her now: 'In the Dark.' It had been good for the first while. She had even enjoyed seeing her parents' reaction to the title. Was she going a bit Goth? Vampire stuff…?

They didn't get it. She had tried telling them anyway. It was about how society tried to keep young people in the dark. How society wanted people not to know what was really going on. Like with the environment, and the drug companies and the oil companies paying people to cover up and to lie. The fashion sweat shops and their child labour. Anorexic models with popsicle bodies – bulimia too, of course. Clothes designed by weirdo creepy loser men the age of fifty. The government, the school system. Everything really, when you thought about it.

They had done their parent thing about that, nodding their heads and looking thoughtful. Her father couldn't fake it, however. He just did his usual thing then when things got a bit tense. That meant looking up from a book or something he was working on. That constipated look on his face, eyeing her like she was an alien. Sometimes it was funny. Sometimes it wasn't.

Her mother took everything a bit personally, as usual. Like: what 'society' was Rhiannon talking about? Did she think that adults were trying to cod teenagers all the time? Rhiannon had told her that it was basically about hypocrisy. She had said that as a hint, and she knew her mother had gotten it because the talk ended soon after that. Later that evening, she had heard through the door some of the murmured words between them. For shock value, love … But is anger like that normal? She felt elated, powerful, when she heard that, and then stricken. Later, in bed, she had cried. Why, how could things get so stupidly complicated?

Something eased then. It was like a screen sliding open to reveal a majestic Himalayan scene. She felt her shoulders release their tightness. She stretched her neck in a slow half-circle, and rested her gaze on the clouds as she came around again. They were actually brown! She held her eyes shut for a count of three, and opened them again. Okay, manila maybe. But anyway: the fact was, she was almost finished this project. But never again. As in never ever. Someday she'd even laugh about it. And when Maeve and the others would finally see it on the screen, she'd realize what work had gone into the project. That'd be a moment, all right.

Maeve. The truth was, Maeve did actually hate her parents. She really did. Rhiannon didn't hate hers. Maeve took her parents for whatever she could get out of them. Rhiannon couldn't do that. She'd just feel crap if she tried. Maeve lied and she stole, and she got drunk, and she scored with different guys almost every weekend. Well that actually made Maeve a slut then, didn't it? *And*: Maeve was jealous. Just because Rhiannon liked multimedia and Photoshopping and that sort of thing? Maeve slagged it because she couldn't do it. She pretended she didn't want to, but she did, and anyway Rhiannon was good at it. The project last year on History of Fashion? Those animations ...?

She settled the tripod again and checked the viewfinder. There was plenty of battery power left. She got her mark on the branches that started over the mountain there, and slowly took a set of five shots. She made sure she had decent overlap each time. She listened to the shutter each time. The speed was slow, so the F-Stop thingie was doing its job. That'd do it for the bay panorama then. She switched off the camera, and waited.

Seventeen calls from Maeve in the past two days? Was that possible? And a billion texts: she didn't want to look. Maeve told her she read too much into things. The weird thing was, this 'Reading a bit much into things' was one of her father's expressions. Each time she heard it, it pissed her off more and more. How could he have a clue what she was thinking? Maybe it was one of those phrases he used at work, when he'd have to be precise and all that. After all, he had said to her, a person could be sent to prison for years if the science was sloppy here.

Whatever. Bygones be bygones and all that. She closed the mobile gently this time. It was an okay phone, it did the job. And she wasn't a spoiled cow like Maeve. For a moment she imagined throwing the phone right out far into the sea: text me now, Maeve, you wannabe, you bitch.

She smiled. It was the sudden recall of her father, and that test she gave him on texting. It was actually his idea, a joke. He knew the lol and cul8r stuff, but the rest was Chinese to him. He just made it up though. She had to laugh, really. That was the thing with him: he didn't mind making an iijit of himself. If only he didn't keep going on about it, like he did with jokes, telling them over and over again. The nerd side of him, she supposed. Aspy, really.

She ran her finger over her eyebrow. The stud there had fairly freaked him out. He hadn't a clue what to say. He had given her a long, hard look when he had first seen it. His world had changed suddenly, had turned upside down. Like he hadn't expected anything like this at all, ever. The precious little daughter, the one whom he had decided deserved a name from Fleetwood Mac, well she was only doing something that he would have done at her age too. That was *exactly* what she had meant by the hypocrisy thing with 'In the Dark.' They'd never get it.

She didn't want to think about it anymore. Instead, she thought ahead to the work she'd do tonight. The panoramas: bring up the colours better, make them glow a bit, and try some of those effects. Miss Conway, bitch of the entire known universe, would notice. Hard to admit this, but when it came down to it, it was true: Miss Conway actually wasn't the worst. As Art teachers go, anyway. She actually wasn't a thick with computers, not like the others. So yes, Rhiannon thought wearily, she'd hand in the project on Thursday. Yes, it was a week late. But she deserved an A, didn't she? That's right. 'A for not screaming in the Art teacher's face.'

Art teacher: her heart still soared at the thought. It would be so cool, being an Art teacher. To actually get paid to do something you loved, something creative and fun. And it wouldn't be spotty secondary school students, no. It'd be the College of Art, the real thing. Miss Conway would write her that reference—

The rustlings came from close by. They came and went again. Maybe it was birds hopping about in the undergrowth. She looked up and down the path. It was funny how things changed with the light, and that feeling of threat came on. It would be creepy here at night. More than creepy, actually.

A small shape came quickly around a bend in the path: a little dog, a terrier, hyper. It was soon nosing around the tripod. He or she was young, all tail-wagging and panting, jumpy. Rhiannon liked the way it licked furiously at her fingers.

"Tess," a woman called out. "Come here, Tess."

Tess was having none of it. Good on you, girl, Rhiannon thought. The woman came around the path. She had a Burberry outfit, a mobile held away from her face.

"She won't harm you, all right? She is just a pup."

iPhone, of course. Southside. 'Roiight.' Bossy tone too. Maybe a doctor? This Tess one was beyond giddy now, prancing and jumping. Rhiannon clamped her hand on the tripod.

Burberry Lady's hubbie/ancient boyfriend/gigolo was Gore-Tex Man. He looked much older than she did. Trophy wife, Rhiannon wondered now. And plastic surgery? Gore-Tex Man slowed to watch Burberry Lady trying to corral the dog. My God, but he was wearing a really, really stupid hat. This Tess was having none of it. Off it went full tilt, stopping abruptly every now and then and turning to look back.

Rhiannon couldn't help but smile. Burberry Lady was getting annoyed.

"You should take a picture of this," Gore-Tex Man murmured.

Rhiannon eyed his hat. He had probably bought it in some ridiculously priced place in – who knows, Germany? Italy? No, not the type to go to Italy.

"A bit of a comedy," he added. "Wouldn't you say?"

Tess the rebel terrier was well into the undergrowth now, skipping and prancing and skidding in the leaves. She stopped to sniff, jerking her head all the time, talking to herself. A shame, Rhiannon thought, that puppies didn't stay like that all their lives.

"That's a good camera," Gore-Tex Man said.

She tried to look him in the eye for a moment, but the glasses only reflected the light. Okay. He was just being friendly. Like they say, don't judge by appearances.

"It does the job," she said.

Gore-Tex Man glanced over to where Burberry Lady was calling out to the dog.

"Or maybe more a farce than a comedy," he muttered.

He fumbled in his pocket. Rhiannon heard a plastic bag.

"Claire," he said, louder than Rhiannon had expected. "Claire?"

Well of course she had to have a name like Claire, didn't she. *Another gloss of bobbly, Claire dear?*

"Tess," Gore-Tex Man called out then. "Bikki, Tess. Bikki?"

The puppy stayed in the undergrowth, sniffing and pacing up and back, half-yowling to itself. It was just too much, Rhiannon decided. Even his dog ignores him.

Burberry Lady Claire seemed to be giving up. As though calculating each step, she stepped carefully back through the grass and toward her hubbie. Maybe she was embarrassed, Rhiannon thought, the way snobs are embarrassed when things don't go perfectly in their perfect universe according to their perfect whims.

"All yours," Rhiannon heard her say. The tone said everything really. She gave Rhiannon a brief smile, and raised her mobile again.

Gore-Tex Man hunkered down and held out the biscuit. The dog made a few darting step toward him, barked, darted back. But after a few runs, it opted for bikki. Seeing Gore-Tex Man scoop the dumb dog up so easily soured Rhiannon. She turned back to the tripod. It was time to just get this thing finished. She checked the aperture again. Nothing was perfect, it never would be. She planted her feet away from the tripod legs, and settled in behind the camera.

She took a five-shot panorama at 55 mm. After she had taken a second set of five, she reviewed them. The ones where she had tilted the camera toward the foreground worked the best. The bit of worn grass seemed to flow out like the sea from under the trees. The patch of evening sky had a bleached, almost luminous look to it too. A sudden, sharp elation glowed in her. The whole thing had actually worked out. Like her father had said: the camera sees things that the operator can't.

The couple had moved on. Mrs. iPhone Burberry Lady Claire and Mr. Stupid Hat Gore-Tex Man, to give them their proper titles. Rhiannon detached the camera from the tripod, and unscrewed the lens hood. She pinched the lens cap on, and she slid the camera carefully into the bag. There was something very satisfying about getting the tripod down, how it slid together so cleanly.

She was almost finished when she heard Gore-Tex Man calling for the dog again. The voice was quite a way off. And he definitely sounded less than thrilled.

Then, Tess burst out from the gloom, right where the path turned inland. She was panting, her short legs going full tilt, the eyes on her big and full of mischief.

Rhiannon got down on one knee.

"You made a break for it, you little bugger, didn't you?"

The dog sidestepped her, and dropping its nose abruptly to the ground, it raced into the undergrowth. It seemed not sure how to bark, but went back to arguing and talking to itself instead. Gore-Tex Man appeared down the path now.

"Well," he said in a strained tone. "Who's training who, I wonder."

Rhiannon said nothing. She settled the bag on her shoulder, and shuffled a bit to make sure nothing was loose in there. The tripod was cool on her palm. She took a last look over the bay, tracing the curve south to Bray Head. Someday – soon, she decided – she'd actually go to the real places in Italy that all this was named after.

Burberry Lady Claire was back. She stood by the path, still deep in her love affair with her mobile. Gore-Tex Man had started talking to the dog now, and he continued making his way over slowly, his hand out with another bribe.

Tess wasn't running away this time. She was clearly torn between the game and the bikki. She pawed at the grass and weeds, the small trunk tightening in spasms from her yelps and whines. Then slowly and uncertainly, she made her way to Gore-Tex Man. Just as she took the bribe, he fingered her collar and drew her in.

Rhiannon watched how he leaned in and talked to the puppy, holding her gently but firmly while he attached the clip to her collar. It was a small enough revelation for her, but it left her more ashamed than confused: maybe Gore-Tex Man wasn't so predictable after all.

Now released again, the puppy immediately tested the length of the leash. Gore-Tex Man began tugging it away from the undergrowth. This time, the puppy yelped and pulled harder, and bounded and hopped on its back legs trying to get free.

"All right, Tess," Rhiannon heard him say. "One last go of it."

He let himself be pulled into the undergrowth.

The breeze seemed to have decided it would settle here on the headland. Rhiannon turned from it as she gathered her gear, and then she headed for the path. Burberry Lady Claire ahead didn't seem one bit interested in the goings on. She kept up her quiet conversation instead, staring at the foliage like she was in a trance. A hint of Burberry Lady's perfume came to her. Rhiannon decided that she wouldn't be the one to say hello first when she passed her.

The shout made Rhiannon actually jump.

"Claire!"

Burberry Lady Claire had started too. She didn't know where the shout had come from. Rhiannon turned to see Gore-Tex Man, walking sideways, pulling the puppy hard.

"Claire! Your phone? Phone 999, the Guards."

Burberry Lady Claire was looking steadily at Rhiannon now, as if looking for some understanding. Gore-Tex Man mimicked holding a phone to his ear. He reeled in the puppy and picked it up, and he held it tight against his chest.

He was breathing hard. He didn't seem to notice the puppy's snout working its way around his mouth.

"The Guards," Burberry Lady Claire said. "Phone the Guards? What for?"

"Give it to me then, I'll do it."

"What's wrong?" Rhiannon asked.

He seemed dazed. Burberry Lady Claire murmured into her mobile, and then slid it into her pocket.

"There's something over there," he said.

A stark-eyed look had come to Burberry Lady Claire.

"What are you saying?"

He looked at Rhiannon. His eyes had gone watery from the wind.

"I don't want to say. Just phone, will you."

She began to push the keypad. Rhiannon held the tripod tighter.

"Are you here on your own?" Gore-Tex Man asked her.

"Why are you asking me that?"

"I mean, your family – You're on your own here? Nobody . . .?"

"I live up the road – Wait, that's none of your business."

"Stay with us until the Guards get here."

Burberry Lady Claire was poking him with the phone.

"You talk to them," she said.

The leash got caught in the man's arm as he tried to swap the dog over.

"Tony Meehan's my name. Yes, Meehan. Anthony, Tony... M-e-e-h...Yes."

Rhiannon watched Burberry lady try to hold the dog, fending off its wriggles and licks at the same time. Meehan, she thought. It was an ordinary-sounding name really. He was getting exasperated, trying to explain where he was. No, he didn't know the exact name of the nearest road. He had walked into the park from the Dalkey side. So they were somewhere between the obelisk and Dalkey Hill. Yes, there were woods. There was a GPS on the phone, he said, would that help? Apparently not.

The dog's eyes rolled wildly, and it trembled. Rhiannon wondered if it might bite.

"A person," said the husband. "Yes, it looks like a person. What?"

He gave Burberry Lady Claire a forebearing look.

"No, he's not sleeping. He looks, you know."

Burberry Lady Claire' eyes had gone wide. She seemed to

want to say something but was waiting for the right words. Didn't she notice that the dog was licking her face?

"Jesus," Rhiannon heard her say then.

"Well yes," Tony Meehan said, his voice going reedy. "I'm no expert, am I? But, Jesus Christ, it sure looks like that to me."

His unfocused gaze slid from Burberry Lady to Rhiannon and back.

"Look," he said, and Rhiannon was sure he was interrupting someone at the other end now. "Look – listen: can you just send someone? Please?"

Something was settling on Rhiannon now. It reminded her of the strange, chill gravity that pulled on her when she stepped out of the bath. The strap of the camera bag was beginning to bite. She was so close to Burberry Lady now that the dog was reaching toward her, trying to nibble at the hand she had raised to her mouth.

Tony Meehan's impatience was turning to agitation, anger even.

"Yes! Me, my wife. And a girl. Jesus – I don't know! Out for a walk, I suppose."

Burberry Lady's nostrils were going in and out.

"I'm Claire," she said, in a strange, choked voice.

"I know that," Rhiannon said. It sounded – and it was – a stupid thing to say. She found that she was taking steps now, getting closer to Burberry Lady. "I know."

Chapter 3

Minogue and Kilmartin had gotten to Ryan's pub early. It was quiet enough. The prospect of a session had Kilmartin in high gear. He had been through a good number of his ritual disparagements already: government ministers, French rugby; Guards and their collections of 'patches'; the legal profession, tour-bus drivers; environmentalists.

"Well, are you sure Malone actually got off this morning?"

Minogue knew better that to rise to the bait. He had been at the Ombudsman's office on Abbey Street this morning when they'd handed down their finding on Malone. Seen Malone emerge into the foyer afterwards with a flinching smile. Waited through the awkward moments with Malone staring out the window at a tram rumbling by.

Kilmartin sauntered to his old spot, and eased his shoulder onto the partition.

"Whiskey, Liam, in the name of God. And something for this oddball beside me."

Minogue made a survey of the pub while Kilmartin checked his mobile. Ryan's was long a favourite with staff from the Garda HQ nearby. It had deflected the Celtic Tiger a good bit with window boxes and a restaurant, but here, a stone's throw from a still-tidal River Liffey, it had managed to stay a pub.

"Celebrating, are we, gentlemen."

Liam had been a barman here since the Vikings had found a way across the river. He lived in an invisible fog of skepticism, one that rarely slid to outright scorn. A working-class Dubliner, Liam's questions were usually rhetorical.

"Yes and no, Liam," replied Kilmartin. "Tonight's two-for-one. There's a financial crisis, did you know? We're doing our bit with a wee stimulus package here."

Liam's baleful scrutiny didn't budge from a pint of Guinness that he was filling.

"Just what the country needs," he said. "Well played."

Kilmartin made a vague gesture in Minogue's direction. "Head-the-ball here is starting a new gig. And to top it off, we have another lad out from under a cloud today."

He waited until Liam left before leaning in to Minogue.

"Straight to business," he said. "One question. Did he or didn't he? Malone."

Minogue had half-expected this. He kept his eye on the door out to Parkgate Street.

"That was decided this morning. Have you heard of the Ombudsman?"

"Go away out of that. They never found any black box on this Kelly character, did they?"

Minogue had heard that one too often already. Kilmartin cocked an eye at him.

"Those Ombudsman feckers decide nothing in my book. Nada. The Book of Reality, that's my book. So: did he heave that Kelly *lúdramán* off the roof? Yes or no."

Minogue mulled over whether he should admit that he still wondered too.

"Ask him yourself," he said instead. This drew a mock scowl from Kilmartin.

"Hopping the ball as usual you hoor, you. What did I expect, I wonder."

Liam placed Kilmartin's whiskey and a jug of water on the counter, and returned to slow, enigmatic notations in his copy of *The Irish Field*.

Kilmartin had his usual insider info to impart. Somehow, he had gotten his hands on a transcript of records from Kelly's mobiles, and even the mobile Chan was carrying.

"A who's who of blackguards," he said, his voice down to a murmur. "A gold mine entirely. Dublin, London – even off in fecking China, if you please. *China...!*"

"I know what China is."

"Well you know what a triad is then, don't you? And I'm not talking about our precious national three-leafed clover, am I."

Minogue said nothing. Kilmartin's vacant stare floating around the counter told him that some matter was far from settled.

"Ever wonder," Kilmartin asked then, a flinty smile taking over his face. "Ever wonder why the only girl that Malone falls for, she has to be Chinese?"

Minogue stole another look at the symbol that Liam had just drawn. Horse-worship was Liam's religion. Form sheets and the *Irish Field* were his scriptures. From these he divined his signs, and on them he inscribed his own hope. His complex bets encoded the fruits of his devotions. Who cared if ponies were a mug's game? The study of signs, the assaying of a future, were what mattered.

"Well?" Kilmartin went on. "Never strike you as odd at all? No? Yes? Maybe?"

"Didn't what."

"Chinese girlfriend?"

Minogue shook his head.

"With all you're privy to in Liaison? In-ter-nash-nal Lee-eh-zon?"

"Why do you always try to make it sound like a girls' finishing school?"

"That question answers itself," Kilmartin went on, breezily. "But if anybody knows about Chinamen and triads here, it'd be that very section, wouldn't you say?"

It was entirely possible that Liam was listening, and surely relishing, the sort of guff emanating from Jim Kilmartin. Maybe he was writing a book about it all.

"It's out there," said Kilmartin. "This Triad thing? Welcome to the big league."

Minogue opted to continue saying nothing. Kilmartin was used to it.

"Longest river in the world, Matt. Deep and dangerous. Lot of alligators there, making a lot of allegations."

"Far as I know the Nile is still in Egypt. Not China, or Macau, to be precise."

Kilmartin put out a forebearing grin.

"Don't cod yourself. They're already here. Money money money."

Minogue gave him a side glance.

"What's the issue here? Tommy's guilty of dating a non-colleen?"

Kilmartin's eyes flickered with irritation, but he came up with a fake smile.

"Nice," he said. "Loyal to a fault. That's great in the abstract, of course. But it's real life we're living here, so just remember what I said, and when I said it. That's all."

He shifted his shoulder against the partition and he sighed.

"Anyway. Stay with the Chinaman a minute. The money's rolling in good-o now to a certain barrister's office there in the Distillery Building. Can you guess whose?"

Of course Minogue could. So he didn't.

"Well I'll fill in the blanks for you. Up popped that lying bastard Connolly, the fistfuls of Chinese gangsters' money still hanging out this so-called barrister's pockets, and him firing out writs and claims like cannonballs. Anything from Improper Seizure to Wrongful Arrest – he's even throwing in the race card, I hear. A new low."

"What race?"

"Not the *ponies* – the fact that he's Chinese."

"Well that's a fright to God entirely. Terrible times we're living in."

"You don't want to know, do you? Don't care?"

"I like both options, James. Don't make me pick."

He studied Liam's hieroglyphics again. Liam was a man looking for signs, Minogue reflected. And why not? Might as well look for them in a racing newspaper, or in the churning hooves of glorious beasts, as well as where the devout were look-ing for their signs these days on holy tree stumps or sun-rings at

Knock's shrine to Mary, Mother of God, pray for us sinners....

Kilmartin darted a look to Minogue.

"I know where I'd put me money if I was a betting man. This Kelly situation, I'm talking about. Accidental death, fleeing arrest. Any contraband in that lock-up? Not a sausage. Was there a tipoff? Go ask the tooth-fairy. So. That Chinaman's going to walk. What have we got after all this? Zero. Feck-all. Nuttin'. They're back laughing at us – in China too. But they'll be back, you can be sure. No slip-ups next time."

Liam folded his paper and made his way over to finish pouring the Guinness. Kilmartin slid a twenty onto the counter. Minogue turned the glass a quarter way on the counter, and pondered yet again what a shame it was to ruin its creamy head.

"Introibo ad altare Dei."

Kilmartin tapped him on the arm before he could lift the glass to his lips.

"Mind your gob," he said, and then he winked. "That's blasphemy, man."

Passage of the Defamation Act had even Kilmartin rolling his eyes. Was Ireland getting its laws from the alphabet now, went his flat joke, from between Iraq and Israel?

"You're afraid God's going to miss me, and hit you with his lightning bolt."

Kilmartin's show of scorn was a slow, basilisk blink.

"It's not that. Do you look at a newspaper these days? The church...?"

"Is there a new holy tree stump I need to know about? Some new miracle?"

"What you *have*," he said, "they have no cure for. The Commission, I'm talking about, the report coming out next week."

Kilmartin's voice turned to a harsh whisper.

"Child abuse? Priests? Dublin diocese? Bishops covering up? Planet Earth...?"

Minogue took his chance. The foam touched the tip of his nose just as the Guinness delivered its silky chill.

"How could that happen? A Christian country? With all we've been through?"

Minogue kept the Guinness coming. An earnestness had entered Kilmartin's voice now, and it brought to Minogue the dismaying thought that a lecture was on the way.

"The church – the one thing that we had to keep us going. Wasn't it? Your life could be shite – the landlord evicting you, your children barefoot, gone to America, gone to jail – but by God, you could go to Mass. Even if it was behind an old rock there in the glen, you could be sure that Himself above would listen to you. You had hope. See?"

He drew up his shoulders and heaved them about. A calmness took over his face.

"That's how we prevailed. Eight hundred years. We had hope. And now look?"

"We'll rise again" was all Minogue could think to say.

Kilmartin leaned back, a glint of the old raillery in his eye.

"You want to know what I heard a fella say? Line 'em up against the wall, says he, and..."

"Who the Chinese?"

"Spare me, will you. The clergy who did that stuff, I'm talking about."

He nodded several times.

"But this is what makes me laugh – or not laugh, I should say. Wince – that's what I do: I wince. The fact is this: I'm a Garda officer sworn to uphold the law, and here I am, hearing citizens issue threats. Counseling others to commit murder."

"Murder, I don't know. Manslaughter, maybe?"

"Manslaughter my arse," Kilmartin retorted quickly, his eyes narrowing. "Incitement puts you close enough to First Degree, boyo, if you want to legal on me here. But the law is the law. So should I do the Three Monkey Routine when I hear people talking about lynching priests or bishops? See no evil, hear no evil and that?"

"You Mayo crowd can't be bested in that regard, this three monkey scenario."

With that, Kilmartin shifted his stance. Minogue reached for his pint again.

"Very droll," he said. "Okay, you've heard the rumours, I take it. About Malone?"

"Can't say that I have."

"Well that's odd. Very odd. You must be the only man in Ireland who hasn't."

When Minogue didn't react, Kilmartin shuffled a little.

"Well let me come at it this way then," he said. "Nice and diplomatic, so's I don't upset you now. I'll paint a picture for you. You ready? A hypothetical copper, working away in the trenches. He's at the coal face, no let-up. The bad guys are winning. Okay? So this copper gets to wondering about things. He's no thicko, he's under no illusions. He's paid his dues, he knows right from wrong. He sees what the courts do, and what they don't do. Or what they can't do, with our stupid 'rights' thing here. Still with me?"

"Sort of. Maybe. Do I get to pick?"

"There you go again, playing the gámóg. What do you think I'm talking about? Law and order, is what. The basics! Now don't get me wrong. I'm not saying Malone is part of anything. But still and all, you have to ask yourself, you know."

"Ask myself what?"

"Jesus," said Kilmartin, his face twisting in exasperation. "Are you deaf, or are you retarded? Both, is it? Easy for you to laugh, and you whiling your time away up in Liaison there, with your pals in Brussels and Lyons and the rest of cappuccino land. But I'm talking about the streets of this very city. I'm telling you, people are angry. Don't mind the banks robbing us, or the developers, or even the gobshites we voted in. Where's the law, people are asking. Why are those lowlifes, those gangsters, still on the street?"

Kilmartin formed a weak smile, but it quickly faded.

"So look. You're being decent to Malone, getting him this job with you, this cold-case effort. I want to say that first, to acknowledge that."

"Will you stop calling it 'cold-case.' That's the television talking."

"Okay, okay. Serious Crime Review thing, whatever the exact name is. But don't try to dodge. I'm saying to you straight out: you're sabotaging your career."

He drew back his head and waited for a reaction. Minogue stared at his hands.

"What I said," Kilmartin added, "I said as a friend. But it's true. It's a case of self-sabotage you're looking at here."

Minogue was pleased, even proud of his restraint.

"It's a six-month thing, James, a six-month pilot project. How's that sabotage?"

"My point is, it's nice you went out on a limb for Malone. Very decent, yes. I've got a lot of respect for that. A lot. God knows Malone could do with a bit of moral support, the way he's been left twisting in the wind. By the way, meant to ask you: is it really true there wasn't a one of them there this morning at the verdict?"

"It is."

"Bastards. Anyway, here's the thing. This new gig of yours? A grand stroke. You're happy now? Good – run with it. Why invite trouble? Like you-know-who...?"

Minogue took cover in another long, slow drink from the pint. Bits of Kilmartin's earlier doom-laden pieces of advice about his new posting still clung to recesses in his mind: *don't end up carrying the can for some thicko coppers who messed up on a murder case.* Kathleen had said it plain enough: Jim Kilmartin was jealous, plain and simple. Matt Minogue was making a good career for himself; Kilmartin's had hit a wall.

"Are you hearing me at all?"

The head on the Guinness rested halfway down the glass now. Minogue stopped looking for any patterns on it.

"I am and I amn't."

"He's a changed man, is Malone. I don't think you get that. You think you know him, but you don't. He's not the Tommy Malone you and I worked with. So how does it make sense to get this unknown quantity posted to your new gig there?"

Minogue could only shrug.

"A done deal, is it?" Kilmartin pressed. "Now that GSOC took a pass on him?"

"Detective Malone starts tomorrow."

Kilmartin slowly shook his head. Then he gave Minogue a stern, pitying look.

"I've got to be blunt with you. The talk about Malone?

Don't ignore it."

"Ignore what? Rumours? There's always rumours."

"I mean serious talk. And it's not going away."

"Tell it to go away, why don't you. Wave a stick at it, like a strange dog."

Kilmartin didn't revert to the disdain that Minogue expected.

"Matt. I'll spell it out for you. So as I can sleep at night. So I can say to myself, to my conscience, 'I tried. I had a heart-to-heart with Matt. I didn't pull any punches.' Okay? So listen to me. A senior Garda officer told me that there are two scenarios here."

"Scenarios. What are we discussing now, opera?"

A tight, lop-sided smile formed on Kilmartin's face, but his gaze held steady.

"You're so funny. Just hear me out. Theory A: Malone threw Kelly off the roof to keep him quiet about what he knew. That put the kybosh on Kelly ever coughing up names, insiders. Yes, I said that: *Garda insiders.* Join up the bits: Kelly was looking at a long stretch. He was ready to snitch, cop his plea and spit out names."

Minogue studied the varnished wood beside Kilmartin's shoulder.

"I know you're taking it in there, what I just said."

Minogue threw him a quick, challenging look.

"I hope the B option is as entertaining."

"You won't like Option B any better, but here goes: Kelly told Malone something up there, up on the roof. He tried to make a deal with Malone, even gave him a name. So if Malone knew nothing about crooked cops before, well by Jesus he does now. When it suits him, he'll plant his own little garden, and start raking in his hush-money or whatever. And what's his hurry? All he has to do is get through the GSOC thing, and he's back in circulation. Like right now."

He leaned in a little and dropped his voice.

"Take your pick," he muttered. "But remember, either way, the shite's going to hit the fan. Sooner or later it's going to be wigs on the green with Malone. Big-time."

"I should be writing this down, should I?"

Kilmartin stood to his full height, and stretched a little.

"Oh you'd make a cat laugh," he said, with a calculated vagueness. "There's no doubt on that score. Well here's a plan for you. Put a big fat lid on the big fat pot of indignation you're cooking up somewhere, will you? And don't shoot the messenger. I'm only passing it on, as a friend would do. Anything too difficult for you there?"

"You always had a thing with Tommy. In the Squad, I remember."

"Ach! That was just the Dublin thing, the slagging. That's part of life on our little island, man! Culture. Just to let a Dub like him know he shouldn't be cocky. That's all that was about."

"And when his brother died? That was a good-natured slag too?"

Kilmartin raised his hand, palm out.

"I won't dispute that. But it was only natural to speculate."

"You did more than speculate. You were judge and jury on him."

"Me? Why did I let him stay on in the Squad so? I felt sorry for the poor divil. His own brother, for the love of God, going like that, that overdose? A tragedy. An outrage. And those bastards, the Egans, pushing the story that Malone was bent? I wasn't taken in by that, no way. But I had my suspicions. And that's normal."

"You still have them."

"Think about this for a minute: would I be waiting here to clap him on the back if I thought he was bent? I'm just telling you what you should know. Here's a question for you: why does Drugs Central want Malone o-u-t? Why's no-one sticking up for him? Face up to it: there's a side to Malone that you don't know."

Minogue busied himself with his pint again. Kilmartin began to say something else, but then he let his words trail off. His sudden, cautious grin told Minogue that behind him, Malone had arrived.

Chapter 4

An hour later, and long after the craic had gotten started in earnest, Minogue had slid into a brood. Kilmartin's blather had revived doubts, and they had stuck in his mind.

Of course Malone was different. Three years in Drugs Central nose-to-nose with gangs? 'Intense' didn't begin to describe that. The qualities Malone had shown on the Squad wouldn't change. He wasn't a glory hound. No diva stuff out of him either – ever. A team player. A wicked sharp eye for inconsistencies. He read liars fast, and he read them well. And he never whinged about putting in the hours, or taking on donkey-work.

A simple fact had escaped Kilmartin: Malone would be glad of a change. This posting was a break for him. He'd recharge his batteries, working with someone who wasn't suspicious of him. Boring as it could be, case review wasn't sitting thinking about – reliving – what had happened on that rooftop, or afterwards. Didn't he deserve a fresh start, a chance to rebuild? Hadn't he had enough stuff going against him to earn this?

Sonia, Minogue thought then, Malone's fiancée. Former fiancée? Things had gone astray between them. Those few seconds on that rooftop had surely barreled into Malone's personal life too, ripping through everything there.

He could only guess at what Sonia knew about Malone's troubles. Her parents knew enough. Dublin might still teem with new faces and complexions and languages, but it was still a small place. It was one thing for a Chinese family to imagine an

Irishman as son-in-law – a Dubliner, a cop with an unsavoury interest in boxing even – but for Malone to have a mysterious gravitational pull toward mayhem, that'd be a no-go.

In spite of himself, another notion circled in the back of Minogue's mind, a notion so brazenly irrational, or so downright superstitious even that he wouldn't utter it aloud: did Thomas Martin Malone trail bad karma?

He listened to Plateglass Sheehy's few Kerryman jokes, proof of the man's indefatigable pride in his native county. Only two were recycled: the revolving door one, and the goat with the driver's licence. He turned to observing Malone then, saw that the tight, ambiguous smile was holding. Enjoying himself. Two lads from Drugs Central had shown up finally, and three others from Records where Malone had bided his time waiting for today. Shea Hoey had phoned, said he was sorry, but the baby had puked.

Kilmartin edged closer, flicking his eyes to his left.

"See the fella holding up the bar over there? Seán Brophy. Forensic Seán?"

"Are you sure?"

"None other. Looks fierce shook, doesn't he? Had a brief how-do with him. Got him up-to-date a bit, why we're here tonight, well one of the reasons. You and Malone, the new Cold Case Crew. Seán didn't know about it."

Kilmartin paused, and let his thumb trace the curve of his lower lip.

"You know it was Seán's daughter who found that man back in June, the dead man out there in Killiney. That old, well I shouldn't say it maybe, that down-and-out."

He made half-hearted air-quotes.

"The 'homeless person'? June, this year? It's on your list, isn't it?"

Minogue played vague. The photo of the dead man had stayed with him long after he had read the case summary last week. It had looked too much like that photo of Saddam Hussein, the one they'd taken after they had pulled him out of his hidey-hole.

"Maybe it is and maybe it isn't. What does this have to do with me?"

Something stronger than irritation rippled across Kilmartin's face. He pushed abruptly out of his lean against the partition.

"Jesus Christ, Matt. Look at the state Seán's in. His daughter is in bits – she's having some class of a breakdown. A post-traumatic thing. Won't leave the house. They have to keep an eye on her so she'll eat. The whole family's in a fierce state, entirely. So how could I not give him a bit of hope. You'd want to be made of stone not to."

"What hope? Were you offering my services, is that it?"

"I know, I know, I know. No doubt you have your priorities. Fine."

"You think a six-month project will clear every open murder case in Dublin?"

"Christ's sakes man, no need to turn Turk on me. Listen, Seán is so out-of-it that – get this, are you ready? – Seán actually thought we were still in the game, the Murder Squad. Swear to God. That's why he asked me. Long story short, I said I'd put it to you."

"Put what to me."

"Don't be a gobshite. Give him a listen. Or is that too hard to do?"

Kilmartin's insouciant stare didn't falter.

"Listen to me, you," Minogue said. "Go get Seán. Put Seán in your car. Drive Seán home. On the way, tell Seán you made a mistake. Is *that* too hard to do?"

"What mistake? You're heading up this effort, right? I can't tell a lie, can I?"

"You said it yourself. I have a list of cases. *Pri-or-i-ties.*"

"What, a poor homeless divil getting murdered isn't one of your *pri-or-i-ties*?"

"I notice he's not a 'down-and-out' now' anymore. Look just tell Seán you made a mistake."

"I made the mistake all right – thinking you mightn't be a cold-hearted hoor."

"Tell him he can get in touch with me later on. Next week, maybe."

Kilmartin seemed to weigh this information.

"Rhiannon," he said then. "That's his daughter's name. Welsh, is it?"

Answering Kilmartin would only draw him on.

"Seán's your pal," he said. "So he's all yours. Carry him out of here."

Kilmartin looked into his glass, and he rolled the whiskey around slowly.

"This little Rhiannon is very artistic, I hear," he said. "Just like your own daughter, if I might be so bold. Iseult, yes. Lovely girl. How's she getting on anyway?"

"Could you be pouring it on any thicker?"

"Well I have to, don't I?" Kilmartin retorted. He shook his head several times, and shrugged. "What turned you so cold? I never knew you were that type at all."

"What exactly did you tell Seán?"

A pained look came to Kilmartin.

"Not much. I said you might be able to help – *might. Sometime. Maybe.*"

"So now Seán thinks—"

"—How the hell do I know what he thinks?"

Killmartin swallowed then, and a sheepish look came to him.

"Look: here's this man murdered, this down-and-out, vagrant – whatever. I know, I know, you can't use those words. But the way it's gone, the man is nearly a martyr, a victim of society type of thing. You know the routine."

Minogue reached for his glass.

"My point is," Kilmartin went on. "This Rhiannon kid gets nothing, Seán's little girl, I mean. Nothing! I mean, nice that people care, but – Look, are you listening to me at all?"

Kilmartin's nudge made him turn back.

"I am trying not to," he said. "Does it occur to you that the country is up the creek precisely because of what you're asking?"

Kilmartin looked more shocked than puzzled.

"All because I'm asking you a simple question?"

"It's the whole insider thing again. 'A pal of mine'll fix you up.'

'Ah, don't bother going through the steps, I'll look after you.'
Nudge nudge, wink wink."

Kilmartin rolled his eyes.

"Christ's sakes," he said. "Am I a bank asking for billions
to bail me out? This is Seán, his family we're talking about.
They're being destroyed! It's common decency has me asking! Or
are we gone so low in this country that we can't even do that anymore?"

"There's only so many cases we can go at."

"No doubt. No doubt. Well, it'll look good in the papers at
least. Yes, very nice."

"What does that mean?"

"Cop on to yourself, will you? You don't have to actually *do*
anything in this job of yours. You just have to *look* like you're
doing something. Look, did you sleep through the past twenty
years or something? It's all PR these days. All you have to do is just
emote. Express 'grave concerns,' recite your script, and move on."

But before he could give Kilmartin a bollocking, Minogue
spotted Brophy making his way over. Brophy strayed toward a
chair, slowed and swayed a little, and moved on.

"Look how bockety he is," Kilmartin said. "Give him something to hope for?"

Brophy's long yawn seemed to make him change course. He
came to a halt in front of them. From the corner of his eye,
Minogue saw Kilmartin nod his head.

"That's great," said Brophy, wavering more now. But
Kilmartin was already on the move, and calling out to Farrell.

"Long time no see, Matt," Brophy said, edging onto a stool
and exhaling noisily through his nose. "You and Jim and... Like
old times. Just the men I need."

He spoke through the last of a yawn, opening his eyes again.

"So did Jim tell you? The per..., the *predicament* I'm in?"

"He mentioned it. But there are things he shouldn't have
told you too."

Another yawn was tugging at Brophy's jaw. He fought it off.

"Jim's an old dote," he said. "Heart of gold, has Jim. A big
softie. Not a lot of people know that about him, did you know?"

Minogue sought out Kilmartin, but he had already corralled Farrell.

"Jim's has his own troubles, his own 'dark night of the soul'."

"Jim has no soul at all, Seán. No souls were handed out to Mayo men. Ever."

Brophy wanted to laugh, but something stopped him. He blinked at Minogue.

A sharp suspicion came to Minogue then, that as drunk as Seán Brophy might be, he might be all too lucid too. A deadly combination.

"Seán. Let's be clear here. Jim overstepped himself. You need to know that."

Brophy was rubbing at his eyes now. When he spoke now, his voice had gone flat.

"Does my little girl have to die too?"

Brophy stopped rubbing. His eyes found Minogue first, but looked through him.

"Is that what has to happen," he said. "For anything to get done? Is it?"

Chapter 5

Minogue eased his Peugeot onto Charlemont Street. The lights along the canal were soon in sight, the Ranelagh Road waiting for him just over the bridge.

"That car of mine," Brophy asked. "Will it be safe back there overnight?"

Minogue slowed for the lights.

"Safe enough, Seán. Safer than if you were behind the wheel of it."

Brophy nodded, and swallowed noisily. Minogue let down his window more as the car slowed. Any doubts he'd had about how much whiskey had been in Brophy's evening were gone.

Brophy took an inebriate's keen interest in the smokers next to the doors of pubs.

"Those hoodies," he said. "Like monks, aren't they? Or priests, maybe?"

"Hip-hop monks, Seán. Or they could be Franciscans."

"Ah hah hah hah," said Brophy, his words going wispy before he coughed. "But I do appreciate this, Matt, I tell you. I really do."

"Tomorrow's another day, Seán."

"'*Don't stop thinking about tomorrow, Don't stop, it'll soon be here—*'"

"You know them all, don't you."

"Fecking sure I do. Those lyrics, man, they're etched on my soul."

"Not under your shoe, now. The real soul, right?"

Another weak braying laugh came from Brophy.

"I can still belt it out, you know," he added. His voice slid back down to a murmur. "Well, I used to. Me and a few diehards, we used to get together ..."

He looked over at Minogue

"The great ones live on," he said. That's music for you. Isn't it?"

"You're right on the money there, Seán."

"None of this *hos* and *bros* stuff. Monotonous ould... Am I right or what?"

"How about Nina Simone," Minogue said. "'*I wish I knew how*'...?"

Brophy punched the air twice.

"Oh yes," he said. "They play that in heaven. That's how you know you're there."

The metronomic tack-tack of the tires over the patched roadway took over in the lull.

"Funny thing," Brophy said then. He had slumped further into the seat, and Minogue had sensed his mood growing sombre. "None of mine show any interest in the guitar. Not a one."

"They go their own way. That much I learned – still learning, in actual fact."

"A billion tunes on their iPods," Brophy croaked, trapping another belch in his throat. "But ne'er a one of them can play an instrument. All Facebook now, MyFace, whatever – MySpace. Texting dah dah dah...."

"Ah now, Seán. Hope springs infernal."

The last of Brophy's heavy sigh whistled out his nostrils. His train of thought continued to plough on through this unlit tunnel.

"I must have incolu – intoc – *inoculated* them ag'in it," he muttered. "I do go over the top a bit by times, you know. Wait – I tell a lie. I go *waaay* over the top by times."

Minogue kept his eye on the next red traffic light. He knew from Brophy's voice that he had been smiling a little when he'd said that about going over the top. And he did remember a night of some uproar a few years back, a night when Seán Brophy had loosened the bolts with a mad version of 'When Irish Eyes Are Smiling.' A fundraiser thing for those two Guards heading over to Africa, to do a UN thing? Right: money for digging wells, it was. Seán Brophy had made the money jingle that night all right.

"All in a good cause," he managed. "As I recall?"

Brophy dismissed the compliment with a soft chuckle. His head bobbed as he tried to observe the passing sights. He spoke clearly then, just as Minogue was about to turn on the radio.

"I tell you, Matt, it's hard to rise any giggle around my house these days."

"Times are tough all around, Seán. It's backwards we're going, some days."

Brophy grunted. It seemed to Minogue that he had lost heart completely.

"That thing," he muttered. "Rhiannon...? Christ. Like I said to Jim. Unlucky?"

"Rough, Seán. Very rough. My heart goes out to your young one. Rhiannon."

"'If only you were running the show,' I says to Jim. You too, Matt. Sure the world and his mother knew it was you carried a lot of hard cases for Kilmartin."

Minogue watched as brake lights began to come on ahead. Brophy sat up.

"The Squad," he said, warmly. "'Thank God, here's the Squad!' Remember?"

"Them was the days all right, Seán. Them was the days."

He regretted the sarcasm a little, but like much of what he had said so far, Brophy seemed not to have noticed it anyway.

"I used to see him too," said Brophy, his voice dropping again. "And so did Rhiannon. Everyone did, really. Tell me, did you see him about the place?"

"Who, now, Seán?"

"That poor divil, Larkin. The down-and-out – did you know what he was called?"

Minogue shook his head.

"'The High King' – honest to God. Or 'The King of Ireland.'

Not as an insult, now. It was more pity, I suppose."

Minogue braced himself for next few minutes. Poor Brophy would be squeezing in as much as he could into the few minutes left before they got to his road.

"I'd never have imagined what a thing like that'd do. To Rhiannon, I mean."

"It must be terrible. But time heals all things, Seán, don't they say?"

"Me and her, well we're closer than the others. You know what I'm saying?"

"I do, I think."

"Now Kevin," said Brophy, pausing to finish a slow, boozy yawn, "Kev, he's more like his mother. Very cut and dried. And as for little Madeleine, sure she's a soccer freak. Leaping about, the whole day long. Happy as anything. But Rhiannon...."

Minogue let down the back window a little.

"Oh, I love them all dearly," Brophy went on. "But you know how it is."

The cross light had changed. Minogue considered a diversion, a Spar by the petrol station ahead: bread, milk, or something. Anything to interrupt this slide.

"I was artsy-fartsy myself, Matt. Bet you didn't know that, did you?"

"Well the State only hires well-rounded lads for the Lab."

Brophy made a bleak smile. Minogue made brisk gear shifts away from the lights.

"Music isn't as artsy as you'd think. It's next door to Maths. Did you know that?"

All Minogue felt safe to do now was to nod. Math and music indeed, he thought, and glimpses of his uncle Jackie, the long departed 'American Jack,' came to his mind. Jack, a Maths teacher, had such high standards in everything that his not-so-secret nickname was The Ayatollah. America had long been his whipping boy for all the ills of the world, particularly for the decline of Decency. Minogue kept an old photo of Jackie the freshly minted teacher, all business, posing by a staged collection of Maths books.

A tee-totalling, cross-grained bachelor, Jackie had occasioned much sly amusement by taking up the fiddle late in life. He made no acknowledgement of the fact that he was losing his sight, not even when blindness had finally settled on him. He merely carried on learning new tunes and playing them ever badly, and worse, over and over again until that warm, Spring day when in a sudden toppling from the chair set out for him, he passed from the earth, his fiddle crushed and silenced beneath him.

Brophy's tapping fingers drew Minogue's eye. The tapping had started on his knee, but now his fingers rose up to frame chords on an imagined guitar. The traffic lights began to oblige; they were soon passing the Goat Inn. Minogue's hopes revived.

Then, with a yawn that ended in sigh, Brophy relaxed his hand.

"On the right," he said.

Minogue went by the driveway, and pulled in to the curb. Brophy's head dipped as the car came to a stop. Minogue heard the sniff, just as he caught sight of Brophy's hand going to his face.

Brophy shook gently as he cried. His breath came in tense, torn-off gulps that gave way to wheezes. Minogue squirmed and pushed the window down a little more.

After a while, Brophy shuddered, and a long, sighing gasp escaped him. He fumbled in his pocket until he drew out a crushed packet of paper hankies. His voice came in a hoarse whisper.

"Sorry about that. Came out of nowhere. Jesus."

"No bother, Seán. You're grand. Nothing to be sorry about at all. Not a thing."

Brophy darted him a look, and then half-heartedly blew his nose.

"This is, you know, just between us," he said afterwards. "Right?"

"To be sure it is, Seán. To be sure."

"And look," he heard himself adding before Brophy could start again. "We'll have the Christmas now soon enough, and we can down tools. Just the ticket, I say."

Brophy sniffed, and swallowed.

"I suppose, yes. The Christmas, yes. But like I say, sorry about that."

Minogue made a short dismissing gesture with his hand.

"The drink no doubt," said Brophy, against the breath he drew in. "Let myself slide a bit tonight. Didn't expect that, I can tell you."

"The drink can turn Turk on you, here's no doubt."

Brophy stared at the cars parked further down the road.

"You relax a bit for the first time in ages and, well, that's what happens."

Minogue moved the gear stick over and back across the gate again.

"And the stupid music," Brophy sniffed. "Reminding me."

Minogue dared a look over.

"Have you someone inside, Seán? You know, to chat with, maybe?"

Brophy came up with a worn-looking smile. He rubbed the hankie at his nose with slow, decisive strokes. Something curled up tighter in Minogue's chest.

"It was like she was hit by a train," Brophy murmured. "Rhiannon, I'm talking about. You hear that expression, but that's what it is. It really is."

Minogue too stared down the road.

"But she has her years ahead of her, hasn't she, Seán."

"It's like looking through a window, and you can do nothing."

Minogue waited, but Brophy made no move to leave.

"Seán."

"She goes to a shrink," said Brophy, breaking his stare at the roadway.

"Good move. They know a lot nowadays, so they do. To help, I mean."

"Oh I wonder," said Brophy. The new vigour in his voice deepened Minogue's unease. "I said it to her shrink. Post-Traumatic Stress, I said. They don't like you putting your oar in, do they. But later on she sort of agreed with me, the shrink."

A car went by. Minogue let the window down a bit more.

"Look, Matt, you know me. I'm a scientist. So I want solutions. Things fixed. Over and done with. ASAP, ha ha. Remember that?"

Minogue was a little late to the humour. Kilmartin used to barrack the Lab to get results quicker. ASAP: Any Shagging Answer, Pronto.

"'If only I knew,' says she to me one night. If only she knew the people were caught, she meant. Bowled me over to hear it. And the missus, she's at her wit's end too."

"Seán...?"

"Jimmy told me about your new job. I don't think he meant to. Did he?"

"Damned if I know. There's no reforming that bullock out of Mayo."

"Ah now," said Brophy. "Jim's a decent old skin, behind that...that façade."

Minogue bit back a comment.

"I'm not criticizing the Guards, Matt. God, no! But when I phone the station there down in Dalkey – that's where the case is run – I get the feeling that they're not keen to hear from me. Not the bum's rush, now, oh no – very polite. But still, zero."

Minogue was tempted to ask if he had been sober when he'd phoned the station.

"I told them how she was," Brophy went on. "How Rhiannon was. And I used the word 'suffering.' I had to. Because that's what it is."

He broke off at that and he sighed. The quiet lasted longer than Minogue expected. Then Brophy seemed to get a fit of resolve. He put his hand on the door latch.

"Ah you're great to put up with me, Matt."

"Nothing to it. And I have great amnesia. All us married men have it."

Brophy fixed him with a knowing look. His smile was lop-sided.

"Can't help thinking though – can't help actually saying it,

Matt: this effort would have been cleared right quick if, well, you know what I'm driving at. So I won't say it."

"Look, Seán," Minogue managed. "Things aren't that straightforward."

Brophy affected an air of sobriety, but the solemnity he reached for only reminded Minogue of Mr. Bean.

"Fair enough, I hear you. I'm no daw. But how can they be that busy?"

"Gangs, Seán," Minogue said. "Drugs, turf wars. You see it every day in the paper."

"I'm telling you," he added, watching Brophy's slow, disbelieving nods. He put an edge to his voice. "It's all hands on deck, Seán, especially in Dublin. Guns everywhere, money: big, big money. We're scrambling, the Guards I mean."

The passenger door was opening, and cold air across his legs came as a relief. Brophy clutched and clumped his way out onto the footpath. His heavier breathing gave new life to the smell of whiskey in the car.

"Don't be too hard on Jim," he said. "Like I said, a heart of gold."

"A neck of brass, you mean."

Brophy began to chortle, but coughed instead.

"He said you'd do what you can," he wheezed. "That's more than enough for us."

Minogue waited until he was out on the Lower Kilmacud Road before he put the boot to his Peugeot. He took it hard through second gear, issuing his curses slowly and dispassionately and then louder as the inrushing air went from a hiss to a roar. He left the windows down all the way, and grimly welcomed the harsh, damp air rampaging around him, yanking at his scalp, scouring his knuckles and the tip of his nose.

★ ★ ★

The curtains on the Minogue sitting room window flickered and glowed with the light from the telly. He drew the car up tight to the garage, and let go of his last curses. A pseudo-secret smoke by the side of the house beckoned, and there by the hedge he lighted up. The first few drags made him dizzy. He ignored the damp air seeping in under his arms and listened instead to the breeze raising a hiss from the ornamental grasses. His mind lurched more. He was soon rehearsing tomorrow – The Big Day. Put in an appearance at Liaison early, pick up any messages. Double-check paperwork on the Donegal arrests, 'The Nike Lorry' that had caused so much slagging. Sign off on it. Go to all the regulars, thank them. Then – out the door and head to that cubbyhole in Harcourt Terrace that they'd given him for the duration. Grand entirely.

And Malone? He'd fall in line. It might take a few days, but so what. The main thing was, he'd had made it through GSOC and come out the far end in one piece. Those rumours about him would die off. In all the talk he'd heard, there was actually no real criticism of Malone. There was even sneaking admiration. And what about the knife the Kelly guy pulled on Malone on that roof? His prints all over it?

The last of his cigarette was bitter. He used one of the stones to kill it, watching the sparks twist away in the breeze. He had two peppermints left. He took them both.

Kathleen, his wife, was actually home. The gas fireplace was on, and there was still a smell of tea. She was reading.

"Well, gorgeous."

She eyed him, and did her Mona Lisa thing for several moments. He spied some measuring-up hint to that look, as though she were applying some theory from the book.

"So how'd it go?" she asked.

He studied the mantelpiece a moment. It hadn't changed from yesterday.

"As you'd imagine. A pack of Guards in a pub. Old jokes. Bullshit by the ton."

"Ah but Tommy must be relieved. The poor devil. But it's like I said to Tony at work there, things are gone so bad, it's Guards being put in the dock."

She put down the book, and picked up another.

"Here's something you really have to read. You just have to."

Minogue eyed the title. *Second* something...: *Second Tide?*

"It's great. It's about the crisis."

"What crisis – which crisis, I mean."

"Now, now. It's what's behind 'the crisis.' Not just the financial meltdown thing. It's what led to it. Do you get it?"

Minogue remembered the cans of beer by the power-saw in the garage.

"Greed, of course," she said. He knew from her tone that a recitation was imminent. "Losing our moral bearings. Loss of faith – in ourselves, as well as in God."

He shook his head.

"What," she said, and she waved the book. "It's all there. We have to rethink everything. We need a sea-change. Don't you love that word, 'sea-change'?"

In a moment he was back at the beach again, but this time watching the sea take its pounding runs at the beach. Mad sea-anglers, of course. Throw in a collie fighting with the foam too for good measure, and demented seagulls hovering just overhead.

"Not 'the government,'" she went on. "Not 'the banks.' Not even 'society.'"

"What's left we can blame? The drink?"

"*Us,*" she said. "We need to take a long, hard look at ourselves. Every one of us."

She waited for some reaction. The numbness spreading in his mind wasn't it.

"So refreshing isn't it," she said. "Worlds away from the usual doom-and-gloom."

He considered telling her the truth, that doom-and-gloom was exactly what he preferred. Hard times were a relief from the wracking changes that had turned the country inside-out. He felt sure he wasn't alone in this apostasy.

"What are you staring at?"

He raised an eyebrow, and gave her his own long, appraising look. He was all too aware that this look had a spotty record as regards effectiveness. But something caught fire in her eyes, and she smiled, and then she laughed. Her slow steps on the stairs behind him only boosted the charge running riot through him.

Afterwards, she picked up the book up again. He had a third of the Gösser still on the bedside cabinet.

"Are you listening," she said. "All I'm asking is that you look it over. It explains so much. It's how we've forgotten what made us who we are."

He ran his hand over her breast again. She elbowed him.

"Irish," she said. "Remember? We're Irish. We have our fundamentals."

"A great little country we are, to be sure."

"Stop that. Loan the book to Jim too when you have it read. Will you?"

"I'll give that man nothing. Except maybe a kick-up in the arse."

"Oh grow up. Jim's one man who'd appreciate the book."

He leaned over to look at her. That long, deep fold down from her neck stopped at the sheet she'd drawn up over her breasts.

"If he promised not to talk to me about it after he read it, I'd give it to him."

"At least he's trying, Jim is. And this book is right up his alley."

"Don't mind a book, some days I'd take him up an alley."

"Oh give over. It's how to rebuild, how to recover old ways – the good ones only. How we used to be real Irish people. Before this Celtic Tiger nonsense."

"Ah," he said. "The good old days again. A nice wholesome pilgrimage up Croagh Patrick there, in the pissings of rain. In bare feet too, for our many sins."

"My God but you're crooked tonight."

He turned to her, gave her the eye.

"There has to be tons of austerity," he murmured. "Doesn't there? And bucket-loads of repentance and guilt and the rest of it – every kind of squashing we can dream up to inflict on ourselves. But only for certain classes of people of course. That's an Irish fundamental there, isn't it?"

She looked away. He lay back on the pillow.

"Really," she said. "Going on like that...? Where that comes from, I have no idea. That anger – I just don't get it. You'd say it's humour, but I can see through it."

The lampshade had cobwebs that he had not noticed before.

"This country needs to wake up," she added. "And well you know it too."

"Overrated," he said, reaching for the beer. "This wake-up business."

He eyed her while he drank. Leaning over to park the can back on the cabinet Seán Brophy rose unbidden to his mind. It was not Brophy himself, it was someone else, someone he'd never seen, or even met: the Brophys' daughter, curled up, staring at a wall.

"What?" Kathleen was asking. "What's on your mind now?"

It wouldn't make much sense to her. He wanted to scrub off whatever damned thing that Seán Brophy had left all over his thoughts.

Kathleen elbowed him, tenderly this time.

"You're cold, are you?" she said. "Is that what it is?"

Chapter 6

Minogue felt floaty when he woke, a little stupid even. It had been a busy night, with lurid dreams piling up mercilessly on one another. To his dismay, one of them even featured Kilmartin. Dressed in a black funeral suit, Kilmartin stood in a very august hall – parliament? concert hall? – and delivered a sombre, stirring sermon on the Irish soul. But during the wild applause that followed, he'd flown away, and in no time, he was gliding between rooftops in some strange city at the edge of an even stranger sea.

It got worse. Malone too had shown up in this crackpot world. He had been sitting in what seemed to be a circus audience, and clapping at Kilmartin's antics overhead. But then the sea was suddenly pouring in the windows of Minogue's new car, filling it to the roof. Sheer madness.

He had enough time over breakfast to ponder any deep meanings, but came up with none. The Costigan's half-wild cat made its ritual breakfast visit to the windowsill. He eyed its fur stirring and parting in the breeze, the flicking tail, the I-don't-care eyes. The Paris getaway ad came on: Freedom of the City of Light. He finished his egg and went to the sink. That was enough for the cat to take off. He watched it thread its way through the flowerbeds and by the pear tree. Had there been a touch of frost? He heard Kathleen's heels on the stairs.

He dropped her by St. Stephen's Green, and began threading his way down Kevin Street. It was a bit too easy, really. By and by, he was coasting by St. Patrick's Cathedral and up the hill toward Christchurch. A string of green lights let him make the turn onto Usher's Quay in short order. This pleased him, but it made him a little uneasy too. These streets used to be a big, stuttering traffic jam. So, was there a traffic crisis too? All too soon, he was closing in on Garda HQ, and he was glad of the red light by Infirmary Road. He spent the idle time watching the few dry leaves stirring and sometimes escaping from the damp drifts along the footpaths, only to be snagged in another farther on.

There was more suspicious ease with a too-handy parking spot. He lifted his work laptop from the boot. He had deleted all of the work files last night, clicking through all the security software warnings with a pleasant carelessness. Was that why it felt lighter?

Things were quiet enough. He made it to his desk unaccosted, and began by backing up the Europol Lyons correspondence on the stolen cargos. Machine tools, dies, and high-quality steel had been plucked from no less than five countries, each robbery from roadside stops. The thieves had no trouble starting the vehicles, and driving them off. Three of these lorries had been contracted to Irish hauliers, and all three had baggage of their own in tow: serial convictions going back twenty years. The hauls would have totalled several millions worth – early last year, when they were nailed. Today, who knew.

It was Áine Lawless, the detective who had torn open the au pair racket last year, who spotted him first. She had a half-pound of Kenyan coffee for him, and a reminder at the bottom of the card that she'd be expecting him at her wedding in the New Year. Ger Sheeran, Sergeant Ger Sheeran, a hyperactive fitness zealot with a genuine year-round tan, heard the talk. Over he came. Sheehan had just begun a joke about Paddy the Irishman on holiday in Spain when Minogue spotted Galloping Hogan making his way over. Hogan, starting out as Patrick Hogan from the baptismal fount in Coolooney, County Sligo, some thirty-eight years before, was as fearsomely dynamic a copper as Minogue had met, a man surely headed for the senior Garda firmament any day now.

With Hogan standing there, Sheehan rushed the joke, taking

all the air out of it, and then he made off. Minogue feigned interest in Hogan's opener, shop talk about next week's planned bust on the livestock smuggling out of County Louth: postponed. There had been a tipoff from across the Border. Then came the infamous Hogan Pause. Minogue picked a spot on the wall, and let his eyes out of focus, and he waited.

"So, Matt," said Hogan eventually. "Ready for the big time, are you."

"Just about. Yes. 'Change is good.' All that."

"It'll be nice to be running the show yourself though, I imagine."

Minogue fetched around for an innocuous answer. For too long now, he had wondered if Hogan had formed some resentment against him. He had put the awkwardness between them down to an age thing. Or had Hogan always felt that he had been overruled when Minogue was appointed, more than hired, to the unit?

"Six months, Paddy. We'll see what comes of it. Nothing more, nothing less."

Hogan gave a couple of slow, thoughtful nods. Another Hogan Pause.

"You've been very decent about this leave, Paddy," Minogue said. "In case I forget to tell you."

Hogan dismissed the compliment with a quick flexing of his eyebrows. His eye still unwilling to stop its slow roaming around Minogue's desktop.

"You know we don't blow our horn here," he said, and then looked up sharply. "But there's a lot of lads would give their eye teeth to be at your desk here."

Minogue had never learned to tell when Hogan was angry.

"Don't I know it."

"But you know what you're getting into. A man of your experience?"

Minogue decided it might now be worth a try at some distraction.

"I'll phone every day, Paddy. Check you're able to manage without me."

Hogan gave no sign that he appreciated the wit.

"I have a message for you," he said instead. "Two, actually. Maybe you got one?"

Minogue could do nothing but wait out another measured delay.

"Nobody phoned you?" Hogan asked. "Last night even, late-ish?"

"Me and mobiles, Paddy, we're not a great match. I do forget sometimes."

"Something about last night," Hogan said. "Below in Parkgate Street."

"I know Parkgate Street."

"A certain premises on Parkgate Street. Bit of a shindig there, was there?"

"There was. Tame enough, though. I left early."

"Well you missed the highjinks then."

Minogue stuck to the only strategy he knew, grimly waiting Hogan out.

"Bit of a barney there, is what I was told. One Garda Malone, and somebody. Two somebodies in actual fact. Two other Guards. A nice how-do-you-do."

Those two dark eminences, the hard-chaw looking bastards with their stares.

"But maybe it's been sorted out already," Hogan said.

Hushed up, as only Guards could do well, Minogue wanted to add.

"You might want to know who told me," Hogan said then. He didn't wait for Minogue to ask. "One Sergeant O'Leary."

"Brendan O'Leary?"

"That's the one," Hogan replied. There was no attempt to tone down the irony. "Commissioner's office, yes. He said to pass that info on to you before the meeting."

"A meeting."

Hogan gave him a quick, knowing look. He was enjoying himself. Minogue couldn't blame him.

"Well that's the other message. Commissioner Tynan wants a chat, this morning."

"This morning, you are saying. The Commissioner."

"This very morning, yes."

"Was there a time mentioned?"

"The term used was ASAP. That sound about right to you?"

★ ★ ★

Brendan O'Leary, the Garda Commissioner's driver and aide-de-camp, was half-pretending not to have seen Minogue first.

"Brendan, how do. Fresh and well you're looking."

"Nothing on you, Matt. Very suave. Are you en route to the Left Bank?"

Minogue didn't mind the dig. O'Leary's wife had dragged him to Paris over the summer. He had phoned Minogue for survival tips. O'Leary had liked Paris a lot more than he had expected. Minogue ended up with a bottle of Marie Brizard for his troubles.

"New job, new suit," he said. "A one-day wonder only though."

"Thanks be to God. You'd only be showing us up if it went longer."

Minogue sat.

"Do I take a number?"

O'Leary shook his head, and returned to his keyboard. Minogue was soon half-lulled by the delicate, arrhythmic clacking. He let himself imagine that O'Leary was making his umpteenth application to go back to Africa. But wasn't he married now, with a baby on the way? He'd married late enough. She was a Wexford belle, and well-got, weathering the crash in some high-up job in the Financial Services Centre.

Footsteps sounded behind the door, and nervousness fell on Minogue again like a chill. He had not seen the Commissioner since Rachel Tynan's funeral.

He caught O'Leary's eye again.

"Same as ever, is he?"

From O'Leary, a shrug: what could he say about his boss being a widower now?

The door swept open. It was not Tynan, but Carney, Deputy Comm for the Dublin Metropolitan Region. Was this the 'sorted out' that Hogan had meant?

"Ah, Matt," he said. "Cometh the hour, cometh the man."

The smell of old-school shaving soap from Carney reminded Minogue of severe teachers. He didn't squeeze back hard on Carney's handshake.

"Ready for action there, Matt?"

He imagined telling Carney to stop spinning his hat between his fingers.

"Sufficient to the task, I'm hoping," he managed.

Tynan was on the phone, his long legs straight out, heels dug into a mat. Minogue surveyed the office. Everything seemed the same, but this made things only stranger. That ugly bog-oak crucifix had always been on the wall over the chairs. Rachel Tynan's watercolours of the Shannon lakes were still aligned to the very millimetre above the cabinet.

"Almost like old times, isn't it?"

Carney's genial tone unsettled him. He was holding out his card. Minogue made sure that Carney saw him file the card with care in his wallet.

"Good luck in your new position," Carney said. "And phone me directly if you need something? Directly. We're open door, you know. The whole transparency bit."

Tynan told someone that he had to go. He ended the call with a few sentences of fluent Munster Irish. It must be that ancient aunt of Rachel's, Minogue guessed, that relic of old decency, a Macroom Prod, the one who'd read poems at Rachel Tynan's funeral.

Tynan put down his biro, and slid his daytimer to a corner of his desk. Though he couldn't pin it down, Minogue was sure that there was something changed about Tynan.

"I know better than to be offering you any ordinary coffee."

"A weakness I struggle with, to be sure."

"A hard man to please, more like it. You're gone Viennese now, I suppose."

That Europol conference, he meant. Tynan had never been able to do humour.

"It's a fine city for a walk-about, and that's a fact."

"You paid your respects at the shrine there in Berggasse, I hope?"

"I had to, sure. Kathleen put it in the prenup."

Tynan let the pause drag a little.

"All right," he said then. "You have your case list. Staffing and resources sorted? That office in Harcourt Terrace?"

"They are indeed."

"And you're ready for your baptism of fire with the media?"

Minogue nodded. His morning's coaching in the Garda Press Office last Friday had been funny as well as instructive.

"That's good," Tynan said, looking down at his daytimer. "The Press Release is out today. The CSI Effect says you'll be expected to fix everything right away."

"I'm getting guff about 'cold cases' already – from people who know better too. But it's good practice for when the media come sniffing around."

Tynan glanced up again.

"There'll be other matters to distract them, I imagine. The Murphy Report?"

"I almost forgot."

"It won't be just reformatories or borstals this time. It's parish stuff now."

Minogue was stumped for something to say, something not trite or stupid, that is. This musing-out-loud Tynan was not a Tynan that he recognized. Like the rest of the country, maybe he too was looking back to see where signs had been missed. It was more likely that Tynan's own background had him pondering things more than others. Walking away from a Jesuit seminary back then, Tynan mightn't have heard 'spoiled priest' said aloud. But marrying so soon afterwards? To a Prod? Later came the innuendo that the Tynans' marriage had been childless for a reason. So was his wife's death 'a sign' too?

Rubbish – peasant holdover: it was a totally different Ireland back then. But wasn't everyone back to looking for signs these days? The country would never run short of crackpots. The religious ones had already been seeing plenty of their signs lately: the shape of the Blessed Virgin on a wall in Sligo. The same Lady on a holy tree stump. A sun sign at the Knock shrine. Signs of what? That their kids might not have to emigrate?

"'Hard to believe,'" Tynan said. His tone turned meditative. "That's the phrase we'll be hearing a lot."

"You're right, I'd say," said Minogue, relieved that he had something to say now.

Tynan frowned then and studied something on his desktop.

"Okay," he said. "Let's start. Item A: one Detective Garda Thomas Malone."

Minogue wondered if Tynan heard his intake of breath.

"Garda Malone had a set-to last night," Tynan said. "You knew that?"

"I just heard something in passing. No details."

"Fortunately, the matter was settled by the time a squad car arrived."

Minogue tried to form his most alert-but-benign expression.

"As I recall," Tynan went on, "your request for Garda Malone was firm."

"It was, yes."

"Any second thoughts there?" Tynan asked after a calibrated pause.

"I haven't really, no."

"Would Garda Malone benefit from some counselling, in your opinion?"

Minogue half-admired the brazen approach.

"I can suggest it to him, I suppose."

"Does Garda Malone understand what's expected of him in this posting?"

"I believe that he does. And he will be reminded too."

"Especially as nearly all of the list are cases here in Dublin?"

Hence Carney's visit, Minogue decided. A Carney damage-control maneuver because of lousy clearance rates in his bailiwick. Maybe a shot across the bows too.

"So if you ever get any foot-dragging from staff, the expectation is that you'll work it out yourself. People skills to the fore, I need hardly say. Tact."

Minogue could do little but dare the odd glance back into Tynan's stare.

"It would be a problem if, say, in the course of revisiting an open murder case," Tynan added. He paused to let it sink in. "If a Guard was led to feel his work, his opinion, was being slighted. Morale is what keeps things right side up, and working."

Minogue had no trouble translating: Malone was on unofficial notice.

"People can be sensitive," he managed to say.

Tynan looked toward the window, then to something on the wall, but then his focus returned and he bore down on Minogue again.

"When you clear a case," he said. "Credit will include – must be seen to include – officers who worked on it. The whole team, local and specialist. Especially the local."

Carney had pushed back with demands of his own, then.

"Understood," Minogue was glad to respond. "And I will—"

The phone ringing was a welcome jarring. Tynan looked at his watch and then, with his hand signaling Minogue to stay put, he lifted the receiver.

Minogue put some effort into pretending that he wasn't listening. Tynan gave little away, anyway. How many? he asked, and after some reply: how long? Whatever he heard seemed to satisfy him. His changing posture signaled to Minogue that the call would be over in momentarily. But before it was, he had a glimpse of impatience, or more. Proof he was right came in Tynan's tone, his last before he replaced the receiver.

"That's right," he said. "It's Section 30. A search of a car is a search of a car. And yes, you can tell them that at the mosque."

Chapter 7

"Well," said Tynan. "Which cases are at the top of your list?"

Minogue had to yank back his wandering thoughts about what he'd heard.

"First is Mary Slattery, Coolock. Murdered on Hallowe'en, two years ago."

"Slattery. One of the crew from the van robberies? Any connection?"

"The self-same, and he has his alibi. He's halfway through a seven-year sentence. There's no give in him. He appears content to do his time."

"But you think you'll make headway with him now? What's changed?"

"We have a plea-bargaining feeler from one Christy Sugrue. Long a thorn in our sides, Sugrue. He says that Slattery told a mate of his how he'd set it up. And that he paid five thousand to have the missus killed. 'The missus was playing the field on me.'"

"'His mate.' Out of the goodness of his heart, no doubt. Playing us, is he?"

Minogue didn't recall such cynicism from Tynan before.

"Sugrue's up on a murder charge," he said. "And it'll stick. He's headed for fifteen years, easy."

Tynan seemed to weigh the matter.

"So there's leverage now," Minogue felt he had to add. "Sugrue's an addict. There's treatment, sentence mitigation. Parole dates, maybe. Money. He has three kids. And apparently he has discovered his conscience now."

Tynan examined his thumbnail and then laid his hands flat on the desktop, one over the other.

"Good," he said. "Thanks for that. I wanted to speak with you before you got into the thick of things. You've heard the much overused 'A perfect storm,' I take it?"

"I have."

"I'm not a great believer in coincidences," said Tynan. "But some matters have come to my attention very recently. As late as an hour ago, actually."

He shifted hands, placed the left on top this time.

"A case in Dalkey earlier this year. You know the one I'm referring to?"

"A homeless man there, up on the Hill? That Park there?"

"That's the one. One Padraig Larkin. June, I believe."

Tynan moved his pencil to a horizontal position above his daytimer.

"So the case has devolved back to the local Gardai," he went on. "After the fine kick-start and sterling work of the NBCI, of course."

Minogue was too aware that he was being passed an easy ball. His unease grew.

"As we well know," Tynan continued, pausing to give Minogue a quizzical look, "there was pressure on resources at that time. And this pressure won't be lessening."

This lob just over the net was a classic Tynan serve. A hint about the Guards' protest marches over pay cuts? Rumours of a strike plan, or another blue flu?

"The gang feuds flared up again around then," Minogue offered.

"Right."

"And the retirements, of course."

Tynan picked up his pencil. The gesture reminded Minogue of a doctor preparing for surgery.

"The average citizen might be wondering if resources weren't brought to bear on that case in a timely manner."

He seemed to want a comment.

"If I knew more exact details there," Minogue said, feebly.

Tynan leaned forward, and folded his arms on the desktop.

"More than enough personnel were on it. All well driven, sound procedures. Regular case reviews locally, reboots, staff switches. All ongoing."

He could have said 'textbook,' Minogue thought.

"And now the case has passed the six-month mark."

Minogue hedged.

"There are no guarantees," he said.

"Well you know that, and I know that. But there are things particular to this case that are showing up now."

Minogue waited.

"We could start with Facebook."

"Facebook. The Facebook?"

"That's the one," Tynan replied. "Yes, there's a Facebook group for Mr. Larkin. Parts of it are quite, what'll I say, quite lyrical. Mr. Larkin wandered the coast road there, and Killiney Hill, the woods, apparently. His kingdom, one could call it, his domain. I believe he had names, 'The High King' and such?"

"'The King of Ireland' I heard, I think."

"Well I had a look this morning. There are other titles being bestowed there: 'The Green Man,' 'The Fisher King.' Quite something."

Minogue struggled to say something pertinent, but nothing came to mind.

"Well people like their stories, I suppose," he said. "Their myths."

"Myths, yes. 'A national weakness,' I heard the other day. A bit harsh, maybe?"

"It sounds a bit, I don't know – bitter. But I don't know the context."

"It was a chat about the governing of our fair country," said Tynan. "One of about a million such conversations going on in Ireland at the moment, I suppose."

"You might be underestimating that million."

"Well now," Tynan said. "Back to this High King. As you might imagine, there's plenty of slagging the Guards on this Facebook effort."

He took a single, folded sheet from under his daytimer.

"Somebody took the trouble to put this item together, and shove it under the door of the public office there in Dalkey Garda station."

There was a piece of a poem and quotes about justice. Rhetorical questions followed, well-spaced and in italics. Was the life of a homeless man worth nothing? Was justice only for the rich, the insiders? 'Marginalized,' a word that still set Kilmartin ablaze with scorn, occurred twice in the paragraph below the poem.

"They might know their legends," Tynan said. "But their notion of how a murder investigation is run, well that's mythology of a different order entirely."

He paused then, his expression changing slightly as though he had remembered something more pressing.

"So Mr. Larkin was a fixture in the area," he went on. "Wandering the roads there, the coast road. Much preoccupied with his role there up on the hill, apparently. That is where he kept an eye on the sea, for arrivals. He took it as his duty to patrol the coast there. Guarding it, so to speak."

"Like I was saying, I wish I had reviewed this before coming."

"Guarding against the Vikings," said Tynan easily. "The Normans, the English. A keen interest in Strongbow, apparently. Not the cider, the real McCoy, the Norman."

"Interesting" was all that Minogue could come up with.

"You might wonder why I'm telling this to you this morning?"

Memory of Kilmartin's disdain then flared in Minogue's thoughts: *it's all about PR these days, bucko.*

"A professional courtesy, I'm thinking."

"Nicely put," said Tynan. "That goes without saying. But tell me something now. Does it strike you as a bit odd that I know these details about this case? As much, you might wonder, say, as a front-line Garda investigating it?"

"I'll hold off saying, if you don't mind."

"I see. Now do you think I asked you here to hear you hold off saying things?"

It wasn't sarcasm, Minogue knew, but the tone was tinged with something stronger than irony.

Tynan had folded his arms. He was waiting.

"Clare men will tell you to your face, I was told," he said.

"East Clare only, I'm afraid. Tulla and points east, to the Shannon."

"It's not a fox-hunt here. So can you read between the lines here? Why are we here talking about this particular murder? Interrupting your preparations, and set-up?"

Minogue struggled to hide his surprise.

"Maybe because the case has been kicked into the long grass?"

This audacity caught Minogue off-guard. Tynan's expression didn't change.

"What I'll be telling you is in confidence," he said. "Understood?

He waited until Minogue nodded a second time.

"I received a phone call yesterday afternoon. A woman the name of Mary O'Dowd. She's a friend of ours – of mine. You may know her as Sister Mary Immaculata?"

"It has a familiar sound. Something to do with the home-less?"

"Right. She helps at a drop-in centre. Now I know Mary since the Flood. Mary – Immaculata – started up Disciples when she came back from Africa, a few years ago. But she's getting on, so she took a subordinate role a while back."

Minogue vaguely recalled a photo in the papers from a while back. It was the surprise of seeing a nun washing someone's feet that stood out.

"Was there something to do with washing feet involved?"

Tynan hesitated before answering. Minogue knew better than to expect a smile.

"Have you heard the expression 'he' – or she – was 'out on the missions'?"

"I have. I wondered if there was something more to it than just the words."

"Well there is," said Tynan. "A mission priest would come home to Ireland, and he'd bring back what he had learned over there on the missions – gotten used to, I should say. It wasn't always good either. He'd be expecting to be deferred to, or to step back in time here, to when he left. The re-entry here doesn't always go smoothly. You see?"

Minogue had little trouble resisting an urge to say 'gone native.'

"Such eccentricities get the hard eye these days, I'm thinking," he said.

"You said it. Returning to Immaculata: she used to come by our house. We'd have a chat and so forth. More than once she told me that for me to be holding the office of Garda Commissioner, that would be proof that God had a sense of humour."

Minogue realized that he was being given a moment to catch the connection, those years Tynan had spent as a seminarian.

"Don't be fooled by the nun thing now," Tynan continued. "Immaculata is a tough nut. The original model of an Irish nun: cast iron, tempered steel. She used to be about a ten on the Nun Richter Scale. Do you know nuns?"

"I do, a bit. I used to think they glided. That they didn't need to use their feet."

"That's only the Holy Faith nuns. But we can't be sure of that though, can we?"

Not a hint of a smile now either, Minogue noted, uselessly.

"It took me a while to get over the fear, to admire them – well, some of them."

"You're hardly alone," Tynan said. "But the issue here is, Mary knew this man Larkin for some time. And this is what she told me. She told me that she was interviewed by a Guard. 'Cursory' is the word she used. She waited for more follow-up, more in-depth. But since then, apparently no-one has gotten back to her. And it's the same with the crew at that drop-in, Disciples. Once-off statements, and bye-bye."

Minogue studied the faded green felt edging out from under the base of Tynan's pen-holder.

"You might imagine there's room for improvement in the matter?"

Minogue squirmed a little.

"A more robust scrutiny then maybe," Tynan went on. "So that the man in the street can see that this murder investigation has not been kicked into the long grass?"

Minogue felt it was safe enough to nod. Tynan drew out another sheet of paper, unfolded it, and slid it across his desk.

"Immaculata's phone number. I said you'd be in touch, shortly."

He watched Minogue glance at it, and place it in his jacket pocket.

"Next item on the agenda here," he said then. "There is a man named JJ Mac. John Joseph McCarthy. That's the other phone number there on the bottom. He calls himself a journalist. Heard of him?"

Minogue shook his head.

"Well I thought not. He works for one of those free papers, the ones they dump on the doorstep. Community newspapers. *South County Scene.*"

"Is he in the picture as regards this case?"

"He is and he isn't. He has tried to insert himself into it apparently, starting a month or so ago. Whatever his credentials, or his intentions, here, he seems to like to emote. Are we in need of more emoting in the media these days?"

"Saints preserve us," Minogue said. He wondered if Tynan too had taken to slapping the radio off, or hitting the channel changer on the remote.

Tynan drew in his legs, and moved some papers on his desktop.

"This McCarthy button-holed me last month, at a resident's association meeting in Dun Laoghaire. It was in the nature of an ambush. He claimed to be reporting on it for his paper. Well that turned out to be bogus. But in any event, he was all over the map. He had a considerable amount of things on his mind, or on his radar.

'Isn't it time the Guards laid criminal charges against the people running the banks?'"

"He'd probably get my vote," said Minogue.

"'Shouldn't the directors of Shell be in the dock for what they're doing out in Galway, destroying the environment with that gas pipeline?'"

"That's free speech for you, I suppose."

"Perhaps," said Tynan. "But then he moved to other matters. 'Are you prepared to drag those bishops into court?' 'Will ye lay charges against the Pope?'"

"The Pope?"

"That's right. And if the Guards won't handle this, well... someone else has to."

"Has he got Clint Eastwood maneuvers in mind?"

"We haven't heard the word 'lynch' yet, have we," was Tynan's reply. "But after that ritual of pelting me with rhetorical questions, he then took to inquiring on another matter. It was the matter of Mr. Larkin."

"The same Larkin matter we are talking about here?"

"The very one. I remember his expression actually: 'Will the Guards get to the root of this, the real root of this?'"

"The root," Minogue said. "What root?"

"Well I didn't ask him. But he wanted me to know that the leafy lanes and the Mercedes out there didn't fool him one bit. 'Things go on out there.'"

"'Things,'" Minogue said. "Bank directors living there? Bishops maybe?"

Tynan gave him a quick look.

"I couldn't let that one go, so I asked. Long story short, when pressed, McCarthy had nothing to offer."

"Nothing? Boring nothing, may I ask, or interesting nothing?"

"The boring one, I'd have to say. And then he was off on another track. I didn't keep track of all that he went on about. Planning permissions, pubs serving up contraband drink, illegal au pairs... But the main point is, he's set on the notion that certain people – the well-to-do, who else could it be – are used to getting what they want."

"Friends in the right places, he's saying?"

"Let me see if I remember his preferred terms. Yes, he used the current favourite, the 'insiders.' 'Bypass' was one. 'Untouchables' – not the Indian caste either. 'The old days never left. They still have the gardener, and the maid, and the messenger boy.'"

"I'm not sure I get the gardener analogy."

"Did you ever read Hugh Leonard? *Home Before Dark*?"

"I can't remember."

"His father was a gardener, his stepfather I should say. The gardeners would be the ones taking care of things, weeds and so forth…"

"Has he any specifics," Minogue said. "Incidents? Examples? Names?"

Tynan shook his head.

"'It'll all come out,' he said – McCarthy said. "'I have to protect my sources.'"

"I think I heard that in a film a long time back."

Tynan snapped back to alertness. He moved his pen to a new spot on his desk.

"Well that was my thought too, I suppose," he said. "I gave him the only response I could: present us with information. Better again, approach the Gardaí there in Dalkey."

"Did that soften his cough?"

"I have no idea. But he did say that he'd look forward to the day when someone would ask him when he had first raised these issues with the Guards. So, who knows. No word to date."

With that, Tynan turned his hands over and began to examine his palms. For no reason that he could think of then, or even later with the help of a drink, Minogue thought of Pilate.

"But then it was Mary," Tynan said. "Sister Immaculata, the one who brought up his name again. She said that McCarthy had his heart in the right place. That he made sure her drop-in was mentioned in the paper."

He looked over at Minogue again. Minogue issued his most thoughtful nod. It seemed to suffice.

"So," said Tynan. "I did say perfect storm, didn't I?

You know Seán Brophy."

Minogue didn't even bother trying to hide his surprise this time.

"I do. Everyone knows Seán."

It was Tynan's turn to make slow, thoughtful nods.

"Well then," he said. "Here's the next reason for asking you here for a chat. So that you'll consider applying yourself to the Larkin case first. Seán Brophy is not well."

Minogue frowned.

"Seán is apparently in crisis."

"His daughter," Minogue began to say, but let it go.

"Seán's daughter, yes. She was the one who found the Larkin man there."

"Seán was at Ryan's last night, I spoke with him."

"And you drove him home."

Tynan's expression was placid.

"I did. He was okay when I left him at his house last night."

"From what people could gather there this morning, Seán never went in the door. He walked the streets all night apparently. It's clear that – well, it's what I said. Seán is under a doctor's care, as we speak."

Minogue's mind scrambled for recall. What had he missed with Brophy?

"We depend a lot on Seán, as you well know. Too much, perhaps.

Tynan's phone extension began to flash. He watched it for several moments.

"I don't want to say that Seán is irreplaceable, but the fact is, we're still trying to build capacity there in the Lab. We're not there yet. But Seán never let us down, in all these years. You know that, I imagine?"

"True enough."

Tynan turned toward his keyboard. A hint of reluctance, or exasperation, tightened his mouth. He spoke facing the screen.

"We have a homeless man, murdered, and no arrest. A young girl traumatized, sinking by the day. And now, we have the father who doted on her, a man overworked already and carrying probably too much for us, and now he's done down."

He glanced over.

"My thinking is this: we need this to stop."

Chapter 8

Minogue's drive through the narrow, rambling streets of Dalkey brought him finally to a stop behind a delivery lorry. Gas canisters bulged under its blue nylon tarp. It wasn't waiting a turn to move on, it was parked. Not a hundred yards from the Garda station, a vehicle taking up half of the road? As if the turn in from Castle Street hadn't been awkward enough. Tubbermore Road, he mused: the Road of the Large Well. A rename would be in order: The Lane That Calls Itself a Road. The Cowpath of the Parked Lorry.

He worked his way around the lorry, and let his Peugeot coast in second. The mix of cottages and terraced homes and semis were well-looked-after, but there were a few too many dainty touches for his liking. Many of the reno'd ones made statements with interlocking stone and planter pots. The road ended in a T-junction, and there sat the older houses, taller and untroubled-looking, snug behind their high walls and gates.

He remembered the Garda station from a stroll he had taken several years back. The noise and claustrophobia of a boisterous wedding reception – Kathleen's niece – had him out for a break from a nearby hotel. The station was an old house with a preservation order on it. An imposing look to it; a lot of steps up. Wasn't the public office at the ground level, or a high cellar, the former servants' quarters?

His mobile buzzed against the edge of the gearshift tray. Squinting against a glaring, metallic light that now welled through the clouds, he thumbed through to the text. Kathleen: Brídín, her friend at work, had been let go. The text ended in All caps: NO NOTICE CAN U BELIEVE IT! He returned to the Messages, and checked the names of the detectives here again. He was glad he had checked: it was Fitzgerald, not Fitzsimmons, who was the senior one.

Feeling he was overlooking something, he lingered over the phone menus. What had he forgotten? No, he had phoned Malone, and Malone was on his way. Names, contacts out here ready? They were. Was the Slattery case-work parked properly? All too easily, actually. Getting the briefing at Coolock station delayed had been no big deal.

Was it the actual speed of this flip to the Larkin case then? It wasn't. Something else had rankled in his mind since he'd left Tynan's office, and it was as simple to grasp as it was hard to credit: yes, some old nun had gotten on the blower to the Tynan, and lo and behold, Garda resources were at her disposal. That Ireland still existed?

Soured as this made him, he had to admit that this abrupt shift to the Larkin case was starting off not bad at all. He ticked off the steps that had already been taken. This Sergeant Fitzgerald had already arranged a two o'clock get-together to kick off the case review. He was offering to get the original case detectives in. 'No worries,' had been his response to anything Minogue asked. Would Minogue want to start in on the case files right away? 'Can do. No worries.'

Minogue's eye was drawn then to the sign on an older house sliding by to his right. A Period Residence as they'd say in the ads, it was freshly painted in taupe, with dark brown details. He slowed and read the writing. Choice residence... Full of the tradition and character of Old Dalkey... Exceptional. Wrought-iron gates closed over a passageway that ran back to some kind of a walled garden – a courtyard maybe – behind. A doctor's house in former times, he guessed, a barrister's maybe. There was something desperate about the gleaming BMW convertible parked back there. A prop, like the garden furniture, and that fountainy thing too, he felt sure.

The road narrowed even more, and a line of tightly parked cars began. He resumed his search ahead for the familiar blue lamp of a Garda station – was that Malone's Escort? He braked and came to a complete stop.

Malone was on his mobile. He seemed to have trouble winding down his window. It was hardly the time to urge Malone again that he should just to go for the 1,500 euro from that scrappage scheme, and put this old banger out of its misery.

"There's a bit of parking in a yard behind the station," he said to him.

He heard Malone say Sonia's name, as in 'But listen, Sonia,' before his window was fully up again. The gate fronting the laneway that adjoined the Garda station was painted the same cop-shop blue as the door to the station itself. It was work to reverse into the parking spot. At least no one seemed to be eyeballing his efforts. He pocketed his mobile, reached back for the soft attaché case that Kathleen had bought him when he was drafted into Liaison, and stepped into the chill air.

Right away, he was sure that he smelled the sea, and some part of his mind was judging this as benign, that any tribulations that this Dalkey stay might put in his path would be bearable. Coming along Castle Street, the ruin of Dalkey Castle filling his mirror, his vague dislike for the place had returned. He had always wanted to like Dalkey, and it baffled him yet why he had never quite made it. If he didn't like Dalkey, well maybe Dalkey didn't like him right back? But it wasn't Dalkey's fault.

He had tried to get a fix on this before. Was it the way the place was set up? Dalkey meant a certain frustration, it had to be said, with its roads and its avenues and its abrupt changes of camber confusing. It felt tight. Its outlying mansions and villas blocked views of the sea too, and he felt there was something grudging about how little a sliver of the coast had been left as a park for the plain people for Ireland.

But maybe that was a bit petty. Those same winding roads and secluded avenues spilled out verdant greenery, sea views, glimpses of the Wicklow Mountains. There was plenty of ambitious architecture on show. So what if a ruck of arrivistes had elbowed in where old money doctor-dentist-barrister trinity had rooted before? Like it or not, those building tycoons, the financial services wizards, the best-in-Ireland media stars – they were the new Ireland. He might have to admit that there was something else going on here, a shameful atavism: Dalkey felt *English*. Naturally he'd keep this insight to himself.

A sudden gust of wind tore about the yard, peppering his face with grit. He grasped his attaché case tight, and headed for the front of the station. Malone was trudging up the laneway to the yard.

"I was wondering if you'd make it this far across the Mason-Dixon Line."

Malone, the Dublin Northsider, blinked and offered a blank look. Minogue looked again: there was indeed discoloration.

"What's that there, on your left side there? Below your eye."

"That's my cheek. I've another one, on the other side."

"The welt there, the bruise. Whatever the technical name for it is."

Malone ran his hand lightly over the pebbledash on the wall behind.

"What the hell were you doing last night in Ryan's? After I left?"

"Minding my own business, in actual fact."

"It's everybody's business now. It came at me second-hand in that meeting this morning. The one I didn't know I had scheduled, with the Commissioner?"

Malone studied the gatepost.

"They started it, you know. Wasn't me at all."

"'They started it.' Are we back in the schoolyard?"

"They were looking for trouble," said Malone. "I'm telling you. So here's a question for you before I get a lecture. What's being done about them yo-yos?"

Minogue studied the bruise again. It might spread even more.

"Who were they? Was it that pair with the eff-off faces I saw at the table?"

"Yeah. The one with the stupid-looking face on him, the tall one, he was Iijit One. Sly fecking eyes on him. I'd gone to the jacks, see? One of them was in there, he starts muttering. 'How's about an autograph,' says he to me. I says nothing."

"Sounds like you, all right. What kind of nuttin'?"

"I swear to God. I know I have to keep me head down. But he just wouldn't shut up. Starts in on me, like, 'Did you push him or did you pick him up and throw him?'"

"What did you say to this fella to get him going wild like that?"

"Don't you want to know what he said to me first? Like, 'Nice job offing that Kelly gouger, pal – only another hundred thousand to go'?"

"You can't take a slag these days? Couldn't you at least have ignored it?"

"That's not just a slag. It's an accusation, that's what it is. But like I'm telling you, he was going to keep drilling away until he got to me."

"Walk. Out. The. Door. Of. The. Toilet. Without. A. Word. Think of that, no?"

"Boss, are you getting what I'm saying here? He wasn't going to stop."

"Since when did you get to be so thin-skinned? How many times did I hear Kilmartin run the Dublin gurrier bit over you? Teaching you elocution even?"

"That was different. That was in that Squad, and anyway, he's all hot air, Kilmartin. Rocky Balboa on the outside, Richard Gere on the inside."

Minogue couldn't not smile.

"See? You know it too. But look, this thicko last night, he sees I'm having a lash, and I can't just walk away in the middle of it. And still he keeps needling? He even throws in the flight recorder routine. 'Don't worry, Kelly's flight recorder will back you up.' How's that funny? Funny if you're some culchie from Bally Go Shite maybe?"

"No offence to present company, of course."

"Goes without saying. But look, boss, this is a big nothing, or it should be. Hop in the ring, would be my preference. But he's the one starts throwing shapes at me. Jaysus' sake! Posers – *babies*: two big babies, that's what they are. Baa baa bah. Boo hoo hoo."

"Just tell me what you said. I don't want to find out second-hand."

"Something about his sister."

"You knew he had a sister?"

"Everybody has a sister. Anyway. He has a go at me, so I give him one."

"One what."

"A get-the-message dig. Not a hard dig, just sharpish."

"And?"

"Well he didn't like it, did he. Next thing I know, his mate's piling in the door. That's when I'm thinking, Christ these cowboys – armed, like – they could let on they don't know I'm a Guard and ... So I had to put the other fella to the wall. I just had to."

"You hit the second one, the one coming in to break up the row."

"It wasn't a 'hit' hit. How did I know that he was coming in for a hundred mile an hour, like Jackie frigging Chan? What, I'm going to ask him, 'Are you here to help?'"

Minogue eyed the restless foot, the glances thrown at the street outside.

"Look," he said. "You know how it's going to be on this job. Am I right?"

"Pretty much. I think."

Minogue ignored the oversized load of irony.

"So you know the situation here. Why we're here, why there's been a change of plan. Why we're here and we're not in sunny, pleasant Coolock reworking Slattery?"

"You told me already, boss. This thing here's getting flack about it, and stuff."

Minogue tugged his jacket tighter.

"And we're here in Dalkey to help," he said. "You're hearing this, right?"

"Here to help, right."

"Not to have fights in the toilets. Not to look over people's shoulders either. And most of all, not to show anybody up. Is that going to be too frustrating for you maybe?"

"No. I'm grand on that. Sound as a bell. 'Here to help,' that's me – us."

★ ★ ★

The railings at the front of the Dalkey Garda station had been recently painted. The walls too, Minogue noted, pausing a moment on the footpath.

He decided to enter by the public office. A man's voice resonated behind the frosted glass panel, a phone conversation. There was time to peruse the Missing Persons circulars, dog licence reminders, the kids' Traffic Safety drawings. Prodigious red crayon blood flowed from a stick man cyclist's head. Xs for eyes.

A duty officer who opened the wicket soon let them know he was one Garda Corcoran. He glanced at Minogue's photocard, but didn't bother with Malone's.

"The lads call me Corky."

Modest-enough sideburns, and a thick mat of dark curly hair put Minogue in mind of a long-ago Tom Jones. Corky made a cautious grin.

"It's all go," he said. "Heard ye were coming only an hour ago."

"Not too long after ourselves," said Minogue. "But we do what we're bid, don't you know. Plans exist to be altered, and all the rest of it."

"Same story everywhere, sure – Listen, I'll come around and let ye in."

Minogue tracked Corcoran's form moving behind the glass. No surprises in the public office. The worn and cramped look, the customary desks head-to-head, a thicket of notices on cork-boards. Manila folders leaned awkwardly in their ugly holders, backed up by hanging wall files of a type he didn't remember seeing before. The radio set was in the open by the back of the room. A duty-jacket and vest lay on the counter next to a boxy set of shelves with sets of forms. Postcards were taped on the walls.

A brief exchange about the weather ensued while they waited for Fitz to answer the phone. Minogue still couldn't place Corcoran's accent, but with the Rs barely making it out of the man's gob, he'd begun to lean toward the soft option, the Midlands drawl.

Garda Corcoran, source of the enigma, put down the phone.

"Fitzie says how-do, and sorry he's tied up. But he'll see youse later on. 'Make yourselves at home' is his instructions. If it's instructions ye want? The canteen's out the back there, across the yard? And a fitness room too – in case ye get bored."

"Where should we pitch our tents, do you know?"

"There's a place cleared here for ye up the stairs here. Well, half-cleared."

Behind him, Malone was uncharacteristically lead-footed on the stairs.

"Fitzie," Minogue said. "Sergeant Fitzgerald, I take it?"

"That's right. Mickey Fitz. Sarge, or even Mickey. He parks his rank."

They passed a small, narrow room that held unopened cardboard boxes stacked to the ceiling, and ancient-looking file cabinets. The floor had a slant.

"The front office there looks out over the road," Corcoran said. "That's Detective Unit Office. So youse'll be well within shouting range. Don't hold back, I say."

Minogue tried not to stare at the hair again. A generous mop entirely. Corcoran pulled open a narrow, moulded-panel door.

"Not the Taj Mahal exactly," he said "But it'll get the job done, I hope?"

A table and the two bockety looking chairs comprised the usable furniture. An arabesque of incomplete and overlapping circles on the surface of the table showcased the work of sloppy, bygone tea drinkers. A small, grimy glass panel in the door was flecked with a heavy emulsion paint applied, Minogue thought, before the Dead Sea was even sick. Spots clung to the edges of the linoleum too where it met the skirting board. A small window gave a pinched view of a gable, and a few slices of rooftops farther along the road. He guessed that the inevitable filing cabinets here were jammed full.

"We use it as an interview room. But it's a go-to room when there's a major."

Major crime, he meant, Minogue realized. An Incident Room, he should have called it. A sign of how out of touch they were with front-line Garda work here?

"Phone, of course. It hasn't been cabled for a terminal here yet though."

"The evidence room, is it handy?"

"Top floor. I have the sign-in sheet and the key waiting below."

"We were hoping to get hold of files too?"

Corcoran frowned, but then his forehead quickly eased.

"I nearly forgot," he said. "Eight bankers' boxes waiting below. Will I...?"

"Thanks, one of us will get them, if you don't mind."

"Not in the wide world. So like Fitz says, make yourselves at home."

Minogue thanked him, and drew the door shut. The room now smelled like a breadbox. Beneath that staleness, there was a mustiness he supposed could be mildew.

"'Make yeerselves at home,'" Malone said quietly. "Says Corky from Dorkey."

Minogue pulled one of the chairs across the lino, and he put down his bag. Someone had wiped the phone with a disinfectant spray, and it stung high in his nose.

"Take a sabbatical from your acting career," he said to Malone. "And start bringing up the boxes, the case files. And see what you can rig up for boards. Clear a wall or something – anything. We'll need the use of a terminal. And ID, a password?"

"Oh," he called out before Malone closed the door completely.

"The door has no lock too. What can be done about it, ask somebody."

Kathleen sounded busy.

"Day one, superstar," she said. "How are you liking it there in Coolock?"

"Coolock is not bad I hear," he said. "But I'm actually out here in Dalkey."

"Dalkey? Why Dalkey? What happened?"

"Something came up."

"Something is always coming up with you. Is it bad?"

"Not bad that I can see. It's just a case got moved up the list. 'Circumstances.'"

"What about all the stuff you've done already, all you read for the other one?"

"The one you're not supposed to know about?" he tried. "That one?"

"Spare me, will you. How can they switch you around like that, I'd like to know."

"Ours is not to reason why. It has to do with the long grass."

"Long grass? Have you had a few pints there? Hit your head against something maybe? I'm not even going to try to figure that one out."

"The case needs a robust review. Read between the lines, can't you?"

"Well," she said. "I half expected something like this might happen. Everything in this country is gone upside down. Why should it be different for you, I suppose."

It was resignation in her voice, he realized, not anger.

"They have you hopping and trotting. 'This is no promotion.' Didn't I say that?"

"This phone could be tapped, you know."

"I hope it is. Here's the message: 'Give my husband a real job, you shower of sh...'"

Her words ended with a sigh. He eased himself onto the edge of the table, and he began reciting in his mind the things he would not say here: Tynan wouldn't have shuffled the pack if he didn't need to; I never actually wanted what they call a career path; this gig will be good for Tommy Malone, to salvage his career – not that he deserved it after last night's cock-up.

"Tell you what," he said then. "If you need any special goat cheeses, or reiki or something like that, well I am perfectly positioned here. It's ground zero for that here."

"You have this thing about Dalkey, I remember. Don't you?"

He hedged on that. Her tone was serious when she spoke next.

"You know what I'd really like? What a lot of people would like, actually?"

"That we're off Friday night to Paris, and by nine o'clock we'll be in that room there in that Rue Daguerre, and ready to go out to dinner?"

"Ah stop that," she said, but her voice softened. "I know you mean well, but that's for later. No, you'll never get it. It's a fantasy, of course."

Minogue had no difficulty recognizing another fine chance to say nothing.

"I'd love to hear you tell me that they're all under arrest. Under lock and key."

"Is this one of those kinky things where you dress up and get frisky?"

"No, no, no. It probably isn't even on your radar. The commission."

"What commission?"

"See? I knew it. What I meant is when that Murphy Report comes out, when we finally get the truth about those priests, and the bishops covering for them. Each and every one of those – I can't say the word, I just can't. But it's going to be bad. Father Gorman mentioned it at the end of his sermon, Sunday. Pity you weren't there to hear it."

"What did I miss?"

"How our faith is going to be tested next week, when the report comes out. And that we should be praying, and preparing. Father Gorman is depressed himself, I think. But this has to come out in the open, no matter what. It just has to."

Malone was back with the first of the case files. Kathleen had heard him.

"Is that Tommy Malone I'm hearing?"

"It is. Yes, that's him, mullocking around in our, ah, our command post."

"Our ould granny flat," Malone called out.

After his call ended, Minogue still held his mobile to his ear.

"Yes I will," he said. "I'll tell him all right. Definitely."

Malone watched him close the phone.

"Tell me what?"

"Kathleen says congratulations on yesterday. The Ombudsman's report. Not your carry-on with those two head-cases in the pub."

"Very nice of her, say thank you."

"And you're to behave yourself, she says too. To mind your manners."

"Really."

"Oh, and remember who's boss, she says to tell you too – and to call me sir."

Malone's stare lingered on the stained desktop.

"Okay," Minogue said then, rising. "Lot of catch-up to do here. I'll go visit this drop-in place, and see this squeaky wheel, Sister Immaculata."

"Are you going to get your feet washed there?"

"So you know a bit about her already?"

"Found her on the Internet," said Malone. "Bit of a saint."

"We'll see. Now I want you to start at the other end, will you? A fella the name of Joseph McCarthy. He goes by JJ Mac, maybe Joey Mac. Supposedly connected with a paper out here, one of these ads masquerading as a community newspaper."

"McCarthy, with a h?"

"With *an* h. You're on the South Side now."

"Thanks for that. And that Sister What's Her Name?"

"Immaculata. Im-mac-u-la-ta?"

"She speaks Latin or something?"

He looked up, saw Minogue's raised eyebrow, and resumed tapping the keyboard.

Chapter 9

Minogue took the first chance he got to turn onto the coast road. And why not? There was more than one way to get to this Disciples place. Disciples: the word circled in his thoughts. Back in school, it was always 'Jesus and His Disciples,' and the pen drawings in the religion texts had Jesus looking young, sort of naïve, distracted. But when push came to shove, those so-called disciples were a huge let-down, and those beseeching words of Jesus had been repeated so often in the Holy Weeks of his childhood: *Will none of ye stay awake and pray with me?*

The sea was grey and surly-looking, and out from shore, a stiff breeze was raking the tops of the swells. On the edge of the bay, a finger's length from the featureless, grey lump that was today's version of Howth, a cargo ship lay at anchor. His view of the sea ended at a sea-wall with an elderly couple walking resolutely behind a fat dog.

The door to the drop-in centre was painted a canary yellow. Was it meant to be some kind of a beacon? He couldn't spot any sign on the door, or the walls adjoining the place. He geared down and dawdled. The place looked closed. A van suddenly filled his back window, and he pulled in. Naturally, the parking had to be metered. Walking back with his ticket, he mentally retraced the road out to Dalkey from here. He figured it was under an hour's walk. How long would have taken this Larkin fella though?

The doorway smelled of disinfectant and mothballs, and

other smells he wanted to keep from consideration. He checked his pockets, feeling again for his wallet and mobile. The door opened before he had to grasp the handle. A wet-eyed man with a rubbery face and eyes fixed in a dull stare came out, swaying a little. Minogue caught the closing door with his forearm. The smell enveloped him, and he held his breath. Homelessness had a smell to it, a peppery musk of unwashed bodies and slept-in clothes, and cigarettes. He tried to quash his thought that taste and smell were allied.

Snared between aversion and shame he paused just beyond the doorway. Ruddy, weary faces half-turned toward him from the open area ahead. There were close to a dozen men sitting around. Several lingered before turning away again, some toward the telly, some to stare at nothing. An older man with a blaze of white hair stared blankly across the room. Another was canted awkwardly at the end of a sofa, his bandaged fist dug in hard under his chin, his eyelids flickering. What talk there was, was subdued.

He took in the bags parked by some of the chairs, the posters with words that he couldn't make out yet, the magazines and books. A figure emerged from a doorway behind the television, an elderly woman of medium height, slim, carrying a plate of sandwiches. Civvies or not, Minogue pegged her for a nun. Was it the hair, the clothes? Or was it some bearing, a set to her face that said competent, or strict, or compassionate? He tried to calculate how many years had passed since he had seen a nun in her proper regalia, an old-style nun under full sail. They had been mysterious and frightening to him when he was a child. They didn't walk, they glided, in a swirl of robes and clacking rosaries.

She laid down the plate and then began loading a tray, murmuring all the while to one of the men. A piece of white something, his coat lining, flowered at his shoulder. DTs, Minogue thought, the man trying to nod and drink from a cup at the same time. The man said something back to her. She glanced at Minogue, and went back to gathering dishes, all the while keeping up the conversation with the Mr. Torn-coat. His nods became more vigorous. He seemed to be getting what she was saying. He wiped at his beard and he looked up at her, and he beamed. Yikes: no teeth.

He'd have to breathe at some point. He concentrated on blocking his nose and keeping his breath shallow, and he pretended to read the pages pinned to a corkboard. Know Your Rights. Health Clinic. Pictures of the Sacred Heart, Mary at the foot of the Cross with lightning in a torn sky behind. That poster with the footprints on the beach. One of the seated men sat up and turned a little to get a better look at him. Minogue offered a small nod, his friendly but distant Garda model.

Then the shouting began. A man with a swollen face and a Kerry or Cork accent was doing the shouting. The target of his anger was a short, brittle-looking man with hollow cheeks and a Fu Manchu moustache. Minogue caught some of the words. A row about the Eurovision Song Contest? The Kerryman called the other one a liar. The other began to chant 'Romania, Romania.' The argument grew louder. The Kerryman sat back hard in his chair, scraping its legs along the tiles, and he started in on the curses.

That seemed to do it for this Sister Immaculata. She left her tray full of dishes and made her way out towards the pair. She was singing even before she reached them.

All kinds of everything
Reminds me of you.
Dances, romances...

Dear God, thought Minogue. That song was Ireland's great moment from decades past: *All Kinds of Everything*. Nineteen... seventy? Yes – Dana, that wholesome Catholic girl from embattled Derry had beaten all of Europe to win Ireland's first Eurovision title. She'd married, gone holy-roller since, and now in midlife, she haunted Ireland.

But the singing seemed to be doing the trick. What's more, this Sister Immaculata had a damned good voice too. She wiped her hands in her apron as she launched into another verse, and then she slowly began to make her way over to Minogue.

Her hand was soft and damp from washing dishes.

"I knew a Minogue years back," she said. "A priest out in Africa."

"I can't claim that one I'm afraid, Sister. I wish I could."

"Mary. Call me Mary."

It was said conclusively, with none of the usual emollient smiles or the 'ah sures' he had expected. She owned the lightest of light blue eyes, grey almost, and they looked out calmly from beneath an unlined forehead. They communicated zero. Was it possible that nuns these days could get their hair styled, or even tinted? Maybe a life spent not having to deal with men directly was a life where grey hair could take its time arriving. An outdoor plant too, this nun, he felt sure, and well-preserved.

"You juggle a few careers," he tried. "The singing?"

"I wouldn't make a living out of it."

"Don't sell yourself short now. You have the pipes, I'm thinking."

She wiped her hands and glanced toward the men. The bickering had not revived.

"Do you know anything about horses?"

"Enough to keep my distance. I got a right good kick off one when I was a boy."

She kept her eye on the man with the red face and the wild eyes – Mr. Furious.

"You need to talk to horses. Did you know that?"

Minogue offered a vague, benign nod. He had known from childhood about nun powers. Nuns could see your whole life in the space of a second, secret parts included. They could probably see your eternal destiny too. This particular nun was some kind of über-nun too by the looks of things, one with the power to move a Garda Commissioner.

"There's a little office of sorts over beyond," she said. "Let's have a chat there. I have a few things to show you, if you're interested."

He followed her, waited for her invitation to sit. She drew open the top drawer in a file cabinet, and craned her neck to find something there. There was a small blemish on her neck, and now that he'd noticed it, it kept drawing his eye. A wen, that's what it was. The word rolled around in his head. Was it something to do with witches?

She seemed to be aware of his thoughts. Pointing out details in the photos she had spread on the table, her thumb and forefinger pressed closed the collar of her blouse.

"Christmas dinner," she said. "Last year's."

He imagined the same slow, deliberate murmur sounding the decades of the rosary in a cold chapel.

"That's him. That's Padraig there."

Minogue studied the other faces again. Stubbled and windburned, several glared at the camera with glittering eyes. Others looked bewildered, anxious to the point of fright even, with expressions that could mean drunken or high, or off in a private mental hell. Over all of them though, he saw weariness.

"The men there, are they sitting together for a reason, or just at random?"

"Both. But Padraig had a couple of regulars that he could manage, for a while anyway. This one is Seánie, Seánie Walshe. The little lad, the one who looks like a jockey, he's another, Davey McArdle."

Minogue switched on the point-and-shoot. He still wasn't up to speed on all the buttons and options, but he found the macro. Then he set the flash.

"And have the Guards, the other Guards I mean, seen these snapshots?"

She shook her head. There was something in the slow shake that he didn't like.

"Taking a picture of a picture," she said. "I'd never think to do that."

"It saves me having to take them away."

He continued to rearrange the snapshots out on the table. When he had them separated, he did a test shot. Glare from the glossy finish had ruined it. He turned off the flash. The lens dithered and buzzed as it focused. The sound of the shutter reminded him of a sly card-player laying down a trump. He went to Replay, and zoomed in. The last photo was a mess – muddy, soupy colour, pools of glare. The others would do.

"I'll need to get the names," he said to her. "To go with the faces."

The blue-grey eyes didn't blink.

"You're asking me for names? Is that normal?"

"It'd be helpful," he said, evenly. She drew one of the snapshots closer.

"Padraig and Seán and Davey, the three musketeers. 'I'm named after a beer, Sister!' Davey says. 'Up ag'in it from day one!' Is that true, was there a McArdle beer?"

He might have to relocate her accent south. Midlands, lake country?

"There was, unfortunately," he replied. "I'd have to say it's best forgotten too."

No smile. He slid his camera into his pocket.

"The Guards spoke to him," she said. "Poor Davey, he was petrified."

"Those men are regulars here, you say. Which of them are here now, today?"

"Neither of them," she said. "Not so far. I haven't seen them for days."

Minogue looked at the faces again.

"Padraig couldn't take people," she said. "But Davey often got on his good side."

"What's the story with this Seán Walshe? He's a big lad, I'm thinking."

"Seán," she said, carefully. "Seánie has what you might call a short fuse."

"How short would 'short' be?"

She glanced at him and let go of her collar a moment. She quickly closed it again.

"Could you give me an example maybe?" he pressed.

"Well I forget that it's to a Guard I'm talking."

"With all due respect, Sister. I don't think I'm hearing an answer to the question."

Several moments passed before she spoke.

"If it's facts you're talking about, and information, well then – no."

He made an effort at friendliness in his tone.

"Mr. McArdle is not a suspect in the matter," he said. "He's been alibied, and it's held up – so far, anyway. Are you suggesting that maybe that alibi won't stay that way?"

He let a few seconds drag by. Her voice had turned formal when she spoke now.

"That's a matter that is well beyond my expertise now, I'd have to say."

"I see. You were talking about the fact that he has a short fuse?"

"Well he can be impulsive, Seánie can. But I'll leave it at that, I think."

"It sounds like you knew Padraig's ways somewhat," he said then, putting an edge to his tone. "His comings and goings, that class of thing."

"I suppose I did," she said. "But Padraig wasn't one to share his thoughts."

"There would be things about him that you'd know, I hope, things that might have escaped others maybe. Hence your contacting the Commissioner?"

He hadn't expected the broad smile. It quickly gave way to a rueful version.

"I've thought about that, the last little while," she said. "And I decided I couldn't let it go by. Even if it comes across to a Guard as stupid, I said to myself."

She seemed to be waiting for a question.

"Or interfering," she added then. "So here's the thing, why I used the word 'stupid.' I really have nothing to offer – I mean I don't *know* anything. So why did I pick up the phone? I felt, well I felt like Padraig was getting lost."

She sat more upright, and she studied the photo again.

"Ignored," she said. "I think I must have read too much on the Internet."

"The Internet," he said.

"Well you could laugh, I suppose. An old nun on the Web? But we do. Somebody mentioned that website, Facebook. So I looked, and I thought, well there's an Ireland that I know. Yes, I did, and was I surprised. I shouldn't say that, maybe."

"Shouldn't say...?"

A smile rippled across her face. She seemed genuinely embarrassed.

"Are we allowed to do politics these days? People think we hand in our brains when we take the veil or something."

He gave her a disbelieving look.

"All the goings-on, I mean," she said. "The economy, the politics – all the madness that's taken over the place the past, I don't know, thirty, forty years? I was away for that, you see. But the old truth lives: there's more to life than money. You see?"

He doubted this brand of rhetoric required any input from him.

"So that's what I mean about the Facebook part. That people do care, and that there is still an Ireland. It might be a bit worn around the edges, but it'll come back now that we've hit the wall with all this materialism thing."

Her expression set into something more serious again.

"Money and all that is one thing," she said. "But now at least we can return to seeing what's important, can't we? The soul. The immortal soul."

The ardour in her voice made Minogue even more determined to keep clear of these shoals.

"Would you have known where Padraig was," he asked. "Any given day?"

She shook her head.

"You knew about the King of Ireland rigamarole though, I take it."

"Rigamarole?"

"His beliefs. His walkabouts."

"I did. I used to wonder if it was some story he told himself. Something to do with his own life, to buck himself up. Did you know he came from well-off people?"

"I'm only beginning to learn about him."

"Well maybe you'll know more about him then than I do soon enough."

"I'm hoping you knew him," he said. "Well enough to get us moving again."

"Ah," she said softly, in a way that Minogue knew would only irk him more if she were to repeat it. "You mightn't know what's real, or not real, for men like Padraig."

He let his pencil roll down his notebook and come to a stop.

"Sister." He waited until she made eye contact. A fold had appeared between her eyebrows. "There's something that I'm not getting. Maybe you can help me out? You've told us that you think more could be done here as regards investigating Padraig's death."

"His murder, yes."

"Yes," he said. "His murder. So here I am. The photos are a start, thank you. But I have a question for you, and I'd like you to think about it before you answer."

He paused to let her know that he had a Garda-model stare available if needed.

"Is there something about this matter you've discovered? Something that you've maybe forgotten to tell us before?"

There was none of the hesitation he had expected.

"That's a policeman's question, I'd have to say to you."

She was making a poor effort to smile. Her eyes had gone more grey, but there was a troubled cast to them.

"They're the only variety I have," he said.

"I must confess," she said, and sat back. "Right after talking to Joh – to your Commissioner, I was mortified. 'What am I to tell these Guards?' I said to myself."

She drew in a deep breath, and let it out in a quiet, controlled sigh.

"But John said that you'd have the right approach."

This was getting him nowhere. He looked toward the ceiling.

"Well, you have friends in high places I daresay," he said.

He wasn't sure that she'd get it, but then she threw her head back in quiet glee.

"Don't we all," she said, and blessed herself. "If only we knew it."

The mirth evaporated in an instant. She fixed an earnest look on him.

"Look," she said. "These lads might look like hard cases to you, but actually they're fragile, wounded. But not the kind of a wound that you might see on the outside."

Minogue wanted to head off any detour into Mother Teresa territory.

"Which is not to say that one of them couldn't cause damage, though. Is it?"

Her gaze slid toward the wall. She seemed to be considering his words.

"I have the feeling that this thought has crossed your mind a fair bit. Has it?"

She said nothing, but made a bleak, resigned smile. His annoyance with her was beginning to swirl again. All right, so she had been on the missions. But did she imagine that the country hadn't changed in her absence? That she could pick up a phone and have Guards at her beck and call? Tell them what suited her, hold back what didn't?

Well okay, he resolved: if a nun had X-ray vision, then a copper had his nose, didn't he. This copper here in front of her sensed that something was nagging at her. She was tough, and stoic, so fair enough, he wouldn't condescend to her. She needed to be told the score. Part of the score was telling her that this country wasn't a convent yard anymore. It wasn't some class-room of kids under the commanding glare of a nun.

He pondered for a few moments how he'd put it to her. *What are you holding back here, Sister?* Or: *Have you found out that somewhere amongst these broken people you want so much to protect is one, or more than one man, who killed Padraig Larkin?*

"Look," he said. "I don't want to make things worse for these lads. But the law's the law."

The firm tone had returned to her voice.

"I understand. But law and justice aren't always on the same road, are they?"

With that, she drew in her breath, and like the farmer that Minogue imagined her father had been, she placed her hands on her knees and levered herself abruptly upright.

He was being dismissed?

"You'll phone me when these lads show? When you know where they are?"

She made no reply, but lifted the card he had given to her, and studied it. He wondered if somewhere in Sister Immaculata's world, he had not quite measured up. Maybe he never would. Maybe no-one would.

"No squad cars," he said. "No uniforms, no sirens. Just a chat."

"You'd be involved yourself, I hope, would you?"

The tinny drone from the television and the clashing plates surged back with the opening door. Too late he realized that this little room had been a refuge from the smells that now fell on him again. His nose was already trying to close itself. He quickly scanned the faces for any from her snapshots. No McArdle that he could see, no Walshe.

"We'll do what we can," he said.

He was at the door before he remembered. He crossed the floor back to where she had left him. She was sitting, listening to one of the men.

"One more thing if you please," he said after she had finished. "One 'JJ Mac'?"

"Ah, JJ. A bit of a character, JJ."

"A character."

She answered his unstated question with a stoic smile.

"Is there anything you think he could help us with?"

"If JJ would only help himself," she said. "Ah, I shouldn't be saying that."

"You mean...?"

"His heart's in the right place, that JJ. He told me he wanted to do a piece on us here. This was back before Hallowe'en. He even had a chat with some of the lads, I think. Yes, he was here one day and I was away. They'd put talk on anyone, some of our lads here, just to feel normal. Nobody will say a word to them when they're out roaming the streets, you see. Someone told me he was chatting awhile, or more listening. Just to get a feel for what they go through, I daresay."

"Was Padraig among them?"

"Well, I couldn't tell you now. One of the lads said he was, all right."

She paused to allow a smile its fuller expression.

"That's a compliment here. Someone else – Seánie, no doubt – said that he was spying on them."

"Spying."

He heard her issue a soft sigh as she waved away the word.

"'A government inspector,' I think Seánie decided. 'Out to get them.' It's par for the course, I'd have to say now."

She threw him a quick glance.

"Confidentially now, that, do you see?"

"I do. So what came of his visit, McCarthy?"

"Who knows, now. It didn't go over well with the newspaper people, the editor. But fair play to him, I suppose. He wanted to try, at least."

"To try what, exactly?"

She frowned and glanced obliquely at him.

"Publicity," she said. "That's the name of the game, isn't it? PR?"

"PR?"

"Of course! For Disciples here."

The voice – the tone – reached back decades to zap his nun-fearing amygdala.

"We're not iijits," she said. Her eyes had come alive with a smile. "We have to play the game too. We have to build cred, so when the cutbacks hit, we have a chance. We need people to buy into our efforts here – local people, County Council, everyone."

"To buy in?"

"Oh yes. I had to learn the lingo quickly myself. 'Render unto Caesar,' as Our Lord says. I thought JJ could help us with our profile. To humanize us, for the public."

"What did he come up with?"

"Nothing," she said quickly. Her smile held, but it had a rueful hint. "'Maybe later' they said to him. The last I heard from JJ was him saying that he kicked at it a bit more with them, but he hadn't much to draw on. It sputtered out, I expect."

Rising from the chair, she made a sudden grimace but quickly wrenched it away.

"Well you likely already know JJ in some form," she said. "You Guards in general, I mean."

She held out her hand. She had a strong, even combative handshake. Oh well. Saints, supposedly, were difficult people by definition.

"God bless," she said on an intake of breath, and then she smiled. "We'll be seeing you again, please God?"

Chapter 10

Malone had company back at the station. This Sergeant Fitzgerald, head of detectives at the station, was on the south end of his forties. The tufts of dark hair peeping out of his shirt collar reminded Minogue of one of those men he'd spot on a beach, one who'd cause him to wonder about evolution. He took Fitz's easygoing manner to be a screen. After all, this wasn't the local Garda station in Ballybejases: sergeant of detectives in a Dublin area station was not a post for sleepwalkers.

Malone was asking him about the area's luminaries. Fitz had eased himself back more against the door jamb, his eyebrow curling up in response to Malone's dry slagging.

"Sure we could phone Bono," he said to Malone. "Tell him you're here."

He turned to Minogue.

"I was just saying to himself here, to Tommy, to hop down to the office proper, and use the terminal there. Log on, and file away there to your heart's content – or bang on my door, why don't you, and use that one."

"Thanks," Minogue said. "And sorry about the short notice here."

"No bother," Fitz said, and smiled. "Sure we knew the thing was in review. Glad enough to get to the top of the queue. Makes us feel special, like."

Minogue smiled in return. Fitzgerald scratched at his head then, and made a quick survey of the room. His gesture reminded

Minogue of a farmer's studied reluctance when he was close to settling on a price.

"I'm only sorry we don't have a proper Incident Room. A dedicated one, like."

"We're grand," Minogue said. "Rare enough to find one anyway. And anyway, you might need a bigger dose of crime here to get facilities like that."

"True for you, by God," said Fitz. "'Be careful what you wish for,' et cetera."

"Quiet enough here, is it?"

"Well," said Fitz, and shifted his stance a little. "Could be worse, I suppose. Oh yes, a lot worse. Public Order stuff, a lot of it. But that's Dublin these days, isn't it?"

Minogue expected Malone to put in his oar in defence of his home city. No go.

"Yep," Fitz went on. "We get the usual closing-time dramatics. But who doesn't? A fair bit of thieving here, I have to say too, gougers going after the big houses. Lots of well-to-do people here, as you probably know. So we'd be busy in that regard. And vandalism, well it seems to come and go, in waves. Again, a lot of it's the young crowd, drinking and running around."

"Affluenza," said Minogue. "The kids these days, money, and that...?"

"'Affluenza' – I like it. I'm going to use that one."

"Many drug offences here?"

"Compared to say Dun Laoghaire back the road, it's low. We have a few Sharons and Darrens here though. 'Darren the baron,' like."

Minogue got the reference to skangers, but not the nobility.
"Baron?"

"Drug barons. Well, former ones, okay. Ones with good lawyers."

"Ah."

"Of course they've 'diversified.'" Fitz released his air-quotes slowly. "All arm's length, since Criminal Assets began tearing into the feckers."

"Do you see much of them?" Malone asked.

"Nah. But you'll see the wives there every now and then, double-parking the old Range Rover while they pick up their kids from school. Or at some hen-party there in a restaurant, comparing their bracelets or their tans or the like."

"You keep an eye on them though, do you?"

"Well we are aware of them, yes. But we're only on the edge of things, to be honest. We'd be falling in line with what the big planning says. The big ops."

Serious Crime Squad, he meant. It was more irony, more sarcasm, Minogue felt.

"Tell you the truth now," Fitz went on, rubbing his spine on the door jamb in a way that reminded Minogue of a cow against a fence, "day-to-day, we're more put-lights-on-your-bike here, or sign-your-passport-forms. Local, like. Not that it's easy now, or anything. We do a lot of checkpoints too, the drunk driving. It's steady enough really."

A cushy number too, Minogue would have said – if asked. Maybe even a wheeze.

Fitz slid upright, absent-mindedly shoving his shirt-tail more under his belt.

"So now you have it," he said. "Just to say hello, yes."

"Good man," Minogue said. "We'll be getting up to speed here now."

"At it already," said Fitz. "Fair play to you. I don't envy you, I have to say."

Minogue shrugged. A thoughtful expression had come to Fitz's face.

"There was a week back then," he said. "The Larkin matter? Well it was like a beehive in here, people buzzing all over the place. The GBCI team, go-go-go – no let-up. But that's what they're about, I suppose. The forty-eight hours rule, isn't that what they say?"

Minogue put on his neutral expression.

"It's not a hard-and-fast rule," he said.

"Twenty-three plain clothes at one time," Fitz went on. "The half of them worked out of the van, the Command Post van there eventually. Tight quarters."

Minogue let his eyes sharpen into a stare. Fitz got to the hint.

"Sorry, yes," he said. "Now: you'll be wanting the evidence room – ah, I see you beat me to it. Great. But be sure and keep a window open. You'll know what I mean when you open one of those boxes, let me tell you."

He paused by the door and turned.

"Oh, I meant to ask: do you want that chat with the assigned officers today?"

"We'd hardly expect that right away. But if there's a chance...?"

Fitz winked, and nodding toward the files now stacked next to Malone, made a slow, sympathetic nod. He paused in the doorway.

"A nice sandwich place there near the Castle. Italian?"

Minogue listened to Fitz's footfalls receding while he eyed the boxes that Malone had already retrieved from the evidence room. They were the new boxes, more like suitcases than anything else. German made or not, he had heard that these so-called Secure Evidence Enclosures had come with cheap, bollocky locks. He leaned over one, weaving his head to get by the glare of the fluorescents overhead on the polycarbonate window. He saw a date from last week next to a Garda Somebody's signature.

"'A nice sandwich place. Eye-talian.'"

Malone's talent at mimickry hadn't slipped. He unwrapped another stick of gum, flicked the ball of foil in the air, and caught it with a studied carelessness.

"That was a snooping visit," he muttered.

Minogue hunkered down by the boxes.

"That was a colleague being helpful," he retorted. "This is a normal practice."

"That a fact. Well I say it's a piss-on-the-fence visit. Territorial."

Minogue found what he had hoped, a folder 'Disciples.' He drew it out.

"Listen," he said. "We're on the same side. Did you know that?"

"I say Fitzie was checking sound levels. We should look for bugs."

Minogue stopped reading the list and looked over at him.

"Now. Have you located this Mac fella? JJ Mac somebody. McCarthy, yes."

"Not in the raw, I haven't. Not yet. But I found his record. You want?"

"Fire away."

"Done first in the early Eighties for importation. He tried to bring in cocaine – and get this for Mastermind at work here – he'd stuffed it into picture frames. Picture frames? Anyway. Came in from Amsterdam. Thing is, he didn't do time for that. Looks to me like he went over, and gave names for suppliers over there. His name shows up in incident reports right through to...let me see...six years back. Associating with knowns, attending on knowns. He was pulled in a few times, invited to assist."

He paused and eyed Minogue. He didn't need to voice his doubts out loud. Minogue knew that 'Invited to assist' ran the gamut from easy money to dire threats.

"He lodged complaints," Malone went on. "Tried a suit, said the Guards assaulted him. It took four years to get through the system. Went nowhere in the end though."

"That was it for him and the justice system then?"

"No. Two charges, late Nineties, but the charges were dismissed. Handy, right?"

"Very handy. How'd he wangle that one?"

"Guess. Yeah, I found the fella who worked him. He's Sergeant in Howth now."

"Worked him?"

Malone gave him a glazed look.

"McCarthy grassed on someone we wanted. All arm's length, and well-put-together, this Sergeant told me. They wanted McCarthy staying in place, so they waited to get him clear of any pay-back from his cronies."

"Lovely, I'm sure. Is this McCarthy still assisting the forces of law and order?"

Malone shook his head.

"Don't know," he said. "It's not showing in the system. But you know, yourself."

Minogue did, but it would be a hell of a job to find out. Drug

Squad detectives in every division across the country had their own networks of touts and hangers-on, a shifting, ragged tribe made up of addicts and parolees and misfits.

"Cork man, McCarthy?" he asked.

"No way. He's a Dub. Just up the road, in actual fact, Sallynoggin. The guy's in his fifties, but home address is his mammy's. Sounds like Loserama to me."

"You can't raise him at work? No mobile?"

"Well here's the thing," Malone said. "I phoned the paper, South County. They're cool on him. 'Mr. McCarthy worked on a temporary basis. He is not currently on staff.'"

"And what does that mean?"

Malone started a stretch.

"Means he's not working there. And they like it that way, is what I'm hearing."

"What, he got the sack? Dirtied his bib with them?"

"They wouldn't say. 'Confidentiality' yeah yeah yeah – Blaah. But they gave me his mobile. It only goes to the machine. I ended up getting an address from the MT."

Motor Taxation office, Minogue realized. Malone's stretch ended in a low growl.

"So I ended up talking to his mammy. That was something. She's got to be ancient. So yeah, he lives there, she says, but he's away. Away where, says I. Amsterdam, says she. 'He has to report for his newspaper.' She doesn't know what the hell it is though."

"Amsterdam. Could he be back to old tricks? Maybe he never stopped."

"I have no clue – yet. But he's got his mammy living the dream. She thinks he runs the country or something. But say he's tweaking, and he's out of money...? That'd fit. You want me to keep going on it, see if I can get him showing on a flight list?"

"The sooner we get to him the better, yes. Use him, or get him out of the way."

* * *

Fitz's warning had not been exaggerated. Even with the window pushed open so far that it dug into the paint, and maybe even bent the fittings, the penetrating reek had blanketed the room. Minogue had tried to ease himself into the job by going for what he had hoped would be the lesser assault on his nose and his senses generally – the box that held not-on-the person effects and belongings.

The old history book and the falling-apart map had come from Larkin's hideaway. They had all the signs of being obsessed over, with smudges and stains that flowed together. But a musk had risen from the box even before Minogue's cotton-gloved hand had settled on the polythene bags within. He dragged the table as close as he could to the window, but the moment the first bag was opened, he knew they were in for it. He had struggled to come up with what it reminded him of: old vinegar, milk gone sour in the car on a hot day, that Italian cheese... But always, the unmistakable smell of something charred. Even Malone was taken aback.

"How old you reckon that book is?" he asked.

"The Sixties, it looks like, but I haven't read it in the report yet."

"Talk about boring-looking. Isn't it?"

"You were never a history fan that I recall."

"Come on now, boss. Even the pictures are boring. For a kids' book? Even I know enough about Vikings to say that there should be something decent-looking here. Swords, and fighting and all that. And horned helmets too, right?"

Minogue pulled the gloves tighter.

"So this stuff here says he had the mentality of a kid then?"

"It's more complicated, I'm thinking."

"Well at least the map is grown-up," Malone said.

Minogue placed the book back in the box. Pausing then as he refolded the map, he let his eyes wander over it one more time. Those marks still meant nothing to him.

"Jaysus," Malone muttered, and began looking over the other boxes. "That stink isn't dying down, is it? Did we close them up again right?"

The phone interrupted his search.

"Fabulous," he muttered. "Our first official call-in?"

Minogue placed the map alongside the book and the other effects taken from Larkin's cave. A sweet tooth, or a kid's palate, for the chocolate and the crisps and the allsorts – even fruit pastilles, for God's sakes. When had he gotten that rice wine? Make sure he remembered that when he went to the files. Sweets weren't all that he ate, of course. A can opener, well-used. A sturdy dessert spoon, and alongside it a fork with a tine bent in a little; a pound shop knife with a fake bone handle. Paper serviettes: were they instead of toilet paper...? More cigarette papers, and two boxes of matches, wrapped in a plastic bag.

He listened to Malone asking about other airlines. Then he echoed something he was being told and he let his biro fall onto the pad of paper, unused.

"Well?"

"No sign of him yet," said Malone. "I'll try the ferries next. Would he be going through England if it's Amsterdam he's headed for?"

"Who knows. Relatives, friends – maybe he's on a bit of a caravanserai."

"What's that mean?"

"Taking his time. Dropping in on people."

"People? Gougers and blags, you mean. Some 'journalist,' this fella."

Minogue secured the lid, and made sure the lock was aligned.

"I'd like to know if he ever left planet druggie in the first place," said Malone, his voice trailing off. "Or did he keep up that grassing career he had back then?"

Minogue had no answers for him. It took him a few tries to get the lock to slide home. The gloves hadn't helped.

"That one's ready to be signed back in," he said to Malone. "I'll be back in ten minutes. I forgot something in the car."

"They're in your pocket," Malone murmured. He didn't look over. "You put them in earlier."

Chapter 11

It was an hour after Minogue had come back from his smoke before the cold draft in from the window had finally won out over the remnants of the smell. Levering the window closed, he discovered that he had indeed done something to the mechanism when he'd pulled it open so wide before. He stood by the window, let his thoughts drift a little.

He was soon up on the Hill, with glimpses of the Irish Sea far below, and between the leaves the perfect blues and whites of a June day. Wait: that was fantasy. June had been the wettest on record. So, had Larkin's foxhole kept out the rain? He let himself imagine Larkin sitting near the dripping mouth of that cave of his. Larkin would hardly be meditating. Could he stay fixated on this Viking raiders kick all day? There was no point in trying to guess what else would have found its way in to occupy Larkin's thoughts. The weather would have figured surely. As much as it had wrecked the summer for everyone else, it had also played havoc with Larkin's walkabouts and the haywire sentry duty thing he did. Did he read the paper, listen to the radio, watch the telly? Had he any notion of the crisis out there, the rage and foreboding that had seized the country?

He noticed that Malone was well into a bubble now. It was half the size of his face already. For some reason, he gave up on it.

"You know," he said, after he had chewed it back in. "I never actually thought about that much before. Not at all, come to think of it. Being nuts, I mean."

"Don't you mean mentally ill?"

"Right. It just struck me, going through the reports there. This Larkin guy is probably in his own time zone. Back to childhood or something, right? Does he notice anything of what's going on at all around him?"

"I was just thinking about that."

"And has he got any idea of time at all? He can't be doing his patrolling thing all the time, can he? What, Vikings in the morning, and then Normans in the afternoon?"

He snorted softly then, and dismissed some thought with a toss of his head.

"Now that's funny," he said. "Maybe now is when we need the likes of Larkin."

"What do you mean? Too deep for me there, I'm afraid."

Malone abruptly stopped chewing.

"Wasn't Larkin going around the place making speeches? Shouting about invaders, and robbing and pillaging? 'Run like hell, here come the Vikings!' Something like that? But think about it. Robbing, pillaging...? Banks, builders, bail-outs...?"

"Letter to the editor," said Minogue. "Better yet, add it to that Facebook page."

"Whatever. So, how'd it go with that nun one out there? Sister What's-her-name – Sister Act, whatever. Is she happy, now that she got her say with us?"

Minogue realized that he didn't have a clear answer.

"Not so good?" Malone pressed.

"Actually, I left the place wondering if maybe something's bothering her."

"Bothering her? There's a good one. But that's nuns for you, isn't it?"

Minogue felt a strong impulse to just agree. Malone would never get the nun thing. Just like the dog-watching-television look he'd give when Minogue used a word of Irish, nuns for Malone were just another weird holdover from an Ireland that had passed. No offence, as Malone would say. It wasn't about the twenty years' difference in their ages, or a Clare culchie at odds with a Dublin jackeen. It was a case of living in different worlds.

So what chance would Malone have then of recognizing any part of the world that Immaculata lived in, one of souls and glory and God and...?

"She was the one making noise and pulling strings, but she only wanted to vent?"

"Maybe," Minogue managed. "I don't know."

"She put a spell on you," Malone said. "That old nun. That's what she did."

Before Malone could draw him in more, he had finger-walked over the file folders and pulled out the one he had been seeking, the very properly and very neatly labeled 'Report of the State Pathologist.' There were digital 8×10s along with the photocopies.

"I'm going to start on this now," he said to Malone. "Any pointers for me?"

Malone eyed the folder, and then Minogue.

"Don't be fretting," Minogue said. "Case review guidelines, they're called, not The Ten Commandments. So talk to me. What were you thinking after you read it?"

"Okay," Malone said. "One attacker. And he was kicked a lot – I mean really kicked – so a serious going-over. It wasn't just a barney, a fight, I mean. No choke marks, no defensive stuff. No weapons or objects at hand. No sign of that rock."

"Just the big drop on the head, am I remembering right...?"

"Right."

Minogue turned to the summary first. Larkin's skull had shattered at the top of his forehead. His brain was coated in a film of blood and more hemorrhages were also found inside the brain. There was blood in his lungs. It could not be said with certainty if that alone had caused him to choke to death. Such injuries would almost certainly have severed nerve cell filaments. Nerve cell filaments? Some sort of a brutal mercy, maybe.

There had been multiple injuries to the head and neck beyond that fatal crushing of the top of the forehead. A spreading, fan-shaped pattern over the right ear was noted, and another patterned bruise behind the right jaw. As if these weren't enough, the report noted that injuries like this to the neck can cause cardiac arrest and instant death.

He put the pages down, and gingerly eyed some of the digital prints. He tried to stifle an image that distracted him, of bog bodies and their flattened faces.

"Pretty bad," Malone murmured. "Yeah?"

"It's bad all right."

"The worst you ever saw?"

"They're all the worst, Tommy. Every one, every time. You know that."

★ ★ ★

By four o'clock, Minogue was beyond restless. The place was getting to him again. He had already made two quick forays against the claustrophobia, down the hall to a window looking over the yard at the back of the station. A heavy shower had come and gone over the town, and left drops shivering on the window there.

There had been no phone call from Immaculata. He took that to mean that none of Larkin's cronies had shown up at her Disciples drop-in place.

Malone tapped a finger on the copies of Larkin's treatment reports.

"That's something, that stuff. The children thing? Neighbours? Jaysus."

Minogue was surprised at Malone's squeamishness.

"Child molesting, you're talking about?"

Malone's reply came after a slow, ironic look.

"I thought it was only priests did that stuff," he said. Minogue gave him the eye.

"What," said Malone. "I'm not allowed say that? What about that commission thing next week? It better not be a whitewash. They better be naming names."

"Give them a fair trial and then hang them. Is that your approach?"

Malone's reply was to study his nails.

Minogue refocused on his own summary. Padraig Thomas Larkin, fifty-eight; chronic alcoholism, serial markers of organic brain damage. A long list of failed efforts at working. Clerk, deliveryman; supermarket yard worker – whatever that was. Parking attendant? He had worked in some capacity at a homeless shelter in a 'recycling enterprise.' Four recorded visits to Accident and Emergency had punctuated his time in England. Two London hospitals, a total of five hospital stays. 'Accident due impairment,' in two, victim of assault in another two. Pneumonia/collapsed lung in the other. A seven-month stay in some St Helier place, in Surrey, with some treatment. A record of faltering attendance at two psychiatric outpatient clinics over a period of three years.

Larkin's return to Ireland had come just as the Boom was starting. A timed return to Ireland? Hardly. He'd hardly timed his exit with the crash either. Those years seemed to have given him a more sedate existence: no record of contact with the criminal justice system. His name had two entries on Pulse, the Garda information database: witnesses to assault. One had a notation of 'unhelpful.' Visits to the Accident and Emergency in Dublin had been relatively sparse. He had long stays at hostels, many to the six-month limit. The Simon Community had tried a Transitional House scheme. It wasn't clear why it had fallen through.

He turned to the notes from Larkin's psychiatrists. They seemed stale, wordy, out-of-date. Larkin had been fifteen that year. The Summer of Love, that year was called? He had admitted to taking – 'trying' – LSD, but claimed not to have known what its effects could be. No recall of going into the garage with the girl from down the road.

"Surprise surprise."

Malone had been following his reading.

"The rot started with drugs? So that was the Sixties, maaan?"

Minogue disdained a reply. Malone began moving his head and neck in those short jerks, moves that Minogue assumed had something to with fitness routines.

"What did they call that kind of carry-on back then anyway?"

"They had euphemisms. 'Interfering with' was one, I remember."

"What," said Malone. "No one said it out straight? Like, rape? Sexual assault?"

"It was a different time."

"Different? Like his daddy's a judge, and all that? Warped, or what."

Minogue shrugged.

"And no charges," Malone added. "How's about that? Not even drug treatment. Wait, was there addiction treatment back then? Coolmine?"

"Coolmine was the Seventies, I think, early Seventies."

"Yeah well, that hasn't changed, has it. Money still talks."

The teenage Larkin had been taken out of boarding school, and sent to this shrink. The files had gone into Larkin's medical record after the shrink died a decade ago.

Malone trudged toward the door, and studied the pages that Minogue had taped to the wall next to it. The maps of Dalkey and Killiney seemed to draw his interest most.

Minogue let the pages collapse back into their sheaf, pushed back his chair and looked across at the maps. Larkin's known movements and sightings were in red. There weren't just days missing, there were weeks. No wonder the case had been treading water.

Floorboards creaked with Malone's extended stretch. He spoke though a yawn.

"Surprises me he got as far as he did. Sleeping rough like that, at his age?"

Genes, Minogue wondered. Luck? That farmers' saying about weeds came to rest in his mind: 'Hard to kill a bad thing'?

"That sister of his," Malone said. "She must have known all this. You think?"

"It's hard to see how she wouldn't have."

"Orna," Malone said, pausing between syllables. "Is that a real name, Orna?"

"For a certain generation it is, a certain social stratum."

"Funny names out here, Southside names. Does it mean something?"

"'Golden one.' See what you're missing because you don't know any Irish?"

"Huh. Seen that statement of hers yet? Not much gold in that. All it is, is the bare minimum. Info and verification. Next-of-kin? His only sibling? They phoned her back a few times. Know what she says? 'The matter's closed.' Really. 'I've told you what I know, the matter is closed.' It's right there where she said that, on the last page. Read that over a few times there, go on. I did. It gets you wondering about people, I tell you."

Minogue made a quick calculation: including the time Orna Larkin had spent in university there, she'd been in England over forty years.

Malone was still thinking aloud.

"A no-show, even for the funeral. That says something, doesn't it? But who are we to judge, right? And she did keep up the allowance for him. Guilt money, maybe?"

"How much was it again?"

"Fifty euro a week – enough for cigarettes and a few jars. She said the mother gave him money to get something started in London years ago. Blew it, apparently."

Malone scratched the back of his head.

"But this sister did all right though, didn't she," he added. "She made her own life and all. Didn't marry, but. And what is she again, some science thing?"

"A chemist. Some outfit near London."

"High up in it though, right? Not bad. Brain-power there, I'll bet you."

"It looks like she ran out of here, first chance she got. Dublin, like, or Ireland."

"Emigrated," Minogue said. "Went where the opportunities were."

"You think? 'Didn't come back' equals 'ran' to me. Bolted."

"There wasn't much stirring here during those times, especially for girls."

Malone's slow stroll had returned him to the maps. This time, he studied the topographic rings around the hills that made up Killiney Hill Park. The photocopier had done a not-great job with the colours and shades from the original.

"We really should take another run at placing him better," Minogue said. "That's number one for me at the moment. We can't place him for days and days before Seán's girl found him on the Hill there. Rhiannon."

"Run a public appeal again then? Right away, like?"

The phone ringing startled them both. It was Fitz. Did they want a chat with the two officers who'd handled the case? Fitz asked if they would prefer to have a chat down the street at a café maybe, get out of that 'little confession box.'

Minogue replaced the folders. He had the trouble locking the enclosures that he expected. Malone was closing the door behind him when his mobile went.

"Find your way down when you're ready," he said to Malone.

He was soon tapping at the half-open door to the detectives' office.

"Come in, come in," said Fitz. "No need to knock."

The office was spacious; tatty enough too, but almost homely. In its high ceilings and tall windows Minogue read signs of its former life as a drawing room, or a parlour. There was the usual pairing of desks, with their matching long-out-of-date CRT monitors like Easter Island sentinels. The view was over wet rooftops and crowns of Canary palms in a nearby garden, their wet swaying fronds a reminder of a better climate elsewhere.

"They're over beyond already," said Fitz. "Frank and Tony. They're only back a few minutes. Gave them a bit of time to get settled, water the horse and so forth."

"Well thanks," said Minogue. "But we don't want to get in the way of things."

Fitzgerald's response was a complaisant smile.

"Good God, no – plenty of time. Nothing pressing, as they say. Don is on an assault case, a wedding party thing. Imagine that: a row at a wedding. And Tony's back from a big break-in, a builders' supply and rental place."

Don – for Donegan, of course. He thanked Fitz, and headed

back down the hall toward the stairs. Malone was by a window, still on the mobile. It was a serious-sounding conversation.

"I know," he heard Malone whisper, and repeat it. "I know, Sonia, I know."

Chapter 12

The same Frank Donegan turned out to be an affable copper – either that or a first-class faker. There was something boyish and disarming about the freckles on the milk-white forehead, the wiry hair still more rusty than grey. He was still chuckling about taking the briefing in this café.

"This is more like it," he said. "Isn't it, Tony?"

Detective Garda Tony Ledwidge's answer was a flexing of the eyebrows, and a shift of his shoulders against his car-coat. Another glance at this dark-haired, balding mesomorph with the ruddy complexion told Minogue that he was still very much on guard. Ledwidge, the senior man, was likely more allergic to any pixie dust from high-octane blow-ins like the great Inspector Minogue and his sidekick.

Neither Donegan nor Ledwidge was fussy about coffee. Malone wanted his usual cup-a-tea-nuttin'-else. Minogue was willing to risk a latte. While they waited, Donegan eased into a yarn about a holiday that he and his missus had taken in Portugal. Minogue surveyed the premises, trying to ignore the dithering, go-nowhere jazz in the background. The stainless steel and black surfaces held no allure for him. Jars of preserves topped with bright pieces of cloth and finished with ribbons looked like props. Cake names were over the top: Maraschino Bliss? Magazines, dried flowers, cracked tile half-hidden under a table. The only other customer was a young woman writing in a notebook by the window, the familiar white iPod wires below her ears quivering as she wrote.

The Donegans' romantic getaway in Portugal had its epiphany in the town's local hospital. Donegan pronounced the Portuguese nice people, and held them in no way responsible for his wife falling down the steps. Malone came up with a mild version of his holiday in Spain with his mother, the too-much-karaoke, too-much-sangria holiday. The atmosphere was cordial but still wary. Minogue still couldn't get a fix on Ledwidge. Could it be that he might be one of those rarest of Irish birds, a Man of Sparing Words? He reminded himself of the goal again: rapport, getting off on the right foot.

He took an opening from talk about floods in the West and slid into a safe topic, his efforts planting vegetables last Spring. All four policemen soon declared a preference for the cold to the wet in Ireland's winters. Talk of rain and weather led handily to Killiney Hill Park, and the camp that Larkin had made there.

"Well I tell you now," Donegan said, his voice dropping. "I never saw anything like it in all my time. Never did. Like one of those Viet Cong spider holes."

He looked to Ledwidge for corroboration, before leaning back to allow the woman to put down the tray of coffees and the teapot.

"A badger," he said after she left. "The first thing I thought – a badger in his sett."

He put down the package of sugar and drew in a breath through his back teeth.

"Did you get to the PM yet? The preexisting state of health bit?"

"I ran by it fairly quick," Minogue replied. "Not a well man to begin with?"

"Liver half-gone," Donegan said, beginning a count on his fingers. "Kidneys damaged. Blockages in arteries. Lung lesions? Something about deposits in his brain: 'undetermined cognitive effects.' Maybe the King of Ireland stuff was brain damage?"

"A rough life I suppose" was all Minogue could think to say. "Hard on a body."

"And a heavy alcoholic. Bit of a miracle he was upright at all."

Minogue slid a lump of sugar into the froth that hid how small his latte really was.

"How did you find that place of his, exactly?"

Ledwidge seemed to take this as his cue to join in.

"The information line," he said. "A call-in, after the first public appeal."

"We'd heard he had some place there," Donegan added. "His mates told us."

Ledwidge gathered himself and sat forward before he spoke.

"These mates of his, they said they had no idea where the hideaway actually was."

"Yes indeed," said Donegan. "Finding it turned out to be quite the job of work."

"Did you get a look inside it?"

Donegan's eyes widened.

"We didn't go poking, no way. Went by the book. Site secured, rang the Bureau."

The writing woman was scowling at her mobile now. Minogue had never figured out what exactly it was about people intent on their mobiles that made him dismayed.

"But you could see into it a bit," Ledwidge said. "Tight quarters, but still you'd fit a man inside. He had plastic for lining, sticking out from under the sleeping bag."

"He knew what he was doing," said Donegan. "The trouble he went to, getting those bits of wood up there? Digging the thing out, camouflaging it? Quite something."

Minogue took a sip of the latte. There was a faintly burned taste to it somewhere.

"It was something he was good at, I believe."

"Like the forts we'd build when we were kids," Donegan said. "But better."

"When was it found, this camp place of his?"

"The fourth day after, unfortunately. Two days of rain. Did you see the photos?"

"Only a cursory once-over so far. But I ran through the list of effects in it. Slim."

"The rotgut he never got to finish, the Chinese cooking wine. The stuff he had there, kid's stuff, crisps, and sweets. And that old schoolbook, the history one, with his scribbles?

'Viking hordes.' 'Wild Sea Raiders'? He had a thing for Vikings."

"Bit of a Lord of the Rings thing going on in his head there."

"Seen any of the psych reports yet?" Donegan asked.

"We gave them the once-over," Minogue replied. "Tell me though, do you think there could be more belongings of his somewhere?"

Donegan settled his cup carefully on the table. His face turned thoughtful.

"Nothing so far," he said. "And it's been a while already now. Larkin never settled, really. We went back as far as we could on him. He shows up at various shelters and hostels in the cold months, but lots of times he wouldn't stay, even in the winter. 'A bolter,' we were told. 'Very touchy.' He'd switch between the South City hostel and Crosscare, the back of George's Street in Dun Laoghaire. Always coming back out this way."

"Sure it's around here that the poor divil started out, I suppose."

Minogue heard no irony in Ledwidge's murmured words.

"His family was well-to-do? Clarinda Park?"

"That's it," said Ledwidge. "But they're long gone. The father, the judge, he's gone these twenty year. Twelve years for the mother. Larkin's sister is all that's left."

"Orna, in England."

"That's her," said Donegan.

Minogue felt the caffeine begin its agitation in his chest in earnest now.

"Have you been up there recently?" he asked. "Up on the Hill?"

"No," said Donegan. "The hideaway was filled in the end of July. 'A hazard.'"

"The NBCI team gave it six days there," Ledwidge added. "Canvassing, like. And we had the uniforms there four days in a row after as well. Three weekends too."

Malone blew on his tea again. Donegan watched him for several moments.

"So tell me," said Minogue. "What do you make of the Facebook effort?"

Ledwidge shifted in his seat. A wry look came close to being his first smile.

"The 'Green Man' et cetera? The fourteen hundred and something 'friends'?"

"But it's all well meant," said Ledwidge. "That's the important thing."

"Conor Reardon," Donegan added. "Nice lad, a student. Save-the-world type."

Minogue didn't miss the hint, another signal they had done their due diligence.

"Still," said Donegan. "Like Tony says, nice to see people care, even nowadays."

Donegan put his cup on the table with an *ahh*. A hint of mockery glinted in his eye.

"You'd wonder what'll be left standing, in the heel of the reel," he said. "If it's not the banks or the church, it's shoot-outs on the street. What are we up to now? Twenty-seven this year, the gang stuff? Or is it twenty-eight?"

As if he didn't keep score, Minogue reflected. He pressed his sombre, thoughtful nod into service. It wasn't enough to stifle Donegan yet, however.

"Just when all the higher-ups are retiring in droves, to get ahead of the pension levy? All that know-how flying out the door...?"

Minogue took the 'higher-ups' to be a sly dig, a test. But Malone had had enough too, and it was his Dublin demi-drawl that cut short the moaning.

"I'll tell youse what'll be left. Lots of room for promotion. That's what."

This drew a soft cackle from Donegan. Minogue eyed the writer woman and tried to imagine what had her writing so keenly again. Maybe she was famous, that one who wrote those shopaholic books?

Mention of Facebook eased the talk back on the rails.

"This Larkin Facebook effort?" said Donegan. "Well I could live without it. How's pissing on the Guards going to help? We're trying our best. Don't they get it?"

Minogue shifted in his chair, and looked from Donegan to Ledwidge.

"Indeed. So, what, or who, is left standing here with this Larkin situation?"

Ledwidge drew in a breath, and let it swell his cheeks for several moments.

"Number one place to start was known persons," he said. "Larkin's cronies. Trouble is, they're alibied. Walshe was in a shed out in Dun Laoghaire, a building site gone bust there. McArdle, the other hobo, was along with him. A squat situation."

"Simon Community did a soup run out there," said Donegan. "It took us a couple of days to get a statement out of the Simon fella."

Several moments passed.

"That shed's gone," Ledwidge said. "It got out about them squatting there."

"Can we get any forensics pointing at them?"

"Not so far we can't," said Ledwidge.

"Site yield? Or from Larkin's belongings?"

"Tests on his gear all go back to Larkin," Donegan replied. "And him only. The same for effects on the person. There was other stuff they couldn't do anything with."

"Sorry about that, CSI fans," Malone murmured. "We'll go to the ad break now."

His effort earned a dutiful smile from Donegan.

"Okay, his booze," said Ledwidge then. "We sourced the place he got the cooking wine. The best we got is 'don't remember.' We haven't been able to budge that."

"No sign of any weapon?" asked Minogue. "Implements, I should say?"

"The rock used on his noggin?" Donegan replied. "That same rock, that stone, it did away with the chance of a decent print from whoever did the kicking? Nope."

"Any sense that whoever hit him with the rock was not the kicker, or kickers?"

Ledwidge twisted his ring slowly on his finger as he spoke.

"Well this is the thing. We can't be beating about the bush here.

The fact is, we still don't know how many were involved. We just don't."

Ledwidge's bluntness brought a small current of relief trickling into Minogue.

"Fibres, track casts, litter," he went on. "All went to the Lab. But no go. No transfer on Larkin – even with him dragged into the bushes, nothing."

"There's an effort to hide him," Minogue said. "Is he murdered in the daytime?"

"Larkin's hefty," said Ledwidge. "If there's no accomplice, then this one doing the killing, and the dragging, and so forth, he has to be a bit of a Schwarzenegger."

"Hooligan factor?" Malone asked. "Young fellas drinking, running wild there?"

"Not a peep about any carry-on like that on that day, or that evening. Nothing."

"Any clear signs of an effort to cover up signs, or tracks?"

"Clear, no," said Ledwidge, letting go the sugar bowl. "But no tracks either."

"He was killed lying on his back? Those contusions, the fractures?"

"Right," replied Ledwidge. "Somewhere along the line he's turned on his belly."

"What did you make of that?"

Ledwidge sat forward a little, and glanced at Minogue.

"It could be him, or them, buying time to get away, making it look like he was having a snooze. But we see it connected to somebody going through his pockets."

Donegan seemed to be ahead of Minogue's next question.

"That bit of money he got every week," Donegan added. "We wondered?"

"Did his cronies know he got that money?"

"None of them admitted to knowing it. Larkin could have kept it to himself."

"It sounds like you have your doubts still though. How did Larkin actually get hold of this allowance? I haven't reached that yet."

"A bank in Dun Laoghaire. They had it waiting for him, every Wednesday."

"Any issues there?"

Donegan shook his head.

"No. He went to the same one. She knew him awhile – not *knew* him knew him. She was used to him. Never said much. Just came in, got his money, and out he went."

"Is it connected to the sister, Orna? Was it out of a trust fund or something?"

"It was her money," said Donegan. "The goodness of her heart? But how to square that with the fact that she didn't come over for the funeral...?"

"Any issue about a will or that? An inheritance? Bad blood maybe?"

"No," said Ledwidge. "The family had money, but it went in due course with the mother, and then the daughter. When the mother died, the house was sold, and the daughter – Orna – she bought a place in London. He came back here around that time."

Donegan took a sip from his coffee and made a face.

"The no-show at the funeral was an eye-opener," he said. "But when we got more background, you could see where she was coming from. Skeletons in the cupboard, is that the expression – Larkin, I mean. She hadn't been back to Dublin since the mother died. Here, Tony: what was the word she used again?"

"Impertinent," said Ledwidge.

"That's it. I keep on forgetting it. We were trying to ferret out any money angle, and up comes this: 'That's a highly impertinent question.' But that was when it came out that she was the one doing the allowance for him."

With that, Donegan shrugged and eyed his coffee.

"The funeral was small," said Ledwidge. "The priest, of course. McArdle and Walshe, his on-again-off-again cronies. People from the shelter, and social worker types. A nun, Sister Immaculata, she works with the down-and-outs. But that was it really."

"Cousins?" Minogue asked. "Neighbours from the old days? Family friends?"

Ledwidge shook his head. He rubbed the sides of his cup.

Summoning a genie, Minogue wondered. The quiet lasted a bit long, even for Minogue.

"Did I get the PM right," he said. "Killed eighteen to thirty-six before discovery?"

"That's right."

"And do we have any notion of time elapsing here? Did our kicker, or our kickers, did they go away, and come back later to drag Larkin off into the bushes?"

At least Donegan and Ledwidge didn't shake their heads in synchrony.

"A good number of walkers up there on the Hill, I imagine," he said to Ledwidge.

"True for you. The cross-checking took until the end of July."

He scratched the back of his neck and gave Minogue a bashful glance.

"Bit of a land after all that to see, well you know by now, how little we have."

"That's the real world for you," Minogue said.

"We do case review the end of every month," Donegan said, sitting up straight as though to face down his colleague's doleful conclusions. "We've done four public appeals now. Got it on *Crime Call* again, when it got started up again after the summer."

★ ★ ★

The walk back to the Garda station followed Castle Street's curves. Minogue found himself paired with Donegan, and whether it was the unhurried pace, or the company, he began to suspect that he might begin to like this street a little. He clung to a belief that a hint of seaweed on the breeze was helping in this regard.

It had gotten colder, and the usual mid-afternoon trickery with the light was playing itself out. It seemed to be steady and even brightening, but the November daylight was in fact on its last legs, and the air had already taken on the metallic tone that would send the world tipping toward evening at any moment.

The woman behind the wheel of the white Range Rover

idling next to a tanning salon had that bored, even angry look.
The sharp hairdo hanging over one eye, the starkly thin neck and
shoulders: a clone of what's her name, the Beckham one?

Minogue pulled his coat tighter. They passed the wellness
place again, the poster of the woman with stones on her back.
Hadn't Kathleen said she'd like to try that?

"That nun mentioned earlier," Donegan said then. "You
know about her, right?"

"She's at that drop-in place there, you mentioned."

"Right. She's not sending any fan mail our way, that Sister
Immaculata."

"Is she any help to us?"

"Well she knew Larkin. He was 'a client' at the drop-in
place."

"Knew him well? Knew him to see?"

"Well she gave us what she had. It was no great shakes."

"She's a good age," Donegan went on. It wasn't a compliment. "Yes indeed, a good age to be doing what she's doing out
there. But sure you know the nuns."

"Concerning this case," Minogue tried. "Or more in general,
you mean?"

He slowed to scan the headlines on the newspapers.

"Gave me a lecture – a sermon?" he said. "A bit of that
'social justice' stuff."

Castle Street had ended, and a glut of traffic held the four on
the footpath while they waited to cross. Malone's eyes followed
an Audi as it slid soundlessly by them.

"Eighty-five thou," he said to no-one in particular. Minogue
turned to Donegan.

"I meant to ask you earlier on, but I forgot. A JJ Mac.
McCarthy, a journalist?"

Donegan smiled, and looked over his shoulder at Ledwidge.

"Farty McCarthy, Tony," he said. "Told you. Another pint
you owe me."

"Sounds like you know him, or of him," Minogue said.

"Oh we know him all right. A chip on his shoulder the size
of a house."

Minogue followed his lead crossing between cars. The path ahead hit a narrow stretch, and Donegan worked around a pram. The au pair was Asian, her face pinched and frowning as though braced for more gusts. Gob open and head back, the child slept.

"Whatever else he is," said Donegan, interrupting himself to regain the footpath with a quick skip. "A journalist he ain't. Maybe in his dreams, he is. But what he really is, is a newspapers delivery man. They're not even newspapers, they're advertising rags."

Minogue stepped onto the roadway to allow Malone and Ledwidge to catch up.

"And by the way," Donegan, added, "he has a record – imagine that. That explains a lot about him in my book, the grudge he has with the Guards. We gave him the bum's rush, good-bye and pip-pip and mind-your-head leaving. We were on to him."

"On to his...?"

"His M.O. He's on the prowl for anything to make us look bad – anything. And if he can't find dirt, he'll make it up. So any chance he gets, off he goes to pelt as much shite as he can at the Guards, hoping any bit of it'll stick. That right, Tony?"

"He's out to provoke you," said Ledwidge. "That'll give him a story then."

"So this McCarthy is not in the picture," Minogue said. "This Larkin case?"

"I spoke with him," Donegan replied, pausing as a gust of wind watered his eyes. "Had to. It'd cause more trouble not to anyway, the stink he'd raise. Oh boy, what a treat that was. He only found out about Larkin maybe six or eight weeks ago but he's at it like a terrier. 'When can the public expect this?' and 'Why is this case shelved?'"

Donegan stopped, and he fixed an earnest look on Minogue.

"And he has this look on his face when he's talking – he sneers at you. It took all I had to be civil, let me tell you. I says to him, look, I says, if you have something to offer the Garda Síochána in the matter, it's your civic duty to assist. The reaction? He laughs."

"Laughs at...?"

"Who knows? My choice of words? Me trying to stay polite? No – he's trying to get a rise out of us. But I let him know that there's ways to be civil here."

Minogue waited.

"Says I, 'If you'd care to go and ask your associates for info well that might help.' 'Associates,' you know? His criminal record, like?"

"Ah. And how did that go over with him?"

"Well he got it, I tell you. Oh yes. It wiped that smile right off his face."

"Had he anything to offer at that stage? To your, ah, suggestion?"

"Bugger-all," said Donegan, almost cheerfully. "Not a sausage."

They turned onto Tubbermore Road. The steps and railings of the Garda station began to come into view.

"Been quiet since," said Donegan. "Maybe he's moved on to another cause. But I'd say he's nosing around somewhere, just waiting and hoping for us to screw up. I'd give him a few days before he hears you're here, and then he'll find a way to get to you."

He looked back at Ledwidge.

"Tony? A fiver says Farty McCarthy'll be back to his tricks before the day is out tomorrow – once he hears about the lads here. Will you take me up on it?"

Ledwidge's reply was a toss of his head. The wind had brought up his complexion, and the wry expression put Minogue mind of a farmer leaning on a gate. Donegan inclined a little toward Minogue then.

"I have my own theory about the likes of McCarthy," he said. "Remember punk? That's him. He's in a time-warp, still thinks he's, I don't know, twenty or something. Still listens to the Ramones, still wears the look. The world's moved on, but he hasn't. So where does he gravitate to? The whinge corner is where. 'Journalist'? You could call it anything, I suppose. Fact is, he's a delivery man. He delivers papers."

Minogue let his eyes roam the narrow street ahead. A street lamp came on. Already? An image came with it, one of a man too weak and too dazed to escape the plunging rock that ended his life.

He stopped at the bottom of the steps.

"Thanks," he said. "For indulging us. Very civilized entirely."

"Any time," said Donegan. "I hope there's more meetings like that, by God."

Their scuffing footfalls receded. Malone surveyed the end of the street.

"Well I reckon we got off on the right foot," Minogue said.

"Well nobody threw any punches. You notice they were on to the Sister Act, what's her name again. I'd say they heard that she got to Tynan."

He made a twirling motion by his head.

"Is she really, you know, like he said, a bit off her head?"

"Well like the saying goes, she was out on the missions."

"'Out on the missions'?"

"They're different when they come back. Priests, brothers, nuns – they change out there. So they don't fit, not easily anyway, when they get home. Anyway: I have another job for you. When you're ready."

"Well Christmas is around the corner, yeah? I better get me shopping started."

"Social and Family Affairs, Health Services stuff, go through it again."

"Hospital admissions? Prescriptions?"

"Yes, that and more. I'm looking for interviews over the years – assessments, counseling sessions. I'd be interested to see if there are notes of things he talked about."

"Like 'Watch out everyone, the Vikings are here'? That kind of stuff?"

"I just want some more background on him. And I want to get it now so's we don't end up staggering around like iijits in a court order situation."

"How far back are we going to go on any records?"

Minogue had already determined that he'd take only one more drag of the cigarette before discarding the cancerous half.

"All the way back to the Vikings, if that's what's needed."

Chapter 13

It was gone five o'clock when another writ of Murphy's Law was handed down. This one was delivered through Minogue's mobile: Sister Immaculata. Davy McArdle had made a brief showing at Disciples. He had been in rough order; he had been put out.

"Out where?"

"Out the door," she said. "He drunk, or he's high. He can't stop himself bothering the others when he's in that condition. It's his way of getting noticed. But he'd started a row, so out he had to go. We close up soon anyway, get them ready to go to the shelter."

"Where is he now?"

"If I had to guess, I'd say somewhere close to an off-licence. Maybe down at the DART station, trying his luck begging off the rush hour crowd. But he'll hardly be sleeping this one off on the street tonight. Sooner or later, he'll be wanting his bed."

"The hostel up the road there from the station?"

"Crosscare, yes. That or the Simon one, the cold-weather one."

He looked over the scattered notes from a conversation with the HSE official Malone had found for him. They expected a court order now. This was why Ireland had a Data Protection Commissioner…? But that'd be tomorrow's battle, one of them anyway.

"Would he have a place of his own, a squat maybe?"

"It's very unlikely. It's rare you'll find squats out this way."

"Was he fit to talk at all?"

"Not tonight," she said, lingering a little over her words. "He's out of commission, in that regard. But I told him anyway, what he had to do for you."

He wondered if she had chastised this McArdle character, like an errant child.

"Yes," she went on. "I told him in no uncertain terms that he owed it to Padraig, and to all of us, really. But you can't reason with him in that condition, of course."

"I'm not entirely clear on what you mean here, Sister."

"I told him to make himself available. Is that the expression Guards use?"

"Available to talk to us?"

"Of course! I told him that ye could have a nice chat, right here."

"And how did he take your invitation, may I ask?"

"Well if he remembers a word I said, the chance is not bad. I laid on a bit of an inducement – tomorrow's dinner. It's his favourite, so if he remembers at all, well..."

"Fair enough."

"I didn't see any sign of Seánie now – only Davey. But I'll track down Seánie the same way, sooner or later, and he'll hear the same from me. Then I'll sit them down, or somebody will, that ye can use the office here such as it is, and do your business."

"Well, we'd need to think that over a bit."

"Think what over? If the right person, with the right approach, sits down here with Davey, or Seán, well who knows the difference that'd make? In a place they know, with people around they know...? Do you see? It's all about trust, isn't it?"

He stopped sliding his pages into order: Malone was eyeing him. He smiled grimly back at him.

"I'm just keeping you in the picture," she went on. "Like you asked me to."

"Thank you. I do appreciate that now."

"Have you more questions for me then?" she asked.

The teacher tone back again, he thought. He'd close on a

light note. They'd be needing Sister Immaculata onside, for a while at least.

"I don't. At the moment anyway. But I'll be in touch."

"Good. When?"

Minogue was too taken aback to reply right away.

"As soon as time permits" was all he could think to say.

"A lot of time has gone by already now, wouldn't you say?"

Minogue sat up. How quickly his resentment could sweep back, he thought. The ghosts of those overbearing priests and nuns from his own past would never be laid. Or was he misreading her? Her long life had been one of service. She had put herself at God's bidding, and would be that way until her last breath too. Was she not a Mother Courage, a bear defending her cubs?

"I hear you, Sister – I mean, Mary."

"Nothing should come between us and the outcasts of the world, should it."

He imagined her sitting there in that small room she called an office, quietly bristling, those grey-blue eyes of hers blinking a signal of her impatience.

"I think we're on the same road here," he said. "Well, I hope we are?"

There was a quaver in her voice when she spoke now.

"I'm sure you mean that. I heard only good things in that regard. But the longer we wait now—"

"We're not delaying on purpose," he said, evenly. "We'll get to those chats you're talking about soon enough, I'm hoping. But should I be expecting new revelations from these men?"

From her reply, he doubted she had heard his question. Or she was ignoring it.

"I've told them, told Davey anyway, what needs to happen," she said. "The sooner he gets that done, the better, don't you think? I have him persuaded, I think. He'll do it, I'm sure."

"Persuaded to do what?"

"To talk to you, of course. I told him it was different now, that he didn't need to hide anything anymore."

"Hide what?"

"That's my point, Mike, that's my point. Mike, is it?"

There it was, he thought, a tell: 'Mike.' She had his card right in front of her to phone his mobile, but still she couldn't get his name right. This woman's great achievement, apparently, was to mask any confusion – agitation, even – with an outward appearance of calm and control.

"Matt," he said.

"Yes – Matt, of course. What was I thinking there? Sorry."

"I get called plenty of other names, so don't worry."

Her fluster was genuine. Dismayed, he saw himself at the kitchen table tonight, telling Kathleen that he had a bossy, and maybe actually senile nun on his plate.

"That was the problem in the first place you know," she said. Her tone had regained vigour. Minogue did not know what she meant. He said nothing. The break he hoped for came.

"None of the men want to talk to the Guards. They don't like Guards. They don't trust them."

"I understand that, but—"

"Davey and his like say plenty here, I can tell you."

"Such as?"

She didn't answer right away.

"That the Guards are out to get them. That the Guards push them around. And worse."

He wondered how far she'd go with this.

"That's why there was nothing good, nothing useful, out of Davey or Seánie or the others. You see? So that's why I'm working on this now, I just can't be sitting back and waiting…"

"All right," he said. "So. Their statements. Are you telling me they're no use? That they're made up? Coerced, or something?"

"Ach, I'm not explaining myself very well…"

"If you think there's Garda misconduct, then the law is the remedy."

"Listen: the likes of Davey or Padraig – or any of them – they're *frightened*."

"Frightened."

"That's right. Everything's gone against them at some point, everything. Families, friends – even their own bodies let them down. Their genes, you could say? Frightening thought, isn't it. The law is just one more thing to go against them, to let them down."

Minogue said nothing. He slid back his jacket sleeve. Nearly half-past five.

"But they talk to you, I'll bet. Do they?"

"Well they do," she said. "Some things. Not that it makes a lot of sense half the time – or that it's true. But talk, they will. You know, people thought I was mad to want to work here. They still think it! A woman, a nun if you please, and all those men! But what do people need when they're down, I'd say. They need a mother, that's what they need. Someone who won't judge them, or dismiss them."

How about someone who might cover up for them, he thought.

"So you don't run a confessional there, is what you're telling me."

"I think I know what you're driving at," she said. "So go ahead, ask me."

"Ask you what?"

"Ask me if I think any of my lads here killed Padraig."

"Fair enough then. A great question. Do you think so?"

There was an edge to her voice now.

"No I do not. Of course I don't."

"Next question then. Do you think some of them might know who killed him?"

"How can I answer that? I want to say no, of course I do. You see?"

She had thought it all through, he realized, and she had prepared.

She seemed to be waiting for more questions. Too bad.

"Well. Now we know your opinions on that matter," he said.

"It's good to clear the air, yes. I'm sorry now if I...?"

"It's okay, you're grand. We're all grown-ups here."

"Mary, call me Mary."

He couldn't be sure, but he believed she was smiling when she spoke now.

After he closed his phone, and eyed what he had scribbled on the sheet. The time she had phoned, of course; 'assault?'; 'one from Disciples?' But most of his doodling was around McArdle's surname.

"That was fun," said Malone. "Was it?"

"Oh, a hoot, entirely."

"She's a case," Malone said. "The sound of that?"

Minogue said nothing. The picture of her there in that cubbyhole of an 'office' was still with him. Fretting a bit now, but guarded too.

"Ran you over, did she?"

"I gave as good as I got," Minogue said. "Didn't I?"

"Didn't sound like that to me. Those old penguins are no pushover, I believe."

"Penguins. What penguins?"

"Nuns. Mickey dodgers. Whatever. Too bad for you, you have a soft spot for them. Makes it easier for them to roll over you. I'm only saying, right?"

Minogue decided it was another good time to opt for the non-response.

"Well," Malone said then. "Was it to do with one of the hobos there?"

"It was. But I'm wondering what else might be on her mind."

"Something's bothering her, you said before."

Minogue nodded.

"You don't remember OJ Simpson, do you."

"You mean Homer...?"

"No. 'The man who walked.' His lawyer, that's who I'm thinking about. Passed on to his reward since, I believe. Johnny Cochrane."

Malone's jaw began to twist in another yawn, and he let it take him over.

He came out of his yawn slowly, and he looked at his watch.

"I'll give it a go," Minogue said, to himself more than to Malone. "It's on my way home, sort of."

Malone shrugged, and rubbed at his forehead.

"You'll find your way here tomorrow?" Minogue asked. "The Deep South?"

Malone shrugged.

"Oh, before you go: any showing on this JJ Mac character yet?"

Malone shook his head.

"I crossed me fingers and rang his Ma again. What a conversation that was – all over the map. Dotty like you wouldn't believe. La-la-la. But I got a start from her, a 'Stephen.' He turned out to be some employment counsellor – the same one they gave me earlier, a reference off his original job application to get a job there with the paper in the first place. Yeah, 'Stephen's a great friend of Joseph's.' God knows what he tells her. She's senile, maybe? She sure sounded that way this time."

"Stephen, what can he tell us?"

"Nothing about the past two years, that's what – since the time he took that job at the paper. But according to him, he reckons this McCarthy dude really wanted to straighten himself out back then. Took a few courses there, and then he landed himself that job there at South Side. Oh, and by the way, he did get the sack there."

"They got over their fixation on confidentiality then."

"A bit. I had a chat there with one of them, got his name off some of the articles. A reporter? So I phoned him, and he was okay with talking. Told me that McCarthy started pissing them off there a while back. That he has notions."

"Notions how?"

"We know he's only a driver, but he has ideas about himself, right? He was hired on as a deliveryman basically, but he started going sideways. Nagging at them to let him try a bit of other stuff. Like why not, he's driving around anyway. The guy told me that McCarthy got this ' journalist' thing going on in his head. He'd heard that he was telling other people that he was one too. 'He has issues.'"

"Who doesn't have issues."

"Well, yeah. But McCarthy didn't like getting the brush-off, says the guy. Started out polite enough, but it got to a point where he was getting to be a serious pain in the hole. Bit of a yelling session there one day, and that's when he got the heave-ho. The guy says that the feeling there is he wanted to get the sack, so he could go back on Social Welfare, or 'other pursuits.'"

"'Other pursuits' meaning?"

"Well the guy didn't say. Just gave me the eye. Dealing, drugs, is what he meant."

More raindrops quivered on the frames. He heard Malone rubbing his eyes.

"So. Phone your outfit, get them to talk to the Dutch?"

"Sleep on it for now," Minogue said. "See what turns up on him tomorrow."

Chapter 14

Minogue brought the laptop out to the kitchen. He took a slow swallow of beer, and keyed in Facebook. It was sluggish. There were 437 contributions on The Green Man now. He date-ordered them to the most recent, and slowly scrolled through the latest. *it's_not_a_crime_to_be_poor* had plenty to say. It had a mathematical theme, and it was passionate and lowercase all the way, but strangely free of spelling mistakes:

- **ireland's war on the poor = "collateral damage"**
- **neglect + prejudice + greed = murder**

Truth_@_midnight didn't hold back: **Irish society had crucified Padraig Larkin.**

Jackeen_redser: **homelessness is the REAL crime. Thousands of empty houses in ghost estates all over the country – but this man had no roof over his head.**

Dublin_Jen felt she had known Larkin. He was harmless. She never felt scared of him. Now that a valuable member of the community had been taken away from her, she realized that her relationship had been more important than she knew. Not long after relationship came the word that Minogue's cynical side had immediately predicted: She felt...*traumatized*.

Kerryblue_fan was **"totally outraged hearing people saying that Larkin was only 'an old head case.' Was there no justice? Was this the kind of a country we wanted? Billions for banks, neglect for outcasts?"**

He stopped reading and looked around the kitchen. The

pizza had cooled a little. Austrian beer, he thought, and Italian cuisine: Up The Republic! Everybody seemed to like Italy these days, or Tuscany, at any rate. Kathleen wanted to visit Rome, he didn't. For him, Rome was the television Rome. The Vatican, with statues looking down everywhere. Cardinals in red robes, droves of priests and nuns, pilgrims of all colour. Had Immaculata ever been there? He let himself imagine her striding up basilica steps, shouldering aside those ridiculous Swiss Guards, and barging in on a conclave of cardinals. The august faces would turn to her, the white hair peeping out from under their caps, and she would lay down the law. What would it take, she'd demand, to dump this folderoldol here and roll up their sleeves in a village in Africa?

Hardly. But what were those vows that nuns took, when they 'took the veil'? Chastity, poverty, obedience – and defer to the men of the church, of course. How many of them had been bad ones though, those ones in the laundries, or the orphanages? Had they been as cruel as the men of the cloth? Should cruelties be compared?

He let the rim of the beer can rest on his lip. Hadn't there been a good Ireland, before this Tiger/Doom situation? A good-enough Ireland at least? The country he'd grown up in hadn't been hell. Yes, he'd been beat around the ears by teachers, but so had the rest of the class. Had any of the bitter know-it-alls, the ones who lived for grudgery, and to tear down anything they could find, had they never met one decent person in a religious life? A Christian Brother who'd spent a life teaching? A parish priest who brought solace and comfort? A nun who had built clinics in Africa?

He heard Kathleen fold the paper again. A signal of impatience?

He let his eyes drift back to the screen. A username *Mise_eire_my_eye*? Ah, got it: Mise Éire, My Eye. As in: not taken in by Our Gallant Little Country. Padraig Larkin was an icon of today's Darwinian Ireland. He was our Pièta.

Our Pietà?

Kathleen came in rubbing her forehead. She headed for the kettle.

"Facebook," she muttered. "Since when are you interested in that?"

"What of it."

"Oh, it's for... That's creepy. For a man who's dead?"

"Par for the course," he said. "We have to keep up. 'Every avenue' et cetera."

She leaned in to read the screen, and began reading aloud.

"'Anti-religion, materialistic society... Destined to implode now that the emperors had been shown to have no clothes.' Very good. 'Implode.' Very well put."

She made a little gasp and straightened up. She had moved on to the next posting.

"'Jesus Christ was a homeless outsider,'" she said. "Technically true, I suppose."

This homeless Jesus bit didn't sit right with him. His Jesus was a figure of majesty, haloed, light-rays, heart aglow, looking down from glass and wall on the child Minogue. It wasn't a marginalized Jesus who had struck terror into that Minogue.

He scrolled down but soon let go the mouse.

"So you're heading over to Pierce for your card game now, are you?" she said.

"I am."

"Home the usual time?"

"That's the plan anyway."

She made a strange smile, one that he would remember later on...

"Say hello to Jim Kilmartin for me at least, will you."

* * *

For Minogue as much as the others at the card session here in Pierce Condon's, these few hours had never been much about cards. It was more a chance to gab and to take his time over a couple of tins of beer, and to listen in on the arguments. There was no shortage of grandstanding, or mockery. No session that Minogue could remember had gone by without someone barking, "Cut the cards, you leaping hoor!" Or "You reneged, you gobadán!" More often, "I might have known it'd be you'd have the knave, you useless fecker."

The card games were always TwentyFive, the one game that Condon remembered. The games took place in the room that Condon called his playroom, the one fitted out for his wheelchair. Minogue had his usual perch next to Condon's boyhood friend Dessie Smith. As a senior civil servant in Finance, Smith had come to be the target of much sly baiting. It didn't seem to bother him. Kevin, eldest of the Condon children, with his mother's light colouring and her turn on the nose, attended too but did not play. In between getting glasses, peanuts, cups of tea, biscuits – and then putting everything away before getting his Da to bed – he sat in the corner with a laptop.

Condon's bent fingers clutched and released his cards with mechanical assurance, his head dipping slightly each time. He took the trick that Smith set up. Minogue tried to ignore the contortions that seized his face, and the snuffling sounds he made. He slid his tin of Gosser next to his small stack of change, and he felt for his cigarettes.

The porch light shone back dully from the pitted cement of the driveway. It was nearly cold enough for frost. Intonations – voices, but no words – came to him from the windows. He looked back at the Condon's home, a semi built in the early Fifties on what was then a sleepy lane off the old Bray Road at Cornelscourt. Besieged by select homes now, it rusticated behind mad hedges and Pierce's old botanical experiments run to seed.

He drew up the handle on the driveway gate and let the tip of the bolt rest on the cement. His Peugeot was still there behind Kilmartin's heap-of-shite Golf. The hall door reopening made him turn. Kilmartin's face revealed itself in the light. He was still in conversation with somebody.

"Why bother having a government at all," he heard Kilmartin say. "*That's* my point! Give it all to Brussels, or the fecking bankers in I-don't-know-where...!"

He was humming – always a bad sign – when he pulled the hall door after him. He placed a cigar between his teeth and commenced his saunter down the drive.

"No shop talk here tonight now, you," Minogue said, as he drew near.

"Did I even open my mouth?"

"I can read your mind."

Annoyance flickered in Kilmartin's eyes but he made a close-mouthed smile.

"What was I going to say to you then?"

"Well it's not about the Nigerian woman who had four kids in four years so she could stay in Ireland. That one you already pitched inside."

Kilmartin took his time lighting the cigarillo.

"My mistake then, isn't it," he murmured through a cloud of smoke. "For suggesting that the big noises in the civil service get out in the streets and see what's really going on in the country. What was I thinking?"

The smoke hung in the air about him. He began batting it away.

"So much for your guess then," he said, brightly.

"You were going to take some other poke at Tommy Malone."

"Me-o-my, but you could be right. Silly me, wanting to keep you in the picture."

"There's no picture, Jamesy Boy. It's fantasy."

"You wish it were. But I hear things. On the QT, yes, but mock it at your peril."

"Someone's using Tommy Malone to make an iijit out of you."

"Well look who's into fantasy now. Who'd want to do something like that?"

"Who do you think? Anyone who wants to take digs at him, to ruin his career."

Kilmartin smiled wanly.

"He's doing the work of that fine by himself, with his carry-on. Don't you think?"

"And anyone who wants to make a gobshite of you too," Minogue added. "People with sore ankles. People you rubbed the wrong way in the past. The Good Old Days?"

"Oh here we go: the grassy knoll stuff again. Where ignorance is bliss, it's folly to be wise. I have my sources, that's all I can say.

But you can take them to the bank."

"The bank? The banks are bust. Did nobody tell you that, on the QT?"

Kilmartin dismissed the sarcasm with a toss of his head.

"Whatever you say, Matt. You're always right. I forgot."

They smoked in silence for several moments.

"And Kathleen says hello. By the way. Before I give you a kick."

"Ah you're priceless. You may tell that lovely woman that she has my admiration, my deepest admiration. Where is she tonight, by the way?"

There was a large helping of guile in Kilmartin's grin.

"None of your business is my first answer. Why're you asking me, is my second."

"Just making polite conversation. Am I in the wrong country for that, is it? Are we gone fecking bankrupt in that too?"

Yet again in their long friendship, Minogue had to relent. Kilmartin had his own woes after all. The talk fell to holidays, not pay cuts; new diesel engines. Minogue soon began to wonder if there was not a new equanimity to Kilmartin.

They returned to the game together, just in time for Kevin to bring in tea. It was a signal to his father that tonight's session would soon be ending. It was a signal to the others as well of course. They should be ready for Pierce's agitation, an outburst maybe.

Minogue watched the cards fly out from Smith's hand. He noted Condon's frown as he picked up his cards. The man never asked for help, and often, his mood ran dark and he shook with anger. It had been like this since he had come out of the coma. There was talk of moving him in with Kevin and his family. But whatever else Condon had lost that night, his stubbornness had only been amplified. He was holding fast to the house they'd left that evening, four or so minutes before his wife was dead in the seat beside him.

Smith had picked up on his friend's growing agitation, and he was warming up a diversion. He had latched on to Kilmartin's remarks about rappers and their moves.

"Rappers," he said. "I remember when people could actually dance."

"That's me," said Kilmartin. "Twinkle-toes they called me, I was that good."

"Not as good as Pierce and me. We were hounds entirely for the dances."

"You were on your hole," Kilmartin said, warmly.

"Says you. Many's the rug I cut, and many's the heart I broke on the dance floor."

Kilmartin's cackle was full of dark mirth.

"Many's the leg you broke, you mean. Where did all this take place, anyway?"

"Over at Dundrum, in actual fact. World famous. Full to the rafters every night."

"Dundrum? My God man, a legend. The dance floor knee-deep in cowshite."

Smith winked at Minogue.

"Sorry Des," Minogue said. "I've no dog in the race, I'm more a Lisdoon man."

"You needn't be one bit sorry," said Kilmartin. "Lisdoonvarna's no great shakes, but you saved yourself a world of trouble by avoiding Dundrum. Sure if the dogs knew about Dundrum they'd go there to piss. No offence – there are parts of Tipp I like, really."

Smith rolled his eyes, and finished the deal. Solemnly, he turned over the top card.

"God, that's a dirty-looking card," Kilmartin murmured.

"Plenty more of them," said Smith.

Cards were laid with deliberation at first. Minogue felt that Smith was the one to watch. And so it was. Smith slid his five out last, just before Kilmartin's precious king.

"By Jesus," Kilmartin said. "More blackguarding."

It was Minogue's deal now. Kevin was on the move now, discreetly clearing up.

"You like Macs, Kevin," said Kilmartin, stifling his belch with sardonic courtesy.

"I was thinking of getting one. No crashes, I hear? And a bit of style too, of course."

"Goes with that Jesus beard of yours," said Smith. "Sandals and yoga next."

"Plenty of them Macs out your way I'd say, Matt," said Kilmartin. "Aren't there? That's where you'll find all carry-on with yoga and spas, and lattes, and what have you."

"Out in Kilmacud?" asked Smith. Kilmartin shook his head.

"No, no," he said. "Work. Matt's new gig. He moves around a bit."

Minogue threw a glare at him. He got only a studied impudence back.

"New job," Smith said. "News to me, Matt. Congratulations, I suppose."

"A temporary thing," Minogue said. "It's in the nature of a pilot project."

A card escaped Condon's clenched fingers, hopped on its short edge and disappeared. Kilmartin leaned down to retrieve it, grunting.

"You saw my hand!"

"Da," Kevin said. Kilmartin righted himself with a bashful half-smile.

Face twisted in anger, a bead of sweat had stalled by Condon's hairline.

"And the one I dropped," he went on. "You took a gawk at that one too!"

"Jaysus, Pierce," said Smith. "How could Jim see your hand?"

"How? When he picked up the one I dropped, is how! You think I'm stupid?"

"It was only a four of clubs," Smith said. "That's why he didn't keep it on you."

Even Minogue laughed. Condon looked around uncertainly and then began laughing too. It was the same high-pitched, unnatural one that he'd developed.

The central heating pipes took advantage of the quiet then to make their digestive noises. Smith led a trump. Answering cards slid out on the table one by one. The sighs continued.

Minogue noticed that the stricken, distracted look had returned to Condon's face, soon to set into the abstracted melancholy look that Minogue knew too well.

It was a mercy when the hand finally ended. Condon had sagged further in the chair, and was listing more to one side. His sporadic attempts to listen to the conversation made him toss and jerk his head upright, only to have it slump soon afterwards.

"Pierce," Minogue said, gathering himself. "The bed is calling to me. And my pockets are picked empty after this chicanery here tonight."

Condon smiled and blinked slowly, but said nothing.

"Ask for a bail-out then," Kilmartin said. "Pretend you're a bank. Pierce there can help out, I imagine?"

Smith exchanged a look with Minogue before turning a wry eye on Kilmartin.

"Jimmy," he said. "For a man so steeped in knowledge there, you must know that Matt is in the wrong postal code for getting any bail-outs."

"Not to worry. Just write an address in Foxrock or someplace. Actually where you are now will do it, those new digs of yours in Dalkey—"

"He's not Dalkey!"

The shout reverberated overhead. Condon turned to Minogue.

"Why's he saying 'Dalkey'? You're Kilmacud, Matt, Kilmacud! Tell him!"

"Don't mind Jimmy," Minogue said to Condon. "He's lost the run of himself."

The troubled look deepened. Condon seemed to be searching for something to say. Kilmartin's voice had softened now.

"He's working in Dalkey, Pierce. That's what I meant to say."

"No he's not," Condon retorted. "Neither are you. Stop trying to cod me here."

"Ah we're not, Pierce," Minogue began.

"You're in St. John's Road," Condon said, louder. "That's Murder Squad HQ. Everybody knows that, for God's sakes. Why are you saying Dalkey?"

Kilmartin let himself back in his chair.

"Would that we were over in St. John's Road, Pierce," he said. "But sure we moved on out of that. The rug was pulled from under the Squad, a while back now."

Condon seemed to weigh the information. His expression reminded Minogue of his children's faces when they had awoken from a bad dream, awake but not really.

"So now it's Dalkey for you?"

"Only me, Pierce."

Smith rose from his chair with a soft, sighing groan.

"Oh now I get it!"

Condon's laugh had sounded like a seal's bark.

"Yes, Matt – they gave you the cushy number! Dalkey, yes – Dalkey's the cushy number. 'Nothing goes on in Dalkey.' Right? I nearly forgot about that, yes!"

"Well compared to other places maybe," Minogue hedged. "Clondalkin say?"

Condon's smile held. Clondalkin's rep as El Paso was embedded in his mind yet.

"Ah go on with you. Nobody messes with... Oh what's his name. Thing..."

A pained look took over Condon's features then, and he began to groan.

"Oh, he was the real McCoy... Used to swim at the Forty Foot there all the year long. Brylcreemed his hair back. Kept shoe polish in the drawer of his desk for any Guard on duty who didn't... Ach, what's his name?"

"It'll come to you later on, Da," said Kevin. "Leave it, now."

"Like Lugs. Amn't I right? Just like Lugs Brannigan, yes. The same style..."

The awkwardness in the room seemed to swell.

"The legendary Lugs," Kilmartin said. "But Lugs is gone to his reward this long while."

"Stop it, you! Just stop it!"

The shout made Minogue jump again. Even Kevin looked shaken.

"You're always doing that to me! *Thwarting me*...! It's no

laughing matter! Lugs Brannigan, he's the one that puts manners on gougers! 100 percent! No messing there!"

"He did that," Minogue said. "You're right, Pierce, he was the man to do it."

"And the Heavy Squad! No messing with the Heavy Squad!"

"Them too," said Minogue. "You're right about that, Pierce."

"Well tell Jim that! He thinks he's being funny. Thinks I don't know. Tell him!"

Minogue looked over. Kilmartin was trying to hold on to a calm expression.

"Jesus Christ, Matt," Condon said, quieter but straining again. "You know who I mean, don't you? Tell him Pierce says how-do – and that I don't forget them days, when I was starting out, and he put us on the right track. Tell him that. Will you?"

A sliver of moon glowed between the branches. Sure enough, Kilmartin was loitering by his car. His breath came in long volleys through the night air.

"Lovely family," he said to Minogue. "And that Kevin? Lovely fella."

"They're great."

"Our own wee troubles pale by comparison, don't they."

Minogue pressed the keypad again, another wirp to remind Kilmartin.

"Which is not to say we should go looking for more troubles, of course," Kilmartin added. "Or walking like a gom into them, by ignoring sound advice."

Smith had a new Nissan. He waved as he passed. Minogue opened his door.

"We'll be talking, no doubt," he said to Kilmartin.

★ ★ ★

The Almera that pulled away from the curb next to Minogue's house could be anybody's. Still, it was his own hall door closing that he caught a glimpse of as he drew in. He lifted the bolt for the gate, eyeing the glittering surface of the footpath and the driveway up to the house. The rattle and clank of the swinging gate seemed louder than usual. He paused after he had drawn them open and looked up and down the road.

The new people across the road were making the most of their flat screen tonight. The street lamp next to Costigans' still sizzled and popped like rashers on the pan. He looked up through the bare branches and over the rooftops to the milky glow of the moon. The north star was dim but where it should be. He wondered how much Pierce Condon slept, and what he thought about in the long hours when he couldn't.

A shadow moving caught his eye: Jacko, the Costigans' ancient, wandering cat had come for a half hour's engine warmth before moving off to his other night stations.

"Be off with you," he murmured in answer to the cat's begging mewl. "Or I'll have to get the holy water on you. You restless fiend from hell, you."

There was a smell of candles. Kathleen's greeting came from the dining room.

"It's me all right," he said. "George Clooney says he's busy, sorry."

"I can smell the cigars from here."

"They're not cigars. They're aphrodisiacs."

Whatever she was doing, she was in some hurry. He sniffed at his coat and took a hanger from under the stairs.

"Dessie Smith's wife makes him hang his coat in the shed for a few days after a game of cards," he said. "Thank God you're more understanding."

He played the message on the machine. It was a Skype from Daithi, with that weird, underwatery sounding echo. He'd gotten the project manager job, but the company was still downsizing. There was talk about a move farther out in the Bay Area.

Kathleen took her time coming into the hall. He looked at her.

"Looks like we'll be getting to know San Fran a bit more."

There was that glow about her, a contentment that showed most around her eyes. Maybe it was her nurturer self, a bit of pity for Daithi's poor father, a man with no son nearby in his own country.

"Let's face it," she said. "There's nothing in Daithi's line here. It's bad all over."

She was right. For him, it was the wrong kind of right, but he'd keep it to himself.

"You had a bit of a session here," he said. "A get-together."

"You must be a detective."

"Candles. Men use cigars."

"Ah, candles. Yes, we had a get-together. Maura Kilmartin was here too."

Her face flushed, she looked around the room, and then strode to the table.

"We have to do something," she said. "We can't just let things fall apart."

"What's falling apart?"

"It's not one thing. It's a lot of things."

"Is this about your pal Brídín losing her job?"

Instead of lifting the tray, she stared at it for several moments.

"Well it was a success," she said then. "That's the main thing."

"I'm glad it was."

"You're dying to know, aren't you? Go ahead and ask. It's okay."

He didn't.

"Maura and me, we realized there's a crying need, you see? You know that Maura helped organize those buses over to Knock last month?"

He could manage only a nonchalant look.

"You didn't?" she went on. "Well that's interesting. Jim will blather about anything – but not something like that. He's probably embarrassed."

"Jim, embarrassed?"

"If we don't do it, who will?"

"There you have me. I don't know."

"You really haven't a clue," she said, and smiled. "Have you?"

"Knock, pilgrimages, visions of Mary in the sky – Not much, I'd have to say."

"There were thousands," Kathleen said. "And that tells you something. Even that head-case, the one who swore there's be a sign from Our Lady at three o'clock, even he couldn't spoil it. That was what decided us then and there. We'd do what was needed."

"So it wasn't Avon calling here then, or Tupperware."

She gave him a pitying smile.

"You can't help it, can you? It makes you – uneasy, is that the word? Well guess what, love. Don't take this the wrong way, but that's how I know I'm on the right track."

"When the likes of me is uneasy, that's the sign?"

"The important thing is to get things started, and that we did. It's exciting."

"'Started'?"

Her eyes took on a sudden intensity.

"The church isn't a building. It's not a cathedral. It's not even those old ruins that you seem to have a peculiar fondness for. It's people. It's the people and it's God."

What about the god in the woods in Glencree then, he thought, or the god of the sea that kept the boat trip to the Skelligs good and dangerous, as it needed to be?

"How many were here?" he asked. "I'm guessing twelve."

"Oh you're funny, all right. There were seven of us."

"Nary a man?"

She folded her arms.

"Why is that important? Would you actually want to be here for it?"

He had no answer. Actually he did, but he'd be keeping it to himself too.

Chapter 15

The sound dredging Minogue from sleep was not an alarm clock. He eyed the clock anyway: 7:03. Dark still? November. He raised his head from the pillow, heard Kathleen's breathing change.

The sound wasn't repeated. His mobile, he realized, on the hall table.

He slowly lowered his head to the pillow again and he recalculated the time on the west coast. Daithi would be just heading to bed around now.

"I know what that was. A text, is what it was."

Her clear, long-awake voice startled him. It changed to a mumble as she rose.

"Bedtime in Seattle. Let's see what gives with that son of ours. Let go, I'll bet."

He listened to her make her way down the stairs, pass over the creaking one that still resisted all his fixes, and into the hall proper. The thermostat buttons made faint beeps as she pushed them. His mobile slid along the table a little before she picked it up.

"Not our beloved," she said, and paused to yawn. "It's work. You want it now?"

He didn't. Nor did he want to launch himself into a dark Irish morning either. He turned on his side again, and listened to the first ticks and hisses from the central heating.

His sojourn didn't last long.

Kathleen had left his mobile on the kitchen table. Road Watch went on about the M50. The ad for television licences came on again. The kettle was beginning to purr.

The text had perfect punctuation and spelling: Kilmartin's prideful trademark.

Phone me, mobile only. Very Important. Re: M.

No it wasn't. It'd wait. Indefinitely – as in never. Enough was enough: and if Kilmartin was going to try talking about this again, he'd let him have it.

He finished his breakfast slowly. For company he had a printout that Kathleen had made of the business about the murdered Irish missionary priest. It had less of the preachy crap that he had expected. He found himself ceding a little of his well-honed take on what any Irish priest could teach to Africans. It make him no more content than it had ever done to realize out that his views on such matters were full of holes, logical and otherwise. Was there no end to this catching your own self out?

Along with the dishes, he took with him from the table the idea that he should phone Malone now before he forgot. He dialed from the sitting room.

"Listen," he said to a dawny-sounding Malone. "I'm dropping by that Disciples place first, see if any of those characters show up there. The McArdle one got turned away from the place last night, but Sister Immaculata says she put a fatwa on him to show today. It might work, especially if it's backed up with a dinner he likes."

There was no reaction from Malone's end.

"So if I'm a bit on the late side, that's a good sign."

"Okay. I'll try and manage."

"You're fabulous, so you are. And I was thinking over other matters too. Let me know later on what you make of them. Are you with me so far?"

"Fire away."

"I want to skip ahead a bit in the review part. Get a hold of that log from the patrol team that responded first that day. And go through their notes again."

"I can do that."

"Next item. Did you hear anything yesterday about any gay angle in this?"

Malone hesitated before answering.

"Zero, on a gay situation."

"That's what I thought. So go to that Facebook thing, and look for an entry for someone called *Fíor-i-gcónaí*. He, or she, to be saying something about gay. Guessing? Knows something? Rumours? No idea. But see what you think."

"What does that mean? I don't have the Irish."

"'The truth, always.' You barbarian."

"Can you spell it for me then too?"

Minogue had to repeat the spelling for *Fíor-i-gcónaí* three times. He looked down at the notes he'd scribbled last night while he did.

"Next," he said. "Where Larkin was found there in the park. Find out if it was known for any encounters."

"Encounters. You mean any gay scene. Cruising."

"Correct. And any other such places in the area."

Dressing later, Minogue considered jeans and an old shirt. He found clothes that he had neglected over the years instead.

"Why are you wearing that stuff?" Kathleen asked. "Going gardening, are you?"

"I have my reasons."

"You should throw them out then, along with the clothes."

"I probably will, after today."

"I get it – you're going back to that place again today."

"I'll start there. On my way to Dalkey, my glamorous new office suite there."

The sky was layered with clouds, but a few tracts glowed at the edges. He wasn't going to get his weather-hopes up in that regard. He got off easy dropping Kathleen at the Luas. Murphy's Law reached out for him there again however, in the form of a newish Bimmer surging out of a side road and donating a fine spray from the roadway to Minogue's windscreen. He let the last of his curse words expire unspoken.

The news came on. Layoffs. Bank shares trading at a new low. What would the crew out at Disciples make of that? Another statement from the Archbishop of Dublin saying that the release of the next week's report would prove that nothing was held back. Minogue's mind began to buzz with slurs, and he slapped the radio off.

He took the left after Blackrock, and then a quick right toward Seapoint. Waiting there for him was a half-decent look at Dublin Bay at low tide. The water was the colour of milky tea, and flat. Far out, a beam of holy-picture light shot down from a break in the clouds and turned a patch of sea silver. He found himself trying to piece together an old poem about ships that had resounded in his classroom so long ago.

Half-bare trees and the apartment block behind them blocked his view of the water. Soon the road turned sharply back toward the sea, and beyond a short terrace, bits of Dun Laoghaire Harbour began to open out. He was soon driving side-by-side with the railway line, waiting for the stone wall next the tracks to end. He knew it'd be a letdown when it did: in that view across a short span of water, the city would have already slid out of sight behind the Pier.

That same West Pier was no match for its partner, the East Pier that set out into the bay a mile or so south. Worse, it had always had a lonesome and even stricken look to it. Maybe it was because rats were to be seen there too easily amongst unkempt patches of grass. As for the boulders heaped up along its outer side, the side that faced the city, he half-admired the shag-off-with-yourself face it presented to the nation's capital.

He searched along the first section for people walkers. Not a sinner. The foreground itself offered only the usual underused-looking fishing boats tied up at the Coal Quay. Below and to his left, he caught a glimpse of the boatyards, but they too vanished as the coast road completed its climb to the railway bridge. A shaky-looking man near the crest there reminded him that the shelter was only a couple of hundred yards off, up whatever York Road was called after it crossed George's Street and petered out here at the Harbour. The ragged beard made the man's face seem more swollen. In his forties? It could be sixties. He didn't recall seeing him at Disciples. Come to think of it, he didn't recall faces from Disciples, nor from the snapshots of Larkin's cronies either. What might that say? Nothing very decent.

He was at Disciples sooner than he wanted. The daylight revealed dings and scuffs and stains on the door that he had not noticed on his first visit. A few cigarette butts lay scattered on the cement footpath, their filters squashed and split into facsimiles of bog cotton. He was imagining smells already. After a few trial runs at breathing through his mouth, he tugged his sleeve over his palm and grasped the door handle.

There were men playing draughts at one table. One, with a wind-burned face and darting, wild eyes the colour of some remote National Geographic lake, watched his every step. His partner, heavy-set, stroked a long, wavy and badly tended beard, one more salt than pepper, while he concentrated on the game.

Minogue made his way toward the sound of the dishes and the radio. Beyond the doorway there, a woman in an apron, square-set and not long into middle age. She turned a shiny face to him, and in an instant her cautious study of him began. He could only offer a smile with the question. Was Sister Immaculata about? The woman narrowed her eyes. Minogue said that Sister was expecting him. A reply came slowly: she'd be along any minute. Then her question: who was he? Mention of Garda changed her expression.

"A Guard?"

Minogue kept up his smile.

"I am. Matt's my name."

"Are you meant to be here if you're a Guard?"

"I hope so. Are Guards not allowed in here?"

"Sister, you have to ask Sister. She's the one."

"I don't mind waiting for her outside."

She frowned deeply, and her jaw went slowly from side to side.

"I didn't catch your name," he said.

"Emer. That's me, Emer."

"Hello, Emer. It looks like you are a busy person here this morning."

"I don't know," she said, her voice dropping. "I don't know about this at all, no."

He re-ran the smile, put a bit more friendliness into it.

"Is Davey here, Emer? Davey McArdle?"

She adjusted the apron and folded her arms.

"You can't be in here. Sister wouldn't like it."

He noticed now that a line ran along just inside one of her eyebrows. Another scar, fainter but longer, and with the same light gleam, ran next to her ear.

"I was here yesterday too," he said. "And I'm only visiting."

She shook her head. Her stubborn earnestness reminded him of a child.

"No," she said, apparently more certain of herself now. "You can't."

The blue-eyed one got to his feet, and headed their way.

"Who said my name? Did you say my name?"

The look of a jockey indeed, Minogue thought, shrunken somehow, and bandy-legged. His widow's peak was being resisted by longer, ragged strands of hair to the side, most of them tucked behind his ears. A cold sore edged out of one corner of his mouth. No more the full round of the clock than his current interlocutor?

"I did. You're Davey McArdle?"

"Are you a social worker? A new one?"

Minogue shook his head. Close up, McArdle's face looked scoured by the elements more than seasoned. His eyelashes were so fair they were hard to spot at all.

"I'm not. I'm here to see Sister Immaculata."

"Well I never saw you before."

"Likewise."

"What?"

"I never saw you either."

His partner made his move at the draughts game, and then turned to look. His hand changed from raking his beard to tracing a fresh Elastoplast over his eyebrow.

"Your turn," he said. "What are you doing over there? Hurry up!"

McArdle blinked, but he kept his eye on Minogue.

"How do you know my name?"

"Sister Immaculata told me."

"Can't wait all day, you stupid bastard. Come on!"

McArdle spun around. "Shut up," he hissed. "You're a bastard, not me."

The woman stepped back. She seemed to want to say something.

"AIDS man," said the heavy-set one, his voice rising. "Queer!"

Minogue found himself stepping forward.

"Lads, lads! Come on: enough. Are you Seánie Walshe?"

"It was you wanted to play, you dirty queer. So play! Play the game!"

"No need for that kind of talk," said Minogue. "We're just having a chat."

The heavy-set one shifted his glare to Minogue. He let it slide back on McArdle.

"Social worker day is tomorrow," he said. "You don't even know what day it is. That brain of yours turned to shite from Chinaman wine. And AIDS eating away at it."

McArdle turned to look at Minogue. A definite lack of symmetry there, Minogue saw, the eyes that seemed mismatched under a wide, flat forehead.

"He's mental," he said. "Doesn't take his meds and then he goes off of his head."

"AIDS is all you're good for! AIDS!"

Minogue scanned the room. Most of the men were pretending to ignore the racket. A few had remained deep in thought, one rocking slowly and delicately. A man in his early twenties hovered half-risen from a chair, his face set in a dazed look.

"Tone it down," he said. "Back to your game. I didn't mean to get in the way."

"He only cheats," the heavy-set one growled. "He cheats and he lies, and he robs. And he wants us all to get AIDS, just like he has."

McArdle turned to catch Minogue's eye again. Was that a smile beginning, some ritual they went through routinely here, these two?

"I don't have AIDS," he said. "He's always saying that. But I don't. I don't."

"Go on back to your game," Minogue said. "Really. Please."

"Cheater, AIDS pusher. Queer."

"Shut up, Seánie," a man called out half-heartedly from near the television.

"You shut up yourself. I see things, I know what's going on. You don't."

Walshe stood, bringing draughts skittering and rolling on the floor.

"Whoa," Minogue called out. "Easy does it there now – enough is enough."

Some of the men were rising from chairs and heading for the back of the room.

"Who are you?"

"I'm just visiting. I'm here to see Sister Immaculata."

"You're a Guard," said Walshe. "You think I'm stupid or something?"

"You're *mental*," said McArdle. "Stupid *and* mental."

The sound that came from Walshe then was a growl and a shout in one.

"Go back now, Seánie," Minogue said. "Let's get that game going again."

McArdle edged closer to him.

"They should lock you up again," he went on. "Because you're mental."

"Just shut up a minute here, will you?"

"Look at him, going mental. Look, *mental*..."

Walshe clenched and released his fists, and began a slow trudge toward them.

"Sister's little pet," he growled. "Got everybody codded, haven't you?"

"Stay back now," Minogue tried. "Seánie, isn't it? Stay back. Just calm down, and everything will be grand. We'll sort it out. Right, Seánie?"

Walshe continued his slow procession, his stare fixed on McArdle, patches of sheen on his coat glistening dully and then fading as he passed the fluorescents overhead.

"You think she doesn't know what you are," he said, his

voice rising. "Her little angel, with his AIDS, up there in some graveyard?"

The fraying cloth in Walshe's right hand was the end of a cast, Minogue now saw, and his heart sank: that thing could hurt.

"Stop it," he warned. "Seánie? This man's your friend. You were playing draughts nicely, the both of you. I saw you."

"I'm not his *friend*," he heard McArdle say. "I just keep him quiet here, like Sister asked me to. So he doesn't take a fit and go spare all the time."

Minogue shifted his stance. He tried to smile but his muscles wouldn't oblige.

"Let's just carry on with the draughts. Tell you what, I'll play you a game—"

Walshe lunged without warning.

He was soft everywhere, but heavy, and he had a long reach – but now he was on the wrong foot. Clamping his lips tight, Minogue went for the reaching arm. He felt the solid, ungiving cast that ran to the elbow, and he pulled on it. He closed on him, got his arm up his back, and finished the hold. Now he couldn't help drawing in a breath through his nose. A moment passed before the brew crashed into his brain. The oily smell from Walshe's hair carried with it a burned-wood tang, but through it all came the sour stench of sweat long-turned to grease. Minogue gasped.

"You little queer," Walshe grunted. "I'm going to kill you, so I am."

Minogue got him turned toward the table, and he tugged the arm slightly. Over went Walshe, wheezing and drawing breaths through his teeth, his cheek pressing draughts onto the tabletop.

Nausea clutched hard at Minogue and held. He was ready to panic. He saw himself moments from now giving Walshe a hard shove and then walking – running! – the hell out of here and racing home to stand in the shower.

"We can't have this," he managed. "No fights. You hear?"

It was McArdle's mocking voice he heard next, however.

"That's right, Seánie, listen to the man. Yeah, Seánie, don't go *mental* here."

"You," said Minogue, glancing over and taking in the smirk. "Shut the hell up!"

His yell turned hoarse at the end. He heard a yelp then, something between a shriek and a cry of anger. A woman's voice.

"Davey, Davey? What's going on? Davey? Who is that?"

By then Minogue had spotted its owner, Sister Immaculata. He registered the pained expression, her hands paddling and kneading the air. Great, he almost said aloud: now he had to worry that she'd get a heart attack or something over this.

"What's this, what's happening? What are you doing to Seánie there?"

"Trying to stop a row, is what."

He turned, eyed McArdle. The blue eyes were hooded now. He seemed happy with the results here.

"With this fella here," Minogue added. "McArdle, is it?"

Hearing no reply, he looked over at her. Her expression was frozen in place. Seeing her look rattled satisfied him in a strange way. McArdle began to move away.

"Don't be going anywhere," Minogue called out. "I need to talk to you."

Walshe stirred.

"He'll give everybody AIDS," he wheezed. His words seemed to waken Immaculata. She began making her way over.

"Seánie," she said. "Don't say those things."

"I'm going to kill him," Walshe said. "Someone should have killed him already!"

"Seánie!"

"That's an arrest coming up," Minogue said, more to Immaculata than to anyone else. "He has to get a grip on himself here, or I'm going to have to take him in."

She leaned in close, drawing a soapy, citrusy scent with her.

"His meds don't always work the way they should," she whispered.

"Just get across to him what could happen if he keeps carrying on like this."

He saw something that looked like resentment in her

glance, but then she made her way around the corner of the table and leaned over Walshe.

"Seánie, listen? This man, he can take you to jail for that. Do you understand?"

"Take him to jail – Davey! Not me! He's a cheater, and he says things, and...."

"Now, Seánie."

Her voice wasn't loud; it wasn't even stern. It cut through the rising talk from men at the back of the room. More nun-power in action for damn sure, Minogue decided. It was reaching back into some quiet, unchanging recess of Walshe's mind.

"We're going to say a prayer now, Seánie. That's what we're going to do."

"Our peace prayer," she said then after a pause. Her voice had dropped to a murmur. "The prayer we made up together, yours and mine, Seánie. Our prayer."

She looked at Minogue. He met her eyes, but couldn't be sure she'd noticed him.

"Are you ready, Seánie?"

Minogue felt Walshe slacken more.

"I don't want AIDS," he said.

"Now Seánie, I said to stop that."

Walshe grunted something, too low and too hurried for Minogue to make out.

"He's going to let you go now Seánie," she went on. "And after we say our prayer, you're going to sit over there by the wall. In your favourite chair. You can pick the station on the telly too. Are you listening, Seánie."

It wasn't a question. They weren't even having a conversation.

"After a count of five. We'll go step by step. Five...four ... three..."

Minogue plotted out what he'd do if Walshe made a run for it. Immaculata caught his eye. He released Walshe's arm and then he stepped away.

"*O Jesus, my brother*," Immaculata declared. Slowly, Walshe stood upright, rubbing at his throat

"*O Jesus, my brother*, You know my life, and my pain, and my loneliness."

Walshe's voice was too low for Minogue to hear.

"*...You are my friend and my brother...*" Immaculata said, closing her eyes.

Walshe had joined his hands. His head was bobbing slightly. Minogue saw scabs under matted hair near his crown. He took a deep breath and released it with a shudder.

"*...You forgive me when I do bad. And you don't forget me, Jesus...*"

Glancing down, he was not pleased to see that he too had joined his hands.

"Good, Seánie," Immaculata said. "Say the ending of it. I'll say it with you."

"*...If that is Your will. Amen.*"

Her face had gone slack. She turned to find McArdle still hanging around.

"Davey," said Immaculata. "Don't you be going anywhere, I want a word."

"But I didn't do anything. I was being nice."

"No you weren't," Minogue whispered. "You were being a bollocks."

Chapter 16

"Seánie acts for an audience. He sees one, and away he goes."

Immaculata was still keeping an eye on the Emer one. She was handing out sandwiches like they were unexploded bombs. He remembered the soft shine that came from those scars on her forehead. She had come by her contrariness honestly enough. Her husband's attack had left her near death. Immaculata's way of summing up the situation had stayed in his head: 'There were some things they couldn't fix.'

"I was his audience, was I?"

"You were that. But can you see behind what he says, what he does?"

"I don't know about that."

"Mental illness isn't a choice, you know. Did you think it was?"

He hesitated long enough to be sure she was getting his cue.

"I feel a lecture coming on," he said.

"Well I don't mean to. But is this your first time meeting troubled people?"

"No. Not really, I mean. There were insane rulings to cases I worked on. Where the defendant was ruled not responsible, I mean. Not the other meaning."

She gave no sign she appreciated his wit, much less twigged to it.

"So you know about Portrane and so forth?"

"I know of it. One man I knew, a convicted man, he killed himself there."

She winced. He wondered how well she knew the psychiatric hospital there.

"But you've been a Guard a good long time. So you know how things can go when you're dealing with fragile minds."

Fragile, Minogue thought. If only she'd seen the inside of the kitchen where that Mitchell fella, the suicide, had slaughtered his girlfriend.

"So what they say can't be taken at face value," she said.

He waited several moments.

"It's a bit early for you to start plea bargaining for Walshe, I'm thinking."

That registered with her. He felt he should divert a little after.

"You won't mind me saying this now, I hope," he said. "But you're about the wildest nun I have come across."

"Wild," she said. "Me?"

"I can't think of a more diplomatic word for it right now."

She picked at her cuff, as though to pluck away a piece of lint.

"There's nothing to be diplomatic about," she said. "You thought I was hypnotizing poor Seánie or something, I suppose. Did you?"

"Maybe. Or something like it, yes. Nun powers."

Her quick, cautious smile told him that he still had her off balance here.

"Prayer," she said. "The power of prayer. People forget how powerful."

She lifted her chin, and with a delicate shrug, she drew her shoulders back.

"I learned a lot on the missions, I can tell you," she said. "Africa, I'm talking about, sorry. But I had plenty already, growing up. My father, God rest him, was a healer, a bone-setter. A combination of vet, and physiotherapist, and maybe even a psychologist too, I suppose you'd call it. It's in the family."

"Well it shows," he said. "You had me praying, nearly."

"Nearly? What would it take?"

He eyed her.

"Remember you asked me, did I ever get a kick off a horse?"

Her smile turned to a short, throaty laugh. Emer saw, or heard it, and looked over. Immaculata made a soothing gesture that reminded Minogue of a conductor.

"God," Immaculata sighed, and she let out a deep breath. "So many. So *many*."

"Sister—"

"—Mary," she said, meeting his eye, and smiling. "Come on now."

"Look," he said. "I never imagined I'd be in this position. But here I am, sitting here, having to issue a warning to a good-living, decent person like yourself."

"A warning. For me?"

"I have to caution you against getting in the way of the law."

"In the way? Do you mean obstruction?"

"I don't want to be talking like that," he said. "I want to sort this out as ordinary people, you and me. A chat. Give and take."

She pursed her lips and looked away.

"So tell me something now," he said. "Not about the antics out there now. Something else. Something about Padraig Larkin."

Her look came back, sharpened into a stare.

"Padraig was gay," he said. "Am I right?"

"I don't know that."

"But it occurred to you."

She seemed to be weighing a response.

"Is that an important issue?" she asked, finally.

"It could be. But if I don't know about it, then it gets to be important."

"Well, I don't know."

"You don't know..."

"A lot of distressed people like you see here can be mixed up, confused. Some damage themselves too in that regard, the choices they've made, or not made. The things they let happen because they didn't know what to do, or who to turn to."

She paused.

"And I hardly need to tell you about the other matter. What's coming out now?"

"I'm not sure what you're getting at."

She spoke slowly.

"A lot of these men have been abused. Are you following me now?"

"I think so," he said. "Sexually, you're saying?"

"That too. And if it's done to you, you do it to others. The cycle?"

"I've heard that said all right."

"You're thinking, my God, what would an old broken-down nun know about such matters. Aren't you?"

His eye was now drawn to how the cross and chain shifted slightly each time she tugged at her polo neck.

"Broken down?"

She released a cautious smile. Minogue examined his hands.

"So Davey McArdle is gay then," he said. Her frown returned.

"Well why is Seánie Walshe yelling about AIDS?" he asked her.

"Seánie yells about everything," she said. "Sooner or later."

"There's nothing to it?"

"Even if there were, should I be telling a policeman the confidential health records of one of these poor men here? Even if I knew them?"

Minogue squinted at her.

"You would use your judgment, I hope. And then I think you'd tell me what was needed to find who murdered Padraig Larkin. That sound about right?"

For once, he felt he had her on the run. It didn't last.

"Judgment," she murmured. She smiled. "I'll tell you something now about that word. May I? I went to Africa as a missionary nun. You probably know this?"

"I had heard."

"All fired up, I was. That's the Holy Spirit for you: 'You're going to Africa, Mary – on the Missions!' And that was that. Did you have black babies in your schooldays?"

"No actual babies. Just the collection boxes."

"I was going to Africa to save people, you see," she went on. "To rescue them. I'm not ashamed to admit I used to think that way, either. I had already judged them, hadn't I. They were all the one in my mind a, 'them' or 'those people.' Oh sure, I learned all about the different languages, and the tribes, and the history. Do you see what I mean about judgement?"

"Maybe like the Chinese sailor on shore leave in Dublin."

"What Chinese sailor? I don't get what you mean."

"Someone shoves a microphone at him, asks him what he thinks of these Irish people. 'I don't know what to say,' says he. 'These Irish all look the same to me.'"

The sight of her buckling with laughter made him imagine her from before her nun life. A bit of a tomboy, he'd wager. Close to her father, probably.

"You're a bit of a rogue," she said.

"Well if I am, we're well met, I'm thinking."

"Where was I? Ah yes, a young nun, a farmer's daughter from Annaghyduff. The one who knew everything. Well there I was, in Africa. I was teaching – I was even building the school, for the love of God. Me with my bricks and my plaster, my spirit level... Oh such craic we had! But it didn't strike me that I had things upside down until one day. One of the women there, her husband came home. I had never even known him. I thought he was another shiftless fella who ditched his family, and headed off to the sheebeens along the roads there. Brothels – that's what they are. But he tottered into the village, and he sat down outside this house. Not a penny had he sent home to his family all the time he was away. All he brought home was disease. But do you know what happened?"

Minogue shook his head.

"He was brought into the house, that's what. And there he stayed until the day he went to meet his maker. He was bathed, and fed, and taken care of. He couldn't do a stroke of work of course, he could barely get to his feet. That was the start of the

AIDS thing, that's how it came to us what was happening. And now look?"

"A calamity, to be sure."

Her eyes took on a new intensity.

"Not one of them judged him. Not one said a bad word to him, or about him. They took him in, and that was that. And here I was, thinking what I would teach these people? Little did I know that God has His own plans! He had asked these people to go on a mission to me and the rest of us here in this part of the world. You see? I had to go there so they could fulfill their mission! That's the mystery of His ways – right there."

She was waiting for some sign that he approved, or at least heard, her message.

"You know what the future will be?" she went on. "It'll be those same Africans coming here on the missions to us. Like our monks in the old days, our island of saints and scholars, rescuing people from darkness. Full circle! Now do you see?"

"We're a bit short these days in the saints and scholars line, I have to say."

The fervor in her eyes dimmed a little at his words, but it soon returned.

"It's on the missions I learned – I *really* learned – that it's not our job to judge. We're not called to run the universe. Just to do what we can."

It was not easy to meet her eyes, but it was something he had to do.

"It's the law decides," he said. "No law means no society. We do what we can."

To his dismay, she seemed to enjoy this prospect of an argument. She sat back.

"Well this I do know," she said. "Society doesn't mean much to these men. And as for the law, well the law is a blunt instrument in their lives. Some have been done wrong by the agents of the law. Can you see that?"

"I don't want to add to their problems," he said. "But I have to wonder if those two lads – those two in particular – know more than shows up in their statements."

"Is it their fault that the Guards didn't talk to them right? The ones who did those interviews, as you call them? Is it their own fault that they were frightened of them?"

"Frightened," he repeated. "Aren't you gilding the lily a bit there?"

"Look," she began. "When you have been inside their heads and seen…"

She let the rest of her words go unsaid, but they seemed to hover somewhere between them. He spoke slowly and deliberately.

"No mention in any statement of the possibility that Padraig Larkin might be gay. Not one. Not from the lads out there, and not from you. That strikes me as odd."

She was blinking now. He wondered if she were really lost for words.

"Nobody tried to conceal anything," she said. "If that's what you're saying."

He gave her a long, cool look.

"Maybe it was out of some notion of decency? But it was a bad idea."

"I can't just abandon them," she said, her voice hardening.

"Was I asking you to?"

She sat back and placed her palms on the table, ready to rise.

"Fine," she said, and drew in a breath. "You'll do what you want, I daresay."

★ ★ ★

Minutes into his interview with McArdle, Minogue had enough. He put his pencil slowly and carefully on his notebook, and he looked over at Immaculata.

"Can we have a chat outside," he said.

"I'm going with you," McArdle said to her.

"You stay here, Davey. We'll be back in a minute."

Minogue waited by the door, as far as he could get from McArdle. There was a sickly sweetness to the smell coming from him, like stale talcum powder, but charged with a medicinal smell that hinted at something he didn't want to know, or think about.

Immaculata closed the office door. She was in no hurry to meet Minogue's glare.

"This isn't working," he said. "He's leaving you to do the talking for him."

"But he has a hard time putting things into words."

"It didn't sound like that earlier."

"Nerves. He knows you're a Guard."

"You have to let him try."

She said nothing. He heard someone complain about the television station being changed. That Emer character was watching him again. Emer of the jigsaw skull.

"Is he high?" he asked. "There's a smell of something."

"High? I can't be sure. But have a go with him, instead of waiting."

"If he was arrested and held over, he'd sober up, I think. Do you?"

"Arrested?" she snapped. "Don't be stupid."

Her eyes went wide and she took a step back, and her hand went to her mouth.

"I am so sorry," she whispered. "I don't know where that one came from."

Minogue didn't put any effort into trying to hold back his grin.

"You're not the first one to say that."

"I am shocked," she said.

The door opening behind shook her out of her embarrassment.

"Can I go now?"

"Sit down, Davey," she said.

"I smell cooking. What is it?"

"That's for later," she said. "You had your sandwich, Davey."

"I don't want to miss it," he said. "It's shepherd's pie. Isn't it?"

"I forget, Davey. I'm distracted."

"Shepherd's pie," he said.

"You'll get your shepherd's pie," Minogue said. "But later on, after our chat."

"I don't like you. You're a Guard. And I don't like Guards."

Minogue thought again of the strange shape to McArdle's head, the tall forehead that was surely mismatched on one side. He exchanged a look with Immaculata.

"Here's my plan," he said. "We'll continue our chat over a cup of tea."

"I had my tea. I don't want any more tea now. No."

"It doesn't have to be tea. We'll go somewhere, get a cup of something nice."

"Go somewhere? Where will we go?"

"A drive," Minogue said. "We'll go for a little drive."

"To the Garda station?"

"No. No Garda station. We'll find a nice place."

McArdle glanced at Immaculata and then at Minogue.

"You're trying to cod me. I don't like you. You Guards are all bastards."

"Davey," said Sister Immaculata.

"Would Sister be coming too?"

Minogue eyed her, wondering if she sensed he was mulling the hard option again.

"If she likes," he answered finally. "I'll get the car and bring it up outside."

It was a relief to be out standing by his car. He let the cold air pour into his open coat. But even with a cigarette going, he was sure that stink had followed him out. Still no word yet from Malone. Was he dragging his heels?

Malone answered on the second ring.

"Where are you?" he said. "Under a hairdryer?"

"I'm standing outside the drop-in centre. It's windy. Tell me what you have."

"Those two patrol fellas, that were at the scene first?"

"First tell me you found there's a gay scene out here in the Park."

"How badly do you want there to be one? 'Cause that's not what I'm getting."

"Nothing, is it? Violence against them? Gay-bashing?"

"Nothing showing, boss. Really. Want me to phone around the stations?"

Minogue considered it for a moment.

"Okay," he said. "Park it down the list a bit. How about JJ Mac, any word?"

"His answering thing is full. I'm working through his contacts. There's a woman Mary...wait: Mary O'Toole. She used to be with him. He gets fierce jumpy, she says. What's jumpy, I says. Apparently he downs tools and just hits the road every now and then. 'When things don't go his way,' says she."

"What didn't go his way?"

"She has no clue. She's on the outs with him a good long while. He was big into the music scene and all, but it's a while back, that stuff. She's not bitter now, she says. But she had to walk. 'Being an adult gets to him sometimes.'"

"That sounds bitter to me."

"Yeah, well. He's an only son – only child actually. Let me see, I got the names of pubs he likes, a few fellas he hangs around with."

"And?"

"And? And we need more staff. But that's just my opinion."

"Thanks. Drop it in a Powerpoint for me will you? I'll forward it to somebody."

"So are we ready to put in a find with the coppers in Amsterdam?"

Minogue didn't answer for a moment.

"Or hold fire on him for now?" Malone went on. "Like, what's the deal with him? I'm not getting it yet. What is he? Druggie? Gobshite? Suspect?"

"For now he's a gap," said Minogue in place of an answer. "Keep trying with McCarthy's contacts. Maybe they'll know where he stays, or hides, or whatever he's doing. I'll be here awhile yet. I want to check something here, something about a cemetery."

"A cemetery. A graveyard, like?"

"Right. There could be something from one of Larkin's cronies here, carry-on up in some cemetery. I'm taking him out for a drive, see if he can show me the place."

"I'm missing all the fun. Again."

"You'd like to be dealing with head-cases and nuns – at the one time?"

"Too good to miss, boss. Is that oul nun walking all over you again?"

"Walking, I don't know. Maybe she has the steering wheel, and won't let go."

The door to the drop-in opened. Minogue watched McArdle edge out, his eyes narrowing in the breeze. Immaculata had a purple knit scarf wrapped high up to her chin.

She had spotted him right away. Minogue began to retrace his steps toward the car. He had taken considerable care to arrange the old blanket that he kept in the boot on the passenger seat where he'd be sitting McArdle.

"So I'm heading out now," he said to Malone. "With this McArdle character, and Sister Immaculata. The Horse Whisperer."

"What? What horse?"

"Go-between, translator – whatever. I'll tell you later."

Chapter 17

After McArdle got his belt fastened, Minogue checked the edges of the blanket again. No way would he permit any gap between that blanket and the upholstery.

He drove with his window open a quarter way. He had no qualms about the cold air whooshing into the back seat on Immaculata. His glances to the rear-view mirror avoided any eye-contact. He geared down for the climb up Hill Road toward the quarry. McArdle was still half-turned toward the door panel, staring out the window like a child.

"Do you be up here much?" Minogue asked him.

"This is a nice car. Where are we going?"

Minogue gave him a side glance.

"We're going for a drive. We're sightseeing."

"You said we'd have something nice."

"We will. In due course."

He pulled into a driveway. Across the road, and not a half mile distant was a cramped view of Dalkey Hill. The steep, quarried rock faces needed afternoon light to show their features, but the ruin of the old semaphore building that marked the summit bit sharply into the eastern sky behind.

"Do you know where we are?" he asked McArdle.

McArdle stiffened in the seat.

"Maybe I do. Maybe I don't."

"You've been around these parts before."

"It's nice here," said Sister Immaculata. "Isn't it, Davey?"

"It's nice sometimes. But not now."

"You don't like it here," Minogue tried. "Why is that?"

"It's cold. I don't like it when it's cold."

"Padraig knew this place," said Minogue. "Didn't he?"

"Padraig is dead. He went up to heaven. Didn't he, Sister?"

Minogue eyed Immaculata for a moment. Would he witness at last an old sin, one he had wondered about a great deal as a child, that sin of presumption?

"God is good" was all she said.

"You were up here with Padraig," Minogue said. "Up on the hill. Weren't you?"

"Sometimes," said McArdle. "Is the place near here, the place you promised?"

"What place?"

"Someplace nice. You said, someplace nice."

"We'll find one soon enough."

"You have fags. I saw them. Can I have some?"

"How many do you smoke at a time?"

"They're for later on too, when I don't have any."

"Not in the car."

"I'll smoke them after then. Can I have them now?"

Minogue ignored him. He pulled out onto the road again. It climbed some more and then crested and took them by the car park under the inland side of Dalkey Hill.

"In here too?" Minogue asked. McArdle nodded his head.

Minogue let the car coast.

"What would you be doing up here now?"

"Nothing."

"Just out for a stroll, is it?"

"Yes. A stroll."

"Would there be people you'd meet here? Other people I mean."

"I don't know."

"Not just Padraig, though."

Immaculata was trying to catch his eye in the mirror. He ignored her.

"Seánie Walshe, would he be here?"

"I hate Seánie. Seánie only fights. And he roars, and screams, for no reason."

This was more than Sister Immaculata could bear.

"Now, Davey," she said. "That's not all there is to Seánie. Seánie is your friend."

"Not when he goes mad...! And he wants to fight...! For no reason...!"

"Davey," she said, her voice softening. "We always talk about this, how to be nice to people, especially when...what do we say Davey? When a person has...?"

"'When a person has difficulties.'"

"That's right," said Sister Immaculata. "Good for you Davey. You remembered."

Minogue glanced over in time to see McArdle's shy smile.

"Everybody has difficulties," said McArdle. "Isn't that right, Sister?"

"Right, Davey, you're right."

He turned to Minogue again.

"Do you have difficulties?"

"Me?"

"Yes, you. Everybody has difficulties. Don't they, Sister?"

"They do, Davey. They do."

"What are your difficulties?"

Minogue saw a sharp, wistful earnestness in McArdle's expression.

"Patience, I'd have to say. Patience, yes."

McArdle was almost squirming with pleasure now.

"I know," said McArdle. "I know!"

He looked out the window with renewed interest.

"Look!" he said. "There's a place! We'll have something there."

"That's a shop, Davey," said Immaculata.

"I don't want tea. I want something else. In there."

Minogue pulled in. It was awkward parking. He gave Immaculata a twenty.

"And something for yourself," he said. He didn't care if she caught the sarcasm.

He took out his mobile and placed it on the top of the dashboard while he waited. The minutes passed. He strained to catch a glimpse of them through the window. Still hovering over the sweets, it looked like. He'd give them another minute.

He looked back in his messages. Yes, he had neglected to phone Kilmartin back. That was fine – it was a message in itself.

They were back. It was ice cream for McArdle. Immaculata was carrying other items, bars of chocolate, crisps. There was only a fiver and some coins in the change.

"And we're going to go to an off-licence," McArdle said.

"No, Davey," said Sister Immaculata. "That's not right."

"I want to," he said. He began scratching hard at the back of his head.

"Watch how you're managing that," Minogue said.

"What?"

"That ice cream thing, the cornetto. I don't want any of that messing up the car."

"I'm going to eat it. I'm going to eat it all."

Minogue watched him. Had those shakes been there before? DTs? Parkinsons?

"You know the place here," he said to him then. "You and Padraig and Seánie."

"Not Seánie."

"No?"

He had to wait for McArdle to work though a big piece of the cornetto.

"Not Seánie?" he asked again.

"Only sometimes, only when he's not being mental."

"Or when he has something to offer."

A clouded expression came to McArdle's face.

"You share what you have, don't you?"

"Sometimes. If they share. It's being nice."

"Like a bottle?"

"Sometimes. Maybe."

"Around here at times? Up in on the Hill here? Or Killiney Hill?"

"I don't know."

"I think you do. Did you go to the cemetery with Padraig?"

McArdle turned to Immaculata.

"He means did you go with Padraig or the others," she explained. "Graveyards?"

"I'm not going to a graveyard. No way."

Immaculata began to say something, but Minogue interrupted.

"An old church?" he asked. "The old ruin up there, above the station? Marino Road, or something?"

McArdle frowned. Minogue watched for any flicker of comprehension in McArdle's eyes.

"It was a church," he added. "Hundreds of years ago."

"It still is a church," Immaculata said.

McArdle worked slowly and thoughtfully at the ice cream.

"You'd have to climb in," Minogue said. "Wouldn't you? Over a wall there?"

McArdle said nothing.

"Or would a person be able to get over those railings, do you think?"

McArdle stopped licking and fixed his eyes on the dashboard.

"The devil goes there," he said, and returned to the ice cream. Immaculata sat forward in her seat.

"Davey?"

"Yes, Sister."

"The Devil, you said?"

"Padraig said the devil. I don't think he's there at all. But Padraig thinks I'm stupid. You see? But I'm not stupid at all. I know about that kind of stuff."

He looked to Immaculata for reassurance.

"You're far from stupid, Davey," she said.

"I know," he said. He returned to working the sides of his ice cream. "The devil doesn't be out during the day anyway. Padraig used to tell me I could see him at night though. At that place. No way, I said to him. But he laughed at me."

He stopped licking then and glanced from Immaculata to Minogue.

"He said he'd seen the devil there. That's how he knew, he said."

"Did he tell you what the devil looked like?" Minogue asked.

"Are you joking me?"

Minogue shook his head.

"I think you are. Isn't he, Sister?"

"He's not, Davey. Tell me then. When did Padraig see this?"

McArdle sniggered.

"He didn't. He only said he did. You see?"

"I don't," said Minogue.

"Ah, he was trying to scare me! I know he was. He'd only get like that when, you know, when he'd go men—"

He looked over at Immaculata.

"The wine, Sister, the bad wine. He'd have that, and he'd start on his stories. And I had to listen."

"You had to? Why did you have to?"

McArdle rolled his eyes.

"Because if I didn't, well he'd keep it all to himself, wouldn't he? Everything!"

"Do you remember Padraig's stories?" Minogue asked.

"They're kids' stories. Come on now! I told you, I'm not an iijit like some people think. Just stories about God, ages ago. I knew he was making it all up. And I told him too. He didn't like that."

He licked a runnel of melted ice cream off his knuckles.

"Vikings, there's no Vikings anymore. Everybody knows that. Right?"

"Right," said Minogue.

"And the Druid stuff he used to talk about, they're just made up, aren't they?"

"Not quite. But the Druids were a long time ago too."

"I know," said McArdle, sharply. A frown darkened his eyes. "I know! Druids, they're priests, he told me."

"Pagan priests," said Immaculata."Not real ones. Before St. Patrick."

The area had plenty of references to Druids, Minogue

remembered. Wasn't the pub there in Killiney village called the Druid's Chair, or something?

"Well the devil isn't long ago," said McArdle, a note of assurance in his voice.

"How long ago was it?" Minogue asked.

"It was when Padraig was here before. When he was with other people."

"Other people?"

"Not us, I mean. Not Seánie or me. When he was a young fellow here. When he was a teenager. He was from here, near here. Did you know that?"

"So I'd heard."

"But I know he was only teasing me," said McArdle. "Well most of the time. About the devil, I mean. Because I knew, you see, I knew."

"What did you know?"

"Padraig was mental, I told you already – that's why."

"Davey," said Immaculata.

"He had difficulties," McArdle said quickly. "That's what I mean."

The ice cream was at a very dodgy stage now, Minogue saw.

"His mind was mixed up," said McArdle. "Is it okay to say that?"

"Much better," she said.

He glanced from her to Minogue and back.

"There's no Vikings," he said. "But there's still a devil. That's what I say."

"This devil thing, Davey," Minogue said. "I am not getting that."

McArdle chuckled.

"You're not supposed to. You're the Guards. Nobody's going to tell the Guards."

"What wouldn't they tell me?"

McArdle stopped licking and stared at him. His frown gave way to a leer.

"That's a trick," he said.

Immaculata leaned in further between the seats.

"Davey," she said. "It's not a trick. He's here to help. What's the devil thing?"

A disappointed look took over his face. He went back to his ice cream.

"It's a mass," he murmured. "But not a real mass. It's a bad one."

"A Black Mass?" Minogue asked. McArdle looked sideways at Immaculata.

"A Black Mass, Davey?"

McArdle frowned.

"But it was ages ago," he said, looking up as though consulting a memory. "Yes, ages. Padraig said so himself. When he was a kid. Ages ago."

"That church, Davey," Minogue said after a while. "I'm going up there now, in the car. And you show me."

"Show you what?"

"Where you and Padraig used to be."

McArdle looked to Immaculata for guidance. She seemed lost in thought, Minogue noticed. Praying maybe.

★ ★ ★

"We don't need to go in," Minogue said. Clinging to the railings, McArdle moved his head from side to side to peer between them. Minogue had not been seriously tempted to bunk in over the railings.

Immaculata stood with a distracted expression below the wall where they stood. From the small movements in one of her pockets, he guessed she was saying a rosary.

"Give me an idea of where you used to go here."

"The wall," said McArdle. "The far wall, behind there."

Minogue looked through the railings at the gable walls and the arched doorway, the gravestones amid the sodden grass. The stone masons had done their work well here. Cill Iníon Léinin: the church of Lenin's daughter. It was one of the oldest churches too, he remembered, going back to an Ireland that Rome with all its strictures would not reach for centuries, a thousand years even before the name was recast into its present Killiney.

There would have been a mighty view from up here before the grandees had built their mansions next to it. You'd see clear down the Wicklow coast, he guessed, and inland too across the hills.

"So you'd be in there with Padraig," he said to McArdle.

"Only sometimes. Only in the summer."

"With a bottle or two of something."

"Padraig always had one. Almost always. I think someone gave him one?"

"Just the two of you. Nobody else?"

McArdle began to shake his head vigorously.

"I know what that means," he said. "I know that. You can say it, if you like. I know what you're thinking. I do."

"What am I thinking?"

"Padraig was bad. You think he was bad. I know you're thinking that."

Immaculata stirred in his side vision, and he glanced over. She caught his eye for a moment, and then looked away. She knew this would come up, then?

"Why do you say he was bad?"

"I don't say that. You say it. The Guards."

"I didn't say he was bad. Who says it?"

"You know, yes you do. It's bad, what Padraig does. Isn't it, Sister?"

Minogue saw her jaw move a little. She pursed her lips and examined the bare trees over the church.

"What's 'bad,' Davey? What is bad about Padraig?"

"Nothing. I don't want to talk to you anymore."

"We don't mind what you say. Sister doesn't mind. Do you, Sister?"

Immaculata shook her head.

"I can't talk about it. It's bad."

Minogue exchanged a look with Immaculata.

"Davey," she said, an authoritative tone back in her voice now. "You can say the words, Davey. We don't mind."

"They're bad words, Sister. I can't."

A bleak smile came to her face.

"Are you afraid to say them in front of me, Davey? The words?"

He blinked.

"I'll just go out there a bit," she said. "And you can say them to this man here."

"The Guards aren't nice, Sister. They're not."

"Nobody can be nice all the time, Davey. And I asked him here, to help us."

"I never told them anything," he said. "I know what they do."

He looked at Minogue.

"They never asked me, so I didn't have to. So I didn't tell any lies, did I?"

"That's one of the things I like about you," she said.

His expression eased, but then snapped back into a frown.

"Would Padraig be sent to hell, Sister?"

"Nobody knows that, Davey. Nobody but the good Lord Himself. Nobody."

"For that mass thing, that black mass? God forgives people, doesn't he?"

Minogue looked around the churchyard again. There were enough places out of sight of the lane here. Too many, perhaps.

"Especially how long ago," McArdle added. His voice had grown earnest, almost plaintive. "When he was young. He didn't know what he was doing. Right, Sister?"

Chapter 18

S moking a cigarette here by the side of his car wasn't getting Minogue any revelations. What he was getting instead was looks from passing drivers. No matter. He tried to parse his thoughts again. The last few minutes in the car with Sister Immaculata had been strained. Her distant, wary tone, the sparse, non-committal observations. All in all, she had disengaged, retreating in her thoughts to somewhere he couldn't reach.

Had there been no sign, he had pressed, no sign at all of gay stuff between Larkin and McArdle? There might have been, she allowed, but she hadn't picked up on them.

Did she think that Larkin was the type to exploit someone like Davey McArdle? Well, she really couldn't say.

Was there something else that she had forgotten to tell him maybe...?

But she had given Minogue no sign that she had picked up on his sarcasm. She seemed genuinely puzzled by the question, even bewildered.

He shivered a little, and let slip a few of the curses that had been rolling around in his head. It was bad ju-ju to be cursing a nun. He checked the sky for any sign of an angry God between the clouds, sizing him up for a good zap. Not yet. Later maybe, when he let down his guard. He eyed his cigarette: near to half-way, the ditching-point.

An elderly woman shuffled by, glancing at the open windows of his Peugeot.

"The day will take up, please God," she declared.

Intended as a smile, her face creased into a grimace instead.

"We could do with it, ma'am, couldn't we."

"As if we didn't have enough to be going on with!"

He could only smile. Her eyes bulged with some passion

"God help Ireland," she said. "That's all can I say these days!"

And she was off. He flicked the butt into the road.

Driving away, he reminded himself to take that old blanket out of the boot when he got home. Dump it, even. The traffic lights were at their most disobliging. He was soon sitting at light after light, drawing the gearstick over and back in neutral and trying to be sympathetic toward the town and its inhabitants. Dun Laoghaire had been hard hit since the bubble burst. Away from its seafront walks and piers, the place had always had too many mangy-looking pubs and bookies. He felt eyes on him: a sweaty-headed dawdler staring from a doorway. Trackies, hoody, Nikes: check. No pretense – just the steady, squinting, eff-off stare that didn't falter when he drew a cigarette to his lips.

He had found the timeless traffic light. He closed his eyes and went to his old ruses, and soon he was threading his way through heather, the wind hissing across the bog and soft turf underfoot. His idyll veered unexpectedly: a churchyard, darkness, figures moving about. What exactly was a Black Mass anyway? And did anyone actually believe that stuff any more? Drugs. A crowd of teenagers, Larkin among them. Images flared and died in his thoughts: candle lights, murmured incantations, hallucinating couples naked in the long grasses. The Summer of Love, Dublin style.

He was turning on to Castle Street when Malone phoned.

"JJ Mac," he said. "Not on a flight list. Not on a ferry."

"Out of Ireland, you mean, I take it."

"Well do you want me to try the Brits then?"

Minogue couldn't spot any gap in the parked cars. He coasted by the station, half-wondering if anyone would see him on his mobile and slap a fine on him.

"Can't we get any pointers from his associates? Is he avoiding someone? Is he on something? Does he owe money? Suspect in anything? Lying low...?"

"Nothing so far, boss. But okay, I'll keep at it. Is that what I'm hearing?"

Minogue remembered Tynan's tone when talking about JJ Mac. But he wouldn't have mentioned the same McCarthy if he hadn't wanted something done about him. The appearance of due diligence at least.

"It is," he said to Malone. "Yes. Keep looking local for a bit longer."

"'Details, details.'"

"That's the speech I had ready, yes. Look, I'm by the station now, in a minute."

"Okay," he said. "Any go-ahead from that drop-in place? That Disciples gaff?"

"I just finished taking one of them out for a spin. Him and me, and Immaculata."

"The nun too? What, she's his bodyguard or something?"

"She calms him down. Sort of translates a bit too. He's light on the loafers."

"A fairy, you mean?"

"Enough with 'fairy' talk, Tommy. It ain't right."

"Well what should I be saying then?"

"Sister Immaculata calls it 'confused.'"

"'Confused?' Nuns, heh... What do they know about stuff like that?"

"She said the same to me – rhetorically, you can be sure."

"Means...?"

"It means maybe she knows more than we think she knows."

"You're back to that again. Interesting."

Minogue spotted a parking spot behind a Post van. It'd be tight.

"My point is," he said. "She knows these men. She can get things out of them."

"Like what?"

"There's an old church ruin here, a cemetery. McArdle went there with Larkin."

"For...?"

"You tell me."

"Booze? And...something else?"

"Two out of two."

"Is this the gay angle? A bit of how's-your-father, yeah?"

"How delicate of you. But here's the thing. I don't know the details. McArdle is not keen to paint the full picture. Can we make him? Entice him? I don't know."

"Why not just get this nun of yours out of the way, bring in these fellas and—"

"—And what, Tommy? Won't work – that's why. There's no other way. Where did the investigation get with these lads on the first go-round?"

Malone's slow, interrogative okay meant his bullshit detector knew better.

"Look," Minogue said. "I'm just parking, I'll be up in a few minutes."

He closed his mobile. He had doubts about the spot now, it was so tight, but he went in anyway.

★ ★ ★

An hour or so later, Minogue was on hold when his mobile went. Kilmartin's name glowed a little brighter as he held the power button, and then the screen died.

He checked his watch: four and a half minutes he'd been on hold. One Eileen Molloy, a medical social worker who had connected with Larkin several times in the past few years, was 'checking the policy' on second interviews with the Guards. They had a policy on that? But he'd heard nothing in her tone that hinted she enjoyed thwarting him.

He had asked her to consider it a continuation of the original statement back in July. Ms. Molloy had let on that she was amused more than affronted by this request. She tried to remind him then of how little contact she had had with Padraig Larkin. He had been an outpatient at the Casualty Office at St. Michael's in Dun Laoghaire. As he had presented signs of homelessness, she had said, part of her role was to follow up and see if he could not be helped in that regard. Connected with homeless agencies, and suchlike. 'Presented'? The word kept circling in his thoughts.

One of thousands, he imagined her wanting to say. A feeble spark of pleasure came to him when he fed her the official line: case review requires every detail be checked. Procedures indeed.

He had overshot the lunchtime, and it was beginning to tell. He felt around for his cigarettes, and listened to Malone repeat the script as he had been doing for an hour now in his phone calls: updating our information on the Padraig Larkin case; a routine case review; yes, it was ongoing; anything that might have been overlooked, or would want to alter; shouldn't be at all embarrassed to bring anything up.

Eileen Molloy was back. They were short-staffed, the cutbacks, and her supervisor was covering for someone. Could he phone back later today, or she him?

Malone let go the mouse, and went slowly into a long, wide-ranging stretch. He had been searching PULSE for nearly an hour.

"It's not party central up there in the woods there," he said. "Up the Hill, I mean. Not according to this anyway. None of that black mass stuff you were talking about either. Sure no-one believes that crap these days anyway."

"That we know about. That was reported."

Malone shrugged.

"There was a barney there last July," he said. "Young fellas, drinking, and it got rough. Some other crowd showed up, a bit of a set-to. Two squad cars, but the young fellas did a runner. No arrests, no charges. A bit of vandalism back after the Christmas. Cars keyed two years back, and a few tires slashed. A total of five cars got broken into, over the year."

Minogue shivered in the draft. He glanced at his to-do list. Dun Laoghaire Rathdown Council, the litter wardens. Rework Walshe's alias. McArdle's too. A proper Bureau sweep of that churchyard? Other old churches and ruins. Any hang-outs there?

"Any mention of our King of Ireland in those?"

Malone shook his head.

"This Walshe fella," he said after a pause. "Seán Walshe, right?"

"Seánie Walshe, he goes by. What about him?"

"He loses it, you told me. Violent bouts. Yeah?"

Minogue watched him balance his biro on his knuckles, and then quickly twist his hand to seize it.

"Try this one," said Malone then. "McArdle and Walshe – in cahoots. Yeah?"

Minogue frowned in response.

"Does McArdle know that Larkin got a bit of money every week?" Malone asked.

"We don't know that. Yet."

"Okay, just say he does. So he gets Walshe to do in Larkin. It's for the money – they take Larkin's money, that allowance that he hadn't spent yet?"

"And part of the deal is that McArdle will alibi Walshe."

"Right," said Malone. "But maybe there was no deal to swap alibis. Maybe in a sneaky way, McArdle could be just stitching up Walshe for it. First he fed him a story – Walshe, I mean – and then Walshe goes spare over it, and kills Larkin. Now McArdle had Walshe in his pocket for that."

"Crazy smart, not crazy crazy? I don't know, Tommy, I don't know."

"What if McArdle is playing everybody? Even if he puts it on a bit, that he's, you know, retarded? But he's actually not? Or not so much, like?"

"It's long shot. Way back of the running. Go on, though."

"Maybe it's not even about money," Malone said, pausing to attend to his biro. "Say Larkin has something, or McArdle thinks he had – booze, say. Or prescription stuff. Let's just say, Larkin wasn't sharing."

"I'd be leaving that one on the table all right," Minogue murmured.

"Ready for the next one then? Here it is: McArdle didn't want to do his share."

Minogue met his gaze.

"Will that pass the politically correct bit with you? The 'do his share' bit?"

"Just about. You're talking sex stuff between them, I take it."

Malone was poised to rise from the chair.

"And what about that black mass stuff that Larkin was into way back?"

"Fair enough," said Minogue. "We have roads to go down there. But later, after we get a better picture of things."

Malone shrugged. He logged off with sharp, stabbing keystrokes and ended in a flourish, before rising robotically from the chair.

"If this were easy we wouldn't be here," Minogue said. "Would we?"

Malone stopped in mid-stretch and looked sideways at him.

"What?" said Minogue.

"Tell me about 'easy,'" he said. "I'm useless at this 'easy' thing, or so I'm told. Know what I'm talking about?"

Minogue shook his head.

"The world of 'easy,' is what. 'Easy,' says she – Sonia. You know this Sonia one I'm talking about?"

Minogue tried not to look taken aback by the bitter tone.

"Your fiancée, you mean," he said.

"Close – ex-fiancée. Former fiancée – Okay. Let's say 'girl-friend' Sonia, I'm talking about then. Anyway. 'Just take a course,' says she. 'Any course, make it an easy one. Father will be impressed.' Yeah, she calls him 'father.' 'Father respects stuff like that.' 'Easy' says the Ma the other night. We were talking about the way things is going nowadays. I don't mean the recession thing, I mean crime, and all."

"Are. How things are going."

Malone drummed his fingers once on the table and sighed.

"'Just go for Sergeant's again,' says the Ma. "'Easy does it. Take a step back,' says she. 'Go easy on yourself. Let the young fellas do that stuff. There's nothing wrong with finding the easy route.'"

The glance he gave Minogue went quickly from scathing to sardonic.

"You know what she was talking about, right?"

Minogue managed a non-committal nod.

"That's right," said Malone. He paused, made a faint snort. "No more running across rooftops after the likes of Artane frigging Kelly. You know?"

"Your mother knows her onions, I say."

"You think? 'But Ma,' says I. 'I am a young fella. Are you blind?' No one wants to really stuck into it, I told her. Coppers, like. Nooo-body wants to get their hands dirty."

With that, he pocketed his hands and he eyed the door. He spoke in a low voice.

"Like here."

"Like here, what?"

"You haven't noticed yet? This kind of country club set-up here?"

Minogue's leveled a look at him.

"What," Malone said. "It's like they got to a certain point, and then they just…?"

Minogue waved off the rest of it.

"Look," he said. "This is just you and me talking. That's the way it has to stay too. We're not here to make local Guards look like iijits. We've just started here."

Malone made a non-committal gesture.

"Yeah, well if it's got to be them or us in an iijit contest, I want them to win."

Minogue sat back, and fixed Malone with a blank stare.

"Am I supposed to hear that?"

Malone checked the scarred linoleum tiles by his feet for a moment.

"Cup of tea?" he asked after a few moments. Minogue dithered.

"Saw a few bikkies over there in the canteen," Malone added. "Does that help?"

"Just a drop of milk then. And thanks."

Malone stretched again, and he finished with a slow slam-dunk that ended in a tight grasp of the handle of his mug. It was the souvenir mug from Rome, Minogue noticed, from the time that Malone had taken his mother 'to see the Pope or something.'

"Pissy," Malone said, with bogus cheer. "You like your tea pissy. Right?"

Minogue listened to Malone's footfalls retreat down the hallway and then begin to fade on the stairs. Definitely an altered Malone. Any cynicism had been wrapped in humour before now. But any plan to marry Sonia was gone in the wind now. How could he not be bitter? Just one more episode on the gauntlet that Malone's life had become? It had been four years now – no, five – since Terry had overdosed. A twin, he thought again, for the thousandth time. Did some of a person die too when a twin died?

He rolled his drawer shut. It got two-thirds-way closed before he had to fix it.

Chapter 19

Minogue studied the flickering extension light. There was no ring tone on this contraption? Malone took the call. "No way," he said to the caller. "Yep."

He held the receiver out, and made a mock salute with his free hand. Minogue put down the pencil that he had been trying to use as a magic wand, drawing lines between the times and the names that he had transcribed from a Detective McKeon's notes. It was McKeon who had chased down and verified the alibis for McArdle and Walshe.

Kilmartin sounded subdued.

"So what's it like out there? Five star-situation?"

"To be sure. Gold fittings in the toilets, helipads. Our own Hollywood Hills."

"Really? I worried it might be a bit raw for you out there. That good though?"

"It's a bit low on the glamour. Lower on the glory. No helipad either."

"Tragic. I heard it's actually fierce old-fashioned out there in Dalkey too."

"You might want to check your sources on that."

"No need. Mobile coverage hasn't even reached there yet. Did you know that?"

"I forgot," Minogue said. "I turn it off and, well, we've talked about this before."

"You think I sit around trying to invent reasons to phone

you, no doubt. But here I am anyway, I suppose. There's something you need to know."

Any hint of drollery in Kilmartin's voice had vanished now.

"So listen to me. I'm not codding now. I'm going to ask you a question, and you say yes or no to it. Okay? I repeat: this is not a cod."

Minogue could think of nothing to say.

"Is Malone there beside you? Remember, all I need is a yes or a no here."

"Yes."

"Good, okay. I needed to know that. Now get that god-damned mobile of yours, and switch it on. Can you do that? It'll say something like 'On.' O-N."

"I'm kind of in the middle of stuff here."

"You're in the middle of something way more important than that, and you don't even realize it. So switch on your mobile."

"Look, what exactly—"

"You need to listen to me."

Kilmartin's anger brought Minogue out of his slouch.

"You think I'm just passing the time here? So *listen*. Now, can I get you to do that one thing for me?"

A chill space opened in Minogue's chest.

"Okay. I can do that, I suppose."

"I want you to act normal – none of your wit now. Just like we're having a chat, like how's the form, weather is shite, how's the new car running – all that. You ready?"

"I am, I think."

"Normal, I said – light-hearted. Chatty. Ready? Now. Do it now. And hurry up."

"I heard that all right. Fogarty will play goal against Limerick, I believe too."

"Good – good. Now just carry on. You-know-who next to you has to think we're having a casual chat. In a minute, you're going to take a walk – with your frigging mobile – and I'm going to call you back. See?"

Minogue didn't. Something fluttered and rose in his chest. Worry? Pity? Had Kilmartin finally cracked? He didn't sound drunk. Had he finally given up on trying to rebuild? That the self-help books, the shrink sessions, the 'making changes in his life' guff had all proven worthless? He imagined an unshaven Kilmartin sitting in his car, making these weird, urgent, Man-From-U.N.C.L.E. calls.

"Talk to me," Kilmartin snapped. "Are you alive or dead there?"

"Fogarty he was injured in a match against Cork last year, so who knows?"

"Good. Okay, one, just one bit of your usual, ah, *wit*, and then you sign off."

Minogue watched Malone swill his tea, and then stand. He couldn't help trying to eavesdrop, of course. That's what detectives did.

"I'll give it a try," he said to Kilmartin.

"Good. So, back to hurling. Ready? Okay, here I go: Clare team couldn't get a goal if the goalposts were cut down and fecking handed to them. Okay – your turn."

"Thanks anyway. The day I go to a Mayo game will be the day I swear off drink."

"Good. Close it now. Ready? Here's something to get you launched: the Clare team couldn't hit a fecking lump of cowshite over a wall. Useless, the lot of you."

"Thanks," said Minogue. "Same to you."

He replaced the receiver and looked sideways at Malone.

"You want tickets to a Mayo game? I never thought of asking you. Hurling."

Malone held the door handle but didn't turn it.

"What's Mayo? What's hurling?"

He listened to Malone's footsteps recede down the hall. Then he rose, and taking his coat, he made his way down the hall. He returned Fitz's how-do with a cheery remark about the unknown pleasures of Dalkey, pausing only to receive to a quip from Fitz about a better class of 'ordinary decent criminal.'

A squad car had parked very tight to the driver's side of his Peugeot.

"Where are you?" was Kilmartin's opener.

Another image of Kilmartin came to him now: elbows on a desk, crouched over the phone, the head down on him like he was trying to choke the receiver to death.

"I'm sitting in my car like an iijit, in the station yard here."

"Well that can't be new for you. Nobody listening in there beside you?"

"No. Look, what exactly are you doing? What's all this James Bond craic?"

"I'll go straight to the point. Your pal there is in it. Right up to his bloody neck."

"In what?"

"I can't give you details. It's not the kind of thing I can ask the fella who told me this. But it's bad, very bad. They're onto him, Malone. Onto him again, I should say."

"I don't get this. Is this a book, a series – a comic?"

"Are you gone deaf? I said they're on to him! They're going after him. They want Malone's hide nailed up on the fecking *wall*. Is that clear enough for you?"

"Who does?"

"Internal Review – a.k.a. Tynan and his crowd! They want Malone to swing."

Minogue listened harder to Kilmartin's breathing.

"What about the Ombudsman inquiry? The all-clear that he got?"

"Ombudsman my arse. Do you think the Garda Síochána is going to be said or led by that parcel of tripe? Review was holding back to see what GSOC might drop on Malone. They've been nosing around Malone for years. Malone's brother, the drugs? All his mates from Primary School are gangsters...? Come on! Let's get real here. We all wondered. Maybe you didn't, you being the trusting type. He's played you for that."

"Think this over," Minogue started to say.

"Facts, man! *Facts!* They think they have Malone this time."

"What facts?"

"What am I, Google? I was lucky to get wind of it at all. It's the real deal, with S and I on board, even. All undercover, ad-hoc.

They only report to Tynan. The fella who told me took a fierce chance. And another thing: realize that Tynan set you up too."

S and I: Minogue echoed within. Garda Security & Intelligence spooks? Malone?

"Are you in one of your fecking trances there, or what?"

"How, set me up?" Minogue asked.

"You're Malone's minder, you gobshite! You keep him from noticing!"

Minogue stared harder at the symbols on the face plate of his car radio. He rolled his thumb carefully along the bevel to dislodge a patina of Dublin's finest grime.

Kilmartin's voice was caught between impatience and pity.

"Look, didn't I try to warn you the other day? Are you ready now?"

"Ready for what?"

"Jesus, man, you're a cross to bear! The whole thing about Malone, the handy way Kelly was put out of the picture, the Triad fella, the Chinese girlfriend—"

"Fiancée, and she was born in Macau."

"Are you going to just keep on doing your la-la routine there?"

Minogue noticed more dirt by the buttons, and put the nail of his baby finger to it.

"Answer me, will you?"

"Okay."

"Okay what?"

"This won't wash, that's what. We've been down this road before. That time, you finally saw through the Egans's efforts to dirty Tommy up back then."

"I know, I know! But this isn't the parish pump stuff, this is an international syndicate. They're everywhere, and they use anybody. They extort, they blackmail, they buy – anybody and anything. And something else, don't be getting any 'race' thing going on your head about what I'm telling you. I like that girl, Sonia, or whatever her real name is. They have their own real names, you know?"

"Just like us, you mean?"

"She might have no say in the matter. Her parents could be clean as a whistle too, but they're being extorted. Loans gone bad, restaurant business down, the crisis…? A Triad fella shows up with money – but then he wants his way. That's how they operate. They *infiltrate*. So don't keep pretending, okay? For Christ's sake, even let yourself think that maybe there's something here. Just let yourself to think 'if,' will you?"

"If I'd been born with seats instead of hands I'd be the Glenamuck bus."

An unexpected calm had come into Kilmartin's voice.

"You haven't a clue – I accept that. But still I'm on your side. Malone got by GSOC, but Review won't fall for it, no siree Bob. Can I make it any clearer?"

This was paranoia, Minogue decided. You could pin it on the wall as a specimen.

"Are you taking this in there?" Kilmartin demanded.

"I am. Unfortunately."

"Spare me the high-minded guff there will you? It's a bit late in the day for you to be getting sense. I told you, the loyalty is a great thing with you. Lot of respect for that, I have. But by Jesus, you deserve better than to be made a mug of, to be set up like this."

"How ever did I mange to walk upright all these years without your guidance?"

"Christ but you're the cross-grained bastard today. Look. They know – they know, I'm telling you, that Malone tossed that fecker off the roof. Kelly – Artane Kelly. And they are going to nail him for it. Got that?"

Minogue closed his eyes. Kilmartin's fervid tone had rattled him.

"How do they know," he murmured. "How?"

"How? Kelly was the issue. Not because he was Kelly, but because he was going to spill the beans on something. You put a rat in a corner, a rat'll bite you. So if Kelly starts blathering…? That's not going to work for anyone, is it?"

The yard was still there when Minogue opened his eyes again. It looked smaller, the sky above closer. In his mind's eye, he saw himself closing his phone in mid-speech.

"Jim," he said.

"Why do you think Malone was so keen to get up on that roof? Through the barbed wire, cutting his hands and that? Why would he do that?"

"He gets intense, you know that."

"Where was Kelly going to go? Nowhere! And the others told Malone to forget it, and just wait. So again, what's Malone's hurry to get up? You can't get around that."

"Maybe he didn't hear it. Maybe he thought there was a ladder, or whatever."

"The operation is so tight that no-one has ever been able to get so much as a peek in. Well Jesus, think about it – no wonder it's tight. Malone's right in the thick of it."

"Jim, I have to tell you something. I'm going to hang up now."

"What? Don't be stupid. You should be thanking me. Not that I expect it."

"And after I hang up, I'm going to wait five minutes. Then I'm going to phone you back. And we're going to meet, you and me. Okay?"

"What the hell for? Amn't I telling you all you need to know here?"

"Look. Who told you this stuff?"

"Whoa there, cowboy. Get off that horse. Didn't I tell you it's confidential?"

"You're making this up, Jim. It's not real."

That worked. Minogue winced. He stopped counting after five.

"I wondered," said Kilmartin. The warm condescension that was his trademark came through in half-growled, half-chuckled words now.

"I really, really wondered," he continued. "But sure, I did it anyway. I went ahead and I phoned you. It's just something you do for a pal. For a man you respect, and you want to look out for. The loyalty thing, that's all we have, at the end of the day."

"If you'd just give me a bit of corroboration..."

"All right, Matt. Nice, sensible question. You're always on the ball. Of course."

"Give me something to work with here. You can't just phone up and tell me this when it makes no sense. The Ombudsman office are not thickos. They dug, and they gave Tommy the all-clear. Why don't people accept that?"

"Why indeed," said Kilmartin. The airy tone didn't mask his disdain. "Why can't we all just get along? Why can't we take a man at his word? Like old times, right? When we had morals or decency in the country. When a Guard's word was the gold standard. When we could trust the parish priest, or the bishop. Is that what you're saying?"

"I'm not asking for some fairytale past."

"Good," Kilmartin retorted. "Because that never existed, did it. We know that now, of course, don't we? But what I'm telling you here is this: I saw this thing with Malone coming over the horizon. So did you, bucko, but you ignored it."

"Saw what? Ignored what?"

"There you go with that denial thing again. You see? Surely to God you remember me wondering about Malone back in the Squad, don't you? That brother of his, God be good to him, the rumours flying around?"

"Rumours – exactly. The Egans play mind games. They're still at it, from behind bars. But you know all this."

"Do you think I get any satisfaction out of this?"

Minogue sat back. It wasn't anger settling in his thoughts, but a cold pity.

"I'd have been told," he said

"Listen, Mr. 'I'd a been told.' The fella who passed this on to me? I told you – he put himself out on a limb to tell me. Not all the good guys have taken early retirement, or been gagged, or softened up with desks in HQ. I trust him. There's nothing in it for him, to be stirring up trouble. He was concerned that a good copper – you, he was referring to, you – is in danger of getting taken down along with our friend there. Unwittingly, of course. That'd be a travesty, he said to me. A travesty and a tragedy."

Minogue bit back the urge to mock Kilmartin's words.

"So there you have it," Kilmartin said.

"I'll be in touch. Good luck—"

"—Wait. You can go off now in a huff, and no-one will stop you. But you owe it to yourself not to get caught up in this thing. Your career, your family."

"Jim, I have to go."

"You're not helping yourself or anyone else by taking this denial line."

"There's no denial. There's work, and I'm behind."

"Listen to reason a minute, will you! S and I coppers are pit bulls? They'll look at a senior Guard – you I'm talking about again – and straightaway the attitude is, 'well he must be in on it too.' Why? 'Because he's been on the job so long – anyone on the job this long must be in on it.' See? That's how they think."

"There's no 'it.' There's nothing to be 'in on.'"

"The fact is," Kilmartin went on. "They're freaking at HQ. Somebody put two and two together there. It's the whole out-of-control scenario with the gangs. The murders, the bank jobs, the floods and floods of drugs, the Chinese massage stuff. It's everything happening at the same time, the whole shemozzle."

"And their great confederation of minds there, or their software, tells them...?"

"Do I have to spell it out for you? Jesus! I shouldn't even be talking to you. Okay, here it is in plain English: *inside job*. Got that? Yes, they're taking it as a given that there's insiders in the Guards for years now. They'll tear down anything. You see?"

"I don't, actually."

"I can't keep banging my head against a wall here. I know you're the goods. I know I can trust you. So I speak my mind here. This is no time for you to be a gobshite. These fellas are going all-out. Like I said, top secret, under the radar, no-holds-barred. Nothing in writing, no section appointments. If they have to take out a few people to get at someone, they don't care."

"Let's call it quits. I've heard what you said. I appreciate the motive."

"Do you hear me – really do you? I don't think so. You don't know what you're dealing with here, that's my message, in a nut-shell."

In a nuthouse, Minogue wanted to say. He took a deep breath.

"Are you still there?"

Are you still there, Minogue echoed within. Are you *all* there?

Images circled in his mind again. Kilmartin's stricken face, slack with the shock and the booze, lifting his face off his own well-tended front lawn after one of the ERU crew finally cut the restraints. Kilmartin standing, wavering, in the revolving blue wash from the Garda lights, trying and failing to form words.

"Well?"

"Thanks," Minogue said.

"I know what that means, that 'thanks.'"

"Jim, I'm on me back foot here. We are, that is. I haven't read a quarter of the case yet. Okay? We won't be seeing daylight in this for a while."

"It's a woods and trees situation, Matt. Adjust your perspective here."

"Perspective how?"

An ominous tone of whimsy replaced the urgency in Kilmartin's voice.

"A lot of birds turn up in odd places in this country. Did you know that? Yes, it was a nature thing on the telly, how oddball birds get blown off-course here, and end up in places like Kerry, God help them."

"Birds," Minogue said. "Why are we talking about birds?"

"I'm getting to that. There's one particular bird not native to our shores, one lad you won't see blown here on the wrong wind. Not in all your life. Know which one?"

"The jackdaw? Or the cuckoo, maybe?"

"Very droll. No. None of the above. The bird I am referring to is the ostrich."

Chapter 20

*C*uticle, *cortex, medulla*. Saying it a few times brought a
rhythm to it.

He let the folder close on itself.

"Heavy going there, boss?"

Malone hadn't looked up from his own reading.

"We had a saying at home: Don't be kicking the dog to see
if it's awake."

Malone arched his back and stretched. He had stacked up
his finished files in a low pile on his desk, and there they waited
for Minogue to exchange for his own.

"Way too deep for me. I was only wondering why you were
talking to yourself."

"I'm sinking deeper into the gripping saga of...Hair
Analysis."

"Fabulous. You done the shoes yet, the patterns?"

Minogue shook his head. He had no urge to correct Malone's
grammar.

"Not yet. I'm saving that one."

He looked at his watch. He still couldn't concentrate. He
rose, his joints reproaching him all the way, and made his way to
Malone's stack, and fingered through the folders until he came to
shoe print analysis. He pretended to study the SICAR copies.

"You okay there?"

Minogue glanced up from the diagrams. Malone was tapping
a biro on his knuckles.

"I think so."

That didn't seem to satisfy Malone.

"No offence, but you look a bit, well I'm not going to say it."

"Go head and say it. 'You look like shite.'"

Malone waited.

"That phone call...? Not that it's any of my business. Wasn't bad news, I hope."

Minogue wondered if Malone noticed that he'd been re-reading the same page.

He waved the folder that he had picked up.

"Is this one going to wake me up?" he asked. "Shoe prints?"

Malone hesitated.

"It's okay," Minogue said. "Relax on protocol for this one. I won't tell on you."

"Okay, boss, on your say-so. That partial on his right temple? The rock did away with anything decent out of that. Can't get a sole pattern, can't get DNA. And the bruising on the body? That's stuck at exclusions. Boots are out. Leather-soled shoes out. A few others out. But nothing on a number for assailants."

He slid back his chair.

"I've been thinking about something else – time of death estimate. The famous eighteen to thirty-six hours."

"You know they can't do miracles with that. What's the issue?"

"I don't have an *issue*, issue. The team ended up leaning more on late afternoon, early evening. It's June, it's nice and bright, there's still hours and hours of daylight left. That's why he's dragged into the bushes. There's people around."

"And the lack of witnesses, or shouting or that?"

"It's tea-time. People are at home. Thing is, Larkin was drinking, right up to when he was done. So says the Lab."

"So who was up there drinking with him?"

Malone closed his eyes and rubbed at them.

"You want Theory A or Theory B...to Z?"

"Go with the alphabet."

"Okay," said Malone, opening his eyes suddenly and gathering himself in the chair. "Here's Theory A: we find holes in the alibis for those fellas at the drop-in. Walshe, and the McArdle guy. When we can do that, we put them in the Park that day, that afternoon. So the situation could start out, there's two there – Larkin, and one of the two. I'm going for McArdle there first. And at a certain stage in proceedings, two becomes three – crazy-man Walshe shows."

"And was this planned ahead of time?"

"Let's say arrangement," Malone replied. "Did McArdle tell Walshe to show up? Don't know. Did he entice Walshe out there, with a yarn about Larkin having something worth robbing – prescription, booze, money? Don't know that either. Or did he just say, by-the-way like, that Larkin and him'd be up there drinking? So Walshe is sitting on this awhile, brooding, building up a head of steam over it."

"How about McArdle just wants Walshe included in a boozing session?"

"Or Walshe put pressure on McArdle to get him in on it," Malone countered.

"All right. A boozing session gets out of hand when Walshe shows up?"

"Right. Walshe, he loses it at the drop of a hat. So, no way is Larkin going to want him around, is he. Especially if what's-his-face, McArdle, has to hold up his end of the bargain, the booze situation, with a bit of you-know-what. Perform certain services."

"Sex, you're talking about, are you?"

In place of a reply, Malone watched the progress of his biro as he let it roll across his knuckles. Minogue found himself staring at it too. Malone let it fall into his palm.

"That's it," he said. "Just how out-of-it is this McArdle anyway?"

"He wasn't the full round of the clock from the start, I believe."

"Which doesn't mean he can't get up to trouble."

Minogue had nothing to offer.

"How hard would it be for McArdle to con an old nun anyway?"

"That I don't know. But you want to go looking at McArdle as capable of murder? Planning one? Actually committing one?"

"Okay, maybe it's pushing things a bit. It's down-and-outs we're dealing with, I know. Maybe they don't even know what they're thinking themselves."

Neither man spoke for several moments. It was Malone who broke the silence.

"Well anyway. I was only thinking of a situation where Larkin was pushing things with McArdle. Larkin had stuff, his booze, a bit of money. He can put the likes of McArdle in a tight spot. Can you see McArdle doing a whinge to somebody about that? To Walshe, say?"

"Easy done, I suppose."

"But not a word to the nun. He'd keep it from her. Sister Immaculata. You think?"

Malone's exaggerated version brought Minogue back to Disciples. Taking charge was Immaculata's default mode. It was in her voice, in her posture even, the cant of her head as she spoke. Nun powers indeed. But had he pushed back hard enough against a reflex of his own, a deference he had brought from childhood? How could he not respect – admire, to be honest – such a selfless woman, a woman who protected outcasts?

"Boss?"

Malone was eyeing him steadily now.

"Are you okay there? I'm getting that ten-mile look of yours."

"No, you're sound. Back to your theory. Inciting Walshe."

"Well I don't know if I said 'incite.' The point I wanted to end on was the Walshe factor. Robbery, booze, jealousy – whatever, if we can find even an hour or two in his alibi...? But Walshe is way too good of a candidate. You know?"

"Push the clock back on the time-of-death estimate, you're saying."

"Yeah. Micro-environmental effects – yeah, I remember my reading. Lividity, that's what, two, three hours? But it can move to four, five hours, right? And Larkin was running to fat too, wasn't he? Plus, it's June, so the temperature thing is going on more. Slowing things, like, the rigor?"

"You want to push events back to when?"

"Late afternoon, say. Walshe shows up, sees whatever Larkin's doing with McArdle and he goes nuts right away. Right-over-the-wall nuts. He has issues with any gay state of affairs, doesn't he, some AIDS thing going on in his head, you were saying?"

Malone paused then, and searched about for something on the table. He picked up his biro again, raised it up close to his face, and studied it.

"So what could have been a scrap, or a beating, it doesn't stop at that, does it."

He flicked his biro up in the air. Catching it seemed to offer him more satisfaction this time.

"Anyway," he said. "Whatever about that, there's Larkin. He knows he hasn't a hope, not a hope in hell. He's not fighting, he's curled up. And there's not much padding, is there? It's our so-called summer. He's not wearing his regulation two or three coats anymore. The kicking goes on, and on. He's in a rage, Walshe. It's that sex thing with him, so he's…"

"In a frenzy."

"That's the word. There's your damage – the hands smashed, forearms. Fingers broken, wrist bones. Comes a point, Larkin's not even trying to cover himself. He's unconscious. That's when you get the kicks in the side, most of them on the left. Cracked ribs, the Adam's apple fractured, broken nose…that torn, or burst kidney. What else?"

"Bleeding in the lungs, 'direct result of high-impact blows to the back.'"

"Okay," Malone said, and he paused. "So Larkin's in a bad way by now. But who knows? Maybe he's going to make it – if he's found then and there. So Walshe, or the other lad, decides there has to be a finisher. So he, or they, find a rock. Larkin's on his side. The rock comes down there on the temple. That's the finisher. The one would have done it, according to the medical. But he does it for three. Three was what the PM settled on, right?"

Minogue didn't want reminding of the photos of Larkin's misshapen skull.

"I'm with you. Go on."

Malone's biro resumed its soaring and falling.

"So now," he went on. "Who's going to move a big hefty fella like Larkin into the bushes? It ain't McArdle, I can tell you. And this rock, what's he going to do with it? Well, he's obviously able to lift it, and to use it, so it's nothing for him to take it away, find a spot, and fire it off the Hill. Are there places up there, maybe you know...?"

"Plenty," said Minogue. "Plenty of drop-offs there, not too far off the path."

"And there's a fair bit of height there to that hill, isn't there?"

"Four, maybe five hundred feet."

"So you throw it, or you roll it, down there, it's going to keep going. Needle in a haystack situation right away. And now, six months later...?"

"What about transfer from the killing, the site, to Walshe? Shoes, clothes...?"

"Throws them out, cleans them – who knows? He's used to scrounging and that."

Malone whisked the biro out of the air. He hadn't even tracked it, Minogue noticed.

"Would have been nice if there were forensics done on his gear right away – Walshe's I'm talking about. Don't you think?"

The raised eyebrow told Minogue enough.

"Is that it for your A Theory so far?" he asked. "Had you maybe thought of a mob situation there? A Clockwork Orange type of event?"

Malone cocked his head before answering, and squinted at a corner of the ceiling.

"Yeah, I'd thought about that. It'd be nice, wouldn't it?"

"Nice, how?"

"You know, videoing with their mobiles. Ever seen any of those happy-slap ones?"

"I thought that fad had had its day a while back."

"Yeah, but remember the one from George's Street last year? The brain damage one, where it got to YouTube for a few hours?"

Minogue could remember. A link had been flying around by email, but the video was gone before anyone got to it. The DPP got a copy however, and even with the ritual plea-bargaining litany about deprived backgrounds, three yobs had gotten serious time.

Malone spoke slowly, one eye narrowed.

"Nah," he said. "It just doesn't feel right. Way to hell up there in a park? I don't see skangers falling out of pubs and then climbing all the way up there. I'm no gom either: a fella I know from the gym works the Southside and he has stories. Stuff the brats out here get up to?"

"How about they knew Larkin was up there, and made the trip up for the purpose, but it got out of hand?"

Malone shrugged.

"Still can't see it. For me, it comes down to leakage. Six months, and there's nothing? Not a sausage. Where's the kid who can't sleep and finally spills to his Ma? Where's the weak link, the one who can't take it anymore, waiting for coppers to knock on his door? So for me right now it's leakage – as in lack of."

"So are we drifting into the wrong-place, wrong-time theory? Happenstance?"

"'Happenstance'? Did you just make that up?"

"Bad luck. Karma. Larkin bumps into someone there. Something as simple as a comment, a look even, could have set it off?"

"It happens," said Malone. "Doesn't it? People are on edge these days. Say, a fella lost his job. Can't pay his mortgage, things are bad at home. So he's out for a walk, just to get away from things. And bang – he loses it, for whatever reason, and takes it out on Larkin."

With that, he let his head back to study another part of the ceiling. A voice, and then laughter, resonated from somewhere downstairs.

"Okay," Minogue said then. "We're in happenstance territory.

Say Larkin sees something, walks in on something. Witness to a crime in progress. Drug deal?"

Malone grimaced.

"I don't know," he said. "It's bit wide for me, I have to say. Who's going up there in the woods for a deal? Some gobdaw buying a few grams for the weekend? Nah. I just don't see it. We're talking about a five-second handover in a doorway here. And if it's a real junkie, is he going to be making his connections all the way up some hill? No way. The call is made, the place is set, the buyer shows. Straight cash, hello, bye-bye."

"I could see him stumbling on a pipe session maybe," Malone went on after a few moments. "But you know, maybe we're making it complicated, too complicated."

"Complicated like...?"

"Why not just a Peeping Tom thing? Any sign of him doing that in the past?"

Minogue shook his head.

"That's not to say it wasn't in his repertoire," he said.

"Okay, yeah, right," said Malone. "Doesn't make much sense. There was rain that day, wasn't there?"

"Yes, there were showers that morning."

"Right," Malone said, with a grunt. "Nearly forgot. It rained the whole shagging summer, didn't it? But let's say Larkin's a flasher then instead. So there he is, waving his mickey around, and doesn't see that the woman is with someone. Her fella goes ape. When this guy cools off, he sees he can't leave Larkin the way he is. So he drags him out of sight, comes back in a bit and brings a rock with him. But he never lets on to the girl friend though."

Malone's frown reappeared.

"Naaah," he said, and he wagged his head side to side. "Like she's never going to cop on that her fella killed Larkin? She can't be that thick. And is she going to keep quiet about it forever?"

"Maybe not forever, forever."

"Okay. We push it out on *CrimeCall* again then, with a decent video of the place?"

"Sooner than later, you're thinking?"

"Why not," Malone replied. "Do a re-enactment of that angle even, like we know about it already. That'd shake her up, and—"

The ringtone was muffled, but Minogue recognized it right away: the Little Richard screech that Malone had played in the pub. Malone drew out his mobile, eyed the screen. The cleft between his eyebrows deepened.

"I'll phone you back," he murmured, and ended the call.

He pocketed the phone gingerly. His face had a clouded, almost plaintive look now.

"Just a couple of minutes...?"

Minogue tried harder to look indifferent.

"Go ahead," Minogue said, and quickly turned away. The door closed behind him.

Chapter 21

The footfalls creaking closer in the hallway had to be Malone's. Minogue had enough time to pretend to be deep in the forensics again.

"Sorry about that. It was sort of important."

Minogue kept his eyes on his file, and turned a page unread.

"Nothing to be sorry about," he said.

He listened as Malone's chair took his weight, heard his small, exhaled *oof*. What had gone on in his mind these few minutes alone must be written all over his face. He had even taken out his mobile, and hovered over Kilmatrtin's number. It had been twenty minutes since Kilmartin's phone call. Twenty minutes only, and already Malone had gotten an alert?

"I sometimes think I should do what you do, 'forget' to switch it on."

Malone's face was flushed. From running up stairs, Minogue wanted to believe.

"But if I don't answer, things go their own way. Pressure from her Da. He wants her to walk. Not up to the altar, away from it."

Minogue half-believed that his own thudding heart could be plainly heard outside his body by now. He took a deep breath, and tried to smile.

"You mind me asking," he said. "That ring-tone on your mobile?"

Malone's face showed his bewilderment.

"My mobile?"

"Kathleen has the same phone, but she can't figure something. I'm no help. Can you...?"

It was harder than Minogue expected to pretend he was paying attention to Malone's instructions. He kicked in a few own-goals about his techie ineptitude: the wrong age, not wanting to be chained to his desk by mobile phone.

"Thanks," he said after the run-through. "I'll be the hero when I show her – another thing while you're at it? How do you dump the call records? She gets caught up in trying to delete stuff."

"Here," said Malone, and held his mobile close again. "Calls are here, right?"

There was no number, just a name: YouKnowWho.

"YouKnowWho? Sorry, I couldn't help noticing."

"Sonia's," said Malone. "Sounds Chinese, yeah? Our little joke. Lame, right?"

"Sonia's parents," Minogue began. He had to clear his throat again. "How's business with them? The restaurant, I mean, with the recession and all?"

"Dunno. It's still open. You mean are the portions getting smaller?"

"No, no. I just wondered, that's all."

Malone's steady look was an audit of something. His eyebrow slid up.

"Looking for another job, are you?"

"But I don't speak Chinese."

"Really," Malone said. "I always wondered about that. But now I know."

"Not like your Chinese though, I'd say. You have to be an expert by now?"

Malone uncrossed his legs.

"Hate to break it to you, boss but I have about ten and half words of Cantonese."

"That's all?"

Minogue shrugged.

"You don't find it's a barrier though, do you?" Minogue asked.

Malone narrowed his eyes.

"Barrier? You mean me and Sonia? No, she doesn't care. The parents are another matter. The Ma came around. But the Da? You know the story already."

"A bit, I suppose."

"Come on, I told you. There'll be no rings on any fingers without his say-so."

"In this day and age? What would it take to persuade him?"

"Me not being a copper. Me being a dentist, or a doctor, or something."

"Tall order. No give in him? He's gotten to know you a bit by now."

Malone let out a breath before replying.

"Sonia's always doing the soft diplomacy bit. Maybe he'll come around if the rest of the family, the uncles and that, get more onside. They have a soft spot for Sonia."

"Big family, the Changs?"

Malone angled his head and let his eyes settle on the maps behind Minogue. His expression slowly shed its frown and gave way to bemusement.

"Now there's a funny question."

"Funny ha-ha?"

Malone's eyes darted back to Minogue.

"No. Funny peculiar."

"Have I put my foot in something?"

"No. But here's what's weird. They asked me that. A few times, actually."

"Who asked you?"

Disguise or not, Malone's sardonic self had returned.

"Come on, boss. You can guess that one easy enough. The Ombudsman crew."

Minogue let the pause last. The quiet settling in the room now made the ticks from the radiator and the muffled voices from downstairs part of the quiet too. He took a discreet, open-mouth breath. Malone began moving his elbows around, and twisting off some stiffness from his shoulders. When he was finished, he looked at the folders.

"Well so much for that," he said, "Where were we anyway before this? Larkin seeing things he shouldn't have...?"

"Tell me something, before we get too keen on that. Who's to say that whatever Larkin might have witnessed was against the law?"

Malone levelled a glazed-eye look at him.

"'Ride on the side'?" he said. "Someone else's hubbie, someone else's wife?"

"People tell me that this sort of thing happens."

"Maybe it was one of them priests," Malone said. "A bishop, even."

Minogue gave him the eye. Malone gave him a mischievous look in return.

"What can I tell you? It's all over the papers, the telly. It stays in the brain somewhere."

Malone's insouciance faded, and his voice took on a reflective tone.

"Okay so maybe it's not funny," he said. "Actually, that stuff's been on my mind this past while. The child abuse report that's coming out? Wondering about Terry, back then."

Minogue watched Malone's hands tighten to fists, then open and flex. It was four years now since Terry Malone had overdosed, five in February.

"Did your young fella do the altar boy thing at all?

Minogue shook his head.

"I didn't either. But Terry did. It was Ma's idea, to settle him down a bit. He was always a bit wild. Reading things wrong, touchy about everything. Picking fights. But he never said anything happened to him when he was an altar boy. Thinking back though, I wondered. The way his life went...? Maybe I should've asked him, kept asking, until he told me."

Sliding back in his chair, his words trailed off. He drew in a breath then, and looked up from his study of his hands.

"But we just don't talk about it. Not a word. I'm not going to push it, I couldn't do it to Ma. She still goes to Mass every single day, even now. But I know she knows, and she knows that I know, that she knows....Anyway."

"'Whatever you say, say nothing.'"

A grim smile came to Malone.

"Yeah," he said. "Yeah, maybe. But you know, we even heard stuff growing up, rumours like. We actually used to laugh about it. Isn't that something? Jesus, if we knew then what we know now...?"

★ ★ ★

Minogue's biro was running out, but he soldiered on, hoping that he had just hit a bad patch on the paper. He had gone back to February in the station's daily log already. He had made notes for only two items so far.

A woman had phoned in several times. She had been 'extremely annoyed' about broken glass, broken bottles actually, on the roadway near Killiney village by the steps into to the park. Her second phone call reported a puncture that had cost her over 40 euro to repair. Could nothing be done about this?

A Mr. Sean Ryan, concerned citizen, had complained of unknown persons – 'young pups' had been his term – puking in the shrubs by his gate. Ryan had saved several tell-tale Rizla packages emptied of their rolling papers. Would the Guards be wanting them as evidence?

Malone shifted a little in his chair, and quietly popped another bubble, regaining the gum without once looking up from his orderly, multi-page piles of pages. He had started in on the mobile carrier records an hour ago, but it had taken him a while to come up with a system. Minogue had watched him subdivide the piles by mast location, and by the smaller zones, the micro-cells. O2 and Vodaphone seemed to have the most traffic.

Malone leaned back over his chair.

"Any give in those phone records yet?" Minogue asked. "Mobiles, I mean?"

"Nah, not so far. But I'm only about halfway. A non-resident out there that showed up in the cell log for a week back then – the mobile was only registering in the cell, like. Some young one girl from Booterstown. She lost her phone out there around that time. The battery died on it eventually, so it's still lying out there somewhere, waiting for the Martians to find it. This young one's a bit of a spacer, according to her Ma. On her fifth mobile. Is that a record out here in Marin County?"

"I have no idea. But I doubt it."

"Are you up on the mobile tracking stuff, by the way?"

"I have the layman's knowledge, plus what I heard around the place, at work."

"So you know this 'Register paging' stuff...?"

"That's the mobile just telling some mast that it's in the area? No actual call?"

"That's it. Anyway. There were four other mobiles with call records that took ages to track. Only one of them was living local to the cell mast out there. They were all belonging to kids who went away over the summer."

"Holidays, work...?"

"Yep. Well them people came up clean eventually, that's my point. It's just that it's interesting to see how they got them. One fella went to the States, he came home in September and they talked to him. Bit of a go-er, this guy, a bit of a disorderly type, but he seems to have turned out okay for the Larkin situation. The fourth one, they got hold of him out there in Oz. They actually got the local coppers to take his statement. He's on a student work thing for six months. But he came through proper too, cleared."

Malone yawned, and readied himself for another stretch.

"Yeah, they done a good job there, I have to say," he said. "Maybe we should send them a fan letter?"

"That might be a first for an NBCI team. They'd frame it, no doubt."

Minogue returned to his reading. Just after his biro seemed to have regained its power, it dried up completely. He eyed his mobile next to his keys on the desk. Kilmartin had laid his egg, and he would wait. He knew well enough to give him time to digest what he had heard.

Malone was forming a new bubble, he noticed. This was Jim Kilmartin's rogue copper? Somebody was playing an elaborate joke on Jim Kilmartin, someone with an agenda to make an iijit of him. All those toes Kilmartin had stepped on over the years, all those eyes he had poked? But spreading rumours about Malone was below the belt: there was malice in it. It wasn't just Kilmartin going to come out of it looking like a thicko, it was Malone's career in the balance. Who would nurse a grudge like that against Kilmartin, or Malone?

He placed the useless biro on the pad, and stared at it.

"Tommy."

Malone turned to him.

"The situation there in Ryan's the other evening."

"What about it?"

"The fella you thumped, well the two fellas. Special Branch, were they?"

Malone hesitated.

"That's what I'm thinking, yeah."

He waited for a follow-up question but Minogue had none. He looked at the window instead, pale and grey now in the afternoon light. It was a month yet to the solstice, and then the slow climb back up to any decent stretch in the evenings.

"It's just the way they are," Malone said. "That crowd. Nobody can breathe without their say-so. You know? They think they run the show. Everything, like."

"Everything?"

Malone scratched at the back of his head.

"Well it goes back to the business with Kelly. Some fellas were saying that we should have had the Branch along with us, or given them notice at least. You know why, right?"

"Because Kelly was grassing on their payroll – as I understand it anyhow."

"Right," said Malone. "But if Kelly was the best they could get, well…"

There was indignation in Malone's voice now.

"Look, boss," he went on. "It's on your mind, I can tell. But believe me, those two bastards were in the pub before I got there. They didn't just happen to be there either. That's all I'm saying. But I just want to move on. You know?"

A moment of chill clarity clutched at Minogue then. Had Kilmartin actually gone off the rails? His mind rebelled immediately: it couldn't be. Kilmartin was holding down his job, he was managing. He seemed to be getting on with things. Yes, he had turned career into a verb, and had skidded into his life-crisis like a juggernaut jackknifing on the motorway. But he was still trying. Still trying to reconcile with Maura, still cracking bad jokes, still pontificating. But surely to God that shrink that Kilmartin was still going to every week would glom onto any signs his patient might be losing it?

Well maybe not. That's what stress did, that's what trauma was, and there were no guarantees, no immunities. Hadn't he seen it at work himself? And it didn't take much to sense that behind the mask, Kilmartin was still full of anger. Anger at his wife, at himself too, for having been fooled. Anger at people he supposed were smirking behind his back. Anger at Garda admin too probably. Anger at life. It was a reflex to want to get back at somebody, or something. Revenge for what though? The mind under stress fled to black and white, angels and devils. It could also transmute anger into envy, shifting to others. Envy toward a Matt Minogue, a man who had a good marriage, one who had moved on? Undermining Malone would be a piece of cake.

"Something bite you there, boss?"

Minogue read suspicion in Malone's stare.

"The place must be getting to me," he managed. "I need a bit of air."

"Musty all right, isn't it. You can sorta feel it too, as well as smell it."

"I tell you," he added, and glanced at his watch. "I'm hitting the sack early tonight. I'm barely able to keep me eyes open here."

Minogue rose and began sliding the file folders together.

"I have an item I'd like to chalk off the to-do list," he said. "Before we go much further here with the paperwork."

Malone watched him place the folders on their edges in the cabinet.

"Up on the Hill," Minogue went on. "The site."

Malone gave a look of mild aversion to the stacks of pages on his desk.

"You think there's anything up there for us still?"

"It's the culchie in me," Monogue replied. "I'd like to see the lie of the land."

"Is it on the way to Sallynoggin?"

"It's not. What has you thinking about Sallynoggin?"

Malone had already begun to gather the folders.

"Oh I just thought maybe we could drop by McCarthy's, or his mother's place, I should say. See if there's anything there that'll tell us more than that he's away in Amsterdam?"

Chapter 22

A short burst of sign language conducted with thumbs and shrugs ended with the decision to take Malone's car. Minogue soon found that he didn't have a clear idea of how to get out of Dalkey and up toward the Park at all. He got them to the bridge over the DART line however, and once by the station and the handful of passengers waiting on the platform behind the fence there, he guessed right about Cunningham Road.

"Will this car of yours get us there and back?"

"What are you saying?" replied Malone. "Nothing the matter with this car. Don't judge it by its looks."

The road climbed quickly. The urge to get Kilmartin out of his head only grew in Minogue. Ludicrous, yes – that was the word he had been scrambling for – but with it came pangs of anger and pity for James Kilmartin. Lost his bearings? So anxious to believe he was still in the loop that he let himself become a target for cruel pranks. Lost his reason? Either way, a dwindling of the man who used to be Jim Kilmartin.

A level section of road soon presented itself, and after a sharp turn, the climb resumed. Minogue forced himself to take note of the hedges and the leaves along the footpaths, the cars in their driveways, the landscaping. Glimpses of Dalkey Hill soon claimed Minogue's attention, sharp in silhouette now against the sky.

"That castle-ly looking thing up there on the Hill…"

Malone paused and tilted his head to listen to the engine's drone.

"What's it called again?"

"It has different names, depending on how far back you go."

"How about today?"

"Fair enough. The Telegraph Building."

"Telegraph? They're ancient."

"Farther back it was the Semaphore Building."

"They're something to do with ships. Flags, like?"

"That's it. The place was built to watch for Boney. Same as the Martello towers."

"Boney. You mean Napoleon?"

"None other. Our would-be liberator."

"Interesting," said Malone, meaning it wasn't. He braked and drew closer to the footpath for a delivery lorry.

"So Larkin kept coming here because of stuff like that, look-out stuff?"

"Maybe."

Minogue imagined Larkin up on the Hill, braced Moses-style against the wind, with robes flapping about him. His hand would be over his brow, surveying the sea's horizon. A ship would appear, and his eyes could burn with resolve. Grabbing his flags, he'd begin the stiff, slashing motions to telegraph the alarm. The French? Maybe he should be picturing Larkin going further back, with the Vikings. It'd be the same stern vigilance on this headland, but lighting a bonfire instead, and scanning the hilltops down the coast for answering fires. Saving his country.

"It's like he had a time machine or something," said Malone. "He had his own take on history anyway, didn't he?"

Minogue found refuge in vagueness.

"Who knows? Who knows what he was thinking?"

"But he'd have to be making it up. Dalkey's no big deal, right?"

"Actually it was. It was the port of Dublin for a long time."

"Dublin? Dublin city? No way."

"The Liffey was useless until they built the Bull Wall."

"All the stuff coming in off the boats came here first? People even, armies?"

"So it is written."

Malone scratched the crown of his head with his baby finger.

"So maybe Larkin really knew his onions then, like this really was the place to be then for all his imaginary friends and stuff."

The words irked Minogue.

"So do you like the diesel?" he asked Malone.

"This isn't a diesel. Why would you think that?"

"Smells like one. You're burning something you're not supposed to burn."

"Like what?"

"Bridges, maybe. Oil actually, it smells like. Seals, gaskets. Who knows?"

Malone's change into third gear was sloppy.

"This doesn't feel right," he muttered. "We're going away from the Hill here."

"The road turns. You'll be making a left up into the car park."

Malone made low murmured comments as he piloted up the curving cement road to the car park: "Weird... Bit of a jungle here... Are we still in Dublin here, or what?"

Minogue eyed the yellowing expanses of wild grass difting by the car. The woods approached closer and soon filled the windscreen. Three parked cars – no, four, one well back. Straggling lines of leaves led to the edges of the woods

Malone had trouble getting his door fully closed. Minogue was content to wait and take in the deeper woods that waited ahead. More than the resinous scent in the air, the quiet here had caught his notice right away, as though it had come out to meet him and to relieve him of his thoughts.

They made their way toward the path that led through the woods, passing an ashtray dump and the inevitable McDonalds' bag, already sodden and separating. Minogue spotted moss in the shelter of the low concrete curbs. Underfoot, the gum-speckled tarmacadam had a greasy feel to it.

"Beech," he said to Malone.

"Where? Up here? Sure we're hundreds of feet up, aren't we?"

"Beech tree. And that one there is oak – and there. A lot of pine too."

The woods here sheltered them from the seaboard side of the hill. Their upper branches barely stirred. Soon, Minogue stopped and opened the copy he'd made of the map, turning it to match the short section of the path ahead. Drifts of spotted, fraying leaves lay everywhere now.

"I'm going to buy that SatNav and just get it over with," Malone said. "Bite the bullet. I mean, how long was Tetra in the works? Can't be waiting forever."

Minogue couldn't remember any exact number of years since the Tetra announcement, that finally, the glories of digital radio were coming to the Guards. There'd be no more black spots, no more eavesdropping, no more Guards having to use their personal mobiles. Heaven entirely.

"Seven hundred years," he said. He angled his map again to match the path ahead. "I might be off by a few years though."

He folded the paper, slid it into the inside pocket of his coat and gestured toward the path. Malone stepped aside to let him take the lead.

"Never knew about this place," Malone said. "It's like, all of a sudden you're somewhere else. The jungle, I don't know. But it's too quiet here."

"Two bends," Minogue said. "Then a stone bench, and we get off the path."

Between stretches of pathway that alternated between gravel and clay, they met concrete steps. Minogue took his time, wary of their greasy sheen and the wet, spongy leaves that clung to them. He slowed and stopped by pieces of broken glass. Turning a bigger piece over with the toe of his shoe, he found it was still held together by a label.

"Vodka," said Malone. "Classy."

Minogue took in the wrappers from bars of chocolate, the barely legible ones from ice cream and bags of crisps, the ubiquitous pieces of tin foil and cigarette butts. When he reached the seat, he took out his camera.

"Somebody made that," Malone said. "Put rocks together like that. Right?"

"Looks like it."

He put the flash on Fill and moving around the stones, he took a half-dozen shots. Crouching on his hunkers, he took a close-up of the marks.

"Seeing if they match the ones they took back in June?"

"That's it, yes."

"'Marto.' 'Marto loves Sarah.' 'Emma is a slapper'? Any Emma I know?"

They moved on, slower. Patches of grass were rare here under the canopy. There had been nothing carved into the tree trunks so far anyway. Ecologically minded vandals, Minogue mused.

Malone was first to spot where to turn off.

"Them three bushes," he said. "Close together?"

Minogue took out his map again. He held a finger on the contour line, and looked at the branches, and listened. He couldn't decide if the soughing was the wind, or the sea.

"Are we close to a cliff?" Malone asked. "Be sort of nice to know."

"We're right on this line here."

He pivoted to look across at a small clearing.

"According to this," he went on, "there's a drop-off behind those scruffy-looking bushes there. We go right here though. It's a couple of hundred yards yet."

The air was definitely cooler here, and more damp, and the dank, biotic smell of decay had lifted. Minogue's shoes gleamed from his passage through the scutch grass. Any moment now, he was sure, the wet would make itself known through the leather.

"It's a big rock we're on," Malone said.

"Keep right, or we'll be walking off the side of it."

The ground began to tilt. After a length of smooth, exposed granite, a soft humus of needles took over underfoot. The two men moved awkwardly now, planting their steps on the edges of their soles.

"No track that I see," he heard Malone say ahead. "You see one?"

Minogue paused, and listening to the thrum in his ears, looked up at a patch of sky above the pines. It seemed closer than back in the town. He could see no contours, no movement in the cloud clover.

"It *is* the sea I'm hearing," Malone said.

"It's not just the wind, or the trees. Yeah, I can hear it for sure."

"We're looking for a few small conifers. Larkin's place is – was – twenty feet to the side of them."

Malone shifted his stance and looked around. Minogue took his time with his own survey, sorting through the tangle. Gorse bushes, their withered spines clogged with tiny droplets, edged in just beyond the branches. Some clumps of heather held out there too, scouts for the heather and gorse that had taken over the seaboard side of the hill.

"I think I see it," Malone said. "Well I see clay and stuff anyway. Something that's been dug up, or turned over."

Minogue backed carefully into the thinly needled branches of the pines. Taking up a spot beside Malone, he let his gaze wander the site – the former site. The earth here was a different colour, and already hard-packed. No bits of torn-off tape, no stakes. No footprints, no litter. None of the pieces of timber that Larkin had brought here to build his cave. No sign in the wide world that Padraig Larkin had ever been here.

He still couldn't get back far enough to get the picture he wanted. Tripod or not then, maybe he'd try one of those panorama stitches later at home.

The flashes put a dull, moist shine on the clay. He switched it off and tried again, but the contrast went murky on him. Back to the flash.

"Just like they said."

Malone's solemn tone told him that maybe he too had fallen under the spell of the place. He cupped his hand as best he could over the display for Playback.

"Said what."

"They filled it in, collapsed it. Their 'safety hazard.'"

Minogue leaned back more against the branches to get another shot.

"He picked his spot well enough," Malone went on. "It's rocky everywhere else. So he knew the place, didn't he."

With that, he scratched his head and turned to take in the place again.

Minogue tried to recall from the file photos more of what the place had looked like before. That makeshift door, the one that held the sods and bits of foliage that Larkin could pull closed behind him, was probably what had drawn Donegan's comparison with Vietnam.

"I can see it being a not-bad hideout all right," said Malone. "In the summer anyway. With all this stuff growing in?"

Yet the place was saying nothing to Minogue, nothing beyond an ominous feeling that something or somebody had been swallowed up here. Had vanished. As close as they might be map-wise to the Vico Road's millionaire homes hundreds of feet below, it felt hemmed in here, remote. Hovering somewhere in his thoughts was a feeling that this place here was like a grave.

He pocketed his camera and took out the map again.

"We'll go on a bit more. He hardly came and went by the same path every time."

They had a choice of taking a steep, almost vertical scramble up through the gorse, or stumbling over the sharply curving ledges hereabouts, and breaking their necks.

Malone led. He soon needed to use his hands at times.

"Watch yourself there," he said to Minogue, bracing himself after a slide, and trying to wipe his hands on an outcropping. "How can there be a place like this, what a few miles from the city centre? Jaysus, they could make a Survivor thing up here."

"Larkin picked the place for a reason."

Malone wasn't sure even when he gained the path that it was path at all. He tried picking mud from the knee of his trousers. Minogue was breathing hard when he made it up at last to the pathway. There he stood, listening to his blood thumping in his head, waiting for the spasms in his chest to slow.

"What's the word, boss?"

Even Malone was breathing heavily. The difference was, he seemed to be enjoying himself.

"Well I'm not much wiser so far," Minogue said and paused.

"We heading over to the actual site now?"

Minogue eschewed talk for a nod, and a gesture of his arm up the pathway. He focused on breathing deeper, and looked at his shoes. Pretty saturated-looking, but he hadn't felt any wet coming in yet. He took out the camera and scrolled through what he had taken so far. Malone sidled over.

"Eight out of ten for weirdness back there," Malone said. "A fella living – actually living – in a hole in the ground here, in a park that doesn't look like a park but a bit of mountains or something, all a few miles from the middle of Dublin. Now that's got be major weirdness. Wait, forget that eight – give it a nine. You think?"

"I was shooting for eleven myself."

Chapter 23

Minogue wiggled his toes again. A heater wouldn't make much headway through wet shoes to even wetter socks. "What's the story here in this part of the world," Malone said. "This Sallynoggin place. A bit rough, is it?"

"Well there's Sallynoggin...and then there's Sallynoggin."

Malone leaned forward again over the steering wheel, weaving his head from side to side to see around the driver's side pillar.

"Whatever that means," he said.

"It's quietened down a lot from the way it was."

Malone was watching the divagations of the van ahead.

They passed the church, one that Minogue had passed a hundred times before, and ignored. Our Lady of Victories? Why hadn't he known its name before?

There were abundant signs of the Tiger years on the houses and terraces here. The usual PVC windows and glass porches went by the car, driveways newly cemented, curly ironwork gates. Satellite dishes perched on most.

Malone turned onto Connolly Close at last, the road where was to be found JJ McCarthy's aged and probably long-suffering mother. A recently waxed car sitting behind elaborate gates caught Minogue's eye.

"That Audi is new," he couldn't help saying.

"What, new Audis aren't allowed on a Council estate? Oh, I get it now. You think it has to be a robbed one."

Minogue began to spot house numbers, and he looked ahead to guess which might be the McCarthy's. Malone had already touched the brakes.

"That one," he said.

McCarthy's house was the only one on this road that had no signs of a makeover. With its pebbledash weathered a half century now, it looked almost organic. High up by the gutters Minogue saw tell-tale signs of damp. The garden was long grass beaten down, dying back in ragged clumps in front of a gapped escallonia hedge that rose to the height of the windowsills. There were faded curtains drawn upstairs and down on the old metal window frames, the putty had long ago rebelled against a greenish paint.

Minogue stepped out, and he waited for Malone to negotiate with his door. If cursing worked, he reflected, then the door would have worked flawlessly.

"You talk," he said when Malone joined him by the gate. "She's old, remember. So give her something nice to talk about."

"What, we're not coppers here?"

"We are, but we're more his friends. He's helping us out. And because he's such a very helpful fella, and so smart, we need his help."

"Okay. But what if she has all her marbles, and susses our game here?"

"Work around it."

Minogue heard no sound from the doorbell. He lifted the knocker over the letterbox and let it drop several times. Malone gestured toward the last of high grass still lining the block wall with the neighbours where a motorbike, wheel-less, saddle-less and tank-less, had shed the better part of the builder's poly sheet that had been tied over it.

A face appeared then in the window of the neighbouring home. Through the reflection, Minogue could make out that it was an old man. Looking more irritated than curious, he shook his head and he withdrew from the window. Minogue was lifting the knocker again when the same neighbour's porch door opened.

The old man was short and wide, with a full head of wiry hair. For a moment, Minogue thought that the clear plastic tubes leading from his nostrils was a runny nose. An age-enlarged nose and matching ears were not enough of a draw to keep his eye from straying to the wattles galore that flowered under the chin. The old man wheezed before he spoke.

"They've been and gone already."

"Who has?"

"Who do you think?" He paused to attend to the tubing. "Your crowd, in uniform. Proper Guards."

"Here?"

"Yeah, here. And that was only the start of it."

A look of pained exasperation came to him and again he paused.

"Well we're looking for Mrs. McCarthy," Minogue said.

"Is that a fact now."

"Who should we be looking for then?" Malone said. "According to you?"

It might have been a snort Minogue heard from the old man. The wattles rearranged themselves.

"Who do you think you're codding there, head-the-ball?"

"Clearly not you," Minogue said, and smiled.

A rusty laugh erupted from the old man.

"You don't talk to one another, your crowd. Detectives and normal Guards?"

"So we're detectives," Malone said. "Are we."

"Well he is. You, I'm not so sure. Maybe you're a sidekick of Joey's."

"Joey?"

"Joey McCarthy. Are you forgetting already?"

"We're both Guards," Minogue said. "What's after happening here?"

"Guards, you say. And you're asking me?"

Minogue latched a resolutely dull stare on the old man's forehead.

"Well what's after happening is that Catherine had to be taken to the hospital."

Minogue watched the old man take another deep, considered breath.

"You said Guards though."

"You'd think in this day and age that Guards would have some cop-on coming out here with that kind of news to an old woman on her own. Bring a doctor or somebody?"

The old man's face had gone from pink to a shade closer to maroon.

"Look, this isn't the best for me, standing out here. I'm going to sit down."

"Here," Malone said. "Let me give you a hand."

The old man threw him a glare. His chest rose and fell in slow, shallow tremors.

"Me? A hand? Youse think that I'm the one needs help here?"

★ ★ ★

"Now I have to say, in the interests of accuracy, he was a burden on his mother. A real burden. Mightn't be nice to say it, but it wouldn't be right that people might not know that. No beating around the bush with me. You see?"

Minogue looked up from where his mobile phone lay on the table. Larry Higgins – 'Higgsy in the old days' – shifted in his chair and pointed toward Malone's notebook.

"Aren't you going to write that down?"

"Write what down."

"'Burden on his mother.' That should be noted – no disrespect to anyone."

"Time enough," said Minogue. "We're just chatting."

This didn't seem to satisfy the retired forty-one-year employee of Brennan's Bread. Forty one years and seven months and just under two weeks, in actual fact. Numbers were Higgins' pride. He and his deceased wife Mary had been the eighteenth family into this estate when it had been built. April 27th, 1956. Minogue couldn't decide if it was the trademark Dublin smugness he was hearing, or the more general vanity of the aged.

He took his opening anyway.

"You have a powerful memory there. Massive entirely."

"Well so people tell me."

Higgins leaned forward a little.

"And you notice there's no talk from me about search warrants or the like," he said. "And me sitting here in me own kitchen with two detectives? I know my rights, but I don't hold with obstructing the Guards. No, I'm not one of those types of people."

"Very helpful," Minogue felt he should say. "Very refreshing too."

"Not *too* helpful," said Higgins. "I'm no friend of the Guards, now. I seen stuff."

"Next door you mean?"

"Aren't you the cute one, slipping in questions like that?"

Higgins was enjoying himself. Minogue masked his quick survey of the kitchen with a rub at his forehead. Spick and span, everything lined up square, the tang of cleaner in the air. A man of firm, even rigid habits. A man short of company too.

"So, like I was saying there, er. In the interests of poor old Catherine next door, she deserves better, that's my point. Much better."

"Is she there on her own?"

"Joey does be there, I can't tell when though. In and out of the place."

"Husband, I was wondering."

Higgins shook his head.

"Gone these years, Bobby. And I have to tell you, that husband of hers wasn't what he let on to be when they started out here. The drink, you see."

Minogue looked down at his mobile again, willing it to ring.

"The drink is a curse. Ruined more families than – Anyway: back to Joey. Listen to me, I never heard of this 'JJ' thing at all. It was always Joey, and Joey was the one and only. After the sister died, that is. You know what are genetics?"

"I have a layman's grasp. Very lay."

"Anyway. The father, Bobby, Bobby Mac. They came in '64, the McCarthys. They're not Dun Laoghaire or any of that, they were country people. A family the name of Nolan had to leave, there was trouble, and they went to England, so Catherine and Bobby were next in line. Little Aileen too, she only had a few years here before it took her. I remember her to this day. Didn't I hold her in my arms a few times? A head of hair so fair it was white. But thin, very very thin, yes. The cystic fibrosis back then, they didn't have much going for that..."

Higgins' breathing had grown raspy. Minogue exchanged a glance with Malone.

"Larry," he said in the lull. "We don't want you to be straining yourself now."

"...I knew from day one, I says to Mary, I says 'Mary, that Joey lad is going to be a handful.' I said that, I did. And wasn't I right in the end?"

"Sounds like you kept track of him," Malone said.

"Who, me?" Higgins' surprise was bogus.

"Well did you?"

"The answer to that is, 'Why are there two Guards sitting here?'"

"There were comings and goings, I suppose," Minogue tried.

"That says it all right – 'comings and goings.' Bobby, the poor divil he was run over by a bus on account of...well I'm not going to say it, am I."

Higgins inclined a little toward Minogue, and fixed a gimlet eye on him.

"Fact is, poor Bobby had no hold on the young fella, on Joey. We used to hear Joey and Bobby going at it years ago. Bobby used to do odd jobs, for the parish and that."

"The church back the road there?"

"That's the one. They gave him things to do, handy-man stuff. But sure he'd go on a tear, wouldn't show up, and this and that. This is before there was any help for families, well like these days. The parish did a lot in them days. People don't know that now, do they. They just hear things and they want to string them up. Don't they?"

"Not me," Minogue said. My wife might though, he added within.

"Well now. The only one Joey'd listen to was his mother, Catherine. And even then, it wasn't the best. But I'll tell you one thing, it was because of her that he never ended up in jail. That always amazed me. Always. The things he would get up to?"

"What things?"

"Joey was never into the aggro. You know aggro? I suppose you do. Joey didn't have it in him really. Bit of a softie, tell you the truth. So he went for the other stuff."

"The...?"

"Ah you know. The marry-you-anna. That sort of thing, and worse. The hash. And then, didn't Joey get done. Caught. Catherine told me one day, God she was very upset. You see, she tried her best to get Joey out of the situation. It was easy enough to walk out your front door here and do the gang thing back then – and this is before the real gang thing got started at all. Can you imagine? All we were worried about back then, with our young lads especially, was they'd be with a crowd who was robbing houses, or cars, or getting into fights and that. But now?"

Minogue offered a sage nod. Higgins stared at the tabletop, took several breaths.

"You'd be shot dead for looking at someone the wrong way nowadays," he went on. "Am I right, or am I right?"

"It can happen. If you're involved in that kind of life."

"Sure the Guards have to carry guns now, isn't that right?"

"Some do. You were saying that Joey was not much for the fighting and that."

"His mother, that's what I'm telling you. Catherine. She used to be signing him up for this and that. Always going to the teachers, and the parish priest and the youth club – everything. She knew what she was up against. Never interested in the sports or anything, Joey. Liked to fiddle with things, motorbikes like, or a bit of stuff with cars. God, sure the place was full of bits of things. The coal shed out the back there? Full of old scrap, and wheels and bits of bikes. But he'd never stay long at the one thing."

"Was he always living there next door?"

"Are you joking me? You know how old Joey is, or was, I should be saying? Sure he was gone for years. Even went to

England and worked a bit there. He liked someplace, what do you call it in Holland – Amsterdam, yes. But as I understand it, that was Joey's 'job,' like. Where you could get hold of drugs and that. Then I seem to remember him doing odd jobs as a sign painter, then bits to do with the computers. A few years ago, didn't he get hold of himself a bit. Matured, I suppose. Or maybe he got a fright? Next thing you know is, Catherine lets drop that he's studying. 'Joey's going to college,' she says one day. Very proud of him she was. Well I could have dropped there and then."

"'College'?"

"Well that's the thing, you see. You went along with what Catherine said. I mean to say, knowing all she'd been through? Losing her little girl like that, that hubby of hers...? You'd be inclined to let her think what she liked. That's my point. You go along with them old people, let them boss you a bit. Sure what harm can it do?"

Minogue thought of Immaculata, and his mood soured a little.

"Not saying you'd believe her now," Higgins qualified. "But you did the right thing by Catherine. Very proud. Came from good stock I believe, fairly well-to-do somewhere. Out in the West of Ireland, yes. Fell for Bobby, she did, but her family wasn't keen on him at all, at all. So after Bobby died, what did she have? Nothing. So she had to do things she'd never expected. Worked in Freddy's there on the seafront, selling ice cream. Worked in a newsagent for years – and then I found out she worked as a maid. A maid, in this day and age? That was when Joey was still a young fella. Housecleaning she did too, up in one of the big houses. She never let on she did it."

"People have their pride, I suppose."

"Too true there, er. Too true. She did it all for Joey too. It wasn't just the money. It was she was trying to show him another way of life I suppose. To introduce him to something outside of where his mates around the place here were heading."

He paused then and looked blankly at the windowsill. Maybe the souvenir salt-and-pepper set from Tenerife there had information he needed.

"Anyway," he said then, vaguely. "This 'college' thing Joey done there a few years ago, it was really more of kind of job-training thing. When the money came to Ireland, the Tiger and all that, there was money for stuff like that. The whole 'make work' thing. Training, he did, with computers. He came back to live with the mother, you see, and that settled him enough to go to school every day."

"How far back was that?"

Higgins looked over at the souvenir salt-and-pepper shakers.

"Three, fours years back, or so. I heard he got a job out of it, graphic something-or-other. But then he had something to do with a newspaper thing. But I don't know if he ever got clear of the old carry-on he was into, like I said to you, the shady stuff."

A look of distaste began to spread over his face.

"Are you all right?" Minogue asked.

"Bloody good question. Maybe I'm not. Maybe I'm talking too much."

"No harm done, I say."

Higgins gave him a baleful look.

"Says you," he said.

Minogue's mobile whirred and began a skittering rotation on the table. It was numbers only, a Dublin number. He got up.

"I'll be out the side of the house," he said.

Higgins shrugged and turned to Malone, giving him a long, frowning appraisal. Malone was the next candidate for Larry Higgins to set to rights. Sure enough, pulling the door behind him, Minogue heard Higgins open a new front with a question, a question that was not a question, about *CrimeCall*.

Chapter 24

The pebbledash wall came through Minogue's coat sharper than he had expected. He pushed off from it, and tried again to ignore his wet socks. He had been switched to one Garda Byrne. A slow-talking passive-aggressive, Byrne was doing a fine job of ladling out just enough of his irritation at having to respond to questions for which he had no answers. Yes, Clontarf Garda station had called them first thing this morning and asked them do that next-of-kin call at that address. The identification of the remains had been made yesterday. The body had been found the day before.

"What's the estimate again?"

"'Several weeks,' it says here...hold on a sec. No, that's all he told us."

"That's it?"

"Well it's not on the system here," Byrne said, with a suspicious ease. "It's just a note I made to give the basics to the lads who went out on the next of kin."

"And there's nothing there on cause of death?"

"'Suspicious circumstances' is all he gave me."

Minogue let a few seconds pass.

"You want the number for Clontarf station?"

"Please. But where did 'appears to be trauma to the head' come from?"

"Ah...well: that was just him saying it looked like that on the report. There are injuries, he said."

Minogue pushed his notebook onto the wall with the heel of his hand as he wrote down the phone number. The contact at Clontarf Garda station gloried in the name of Garda Sergeant Malachy Muldowney. He'd phone Muldowney from the road.

Larry Higgins seemed to have become re-energized. He had moved on from a cross-examination of Malone on Garda patrolling – 'we never see a patrol car here, did you know that?' – and on to social revolution.

"It's true," he said as Minogue took his seat again and signaled Malone his desire to be gone from here. "It goes in a circle. Lookit, when was the General Strike?"

"What General Strike?" Malone asked.

"1913," Minogue said.

A mistake, he knew. Higgins' eyes grew big. The warning voice within was loud and clear to Minogue: just what they needed, this geezer having some kind of collapse.

"A hundred years since that, and look at us. The same thing over again – you're on the inside or you're on the outside. You have everything, or you have nothing. The law only protects the rich – the church too, of course. All in cahoots, you know?"

Higgins' chest rose and fell steadily as he levered himself upright.

"But you know all this too," he said then. "You Guards, right? The thing is, you can't say it, can you. It's time to do something, I say, something serious. Where's our Jim Larkin nowadays? Time for people to stand up. Something's got to give here."

"You sound like a man with a plan," said Malone, rising from the table.

Higgins eyed Malone and then Minogue, and made a thin, mirthless smile.

"I'd only tell that in confession, wouldn't I. Just me and the priest."

"Divine intervention you're looking for too, are you?"

"Like hell, I would. And if you believe that, you'd believe anything. I haven't put a foot inside a church door in fifty year – only for weddings and funerals, I have to say. Baptisms too, of course. I was on to them years ago. A lot of people were. But nobody listened, did they? And nobody did anything."

He paused to swallow, or to breathe. Minogue gave Malone the nod to get moving.

"Nobody did what needed doing," Higgins said. "You know what I mean?"

"I'm not sure," Minogue managed. "Whatever that might be, now."

"Really? Well if you, the Guards, if you have to ask, then what does that say?"

Minogue was more than willing to allow Larry Higgins his victory. It was familiar ground this, the old Dublin story, the old Irish story probably: the man-who-isn't-codded had shown up the man-who-had-been-codded, a.k.a. the man-who-thought-he-knew-better-than-the-ordinary-man-in-the-street.

He was willing to bet that Higgins wanted to slow them down on their way through the hall so they could take in the photos en route. A wedding day, complete with teddy-boy looks: the freshly minted Mr. and Mrs. Larry Higgins. She was all too easy a match for the photo of the middle-aged woman in the next picture, happy-looking, red faced, proud. The poem beneath was memorial card verse. Still, he read it.

> *I am so happy here in Heaven, dear ones,*
> *Oh, so happy and so bright.*
> *There is perfect joy and beauty,*
> *In this everlasting light.*

"That's her, all right," he heard Higgins say. "You are detectives after all."

Minogue glanced at him. There was no smirk.

"Mass every day," said Higgins. "Yes, that was Mary. And we got on great, every day – every day. I went my way, she went hers. That church business was never an issue. I was reared on Jim Larkin, he was my bishop. Mary was more old style. Never a cross word between us all the same. Can you believe that?"

"I'm glad to hear it" was all Minogue could offer.

That's how they left Higgins, well-pleased that he had demonstrated that he was nobody's fool, and lonesome.

He called to them from the doorway.

"You'll sort that with them then, right? Tell them to do the next call different. Bring a nurse or somebody with them? It's only common sense."

Minogue leaned forward in his seat while Malone reversed, and took in the McCarthy home again as it slid by.

"Thinking of a little house-tour there, are you," Malone said.

"Matter of fact I was. But not with Larry fecking know-it-all Higgins staring through the window at us. So head to Dalkey. Meanwhile I'll see if I can get hold to get this fella in Clontarf. Muldowney. Get more detail about McCarthy, if I can."

They were soon entering the roundabout and leaning into the curve that would lead them off toward Dalkey.

"Still on hold?"

Minogue felt no urge to answer Malone's question. He continued his study of the houses they were passing. Working-class Sallynoggin had vanished the moment they had come out of the roundabout onto Glenageary Road.

"McCarthy got on somebody's wrong side," Malone said. "Drugs. You think?"

"Well, there's history there, isn't there. Can't ignore that."

"Be interesting to find out where he went in, in the first place. The water, I'm saying – wait, what do I take after this next roundabout?"

"Go through there, the left of those places, the Towers. Barnhill Road. And be ready to take a right turn. It'll come soon enough too."

A rubbing sound came from the front of Malone's car as he steered into the curve. Minogue switched to speakerphone, and rested his mobile on his open palm.

"Won't be easy," said Malone. "Will it?"

Minogue looked across at him.

"Figuring out where he went in," he added, cocking his head to listen to the car as it straightened again. "That bloke in the hit and run last year, remember? Down the Quays...? He ended up on Bull Island too. Took a while, but that's where he ended up. They said he was probably floated around the Bay for a week, and then back in. Jaysus."

Minogue raised his hand and held it there, feeling the weight of the mobile. The magic spell he'd imagined, summoning a voice on the other end, wasn't working.

"When did McCarthy got the boot at that newspaper?"

"Last month, give or take."

A small piece of Dalkey Hill slid into view. Malone was hesitating.

"Over there," he told him. "Go that Barnhill Road over there after the curve."

The speaker tickled in his palm. He switched back and brought it to his ear. After the introductions, he gave Muldowney – 'call me Mal' – the minimum to go on. Muldowney seemed to expect more, however.

"Dalkey," he said. "But it's Dun Laoghaire station for the family, isn't it?"

"I was just on the phone to them. McCarthy's name shows on this case we're looking at here. He's peripheral, but we're doing review. Tell me, do you think maybe McCarthy was put into the water, in your part of the world there?"

Muldowney's tone told Minogue that he had been expecting the question.

"The way I was told," he said, "is that everything turns up on Bull Island. The tides, the time of the year?"

"Well McCarthy's in the system, I understand."

"That he is."

"What's out your way for a man with certain wants in the line of drugs, say?"

Muldowney made little effort to dress up the irony in his voice.

"Well that'd be for the Drug Squad team here, they'd be the ones to know."

The tone was burning through another layer of Minogue's patience.

"I'm out on the road," he said. "So I don't know much about McCarthy on the system. Would you mind...? The last entry for him, was it recent?"

"Seven years ago."

The forebearing tone again. Maybe there something in the air out in Clontarf?

"But what does that say these days," Muldowney went on. "Maybe he figured out how to stay under the radar."

"There's always that, I suppose."

He let the pause go on.

"Tell me something," said Muldowney then. "Are you anything to the fella used to be in the Murder Squad there?"

"The same one. I still get the migraines."

He heard a low, insincere chuckle from Muldowney.

"I know it's early days now," he said to him. "But have you anything you could offer on him yet? Anything at all?"

"I wish I could. This one could shape up to be a migraine style situation too."

"Slim to none then, so far?"

"You said it. We'll see what turns up with the science, won't we."

It was a talent that Minogue could admire in the abstract, this tacking close to the shore of open sarcasm. He imagined Muldowney for a moment then, muttering to someone in the station after he would end the call. *Junkie washes up half-eaten on the sand there at Bull Island, the middle of Dublin fecking Bay, and bejases someone call us the same day, thinks he can get chapter and verse all the way up to courtroom verdict...?*

"Discovery was the day before yesterday, I heard?"

"It was. The proverbial man walking his proverbial dog."

"Grim, the condition of the remains?"

"As grim as you'd want. Features were not intact."

"And were there marks on him? 'Signs of trauma,' I was hearing."

"Well it looks like he was clobbered all right, right across the forehead. A long mark gone black, one of the lads said. Even with the rest of the, er, effects, you'd see it. So if I were a betting man – which I'm not – I'd be expecting lungs full of the old H2O."

Minogue had been thinking about the long grey strand that made up the Bull. It'd be windy, cold as hell, with the white Bureau tent flapping and straining to be free.

"And no ID on him?"

"Not a flitter."

"Personal effects? Money, keys...?"

"None listed here. You could to add robbery to the deck, if that's to your liking."

"How did you get to the final ID on him, you mind me asking?"

"Well we put him into Missing Persons, his X-rays and all. They can be quick – if there are records waiting there for persons we throw at them. Not McCarthy though, he wasn't even on their register."

Muldowney's voice had taken on a slight sing-song note, as though he were explaining complex matters to a child.

"But they were able to lift two prints off him, two that were close to fifties. That got the ball rolling. Ident threw twenty-seven at us for those partials. So down the list we went, made our contacts, and came down to McCarthy and one other one. Thing is, Ident was pointing at McCarthy for us as the likely. But it can't be 99.9 percent, can it. We finally got hold of the other fella, in England now, and that was that. McCarthy went to the 100 percent. We'd gone the PPS route for an address on McCarthy already, but it was a dud. So we set up the next-of-kin contact."

"Who's at that PPS address?"

"Ah well – there hangs a tale. McCarthy hadn't been at the listed address for a long time. So we got hold of his employer – his former employer, I should say. A newspaper place? I got a bit out of him chatting. According to them, McCarthy walked. He hadn't actually gotten the sack. 'Well could he have walked back in and sat down and kept working then?' That when he pulled the curtains on me. 'Oh now that's a hypothetical, and in the interests of confidentiality." Blah blah blah. I hadn't told them at this stage, that McCarthy was in a drawer over at the morgue."

"No partner?"

"Haven't found one yet anyway. One'll turn up eventually, I suppose."

"Wasn't there talk of him going to Amsterdam?"

"There was. That came from them there at the newspaper. So, I finally let the boss there in on the reason for the call. It fairly shook them, I can tell you. So he opened up a tiny bit again. Now this is all conversation, right? I'm only going from notes – I haven't even entered them up on the system yet. Okay?"

"That's my life in a nutshell," said Minogue. "But whatever you can do..."

"It turns out the last they heard of McCarthy was a phone call, some travel agent wanting to talk to him about a flight he'd booked. Asking him to call them back 'in regards to a payment issue.'"

"Travel agent? Doesn't everyone under the age of ninety book online these days?"

"You're asking me? The girl, the office one there, she thought nothing of it. She just passed it on to the boss. But he didn't try to contact McCarthy. McCarthy had gotten touchy the last while, he said. Hard to approach. Letting things slide, making demands, doing no-shows even. Wondered if he had money troubles, or 'issues.'"

"Issues. That covers a multitude. Issues was code for...?"

Another fake chuckle from Muldowney.

"Oh I asked him straight out. Drug problem you mean, says I. Backed off again. 'Oh well we need to consider whether this is proper, with confidentiality and...'"

"You had another address for him by this stage though?"

"Well that's the thing," said Muldowney. "He seems to have been living out with his Ma. McCarthy worked off his mobile a lot, picked up his pay at the office."

"But no mobile to be had, at all?"

"Right. But we've started looking for one. He had a contract, but it was cut off a while ago. Money troubles again? He went the PrePay route since, and we got the number from the newspaper crowd there. We put in the requisition with Vodaphone."

"On the ball there, big-time."

Muldowney's chuckle was less insincere this time.

"Do you think," he said. "Well we'll see. Early days yet."

"You mind me asking now," Muldowney said then. "Here's a question for you. Do you miss the old days at all?"

"Piking hay back on the farm, et cetera?"

"No, no," Muldowney replied quickly, his impatience revealing itself at last. "The whole Murder Squad thing I mean."

"Hard to say. Hard to say."

He heard Muldowney swallow a long yawn.

"I'm much obliged," he said to him.

"Nothing to it. You have my number there?"

"I do."

Minogue felt sure that the pause was tactical.

"So, you're there in Dalkey, are you. Dalkey, County Dublin. A lot going on there out your way, I daresay?"

Minogue couldn't really blame him for letting slip some sarcasm at last.

Chapter 25

Minogue opened his eyes, to find that Malone was watching him.

"What," he said to him.

"Nothing. I'm just waiting, that's all."

Minogue closed his eyes again and resumed rubbing.

Whatever had been unfolding in his mind had no shape to it. McCarthy floating out in Dublin Bay and then finally returning to shore. Larkin passed out in the long grasses by a ruined church. Walshe screaming about AIDS. Immaculata's singing. Seán Brophy sitting at home, the curtains drawn.

"The phone call," Malone said.

He stopped rubbing. The yard of Dalkey Garda station was still all about him, the soft ticks were still the Escort's engine cooling. He hardly remembered any of the drive back in from Sallynoggin.

"The one at the newspaper," he added. "The one from some travel agent?"

"Go on."

"Sexton Blake."

Minogue looked up from his notepad. His doodles had turned out to be mostly triangles.

"What are you talking about?"

"It's fake. There's no 'travel agent.' It's part of the gig, whoever did for McCarthy. To me, it's amateur hour as well. It's not the real deal, like gang work."

"Why do you say that?"

"Okay. Let's say McCarthy's really in the game, or back in the game at least. Dealing, carrying, driving, couriering, running a crack pad – whatever. But if they think he's got his fingers in the till somewhere? Owing money that he'll never get back, and they think he's going to fold on someone and go grass to us...? A decision is made, and that's that. They don't care about trying to buy time, or covering up. Plenty of fellas are itching to make names for themselves, so they'll do it in broad daylight. They get their starring role, and the boss gets his rep, his cred. Cost of doing business to them."

"PR."

Malone tapped out a quick drum roll on the steering wheel.

"Call it PR if you like, sure," he said. "Who's going to mess with someone that thinks nothing to send someone out to shoot you in public, in the middle of the day?"

Then he gave Minogue a side glance.

"But there's more than one way to go at it, though, isn't there?"

"If McCarthy staged it all himself, you're thinking. Disappearing act."

Malone made another drum roll.

"You can't hide in this town long, I tell you. If you're a junkie, you're going to be out there. You have to. You lose the run of yourself, you can't think straight. You're going to be seen somewhere, or you're going to be making phone calls to somebody, and that somebody will be talking to somebody else, and..."

"I hear you."

Malone stopped his shoulder rolls, and began staring intently at the windscreen.

"Terry done it, you know," he said.

"He done – he *did* what?"

"He tried it once, the disappearing act. He thought he could go cold turkey."

It seemed to Minogue that the words were being addressed to someone else.

"Took exactly nineteen hours with Terry, to be back in

circulation. I actually checked in detail. Dublin's a small place for certain people."

He gave the steering wheel a sharp, decisive tap.

"Went back like a homing pigeon to the same track. That's what they do."

Track? Minogue thought for a moment before placing it: the streets where the dealers plied their trade. A fleeting memory came to him of driving down Abbey Street with Malone, not long after the funeral. Malone had been scanning faces there, searching amongst the restless people who themselves watched every passing car and face.

"'See what the science says,' I suppose," Minogue said. "On Mr. JJ Mac."

Malone dead-panned him.

"'See what the science says.' You like saying that, I bet. Brings you back to the Squad, right? But it was you that the Killer sent to crowbar the Lab, remember."

Minogue's mind had already had its run, skipping through the template of routines for cases arriving in to the Squad. Calls in to the mobile company for the victim's activity log. The Press Office, preparing the appeal. Setting up rota, zones for the area canvass. That hour or so – 'the early Mass,' as Kilmartin used to call it because it was short – with Mary at the State Pathologists to get them started. The calls to Seán Brophy looking for a jump in the forensic queue. Statements, second interviews.

The yard lights were fizzing. One clicked and poured a weak orange light across the yard. Malone took out the key, and looked at his watch.

Minogue was out first, the ache for a cigarette keen. He tapped his pockets for his camera and his mobile. Another light fizzed and snapped on, then a third.

"You'll be up in a while, right?"

Though Malone hadn't meant to be condescending, Minogue still felt a nip of disapproval. He found a spot by the door of the canteen, and lit up, and waited for someone to pick up the phone at Disciples. McCarthy had talked to some of the clients there. Now it was time to find out who.

An answering machine was his reward for letting it ring four times. He knew that he would not be leaving a message, he heard it out anyway. The voice was warm, the words carefully enunciated. Immaculata's lilt slipped its leash at the end: 'God Bless now.'

The back door of the station squeaked open, and after a few footsteps, the silhouette gave way to Sergeant Fitzgerald.

"How goes the battle?"

"Steady enough. Working on strategy here a minute."

Fitz came to a stop and looked about the sky a few moments.

"The evenings are coming on quick these days," he said.

Fitz was a rugby fan, Minogue saw from the Garryowen slogan on the mug dangling from his fingers.

"This is the week the roster starts to bite," added Fitz. He tried and failed to suppress a shiver. "I don't mind the 2 to 10, actually."

"Have you young ones at home?"

"Don't be talking. The little one's a divil. Tries to stay awake until I get home."

Minogue cupped his hand more around the cigarette. Fitz held up his mug.

"They might ban this next," he said, wagging it a little. "On account of, well Christ, who knows why. That it offends someone. Or allergic, like the perfume thing."

Minogue offered a tight smile. There was no sign of Fitz moving on.

"You mind me asking, er, Matt, but does it make much difference to you?"

"The tea?"

"No, I meant coming outside for a smoke. I often wondered. Like does it make a person cut down on them maybe?"

Minogue took a slow drag before answering.

"Not really."

"Well there's a thing," Fitz said, and shuffled a bit, drawing his jacket tighter. Minogue took in the blotches forming on his nostrils, and the watering eyelids.

"Anyone I ask," Fitz went on. "Anyone who smokes like, they never complain. None of them. Isn't that something?"

Minogue took another drag. The quartz lights were gaining strength quickly. He tried not to scrutinize how the light caught Fitz's errant hairs and put a shine to them.

"Plenty of other things to complain about," he said to Fitz.

"True for you. But it does surprise me, how little hankering there is for the good old days. Remember the place full of smoke? The ashtrays? Smoking on the buses?"

He gave Minogue a sly look.

"'God be with the good old days,' right? When men were men, and all that."

Minogue wanted to be agreeable. Here in this yard at the close of a November day, with stuff sliding into the gloom the minute he looked at it, he wanted this state of agreeableness quite a lot. It wasn't Fitz's fault that the man in front of him was a middle-aged smoker, a man all too easy to peg as an adept of any so-called good old days.

"Ah it was a myth," said Fitz, more to himself than to Minogue. "We'd find that out damned quick too, if only they'd hurry up and get a time machine into the shops."

"There's a thought now."

"They'd fly off the shelves, I'll bet. The way things are going…?"

It was one phrase too many for Minogue. It drew his mind to the others that were getting on his nerves more and more: 'We are where we are' or 'Pull together for the good of the country.' "Well I'd be inclined to leave Dr. Who and his time machine on the shelf," he said. "We can face the music the way we are."

Fitz tugged the handle of the mug and then released it to dangle again. He nodded toward the station house looming behind.

"Good old days indeed," he said and smiled a little. "Sure this place could be a museum itself, when you think about it."

"How long are you here in Dalkey, do you mind me asking?"

"Not a bit of it – six year. Promoted the 14th June, landed here on the 17th."

"Many changes?"

"You mean the coats of paint and the, ah, refurbishments?"

"In general, I meant. Someone was telling me that it was a model station."

Fitz frowned, but then his features eased.

"I know what you mean now," he said. "But you're talking about a good while back. Twenty, thirty years – more, actually. Who told you anyway? Must be a veteran."

Minogue thought for a moment of Pierce Condon and his jumbled mind.

"But that's not to deny that we're a model now," said Fitz. "Let's say we're a different model these days. How's that for spin?"

"I'd give you the gold medal this very moment."

Fitz raised his mug as though to toast. He shook more than shivered this time.

He gestured toward the canteen.

"You want a cup yourself?"

"No thanks," Minogue replied. "I'll head back upstairs now and get a few things done, and then I'll probably head off for the day."

Fitz raised his eyebrows and gave him a sly smile.

"You won't get a look at the good old days here so," he said. "Much is the pity."

"What would I be missing?"

"Little enough, really – a few old pictures and clippings. They were up on the wall there for ages, but one day a few months after I got here, I said to myself – enough."

He waited while Minogue stepped on his cigarette, and then picked it up. Fitz pushed open the door to the canteen.

Someone had left the radio on. Roadwatch was announcing the ritual tailbacks near Lucan. He watched Fitz fill the kettle and forage for tea bags.

"It'll only take a minute," said Fitz then. "Give you a bit of a laugh."

He dropped to one knee by a tall built-in, and pulled open a drawer.

"If they haven't been thrown out entirely already."

Minogue looked around the canteen while Fitz rummaged. The draining board was full. A half-empty 7-Up bottle stood on the table. There was nary a sound from the gym a.k.a. exercise room next door. Fitz was talking to himself, drawing out what looked like old dishcloths that had been stuffed in the drawer and forgotten. He reached in again.

"We're in luck," said Fitz. He slid, and then levered out a cardboard box.

"Here you are now. Feast your eyes on these."

He laid the envelope on a chair, and opened another cupboard door. Plastic containers tumbled out, rolling and bouncing with hollow clunks across the floor.

"My God, look at the crap that's piling up. No end to it."

He held up a lid with a melted edge.

"What's the point of holding on to this? An heirloom?"

He pointed at the cardboard box.

"Go on, open it up a look. I was going to feck the whole lot of them out, in actual fact, but I thought there might be a jinx on them. So I sort of pushed them to the back."

There was a stale, citrusy smell from the box. His fingertips registered the matte finish on the 8×10s as he drew them out. They were professional, posed and staged, with a well-diffused flash and good depth of field. Flipping one, he saw the Garda Press Office stamp, its original blue faded to purple: 1971. Did anything momentous happen in the world in 1971? He couldn't think of any. Bad clothes, maybe?

There were photocopies of newspaper articles in the box too. What did they call them then? Photo*stats*, yes. These ones were from the evening papers. There was a greying copy of a page from the Garda Review too, something with a soccer team. These young fellas were not in their teens yet. Their brand-new jerseys stood out from the mismatched shorts and the varying shades and heights of socks. Flanking the back row of boys were two men. The one standing with his arms folded and smiling broadly, a whistle on a white cord dangling over his forearm, had to be the 'Father Peter Murphy CC, Our Lady of Victories, Sallynoggin.' Who else could the other man opposite be, complete with collar and tie and tweed jacket and standing next to a frowning boy in the middle row, but the 'Sergeant Ferg Twomey'?

"This is the one I wanted you to see."

Fitz was holding up an 8×10 that he had plucked from the pile. He read something from the back of the photo with ironic gravity.

"Public Office, Dalkey Garda Station 1973."

"Sure enough," said Minogue, taking in the details. "The Real Thing."

"Look at the radio there – state-of-the-art. Two ashtrays on the counter. See the fag actually burning in that one? Stack of cigarette butts in it too? The new lads have no idea. They can't imagine working in an office that was full of smoke all day long."

He caught Minogue's eye then.

"Ever smoke a pipe, did you?"

"Not knowingly, or sober, I suppose I should say."

Fitz began fingering through the photos again.

"Well this one will top it for you then. Unless I'm mistaken now, and somebody dragged it off to the Garda Museum maybe ..." His finger stopped flipping and nudging, and drew out one.

"Now," he said. "You can't best this one. This fella here is in other ones, but the one I'm going to show you, it says it all. You ready?"

Minogue let his eye find details. With a dull gleam from the belt and its shining buttons, the uniform had to be parade dress. This Twomey character again. The face was by no means thin, but the unfocussed eyes had a hawkish intensity. Maybe the photographer had sensed it too, and told him to look away from the lens.

"That's upstairs," said Fitz. "I took him for an RIC man when I saw it first."

Minogue eyed the photo again. That parting in the hair, and the gloss of hair-oil palmed into it had a timeless look to it. Was it possible the man still used Brylcreem? He began to notice how the photo had been set up: hands splayed on the desktop as though their owner was about to rise. The angle of the pipe resting in the ashtray inclined in toward him. The fountain pen resting on a blank pad of paper, the same old beige-covered Stationery Office issue that had always creaked when it was opened.

"That's somebody Twomey, a Sergeant Twomey, I believe?"

"How well you knew that now."

"He's in a clipping there with some football team. He's in civvies there."

Minogue let the photo fall back into the box. The kettle was beginning to sigh. Fitz ran the tap and slid his thumb around the rim of the mug.

"Oh them was the days," he said over the sound of the water. "It didn't matter if you smoked or not. That's the way things were done. Whether you liked it or not."

He turned off the tap, and shook his mug, and turned to Minogue.

Something in Fitz's rueful smile struck a note with Minogue. A hint, he suspected, that as affable as Fitz had been trying to be, he couldn't always hide the fact that he had been stung by the parachute arrival of one Matthew Minogue.

Chapter 26

Minogue closed two of the flaps on the cardboard box and headed to the cupboard with it. He heard more than felt a shift, or maybe it was the sound of a page turning, and then the photographs were cascading around his feet. One made a quivering sound like a long saw.

"Doesn't surprise me that," Fitz declared. "Some days, you have only to pick something up around here and it falls apart."

Minogue gingerly turned over the box and examined where the bottom had given way. It was well past rehabilitation. He let it down on the floor next to the table leg. The law of falling objects dumped most of the snapshots face down. The few face-up had that tint that lay over them like weak tea, relics of the film chemistry of their time.

He hunkered, began sliding photos together. Down on one knee beside him came Fitz.

"That was a sign," Fitz said. "Might as well turf them for good."

He handed Minogue a sheaf of photos. The same Sergeant Twomey was in the top photo. The face bore the same thinking-his-own-thoughts look, as though he was keen to get this picture-taking over with. Behind him was a sliver of sea, and a gently sloping cut-stone wall, a section of what Minogue took to be a harbour wall.

The nun in the photo was half-smiling, and her rimless glasses had caught some of the sky. Her veil reached not much below her shoulders. There was no trace of hair peeping out from the coif. One hand held the other, fingers modestly entwined.

"That's him," said Fitz, in a put-on Cork accent. "Garda Sergeant Twomey."

Minogue glanced up again to find Fitz now leaning against the counter and craning his neck to see the photo. Steam was rising from the kettle behind him.

"You wouldn't mistake him now," Fitz added. "Would you?"

"Who's the nun?"

"No idea. One of the locals, I'd be willing to bet. There used to be plenty of convents and homes for the nuns out here. They're empty now – any ones they haven't sold. A sign of the times, as they say? That's Coliemore harbour there behind, I think. Dalkey Island behind, but you can't see it in that picture. Something is written on the back there, did you know?"

Minogue turned over the photo.

"'En route to St...' Saint who?"

"Begnet," said Fitz. "Saint Begnet's. It's that old ruin of a church out there on Dalkey Island. Saint Begnet is the patron saint of Dalkey."

"Dalkey has a patron saint? Is it in need of one, all to itself?"

"I only know from one of mine at home, Aoife. She did a project on this Begnet one. A fierce good-looking one, goes the story, and she had tons of offers, even the king of Norway. But things went sideways one night, when she got a visit from an angel. That's when she got her marching orders from The Man Above."

"Happens the best of us," Minogue said.

"The angel gave her a bracelet, with a cross on it. And up she got, left everything and headed across the sea. A missionary, like the monks. She ended up in England somewhere, whatever it was called back then. She started up a convent there. Soon enough she was an abbess. 'The Golden Age.' Well before them Vikings gangsters."

"I hope that young one of yours one got top marks for that. Aoife, you said?"

"That's her. Loves her history. She had all the history of Dalkey laid out there."

He leaned in to see the snapshot better.

"You can't see the church in this picture," he said. "But you've seen it before?"

"I have, I think," Minogue replied.

It had been years really since he had walked down that part of the coast, and sat for a few minutes above the tiny harbour there. It had been winter too, he remembered, because he had been thinking how bleak the island looked across the sound.

"And the Martello Tower there of course, waiting for the French?"

"Indeed," said Minogue. He began sorting through the photos again.

"A lot of history to Dalkey," Fitz went on. The daughter hadn't picked up her interest off the side of the road, Minogue decided. "It used to be the port of Dublin."

There were two nuns in this photo now, no Guard. And there was a bit of Dalkey Island in the background too, the church ruin in the corner. Both nuns had their rosaries out, and one held a pamphlet. The pair looked happy enough. A day out?

"It looks like a prayer thing going on," Minogue said. "A feast day for that saint, or a pilgrimage maybe?"

"I haven't heard of one now," Fitz said. "And I don't remember her writing anything about that. There was some old King of Dalkey Island thing way back though. It was only a spoof, a fair day, with people going over for the day for a dance and so forth. An excuse for carry-on I suppose."

He pulled the plug and the bubbling began to die down. Minogue heard the kettle's spout ring dully against the rim of the cup. The smell of tea began to fill the room.

More pictures, the same camera. Several people kneeling in prayer; a stone wall filling the background; a slice of the Martello Tower visible through a window. Rain?

"These ones would hardly have been hanging up on the wall here," Minogue said, turning to Fitz again. "Were they?"

"No Those newspaper clippings were, and the photocopies – the 8×10s."

"So where did these snapshots come from?"

"I think they turned up when the place was being rewired with the telecom stuff and proper heating. They had slipped down the back of an old cabinet, someone told me."

Minogue took up the photo of the two nuns again. The taller one was leaning in a little, perhaps to be sure to get in the frame. Her smile was genuine. The other's looked formal, as though in response to a prompt from whoever had taken the photo.

"It looks like the nuns had started to lighten up with the regalia by then anyway."

Fitz held up his tea bag as he spoke.

"Can you imagine having to wear the other stuff? Straightjackets. Worse than those things, I always get the names mixed up, the muslim things... Burqua?"

The opening door drew Fitz's glance.

"Corky," he said. "How's the man?"

"Not bad at all. And how's, er?"

"Matt. Grand thanks."

Minogue wondered where Corcoran had hung up his uniform.

"Time for a drop of tea?"

"No thanks, Sarge. The clock's working for me this shift. I'm off – but I'm actually here to save me marriage. If I can find me lunch boxes here, I stand a fair to middling chance of being let back into the house."

Fitz pointed a magisterial finger at the jumble of Tupperware on the table.

"Well take a long hard look through that so," he said.

Corcoran began plucking his from the pile. He paused then and looked over at Minogue.

"Is that your Escort parked out on the road?" asked Corcoran. "The red one?"

"The one that looks like a heap of shite?"

"That'd be it, I suppose."

"Very much not mine, thank God. It belongs to Tommy Malone. The other fella."

Corcoran strained to reach in under the table. He drew a photo across the linoleum a foot or two before he was able to pick it up.

"I have one just like it," he said. "I'm looking for another one, but."

"Why?" Minogue almost retorted, but a hint of hopefulness in Corcoran's face put that imp to flight.

"Escort," said Fitz. "Right, Corky. Let me 'escort' you to the scrap yard with it."

He turned from squeezing the tea bags over the sink.

"Go Japanese, you'll never look back."

"Fifteen hundred euro from the scrappage scheme won't go very far toward new wheels," said Corcoran, and returned to salvaging his lunch boxes. "I'd buy that red one for parts though."

Minogue saw that Fitz was busy again. He slid the photos into his pocket and headed out. The yard was flooded in yellow light. It had gone colder already.

★ ★ ★

There was no answer at Disciples.

"Where do they sleep?" he heard himself murmur. "Where do nuns sleep?"

"Who says they sleep?"

He turned and watched Malone sliding his finger down the side of a page, and then stop while he made a note.

"They're probably vampires. The type you can't see, until it's too late."

"How much more of that mobile traffic records needs a go-over?"

Malone pressed down his finger on a page decisively, and he looked up.

"Triple-check," he said, not bothering to hide the irony in his voice. "Wasn't that the plan? We get this stuff out of the way before we start up re-interviewing and that?"

Minogue rearranged the photos on the desk. He placed the one with the priest last.

"Should I be asking what those pictures are"

"They're pictures. Pictures of ancient Ireland."

"Are you in some kind of nun fan club now? How ancient are they anyway?"

"Sixties, Seventies. I don't know."

"Who's the copper there?"

"Twomey, a Sergeant Twomey – and thanks for reminding me. I meant to phone Pierce Condon, or his son I mean, and give him the name. He was trying to remember it."

"You lost me there. But I don't think I'm going to lie awake over it."

"It came up in a chat. We were trying to remember the name of someone here. Years ago."

Malone released his finger from the page and he eased back into a slouch.

"Nuns. You have an obsession or something. No offence."

Minogue placed his finger on one of the photos.

"That nun there, the shorter one?"

"What about her."

With his free hand, Minogue slid the photo with Twomey over.

"I say that she...is related to him. To this Twomey character."

"She is? Who told you?"

"I told myself. Look at the set of the eyes there, the chin. There's something."

"That's interesting," said Malone slowly. "I suppose. Maybe."

"Actually it is interesting. But not as interesting as the other nun here. The one beside her, the one in the grey raincoat."

Malone scratched hard at the underside of his arm.

"Oh, the rebel one there? Grey was a fashion statement back then, was it?"

Malone's scratching stopped.

"Jay-*zuzz*," he said. "How can you tell the difference between the two of them? Look at the head gear: the same. Look at the what you call 'ems, the scarfs— "

"Coifs, they're called, I think."

"Quaffs then. Same again. So one has glasses, and one's a bit taller, fair enough. But a nun is a nun."

Minogue said nothing

"Don't you think?" Malone asked, after a while.

It was there all right, Minogue thought, the way the taller one seemed to be challenging the camera. He wondered again who was taking the pictures.

"The tall one," he said. "She'd be the one I'd be interested in."

"'Interested in.' I don't like the way that sounds."

Minogue had a heavily ironic look of his own to match Malone's.

"That there nun," he said, and paused. "That there nun is Sister Immaculata."

Chapter 27

"Nice work," Malone said. "Does it pay much, surfing the Internet?"

He pushed home the cabinet drawer with a final grinding squeak. His thumb hesitated over the lock, while he waited for Minogue to look over. Minogue had a hesitation of his own to deal with: a suspicion that Malone was overdoing it. He had been trying a bit too hard to be agreeable, to be his dryly funny old self.

"I'll do it," he said to Malone. "I'm heading home in a few minutes myself."

Malone stood next to him, looked at the screen.

"A local history outfit?"

"More a group of people reminiscing, so far as I can see. Talking about 99s and Golly Bars and Ford Prefects."

"What's that there, 'The Noggin'?"

"Research, is what it is. 'The means must, when the devil drives.'"

"I'm going to have to take your word on that, whatever it means."

Minogue had copied and pasted bits into a text file.

"Did you find what's-her-name there, Sister Thing?"

"I wasn't looking for her."

"You're still sure that's her in that picture, are you, back in nineteen seventy nothing."

"Or someone very like her."

He saved the file again and went to his personal email. Slow.

"I found mention of a Father Murphy though," he said while he waited. "The priest in that newspaper article."

"The priest that oul Lar Higgins was talking about, the one that Mrs. McCarthy worked for?"

"But no picture of him."

"Why do you, why do we, want one?"

Minogue gave him a quick look.

"Because I want to see if he looks like that guy there."

Malone's skepticism came through loud and clear in his widening eyes.

"The priest there with that prayer group, or whatever they called themselves going over to the Island. To that old church."

Malone made several slow nods and then he turned on his heel. Minogue heard him slip into his coat, and slide his keys from the desk.

"Tomorrow, boss."

"Fair enough."

He listened to Malone's footsteps as he took the stairs, and then he returned to the screen.

Father Peter Murphy had been curate of Our Lady of Victories for two years. According to *ProudNogginer*, probably the most frequent contributor to this forum, Father Murphy had been 'a breath of fresh air.' It was too bad that he'd gone on the missions so soon really. *TomTheBomb* wrote that he reckoned that Father Peter probably went on the missions to get a holiday from the Noggin, ha ha. But seriously, he added in a reply to a question about what missions, Hardyman opined that Father Murphy had rubbed them the wrong way, that he was too 'new' for the parish priest there, or something.

"Or something," Minogue murmured. He was hardly the only man in Ireland these days, he hoped, the only man to know that it was rare for a diocesan priest to turn to the missions.

He tried a few more searches, varying the order of the words each time, but nearly every link that came up was a repeat. He was catching the usual ADD and an unfamiliar kind of vertigo at the same time: too much data, not little information, zero knowledge. He signed in to his personal email, and somberly noted that he was not a recipient of any email from his son. A week now? Hardly a record, to be fair. He composed an email to himself and pasted in the contents of his file, and he hit Send. He closed his folders and slid them into the same drawer that Malone had closed. Then he thumbed the lock home and pocketed his key.

He gathered the photos again, taking brief look at each before dropping them into his new fancy, almost empty attaché case. They looked a bit different now, he realized. Less useful? He pushed back against the eddy of discouragement trickling into his mind: Sergeant Twomey for sure, Father Peter Murphy, for sure. Some nun who might or might not look like Twomey. But a young Sister Immaculata? A very big maybe.

He had the door almost closed when the phone went.

"I was lucky you were still there, I suppose."

Kathleen's voice had an edge of annoyance in it.

"I tried your mobile first, fool that I was."

He slid it out while he listened to detail what her friend was now facing.

"I just found out that Brídín has nothing in reserve. Nothing. She'll have to sell the apartment. She'll lose all the money she put into it too. And who's going to buy an apartment these days anyway?"

Sure enough, he had switched his mobile off. He hadn't remembered doing that. What did that mean? That his subconscious had taken over the task of shutting Kilmartin out?

"She was always the life and soul of the place," Kathleen went on. "Always one for enjoying herself. And now she'd right on the edge. She can't sleep, she can't eat – she told me everything. I was shocked."

"Terrible," he said.

"Maxed out her cards, and she hasn't anything put aside. Did I say that already? I did. 'Never one for planning,' she told me. I knew that, but I thought it was just the whole spontaneous thing with her. You know, 'Off to Prague this weekend, d'you want to go with us?' Little did I know."

"True for you."

"What do you mean?"

There was a missed call, but he didn't recognize the number.

"Are you there? I said, What do you mean 'true for you'?"

"I only meant that we only think we know people. Maybe deep down we...?"

Her tone reverted to a stoic, unsurprised Dublin inflection that he knew too well.

"Well that's a big help," she said.

"I only meant that there are limits, love."

"Limits."

"People don't even know themselves half the time, when you think about it. That's all."

"Do you think about it then?"

He thumbed through the Receiveds. Six Kilmartins in two days. That was a record of sorts. His subconscious was acting fairly sensibly then.

"Are you there?"

"I only mean that you see it every day here in the job, how people do things and they can't figure out why any more than we can. The subconscious and all that?"

"Right," she said, at her most leaden. "'In the job.' The new job. I almost forgot."

He closed his mobile with a sharp snap that he hoped she heard well.

"So you'll be late," he said. "Will I pick you up maybe, at the Luas?"

"I'll phone you. On your mobile."

"I'll staple it to my head."

"Switched on too?"

He replaced the receiver and opened his mobile again. The voice answering was strained and even breathless, but it was familiar.

"Mr. Higgins. You phoned earlier?"

"That was ages ago. Do you know what time it is now?"

Minogue listened then while Larry Higgins related his views on several matters. He returned to the views that he had expressed earlier on what could and should be done about training Guards how to deal with elderly people. Minogue was invited to imagine if poor Mrs. McCarthy had been his own mother and had been landed with a shock like that. Minogue forebore replying that he couldn't because if that situation were replicated on his own family, he would have been pulled out of Dublin Bay as JJ Mac had been, and would scarcely be talking to anybody.

No. There was nothing for it but to give way. Did he know that Mrs. McCarthy had nobody now? That she had more or less been out of touch with her own family back down the country for decades now, on account of marrying Bobby. It was very sad all right, he offered during one pause. And what was going to happen now, Higgins wanted to know.

Minogue made the mistake of trying to be soothing.

"The Guards will have started gathering information," he began. "It takes time to get results."

"I know all that! What I'm saying is, what's going to happen now, this evening? She's after falling into some coma at the oss-pital!"

He paused to catch a breath.

"I didn't know that."

"They think she's after having a stroke or something. I phoned them and they told me nothing, so I got my daughter on it, and she went in, and that's what she found out."

"That's unfortunate—"

"'Unfortunate'? You're telling me it is. She won't be coming out of that hospital for a good long while, I'm telling you. You see? So who's going to look after things here, next door I mean? Make sure the cooker is off and the gas is turned off and all the rest of it – and make sure the place is not broken into. Do you know there are people who look to see who's in hospital or has passed away, or even at a funeral, and that's when they come to rob the house? Did you know that?"

"I had heard that it happened. Look, can't you do it for the time being?"

"Me? But then the Guards will be thinking, well I don't know what they'll be thinking. Can't you see what I'm trying to get at here?"

Minogue looked away from the map of the Hill that he had been staring at.

"I'll give you the number of Dun Laoghare Garda station," he said. "they're the ones for your area."

"I did that," said Higgins in a quiet monotone that he surely reserved for dealing with the simple-minded.

"And what did they tell you?"

"They'd 'pass it on.' You know what that means, do you, 'pass it on'?"

The indignation was back in his voice now, something that Minogue had already concluded was giving Mr. Lawrence Higgins a fair bit of grim pleasure. He could hear Higgins breathing more clearly now.

"Well they probably mean that they'll notify the officers who are actually involved in the case with Joe, or Joey. The Garda station out in Clontarf, I believe."

"Notified," said Higgins, in a half-whisper.

Moments dragged by. Minogue let his thoughts slide toward McDonald's on the way home. Nobody need know.

"Would you like me to phone them for you?" he asked, finally. "I'll tell them you'd appreciate some direction in the matter maybe?"

"Tonight I'm talking about," said Higgins. "It's night time, almost. The house is dark – next door I'm talking about. I don't even know if she left out food for that cat that visits, or if she had that old electric fire on and left it that way. Yes, three bars on it, sure the thing must be ancient, ready to go up in flames, and she hangs up the wet clothes in front of it..."

Minogue rubbed at his eyes, and against those same eyelids he could almost see Higgins standing there in the hallway, his chest rising and falling, and his face changing colour. The eyes grown big with panic even. The prickly self-sufficiency he and Malone had been treated to this afternoon would be something else entirely now that the night had come.

"Well do you know if the doors are locked?"

"Of course they're locked, back and front. Wasn't it me who locked them?"

"I meant next door, Mr. Higgins, at McCarthys'."

"That's what I'm telling you. I pulled them shut, I made sure. Were you listening to me at all?"

"Funny you should ask. My present wife asked me the self-same question three minutes ago."

"Is this the time to be cracking jokes there, Sergeant Malone? Is it?"

"Minogue. Malone was the other fella."

"If the house burns down, is that going to be funny?"

There was a tremor in his voice now.

"You're right. Tell you what, can you go in and make sure it's okay?"

"Are you mad?"

The retort seemed to reverberate in Minogue's mind. He waited for a count of three.

"Why is that mad?" he asked, quietly.

"Tampering with evidence? Interfering like that, that's obstruction. Or burglary, or accessory to the fact."

"What fact?"

"Joey's after being found dead, isn't he? Nobody goes in for a swim in Dublin Bay this time of the year – any time, for that matter."

A Big Mac was all Minogue could think about then. He'd surrender to the grease. Fries too. Might as well be hung for a sheep as a goat.

"Look, Larry," he said. "I doubt the Guards have your name as a suspect. Should they, maybe?"

"Are you trying the comedy bit again?"

"I think they'll understand your concerns. That's what I'm trying to get across."

"Like you'll 'pass it on,' will you? That kind of 'understand'? Well I wouldn't put any shagging money on anything coming out of that in the next few years, would I."

It was a while before Higgins spoke again.

"Sorry about that," he murmured, the breath whistling hard in his nose. "I get a bit carried away. It's just that, well this kind of thing, it doesn't happen to us every day."

"It's not something you'd want to get used to, is it?"

"Oh that's a fact now. Do you know, it must be that stupid box. The television. I do see the cops – the police – getting down to business right away, and then going at it good-o, and next thing you know, it's all done."

"And then the ads come on again, right?"

"That's the way of it all right. All wrapped up in an hour."

"That's the Yanks for you."

"Gobshites, I'm telling you."

"Well there are nice ones now, come on."

"No! Us, I'm talking about – us watching that stuff."

"Better than Frontline though."

"Don't be talking! Nothing worse! And do you know how much they pay him? And the other shower of shites there on RTE, the licence fee going up all the time...?"

"You're not alone in that, Mr. Higgins. You're not alone."

His own words hung in his mind, but now as glib, ironic, and even wrong. Higgins was alone, that was the problem. That's why he was phoning people.

"I'm not an iijit now," Higgins went on in a hesitant voice now. "I know that's the television and that. But still I thought, well you'd expect that maybe the Guards would be...you know?"

Minogue did know. He knew that there was no answer here too. And he also knew that Lar Higgins was embarrassed and afraid.

"Especially with things the way they were with Joey."

"How do you mean?"

The harsh tone crept back into Higgins' tone.

"Oh come on now. You're the real Guard, aren't you. Like those little questions you had this morning. You're still at it."

"You mentioned Joey, that's all."

"His situation," said Higgins, impatiently. "The things he was into? You know about that surely. Other people know too, don't they? That's all I'm saying."

"Other people in his, em, situation?"

"What else? People would be thinking that there's something in the house worth breaking in for – you know, that kind of stuff that Joey, God forgive me, was up to?"

"You mean drugs?"

"Did I say that?"

Minogue waited.

"Do you get my meaning there, Sergeant?"

"Inspector. I do, I think. The house is locked, you said."

"It is. I made sure the hall door was on the latch, didn't I, and I pulled it closed. And I checked the back door, the kitchen door too, from the outside. That's always locked anyway."

"You weren't inside the house?"

"Look, I have to tell you something. I don't like going in there. The place is, well it's not kept up, if you know what I mean. She's a bit forgetful, let's say."

Minogue remembered the tidiness of the Higgins' home.

"I should have, I suppose," Higgins resumed. "But with the commotion, and the ambulance fellas and all that, I wasn't thinking straight. And I didn't want to get a turn myself, you know. I have to keep an eye on things, the breathing and so forth."

Minogue was already tracing his way through Sallynoggin, finding the landmark church dome well above the terraces of houses. It wasn't much of a detour really.

"Well, how could you get in anyway, even if you wanted to check on the fireplace or the cooker or the like?"

"I have a key, didn't I tell you?"

Chapter 28

A street lamp had already cast hard shadows on the footpath next to Larry Higgins' home. The front room window was dark, but the curtains were slightly parted. Minogue stepped out into the chill evening air. Someone was cooking onions. Burning onions, actually. Kids' voices echoed from a street nearby, along with the scuffs and dull thuds of a ball. A shadow moved from the gulf of darkness by the wall: a cat interested in the underside of Minogue's Peugeot. Closing the gate behind him, he saw that the parting in the curtains had changed. The latch turned before his hand made it to the doorbell.

Inside, the house was tropical. The early news was on the radio. Larry Higgins looked less sure of himself than earlier, clasping and then unclasping the handle for his trolley set-up. Following Higgins to the kitchen then, Minogue took in some of what kept Larry Higgins attached to the planet. An egg-cup waiting next to a cup and saucer; a neatly folded evening paper, waiting to be read. Probably the same sight he'd see every day here at this time. Higgins ushered him into the sitting room. His voice was full of a fretful bravado.

"Me, I'm acting in good faith here. I want that on the record. People can say what they like. I'm only helping out. Doing my bit, helping the authorities. That's what I'm doing. Right?"

"You took the words out of my mouth."

"What's that you have?"

Minogue waited for the battery charge display.

"It's a camera."

"You didn't tell me you were coming here to take pictures."

"Think of it as insurance," Minogue said, pocketing it. "Safeguarding Mrs. McCarthy's place. If anything were to disappear, or get moved?"

"Insurance?" said Higgins, his tone turning sharply skeptical. "Wait'll you see the place next door first. Then let's hear you talk about insurance."

He fingered the tube under his nostrils, and paused to focus on his breathing.

"You stay here," Minogue said to him. "I go and check everything's okay next door."

"I wouldn't feel right doing that. No. I'm going along with you."

He drew the small trolley out in front.

"You know what this is?"

"Something to do with oxygen, I'm guessing."

"A concentrator is what it is. On a normal day I'd be using this maybe once or twice during the day. But now, since this morning, I have to keep it going nearly all the time."

He kept a keen eye on Minogue while he fumbled in his trouser pocket. He soon drew out keys and held them up. One was an old barrel key, with its long shank.

"Give me a minute to put on me coat," Higgins said.

Minogue waited on the path outside, opening his coat to get a measured dose of the cold evening air. Higgins grunted as he pulled the hall door shut, and tested it. He shrugged his coat over his shoulder more, and led with the trolley.

The scutch grass and the drifting hedge soaked up much of the light coming from the road. Night had transformed the skeleton of the motorbike into a mysterious artifact. Though the edges of the concrete path to the McCarthys' hall door had given way in places, pallid gleams came from pebbles embedded in at and now worn smooth by the years.

"Junk everywhere," he heard Higgins mutter. "Starts a thing, never finishes."

He stopped and looked over his shoulder at Minogue.

"She doesn't notice the state of the place, Catherine. You know?"

The tremor in his voice was not just from his exertions. His hand wavered with the key, missing the lock twice. The hall door was the original, stout and heavy. Its flap scraped across the lintel and then went quiet as the door opened wide.

Higgins leaned in close. There was a tremor in his voice.

"Dementia," he said. "That's the proper word."

The hallway seemed smaller and narrower than the Higgins'. He thought he heard a low groan coming from Higgins as he stepped in, his hand groping for the light switch. He was about to ask him if he was okay when a waft of stale air came to his nostrils. It was the smell of a closed-in house, of newspapers than had lain a long time in the sun. A heavier odour came to him then, what Kathleen called dishwasher breath.

The light here in the hallway was staying pale yellow. The walls were covered in heavily patterned wallpaper and interrupted by pictures. A coat stand, with a woman's coat, and then a raincoat; an umbrella leaning against it also. A small, low hall table presented itself next near the foot of the stairs. There was a phone on top, and a written list of telephone numbers.

"I told you, didn't I."

"Told me what?"

"Mildew, damp! That roof of hers is leaking, I'm sure of it."

Minogue's eyes had grown used to the light now. More details came at him. The wallpaper had been worn down in places, with nicks that showed plaster. A picture of the Sacred Heart hung next to the kitchen door, partnered by a fake plaster relief of hands joined in prayer. No holy water fount? A rug had been placed to cover cracks, or tears, in the linoleum.

"I'm leaving that light on all night," Higgins said. "I don't care."

He used his elbow to push open the door next to the kitchen.

"Nothing's on fire here," he said. "That's something, I suppose. You going in?"

The floor creaked at every step. Higgins hadn't been

exaggerating. It wasn't just that there was hardly any counter space to begin with – every and any flat surface was covered. His mind reeled as he tried to sort what he was seeing. Two plastic basins, an unknown number of containers and jars, pots inside pots, a saucepan with some liquid that looked vegetabley. Old tea tins, bowls, a bag of sugar and another of flour. Bisto, instant coffee, soup packets. An electric kettle with brown stains near the seam. Higgins' tone had become subdued.

"It's no use telling her. No use."

The fridge was one of those old backbreaker models from decades ago, the type that Kathleen's family called a tabernacle. Magazines and newspapers lay in bundles near a cupboard. No shortage of holy pictures: he recognized St. Therese, 'The Little Flower.' St. Christopher showed of course, carrying You-Know-Who across a stream. Chritso-ferens.

"How does she heat the place?" he asked Higgins.

"That bloody electric fire that she moves around. She used to burn turf and coal like the rest of us. But not for years. That electric fire's the thing that keeps me worried."

The table was 1960s Formica, chipped at the edges. *Woman's Own* magazines, sewing things. A cutting board, a bread box. An abandoned breakfast lay in a corner of the table.

Higgins was waiting for Minogue at the doorway.

"I'm not touching a thing," he said. "Not a thing."

He gestured toward the open door to a sitting room. A fold-out clothes dryer surrounded what Minogue supposed was the fireplace. Angled a little toward it was a sofa covered by either a bedspread or a blanket, home to knit cushions at the either end.

"Take a walk in there and you'll see that damned electric fire, the bane of my life, in behind them clothes she has hanging up."

The television in the corner – Bush still made televisions? – had the lurid plastic from thirty years ago. A small coffee table topped by a doily and a vase of plastic flowers kept company with the single armchair. Behind it rose heavy-looking curtains, their gold and floral pattern fading in long lines along the hems.

"Pull them closed, will you?"

Minogue made his way around the clothes. There was no man's stuff. He tried harder then to trick his mind into not noticing the floppy knickers and the drooping nylon stockings. There was the electric fire that haunted Larry Higgins. He had to tease the curtain runners by a kink in the rod.

"She doesn't have a Hoover. It broke on her last year. I gave her a loan of mine once, I said, 'Get Joey to do it for you.' But I never heard her use it."

"Did Joey stay here all the time?"

"I don't know. I didn't see him every day, did I?"

Minogue's eye had come to rest on the picture above the mantelpiece. It was a thatched and whitewashed cottage, with a hill behind and clouds galore. A boreen led off curving into a green and gold distance. A donkey stood in the middle distance, creels loaded with turf.

"A Galway woman originally, you said."

"She is. Not Galway city, she'll tell you right away. Somewhere out there though."

"Do you know if she smokes?"

"I know that she doesn't. She isn't a thick like me, or like I was anyway."

Minogue turned to him.

"I'll have a look in the other room there, the front room."

A table covered by a plastic gingham pattern had been pushed up under the window. There were glasses and delph in the dresser, china knick-knacks, a few small framed photos.

"Joey and her," said Higgins. "In better days. The Isle of Man, I think."

The face on this JJ McCarthy was a fuller version, a relaxed version, of the sharp-featured one that the database had thrown up on-screen back at the station.

"It is," said Higgins. "Yes, he had a big moustache like that. They all did then. Now I know what you're thinking, but that's him. He lost a lot of weight over the years. And you know why too, don't you. Here, what are you doing?"

Minogue examined the cutlery and the serviettes in the top drawer, and ran his hand under the folded serviettes.

"Making sure there's nothing going to catch fire," he said.

He opened the drawer beneath. Table cloths, place mats, a pack of cards. No booze or ashtrays anywhere downstairs then. No mobiles, no laptops, no camera gear.

"If they ever ask me," said Higgins, "I'll have to say yes, you know. About this."

"If who ever asks?"

"The other Guards. The ones supposed to find out about Joey, if he was done in."

"Did you ever see JJ – Joey – using any gear? Cameras? A computer, maybe?"

Higgins shook his head.

"No sign of that cat," he said then. "That's good news, if she's started locking it out."

"Why's that?"

"The cat pisses all over the place, is why. Can't you smell it?"

Minogue headed back to the kitchen and stood there just inside the doorway, and pondered. It'd be a half an hour easy just doing the most basic search here.

"Are there windows upstairs?"

"Of course there are windows upstairs. What are you thinking?"

"I'll go up then so, and make sure they're locked."

It was the standard straight run up, steep, over a fraying carpet runner to where the last few steps turned to gain the landing. Every few steps offered more pictures of Irish country life. He paused to examine one. It was the Spanish Arch in Galway, with men in caps and *bánín* jumpers sitting around chatting. Aran islanders he supposed. The bleak grandeur in the next picture was surely Connemara.

He stopped a few steps short of the landing. There was as different air here, a hint already of rankness, the smell of bed warmth from a sick-room, or neglected laundry.

"What's wrong? What are you doing?"

"I'm looking for windows."

"It doesn't look like it from here."

He made the final steps and stopped again on the landing proper, and he switched on the lights. The fittings in the toilet were original to the house, with brown rust-lines fanning out from under the lip of the bowl. Sections of the enamel in the bath were yellowed and edging into brown, with bare spots revealing the blue beneath. A shower head at the end of a grey rubber hose lay curled on a ledge. No cabinet for stuff, just a narrow glass shelf above the sink loaded with small jars of cream and two tall plastic containers of shampoo. But he had spotted his first signs of a man's belongings there, a can of shaving form and an opened package of disposable razors.

"Look up at the ceiling there. Go on, look."

The grey stain coming in from the corner of the ceiling next looked like a cloud. The black spots at its edges were the indeed the mould that Higgins fretted about.

"You see? That's going to give any day. In on top of her."

He crossed the hall, and bracing himself, he pushed open the back bedroom door. A bottle of holy water from Knock shrine on the window sill, doilies on a dresser under a bottle of 4711 cologne. The wardrobe door hung open a little. A picture of Mary with the infant Jesus on her knee presided over the small double bed. The wall over the dresser had that serenity prayer and a wedding picture from long ago. Slippers, a nightgown on the bed. An alarm radio, more magazines, a crossword book. A small book with a string bookmark – a prayer book.

"Is her window locked there?"

Minogue swore under his breath.

"Thanks for reminding me," he replied then. "I'm going to check that now."

He ignored the sight that came through the banisters to him as he walked back across the hall: Larry Higgins' upturned face, his beady, suspicious eyes squinting against the light overhead. The door handle ground as he pulled it down.

The smell of ashtrays, and the stale reek of clothes infused with smoke, was strong. Aftershave used to suppress it had only made it worse. He stood a foot beyond the threshold and looked around the room. He hadn't expected the neatness, the bed made, and things arranged sort of square on top of the chest of drawers. But still no sign of bag, a case even. No desk, not even a chair. No sign of any camera stuff, flash drives, cards. And still no damned computer either.

He made his way gingerly toward a wardrobe the same vintage as in the mother's room. Drawing it open, he ignored the squeak. A too-well-used leather jacket was hanging on a peg half hidden by a white shirt. Holding back the shirt and another behind it, he checked the floor of the wardrobe, pausing for poke around in a shallow cardboard box. Porno mags. Everyone on the covers was blonde, with the usual energetically bored look. Dutch words too – those Js they were so fond of – not Swedish. He found one pair of running shoes, in bad order. The top shelf in the wardrobe was buried in T-shirts. He stood on the bed and looked down at the top of the wardrobe. A Tupperware container had been placed next to the wall.

The lid gave way with a soft crack. He smelled the dope right away. He poked a finger through the brittle leaves, and a bitter, pungent scent came up. He resealed the container, and slid it back on top of the wardrobe.

Next to a haphazard collection of coins on top of the chest of drawers, lay an ashtray with two roll-your-own butts. Matches, two disposable lighters; scrunched-up bits of paper and receipts. Paper hankies, some small screws that they used on electronics. He leaned in to see if there was anything between the chest of drawers and the bed, and then went on his knees and pulled up the edge of the bedspread. Odd socks under the bed, more magazines, a pair of suede shoes hardly worn…and then the small baggies he had expected. All unused, or ready for use, at least. He drew one out and examined it. Not a trace of powder. A careful operator, McCarthy?

The top shelf held a blue-and-silver ghetto blaster next to a stack of discs, and a small MP3 gizmo attached to an over-the-ears headset. Beneath were mostly fat thrillers. He spotted a biography of the most annoying Irish soccer player in history.

"Is it closed in there, the window?"

"I'll just test it."

He opened the bottom drawer and went through it. What he imagined could turn out to be small pouches of cocaine turned out to be folds in the socks themselves. McCarthy's passport turned up predictably enough in an underwear drawer, next to the predictable condoms. Fanning open the passport, a piece of paper fluttered to the floor: a receipt from last year, an airport train from Schipol. His eye lingered on the photo. The mugshot on Pulse was of a much younger McCarthy. Twenty, thirty years even.

"What are you doing up there? Closing windows, or manufacturing them?"

"Almost finished."

The other three drawers yielded nothing, except bringing to the front of Minogue's mind a deepening dismay at the course of this man's life.

The bedroom over the front door was as tiny as he had expected. A faint trace of perfume, a floral base he associated with old ladies, hung in the air. Save for an old headboard turned on its side and leaning against the wall, the room was bare of furniture. Coat hooks had been hung on a plank set into the wall, and a woman's coat hung inside a plastic dry cleaning bag. Three cardboard boxes were stacked in a corner. Delph, or china, wrapped in newspaper.

The voice coming up the stairs was testy.

"That window's never open. It's only an old storage room there."

He took his time coming down the stairs, his thoughts eddying yet around what he had been hoping to find. Still no bag. No papers, no files, no notepads – not even yellow stickies. No memory sticks or data discs either – unless McCarthy kept them mixed in with his music collection. Any mobile phone, he'd have carried with him. Laptops had gone cheap – a netbook maybe, just the right size to slip into a bag and take with him.

He stopped. How easily it happened. Here he was, blithely

assuming that McCarthy had been carrying stuff. *Stuff*: The word rolled around in his mind. He hadn't even begun to think about email accounts, or *stuff* he kept in the so-called cloud. He blinked slowly to clear his mind. Enough: any further, and there'd be trouble. This crap was for someone else to figure out.

Chapter 29

He dipped his head before taking the last of the stairs. "I knew all the windows upstairs were closed, you know," Higgins said.

"It's best to be sure though, isn't it? You were right to get me to check."

"Well listen to you. Was it me told you to go through drawers and that too?"

Minogue's answer was to pull his coat closed. He began a survey of the hallway. He hadn't looked under the stairs. More plastic tubs, stacked; jam jars, a mop in bad order, an old galvanized pail. A vacuum cleaner, a wheelie shopping bag. A frying pan with a broken handle. Wellington boots, a pair of shoe lasts, biscuit tins...

"So now you've seen the place," Higgins said. "It's something else, isn't it?"

"It is, I suppose."

"Some people actually think that poverty's been fixed in this country. They should be made to come out here and see the likes of this. All of them, up to the President, what's her name."

Minogue moved to the hall door. This place was giving him the willies. It was something beyond the threadbare look, the make-do, the neglected. It was an air of abandonment, of loss, and it bore down harder by the second.

"We'll be off now though, I'm thinking. Come on, and we'll lock up."

He turned the latch, and drawing open the door open a little, threw a parting glance at the pictures, those spells that led out of an ugly, over-run present and back to an imagined life in the imagined West of Ireland. Dreams.

"She's not fit to be here on her own," Higgins said. "But she'll never let anyone do anything for her. She was always like that, that pride – And now look what's happened. I thought when Joey came to stay that he had straightened out. That he'd be able to look after his mother now in old age. You hear me?"

"I get it."

"She can't come back. A hard thing to say, but decisions have to – where are you going?"

"I need to get a bit of air."

He almost missed the step down. The smell of cooking onions was almost welcome now. Someone was burning rubbish now too. Higgins pulled the door almost closed, and then with a tight pull he yanked it home against the jamb. He tested the lock twice.

"Didn't I tell you?" he said. "The Guards need to do something before there's trouble."

"What trouble?"

"The people mooching around here," said Higgins. "Joey's comrades, or whatever you want to call them. Crackheads they're called. That's what everyone calls them."

"Is that what they look like to you?"

"Don't pull that one. They're hardly dropping by for a cup of tea and a chat."

"When did you see them?"

"I'm only saying. I don't know for sure. None around lately, in the daytime anyway."

"Was there stuff going on at night?"

"Didn't I tell you there was? It was a fortnight or so back. I seen their cigarettes going in the dark out there, out the back by the shed. Except they weren't cigarettes."

"There was an odd smell off them?"

Higgins pulled at his coat collar and shrugged to get his free arm covered better.

"The shed is locked, is it?"

Higgins nodded.

"You might have a way to get in though, I'm wondering...?"

Higgins raised his hand. He used his forefinger to wiggle the long barrel key.

"In the interests of security," Minogue said. "That's all."

"Pull the other one. You have to go through the kitchen. Now, have you a torch?"

"Not on me."

"I thought Guards had torches. Like you were born with one? Only a joke."

It gave Higgins notable satisfaction to hand him a large 9-volt battery flash lamp.

Minogue tested the beam, and then fastened the top buttons of his coat.

"You don't have anything bigger, I suppose. Or heavier maybe?"

"Mind where you put your foot," said Higgins. "Unless you want to break your snot falling over stuff. It's Asia Minor back there – and watch for timber and plywood lying around, they might have nails sticking up. Stuff's lying there these years."

Minogue made his way with heavy unease through the hallway again, and into the kitchen. The back door out opened easier that he expected, and soon he stood in the doorway, playing the beam on the narrow apron of concrete below. Dark moss lined the joints. Beyond the concrete stood a post for a clothesline. Bundles rose out the grass, reminding Minogue of an untended graveyard. Most of those bundles were wrapped in plastic tarps that had started out as blue, but were now faded and fraying. Plenty of cigarette butts rotted amongst the grasses.

The shed had had a window, but it had been sealed from the inside with what looked like pieces of timber. He placed the key in the lock, but before he tried to seat it, he looked back at the upper windows in Higgins' house. Sure enough, there he was, framed in the parted curtains.

The lock was trouble. He put the flash lamp on the concrete after a few tries, and used both hands. It wouldn't be about force, but more about balance. It took a dozen and more tries before the key turned.

Opening outward, the door screeched. Minogue found the pebble at the end of its scratch across the concrete and he hoofed it into the grass. The flashlight beam washed over blackened sections of the walls inside the shed. A coalhouse at some stage then. The sharp tang of petrol had lodged in his nostrils right away, and it soon began to give way to separate smells: the heavy, almost animal smell of engine oil, earth from old planting pots, the ginger hint of turf.

A layer of dust covered a push mower, its blades brown and mottled. A rake had settled and gathered cobwebs alongside a spade. The surface of a workbench made of plywood and scarred two-by-fours was covered with plastic containers and tubs. The black and brown liquids in them reflected the beam feebly back.

He used his biro to find the bottom of one of the tubs, and tilted it until a glistening section of gear chain appeared. Bolts, washers, polished and rusted nuts half-filled the container next to it. Protruding from another was the housing for what he guessed was a fuel pump. A lid held different-sized ball bearings. By a can of WD-40, its long red nozzle bent upwards, a tangle of clips and springs and clamps. Sockets for a wrench were heaped in a shallow tub next to a set of four spark plugs. Two gaskets, one new; rusted steel wool. A short piece of hose – a fuel line. In front of a beer-can-turned-ashtray, the flashlight revealed another chain coiled on a rag. A rechargeable screwdriver lay halfway over an empty cigarette packet.

A three-ring folder had been propped almost upright at the back of the bench. Schematics for an electrical system? The pages were a little offset, with the telltale irregular strips of black around the edges: a photocopy of a mechanic's manual. He lifted it up and out from where it rested and fingered through a few pages. The few notations he found meant nothing to him.

He realized that he had no paper hankies to wipe down the edges of the folder. He stood again, and looked for a rag. It would have to be the one under the chain. He wrapped it loosely around his hand and then replaced the folder against the wall.

A wet-looking cardboard box on the floor was for rubbish, apparently. Amongst the half-crushed beer-cans were twists of paper, crisp bags, wrappers. He hooked the box with his shoe, and drew it out from under the bench. Settling on his hunkers he pressed his biro into service again to probe amongst the cans. Balled-up pieces of paper revealed receipts from an off-licence, an ad for garden services that had probably been dropped at the door with one for a dry cleaners. One scrap had scribbled numbers, and he was able to make out some of the words: –gasket –brake cable. Bus fares, a DART ticket; torn pieces of what seemed to be a form letter from the Revenue Commissioners; an ad for replacement windows, a furniture warehouse sale. McCarthy, or somebody, had emptied an ashtray here. He apparently liked Cheese 'n Onion crisps the best.

When the flashlight settled on another crushed ball of paper, it clicked with him that he had already primed himself to have an eye out for something like this. His eye was drawn to a detail on it right away: a section of serrated edge where this page had been torn from a coil bound notebook. He laid the flashlight on one of the flatter cans, and he began to open out the ball of paper.

The flashlight's glare only intensified the mosaic of folds, and threw a strong kaleidoscopic effect at Minogue's eyes. He tried to flatten it better along the ground. There were numbers, phrases, more printing than handwriting. The writing hadn't all been done in one go. A Dublin phone number was at an angle to a phrase, and it had been underlined and followed by two question marks. There were plenty of abbreviations, none of which he got, and dates. Aug. 17 1971, with a P.M. next to it but no numbers. A date next to it was Jan. 22 1972, and it was followed by a dash and another abbreviation, S.A. Or was it an S with a small scribbled r? Beside that was 'Kenya,' and Nairobi, spelled wrong. Off to the side was 'Uganda' followed by a question mark, and another misspelling for the Philippines. Near the bottom of the page was a phone number, with a name. Neary? What was Fr? Frank Neary? And the H.O. was head office?

He turned the page over and looked at the drawing first. It

was a map, or directions at least, and some of the scribbles were legible. Finglas Road, and Glas...it had to be Glasnevin. An arrow pointed down off the Finglas Road, and angled sharply several times before it stopped in a small, hand-drawn oval. He couldn't read what had been written for the names of the roads: he'd check it online later then. There were two more phone numbers.

The glare from the paper was making his eyes itchy. He dialed one-handed. It was answered in the middle of the second ring. Something in the woman's voice stirred a dim recall of other voices like it. A nun, a teacher?

"A nursing home did you say?" he asked.

"It is. Have you the wrong number, maybe?"

"Well, I don't know. I have this phone number on a piece of paper."

"What number are you trying to reach?"

Minogue held the paper up to the light again, and read out the number.

"Well that number is right," she said. "Tell who are you looking for?"

"I'm looking for a nun. It's a nursing home for nuns there, isn't it?"

A hint of suspicion had entered her voice.

"Who is calling, may I ask?"

He slid quickly into his bogman wiles.

"Ah, I'm an old friend of Sister Margaret's family, and I'm up in Dublin for a couple of days. I thought she might be there? Sister Margaret Mary...?"

"Did someone give you this number to phone?"

"I'm a bit short of information, I have to admit," he said.

"Is she Holy Faith?"

"Holy Faith? No, she's not. Sorry about that. She's Mercy, a Sister of Mercy."

"You needn't be one bit sorry. I don't have their number in my head now, but I know they have a place out near Drumcondra. Would you like me to find it for you?"

It took him five tries with the camera before he was satisfied with the job it did on the sheet of paper. He crushed up the sheet again, and dropped it back into the box. Replacing the beer cans one by one on top, he tried to imagine what Immaculata was doing this time of the day. Mass, he wondered, or prayers of some kind. Nuns were great for prayers, weren't they? She'd be getting ready for supper maybe, or doing routine jobs around the place. Around what place?

It could wait. He'd drop by Disciples in the morning. He placed the last of the cans on top, and gently toed the cardboard box back under the bench.

The damp, or the cold itself, had found its way to his finger joints. He made sure that he had pocketed his camera and he looked for some spot to park the flashlight while he replaced the rag back under that chain. The best he could manage was to balance it over one of the tubs on the bench and train the beam on the wall. The chain was unforgiving with the laws of physics. The moment that he saw a section snake quickly out from his grasp, he knew he was banjaxed.

He made a grab for the flashlight just as the beam jerked up. He got his fingertips to it, giving it help it didn't need to nudge the edge of the plastic tub and bring it over. His next grab sent the flashlight skittering. It ended with a crunch somewhere in the darkness near his feet.

He drew himself back upright, a glimpse of the escaping black liquid too clear in his mind. Cursing more in reflex than in anger, he let his knuckles find the door behind. Even fully opened, it barely helped. He hunkered down again, and extended his arm to full length, and he began a slow sweep over and back through the darkness.

The flashlight had come to rest close to the side of that cardboard box. It was in one piece. He brought it up and tried the switch several times. Then he shook it next to his ear. He couldn't tell for sure if the bulb had smashed. He cursed himself again for delaying buying one of those little geeky keychain LEDs. The curtains were straight now in the bedroom window of the Higgins household. No Higgins keeping vigil. He dithered then, but soon fled in irritation to a decision: hand Higgins back the damned flashlight, say nothing, and hit the road for home.

But a last try with the switch was his undoing: the light came on for a moment, flickered when he lifted it, and then died again. He pried open the case at the edge of the lens housing and let his fingers find the bulb. He twisted it snug and clipped back on the housing. It worked.

He stepped back into the shed and shone the flashlight on the workbench, braced for the sight of the slick, spreading pool there. It was not as he had imagined. Next to where the lip of the tub had come to rest was a dark shining line, a joint between two pieces of the plywood. He bent down and turned the beam up to where he expected the drips would still be falling.

There was no stain on the floor. His annoyance had evaporated. He found a spot on the floor, put down a knee, and he craned his neck to look up under the bench. It was dry up there. He shone the light down on the floor again, and slid the box of rubbish out of the way. Nothing.

He got back to his feet and looked again at where the tub had fallen on its side. Grasping the edge of the bench, pulled at it and let it go. It barely budged. He let the light sweep back along the floor again, and back under the bench. A flicker amongst shadows behind the box caught his eye and he held the light there. He had no trouble spotting the long, slow drip that soon followed. Yet again he hunkered down and he pulled out the box. There it was, a black, almost circular spot, and it was wet. But it was too small: a fair amount had spilled from the tub.

He got up and began to examine the bench again, his eye skipping from place to place over the junk that covered the bench. It was fit for purpose, and nowhere near as old as the house or shed itself. The cold was curling up into his shirt front now, and his knees were stiff. The knuckles of his supporting hand seemed to press harder into the cement floor when he got down on his knee this time. He leaned in more, and with an effort he managed to tap the flashlight on the underside of the bench. It gave slightly at each tap.

This time, he made sure that the flashlight was bedded properly. He made his start at the back of the bench, and soon he had a ragged line of margarine and yoghurt tubs trailing along the concrete outside. He left the loose stuff until last, often scooping bits to the edge of the counter and carrying them out in small heaps.

Three pieces of plywood made up the top of the bench. The heads of the screws that secured them were spaced in a workman-like way. He took the Phillips screwdriver, and pushed it down hard before giving it a slow, exploratory twist. No resistance: the head turned over and over again. But the joint between this piece of plywood and its neighbour had shifted when he had nudged it. He worked his baby finger in along the wall where it met the panel until he felt its nail slip down along the edge. Then he reached in his other hand and got another nail under it. It took several tries before he was able to clamp his nails onto enough of the edge. The opening grew. He got his finger pads under it and tugged. The panel came up.

There were sheets of paper there, printed. A set held together by a clip had taken the brunt of the spill. The crud had pooled there before veining out over the biscuit-coloured finish of the drawer to the spot where it had begun its slow, late leak down to the floor.

He set the flashlight on the bench, its beam flattening in a diffuse circle on the wall, and laid the panel on its edge by the door. Then he took out his camera, but then he hesitated. An image of Technical Bureau fellas gruffly prowling the place in their white boiler-suits had floated into his thoughts. Was cat-farting around in this shed part of his job? Or was he trampling on a secondary crime scene? Both? Neither...? At this rate, he might as well set out deck chairs for himself right in front of the fan, and make ready for the shite to cannonade his way.

Well maybe not.

He started with a small paper-clipped sheaf that had been half-nestling under the other. Only its very bottom edges had been hit by the spill. The top sheet was a printout, or a photocopy of a printout, and it bore the unmistakably spotty marks that he'd known too well from his time looking through microfiches and microfilm.

It was a short, businesslike obituary. November 18 1996,

Margaret 'Peggy' Larkin nee Murphy, after a short illness, in her seventy-fourth year. Beloved wife of the late Anthony Larkin LLB LLM, Justice of the High Court (d. 1988). Mourned by daughter Orna, London, and by son Padraig, London. Loving sister to Monica (Hynes) Carrickmacross, Co. Monaghan, Fidelma (Boylan) Leixlip, Co. Kildare, and the late Rev. Fr. Peter Murphy, Kenya and Blackrock (d. 1995).

The paper clip holding the other sheets behind was barely hanging on. He made to gently nudge it off with his thumbnail, but it flew through the air. He stopped and went still. Above the sounds of quickening breaths whistling out his nostrils, he could hear his own heart. He began holding his breath, and releasing it slowly through his mouth. It took a half dozen repeats to make any headway against the adrenalin.

He slid the next page to the front. 'In Appreciation – Tony Larkin,' a copy of an article from a parish newsletter from Sandycove. He skipped through it, lighting on details. This eulogy was delivered with keen feeling by one Patrick Moran, a member of the parish council. Humble roots and never forgot them. Encyclopedic knowledge, unparalleled legal expertise. Fair minded, impartial. Quietly devout family man. Daily communicant for most of his life. Lifelong member of the Franciscans' Third Order. Like St Peter himself, Tony had been a man keen on boats and fishing. The parish, and Ireland itself, had lost a man of towering faith and devotion to justice.

The third page turned out to be a long newspaper obituary for the same Justice Anthony Larkin. This was where the parish newsletter had lifted the 'towering faith' and the 'unparalleled expertise' from. The last page in looked like a blotchy printout from some newspaper archive. It comprised two short paragraphs under a heading, 'Conviction in Drugs Case.' Michael Farrell, 24, Walkinstown, Christopher Tuohy, 20, also of Walkinstown; James Traynor, 21, of Crumlin And finally, Joseph McCarthy, 20, address in Pearse Street, Dublin. A remark at the end from the presiding judge that trafficking in cannabis was a serious crime that attracted more crime, and would be dealt with seriously by the courts. A serious message from Justice Anthony Larkin.

He laid the pages one by one on the floor, and taking his camera, he crouched over each in turn. He let his thoughts hop-scotch while he waited for his eyes to readjust after the flashes. Father Peter Murphy, Kenya; Sister Immaculata, Kenya. Father Peter Murphy at some prayer thing on Dalkey Island years ago; Sister Immaculata – literally in the same boat. Father Peter Murphy, Sallynoggin parish. Joey McCarthy, Sallynoggin parish. Father Peter Murphy and his nephew Padraig Larkin, Sister Immaculata and her sometime client, Padraig Larkin.

He now heard a soft, intermittent patter of rain starting up. It was no time for finesse. He stepped outside and picking up the rag, he went for the stapled papers that had taken the most of the oil. More photocopies. He lifted the bundle by the corner and held it dripping over the rag.

The oil had made the first page almost translucent. Peeling it away he saw it was a copy of a magazine page. It wasn't one he recognized. He moved his grip, read the title: Missionaries of Divine Help? A row of children, dark faces, girls. Two nuns, one at each end of the row. They wore the same head-gear as the smaller nun standing to the side.

The writing beneath the picture was blurred by the spill, but legible enough: First Holy Communion St. Martha's, San Luis. South America? Mother Albert, Sisters Rosa and Paula. Mother Albert? She was the head of something, a convent, a school. He bent closer, but the picture's focus defeated him at that range too. He scanned the column to the left, struggling through holy talk that wearied his mind: sacraments, souls, Christ, mission, joy, prayers, sacred.

He took a photo, checked to see that it worked, and took another just in case. The next page had fared better in the mess. It had only a small printed section, a quick print from a web page 'Contact Us,' with an email address and two phone numbers. 'Counselling services are available.' 'After hours contact.' Across the bottom of the page were notes made in pen, and some doodles. He recognized phone numbers, and what looked to be dates.

The last couple of pages were photocopies of snapshots. It looked like the start of a procession, all serious business, with hands joined in prayer, serious frowns, tightly combed hair. The priest was decked out in vestments, and just as solemn-faced as the altar boys. One boy was holding a processional cross, another the chains of a thurible, the silver-plated bowl that held the incense. Looming behind the group, he recognized Sallynoggin Church.

The smaller picture beside it had slid and turned a little on the photocopier. The two boys in this picture looked back at the lens with cautious half-smiles. There were signs of a party on the table in front of them – a paper hat, a whistle, what looked like half-melted ice cream with wafers sticking up from it. The big window behind them had leaded sections at the top. The faux Tudors. A church? 'BD '67' had been written hurriedly in the space under the picture.

The glow in his chest had eased a little, but the turbulence still coursed through him. Again he tried to examine each of the faces, but almost immediately, his eyes lost their focus. He gave up, and let his stare come to rest on the spill. He was aware of the cold, of the quickening patter of the raindrops, of how the flash-light beam was wavering in his grasp. Each time he tried to coax something to unfold in his thoughts, it simply vanished.

There was one more sheet here, another print from one of the evening newspapers. There was no date. It was a short piece: 'Vandals desecrate historic Killiney church.' Along with the 'desecrate,' a county councillor took the opportunity to decry the influence of bad elements and a 'hippie' mentality that Irish youth seemed to think they had to ape. These signs of a 'Black Mass' were not merely matter for the Gardai, they were matters for their own eternal salvation.

He took his time reviewing the pictures he had taken. He considered phoning Malone, to keep him in the picture. No, he'd do that at home, after he'd copied the pictures on to his laptop. And then, it'd be a call to Ms. Orna Larkin. The self-same Orna Larkin who should have talked about this stuff. The Orna Larkin who wanted to leave her brother as he had been found, to be buried by strangers, and any coppers who wanted to do better for him out in the wind too.

He didn't even try to remember where any of the plastic tubs had been on the bench, but continued to ferry them in at a steady rate and to place them where it suited him. Locking the door at last, he thought of Immaculata, and imagined the questions he'd be lobbing at her first thing tomorrow.

Higgins was suspicious. Pips sounded from the radio in the kitchen: the news.

"Very much appreciated," Minogue said.

Higgins' breathing had grown more raspy.

"Whatever you were doing there, I don't know. I don't *want* to know."

Minogue stopped rubbing warmth back into his hands. The rain didn't seem to have made up its mind in earnest yet. The announcer handed off to a reporter, someone in Bagdad. Bombs had gone off outside of mosques.

Higgins tilted his head sideways a little, and sucked in a breath and grimaced.

"You hear that?" he said. "A mosque, that's a church for those people. Bombing churches. What kind of a religion is that? Savages, is what they are. *Savages.*"

Chapter 30

Minogue tapped out the last few sentences of his Wednesday email to his son. They were taking longer than the rest of the message. The blinking cursor had seized his attention and was beginning to drive him mad. He reviewed what he had written. Iseult had emailed from that WiFi restaurant near the place they had found in that village near Arles. Her painting was going well, and Pat seemed happy enough at the language school there. And Daithi's favourite cousin Mary was expecting her second in May. She had decided not to do the amniocentesis for Downs. Yes, she was very religious still.

But he had struggled to fill a paragraph about his own new circumstances. The job was 'interesting.' It was 'not quite what he had expected.'

He had tried to be brief about the country's woes. What was the point of dwelling on them? After all, Daithi read the papers online. But it was still important to mention these things at least. Maybe it was his own coded way to warn his son that moving back to Ireland was not a good move. No, not a good move at all.

"What was that you said about moving?"

He sat back again.

"I said, that wife of mine has excellent hearing."

"You said something 'good move,' like 'a good move.'"

"I was just talking to myself."

Naturally, he'd end the email on an up note. There'd be nary a hint that he had taken to drinking beer in the garage and that he had started smoking again. No mention of his suspicion that this had something to do with things he could no longer ignore, for example: that neither his son nor his daughter were living in their bloody home country. For example: that Iseult's marriage was shaky. For example: that he woke up too early and too often, ready to admit that the States was going to be his son's home always.

Maybe he'd put in a bit about Larry Higgins, proof positive that Dublin characters lived yet in all their glory. But he didn't. Instead, he slipped mention of a plan that wasn't a plan at all for him and Kathleen to steal away to Paris for a few days before Christmas. He typed 'Love' at the end, and then deleted it. His hands hovered over the keyboard, waiting for a proper finisher to come to mind. 'Your Da'? 'Look after yourself'? 'Regards to Kathi'? Not: 'When are you getting married?' or 'Why can't she spell her name right?'

He quickly retyped 'Love' and then he sent it. Kilmartin's email was still awaiting there in his Inbox, bold and Unread. Twice at least he had almost deleted it.

He signed out and returned to the pictures from his camera. Magnifying and zooming hadn't helped much at all. All he got were bigger spots, a closer view of blurred features. Malone's jibe had kept coming back to the surface: all nuns look the same. He zoomed out and felt a little less doubtful again: that face was a younger Immaculata.

He brought up the photo from the newsletter, the missionaries in the Philippines. Reducing the window to the face only, he set it next to the image with Immaculata and that priest in front of Dalkey Island. He just couldn't tell. The closer he looked, anything he believed was common – posture? expression? – evaporated in the sea of dots.

"Are you finished on that thing?"

The kitchen tap ran for several moments, and then the new stainless steel dish rack pinged with the rim of Kathleen's tea cup.

"Because there's something I have to show you. It'll only take a minute."

The clumping heels of her power-shoes from work turned to

a swish over the carpet. She rested her forearm on his shoulder and reached for the mouse.

"No cat videos if you don't mind. Or birds talking. Or dogs dreaming."

"Type in Lá le Bríd. The www bit first of course. One long word, no spaces."

He looked up at her.

"Just type it, will you. Nobody's going to brainwash you."

He watched the percentages climb on the clock that appeared. The first image faded in, sliding slowly left until it was eclipsed by another.

"Where's the sound? Have you got it on?"

"Can't I just watch?"

"Oh come on. It's an experience, you gom. The music is part of it."

It was a flute, a tune that he knew well but whose name he forgot.

"Is it a funeral maybe," he said. She didn't reply.

The pictures weren't bad at all. The Aran Islands shot must have been taken with a camera inches above the surface of Galway Bay. The single, bare whitethorn spread starkly over the bog behind.

"Is that wind I'm hearing?"

"It is. In a minute you'll hear waves. It's so...so evocative, isn't it?"

"Why am I watching this?"

"Why, why, why. It's always why with you. Just look, and listen."

The first word faded in and out. *Cneasta*: kind, gentle. The sound of the breeze began to take on a harsher edge.

"We brainstormed the words. We wanted Irish words too."

"They're nice photos," he said.

"I'll tell her then. Caoileann. Can you believe she's only nineteen?"

"Caoileann. What kind of a name is that?"

"She's like, oh...how to describe her? She arrived sort of complete."

"A saint, is she. And does she perform miracles too?"

"Oh stop it. Caoileann can do anything. She grew up in Peru, travelling with her parents. Sort of back-to-the-land thing. They're very, very spiritual people, her parents."

"Okay. I think I get it."

"Perfect music, isn't it? She did it all herself, the programming. Taught herself."

Another word appeared: *Bríomhar*. Lively, he thought. A good choice of word for the response he'd get were he to let out his thoughts about scented candles and chanting in sacred groves.

He was hearing waves now. Then the flute died out decently enough, leaving only the wind. It soon fell back to the soughing he had heard at the beginning.

"It's only a prototype now, we get to say how we want the final version."

Names appeared one by one. The second last was Kathleen Ferriter.

"Is that the Kathleen Ferriter I know?"

"I decided to go with my maiden name. Just so people don't get at you about it."

The screen was still now except for a glowing 'Repeat' button.

"What do you think?" she asked. "Be honest now."

"I was kind of used to the Kathleen Minogue bit."

"Oh look at you," she said and chortled. "I get it! Yes, I know what's going through your mind. You think I'm running away with a cult, don't you."

"You're taking vows maybe? A new order here, this Bridget thing?"

She ran her fingers through his hair and down over his forehead. The tenderness in her face looked too close to pity for his liking.

"Okay," he said. "Men have made a bollocks of things. Let the women take over?"

"The church isn't a priest," she said. "Or a bishop – or even a pope. It's people. We need a new day. A fresh start. Back to our roots. That's how we picked the name."

He sat upright. His patience was holding up better than he expected.

"Did you see Maura's name? She went back to her maiden name too. She was actually – what're those pictures you have there?"

"It's work, sort of."

"But that's a nun. What work is that?"

"It's complicated. I think maybe we were sold a bill of goods on something. So I'm going sideways at it, see what I can find."

"But I thought you were working on that poor man out in Dalkey, the homeless man?"

He rose, and he began rotating each shoulder in turn. Then he leaned in and clicked the windows closed. He left Kathleen's page open.

"I'm going to do a job in the garage," he heard himself say. "A little bit of reverse engineering, out in my man-cave there."

"It's not what you think," she said. "That website."

"What do I think?"

"I know you. You think it's a holy roller thing. It's not."

"Maybe it's episode fifty-nine of the men-are-toxic-women-are-angels thing?"

"Stop it. I don't know why you come up with that sort of nonsense."

Feeling the chill of wrong words approaching, he headed them off with a smile.

"Hope springs infernal," he said. She held to her own tight smile.

Closing the garage door behind him, he immersed himself in the comfort of its compound aromas: the lawnmower's grassy presence, sawdust, fertilizer. He felt entitled to smoke, and just as entitled to open a can of Gösser.

He let a few minutes go by. He didn't push back against the usual thoughts. Iseult, crying quietly in some dilapidated farmhouse in the South of France. Iseult bravely trying to keep it all together, fighting off the realization that her husband was slipping away from her into his own depressive's world. Iseult standing numbly in front of her canvas, unable to lift her paintbrush.

He parked the cigarette and reached into his pocket for his mobile. He had put in the space before Iseult's name to force her number to the top of his Contacts. He pressed Call, but even before he had raised the mobile to his ear, he had clamped his thumb on the End button. Who would it help, a phone call like that? Not his daughter.

He swore quietly. It was colder out here than he had realized. He had another gulp of beer, and then he turned to settling his notepad on the shelf that housed his bits and blades for the power tools. He wrote the time, and then he wrote O. Larkin, and he dialed.

The answering machine cut in before the first ring. He listened to the not-quite-English accent and swore quietly. He'd leave a message anyway.

He had gotten his name and number out before a voice interrupted.

"Wait a moment," she said. "Let the machine do its thing."

He heard several clicks and a droning ping.

"Who's calling?" she asked.

He repeated his introduction, lingering a little on the Inspector title.

"But why are you phoning?" she asked. "Why this hour of the evening?"

It wasn't irritation: it was a coldly factual.

"Well I want to introduce myself first, I suppose."

"At eight o'clock at night? Are you working at this hour?"

"It never stops," he said.

"Calling my home though?"

"Would you prefer I call you at your office? Tomorrow morning, say?"

She didn't reply right away. He took a quick drag of his cigarette.

"Is this normal procedure, calling someone at home at this hour – what am I saying, this is London, and you're in, where, in Dublin?"

"Dublin it is. But I should tell you that I'm at home. I had been thinking of phoning you earlier on, but I decided to wait."

She was fumbling with something. A pen and paper of her own, he guessed.

"Look, what's your name again – how do you spell it?"

When he had finished, he waited again.

"I wanted to talk with you concerning your brother, Padraig."

"Well I assumed that."

He studied his cigarette for several moments.

"This is going back a bit," he said then. "And I need your help. Your advice. Some items have come to light concerning your family."

"My family? Surely you're aware that I am the only one now."

"I am. But I mean your extended family. Your uncle."

A fleeting image of Murphy from the picture flared and dissolved in his mind.

"Your uncle Peter," he added.

"What about him?"

"A priest, wasn't he?"

"Well obviously you know the answer to that."

Her accent had slipped a little.

"This is bizarre," she said. "I have to say that. Quite bizarre. Why on earth you'd phone me, and why should I take your word that you are indeed a Garda...? I mean, if this is a legitimate enquiry – what's that sound?"

He held the can clear of the bench and let the last of the foam drip on the floor.

"I'm at home," he said. "Multitasking."

"Well as I was saying – "

"Ms. Larkin? Excuse me butting in now. I have limited alternatives. That's why you're hearing from me this hour of the day, from the garage of my home."

"Pardon? Your garage?"

"Exactly. Here in Kilmacud. In all its glory."

"I know Kilmacud, I think. Well, I did."

"That's grand. It's raining here. Spitting, as we say. Have you rain in London?"

"Rain? Here? Well now, not at the moment, no."

There was a different inflection in her voice now. He wanted to believe that it might be a thaw. The malty scent funneled into his nose as he put the can to his lips.

"You're the lucky one so," he went on. "It's the kind of rain that is reserved for Dublin only, I suppose. That kind of rain."

"But you are not from Dublin though," she said. "I can tell that much still."

"A serious enough allegation that."

"Irish charm doesn't work here, you should know."

Minogue took another sip.

"And I also have to tell you, Inspector Muldoon – if that's your name and you are not some anonymous person whose number refuses to show here on my call display—"

"—Don't worry, it'll show on the log at BT. Same system as ours here."

"You are an expert in this, are you?"

"Far from it. But I was in the Technical Bureau here for a good number of years. The section I worked in went by the dramatic title of Murder Squad."

"Telling me that, is that your way of applying pressure here?"

A swig of beer had trapped wind on its way down. He couldn't summon a belch.

"It is actually," he said.

"Well it fails in that task."

"If you'd prefer to go the official route, you need only say so. It's grand by me."

"What official route would that be?"

He flipped up the sticky to read the address of the local copshop.

"It would be me putting in the request, into the Met – do you actually call them the Met, or is that just the telly?"

"The police?"

"Just so. I'd be requesting them to have a chat with you. Over at, let me see…Lewisham. The High Street? Yes, that'd be your local, I suppose. But I suppose they'd offer you the chance to chat at home first, naturally."

He held his cell a little away from his ear, and he took a long drag on his cigarette.

"This isn't pressure you're talking about," she said. "It's intimidation."

"That's not the plan here, Ms. Larkin."

"It isn't? Can you spell your name exactly now, your rank, and your number?"

"You have my name already. Now I have questions for you. It's up to you how and where you wish to answer them, or to refuse to, of course."

He braced for the click.

"I'm asking for your help in filling in some blanks here," he said.

"Blanks. 'Blanks' is code for...?"

"Information we don't have. Gaps. Some people might read these gaps as something else. They might see willful concealment in there."

"I have absolutely no idea what you are on about. Is that what the Gardai are like nowadays? I don't remember them being paragons in my day either."

"Ms. Larkin. What happened to Padraig?"

The sound from her end sounded like a pen being planted firmly on a notepad.

"I beg your pardon?"

Her return to that English accent jolted him a little.

"Your brother," he replied. "I'm asking you what happened to him. And I don't mean how he met his end. I mean how he came to be the man he was."

The silence lasted several seconds.

"Do you have any idea just how rude you are being here?"

"I have read his details. He avoided the criminal justice system rather well."

"I'm hanging up. But I shall be— "

"—But I'm not interested in that. I am interested in why he did the things he did."

"This is deeply – *deeply* – offensive. I won't participate in this."

He could do little else but dig in further.

"Was it drugs? Me, I don't think that's the whole story at all. Though I don't doubt for a minute but that they can tip a person over the edge."

"What are you saying, 'over the edge'?"

"Well, was your brother a child molester from birth then?"

The sharp intake of breath was followed by an open-mouthed sigh.

"I'm having difficulty believing you actually said that."

"You knew about the Black Mass stuff he did, I take it. Or heard about it."

"We have nothing to discuss."

"And why am I only learning about your uncle now, by chance almost?"

"What uncle?"

"The one who was a huge success as a new curate in the parish next door to the one where you grew up. The 'highly pop-ular,' the 'much-liked,' Father Peter. The one who was whisked away, and then showed up on the missions a few weeks later in some corner of Africa. That one, the one who died out there, out there in Kenya somewhere."

He held the mobile out again, and reached for the can of beer.

"Do you have any idea," she began, but then stopped.

"Any idea of...?"

"Of how hurtful this is? How unnecessary?"

"I don't understand."

"Have you heard me calling for vengeance? Complaining that no-one has been caught for what happened to Padraig?"

"You'd be entitled to, I think. All I can say is that we're trying."

"Don't you get it?"

Her voice had regained its firm timbre.

"Tell me what I'm not getting here."

"It's me you're punishing," she said. "Don't you see it can't undo what's happened? That you're not going to help anyone by threatening me?"

"I'm not threatening anybody" was all he could come up with.

"What happened, happened," she said. "It was a tragedy, yes, and I hope that you catch somebody. But I didn't commit a crime. I mean no harm to anyone. I live my life, and do the best I can."

"So what harm is there in telling me then? In talking about it at least?"

"Talk? Talk does nothing. It only makes people go through it again."

He hesitated then, but the chancy moves had moved quickly up his mental list.

"Your family was devout, I believe."

"Is that an observation? It's an impertinent one then."

"You know what we have going on here, with the church. On the news, lately?"

"Lately? It still surprises me when people use the word 'lately.'"

"Your father—"

"—Leave my father out of it."

He let a few seconds go by.

"He was a judge. I read the testimonials to him. A fine man." She said nothing.

"So it baffles me," he went on. "It really baffles me, I have to say, how such a close and loving family could have such a thing happen."

"Do you..." she said, and paused. "Do you have even the slightest idea of how outrageous you're being?"

He made a quick survey of the dead flies in the cobwebs by the light bulb.

"People talk a lot here," he said then. "Sure aren't we famous for the yapping we do? But I'm not sure we really say that much. Do you know what I mean?"

He scrutinized at the crest on the can while he waited, but she made no reply.

"There's no end of cleverality and wit and humour and God knows what else. But I'm not at all sure we listen though. Do you know what I mean about us here?"

"I think I see your point. But why you're telling me this, I don't know."

"Well like I was telling you, I'm out in the garage here. I'm actually smoking a cigarette. Yes, me, a grown man, well able to figure things out. So I'm ashamed of myself for this. But habits are hard to break, aren't they. The more you focus on something, the harder it is to get by it. What they call the ironic effect, in psychiatry. Have you heard of that?"

Her response was a quiet, toneless murmur.

"I'm a chemist by training, not a shrink. Or a neurologist."

He began a slow patrol up and down the garage floor.

"My point is that maybe we haven't been looking at the right things, in the right places. Going so hard at the obvious that we miss things. It happens in a lab too, maybe?"

"It can."

"Ah. Well tell me something now. Why don't you come back to Ireland at all?"

He could hear her moving about now. He prepared for a return of her indignation. But a cold, almost resigned, tone had come into her voice.

"You tell me something instead. Did they coach you for this? Or did they pick you because they thought you could do this on your own already?"

"Coach me for what?"

"Don't you have psychologists, consultants now? All the police do, surely."

He stared at the crest on the can again.

"Nobody asks me to make a phone call like the one I am on right now. And for damned sure, nobody can 'prep' me for one either. You'll pardon that extra word there."

"Really."

"I decided to phone you about one hour ago. It was after a visit I paid to a house earlier this evening. I had already come across something odd at a Garda station in Dalkey. But it was the visit to that house that has me on the phone to you now."

"Odd," she said, with what he thought could be a mock sympathy.

"Those gaps I'm trying to fill in," he said. "Someone else has been trying to do the self-same job already. Did you know that?"

"Other police – other Guards – you mean?"

"Yes of course, but someone else too. A person...well, let's say he had a chequered past. But the main thing is that it appears he knew Padraig a long time ago."

His words seemed to have stifled hers. He gave it a count of five before resuming.

"It's not clear at all," he said. "But he was trying to find out more about Padraig."

"Who is he?"

"Let's hold off on that for the moment, if you please."

"Well, what is he telling you then?"

"He's not telling me anything, I'm afraid. Nothing directly, at any rate."

"You're falling back on some police technique here, are you? Offer some information, and then take it away?"

"Hardly. He went missing, that's why. But he was found yesterday."

Something sounded at her end, like a pen falling on the notepad again.

"'Found?'" she asked. "Does that mean...?"

"You're right," he said. He took his time now, as he had planned for this stage.

"Yes. He's dead. And yes, it's looking like he was murdered."

Chapter 31

It was a gasp he had heard all right. He imagined Orna Larkin sitting suddenly upright, her eyes wide with fright.

"I'm going to tell you his name now," he said. "Why? Because there's a chance that you know him. McCarthy. Joseph, or Joey, McCarthy. Do you know him?"

Her reply was barely audible.

"Yes."

"I wondered if you would."

"Yes," she repeated, in a murmur. "He'd be the one."

"The one. What one?"

"The family. His mother, is she...?"

"She's in hospital. She collapsed when she was given the news."

"She's a great age by now. Catherine."

"She is that. You knew her too, then?"

"And she has a country accent. She had."

Minogue prepared to put out his cigarette.

"Catherine'd say 'praties,'" she murmured, swallowing. "So we'd say it too. Mother didn't like that. Papa, I think he liked it but he didn't let on. He was different that way."

Minogue was close to losing this thread, but he didn't want to interrupt.

"It was strange really, because they were both from the country, my parents."

Her accent was softening more.

"But Mother didn't want that to be so, so apparent. We did elocution lessons, can you imagine? Do you know what elocution is?"

"'The splendor falls on castle walls –'"

"'– And snowy summits old in story.'"

She took over as he had hoped. A warmth came into her voice as she recited.

"'The long light shakes across the lakes,'"

"'And the wild cataract leaps in glory.'"

"You're good," he said. "Not the best I've heard, but good."

"But, how – why – would you know it too?"

"The Christian Bothers wanted to knock some civilization into us, I suppose."

He realized that he no longer expected her to hang up.

"Just about the worst poem in the world," he said. "Don't you think?"

The caution had returned to her voice.

"But it stays with you," she said. "That's something, I suppose."

"Fond memories?" he asked.

She made to say something but held back.

"You were saying," he tried now. "About Mrs. McCarthy?"

"She worked for us for a number of years."

"After Father Peter left, was it?"

"You don't let go, do you?"

Her sudden lurch back to prickly surprised him.

"I should have known. I let down my guard a little and this is what happens."

He decided to push on.

"As I understand, it was after he left the parish. Correct me on that, by all means."

She sighed in exasperation.

"It was after, of course it was *after*. And you knew this before you ever brought up the subject, didn't you?"

"I didn't. But I had heard that Joey McCarthy was brought over to a family so that he could mix with the kids there, people with a good way of life. To keep him out of trouble, I suppose. Role models?"

"He was at the house a fair bit, I remember."

"Friends with Padraig?"

"No. He was foisted on Padraig. Padraig resented it too. Papa was behind it, I think. He was trying to help out that family a bit."

"Your father would have known that Mrs. McCarthy was let go from the parish house there, wouldn't he? Father Peter, and that?"

"He would, I daresay."

Sparks from the cigarette came out from under his shoe as he ground it underfoot.

"A bit sudden, wasn't it," he said quietly. "Father Peter going away like that?"

The tension was suddenly back in her voice.

"Was it? I don't know how those things work."

"A diocesan priest is gone on the missions almost the next day after saying mass in his local parish? It is very odd. Do you recall that time?"

"No. Not really. I was a child, remember."

"Do you remember Father Peter, your uncle I should say?"

She did not reply right away.

"Why are you asking me about him?"

"I'm trying to get a better picture."

"A better picture of what? Of whom?"

"I want to see if something happened that has a bearing on how Padraig lived."

The silence now was calculated. He began a countdown to the line going dead.

"You know more than you're letting on," she said at last. "A lot more. And you're using that, to see if I say something that doesn't jibe."

"I only wish that were the case," he said.

"That's very candid, I have to say. But it does you no credit."

"I think you deserve candour, Ms. Larkin. I think we all do

actually. It has been in short supply here for too long."

"You're daring me to say something, aren't you?"

He opted for silence.

"You know about my parents, my family. So you'll have all the dirt already then. Why not admit it?"

"It's not the case at all. I'm not out to dig dirt."

"But you know about Father Peter. That man. So why keep on pretending here?"

"I phoned you in the hopes that you'd fill in some gaps—"

"—Gaps? Of course. You have a job to do, don't you."

It was the first time he heard bitterness in her voice.

"You know well why I'd never set foot in Ireland again after Mother died. You know damned well."

"Actually I don't. But I think I'd like to, if you're willing to tell me."

"Do you think I wanted to be the one to do what I did? That I chose to take it on? Look, I'm not that kind of person, I admit it. My father and mother were – charitable, decent people. Good living people. But you'll never see me in a church, Catholic or otherwise. Never. No, I'm not anywhere near as good as a person as either of them."

"You're being fierce hard on yourself. But I know that you took care of Padraig when he lived in London there."

"While my mother and father were alive, I did – but that was all. When we buried Mother, that was it. I told Padraig there and then, that I'd see to it that Mother and Papa's wishes were kept with an allowance. But that was it. You cannot reason with a person on drugs. I tried it – many times I tried it. Nothing good came of it in the end."

"You tried to persuade him to...?"

"Oh don't tell me you didn't know it now," she bristled. "Come on."

"I doubt it."

"My mother was an alcoholic, for God's sakes. There – the words you want to hear. I'll even say them again for you. Yes, an alcoholic. So now you can check that off on your list, as 'confirmed' or whatever you write."

"That's not what this is about."

"Oh isn't it? Look, you don't have to be a PhD here to see the connection. You've said it yourself. You dropped enough hints anyway."

"I am completely at sea here. I—"

"Do you think Ireland is all postcards and bogs and fiddle music, nice green fields? 'The Little People'? Is that what they still believe back there?"

"Some probably, because they don't want to know what goes on here."

"And do you know what depression is? Why my mother drank?"

"I'm sorry, I didn't know any of this."

"Well all right, then – I could maybe believe that for now anyway. After all, why would you? Why would anybody, really. It might have been the best-kept secret ever in Dun Laoghaire – in Ireland itself maybe. My father did everything. And that's why we had Catherine Mac come in as a mother's help. My mother got to a stage where she couldn't function. It'd last for months on end. 'Nerves.' Can you imagine? It was post-traumatic stress and depression rolled into one. That's what it was. I know that now. But why was she like that, I wondered."

Minogue was not sure which tack he should take.

"Things run in families," he tried. "They're finding out more these days, aren't they. Genes and that…?"

He heard her give out an exasperated breath.

"Genes. Ah yes: *genes*."

She hadn't tried to mute the sarcasm.

"And to think," she went on, but in a tone so soft that it took Minogue by surprise. "To think, that the fondest wish a family could have was to see a son go into the priesthood."

"Father Peter you mean?"

"Yes, Father Peter."

"But I read he was well-liked and everything, very dynamic. Sports and so forth, with the youth?"

"You think," she began, but her words trailed off.

"Anything you can offer us," he said, quietly. "Anything."

"Clare," she murmured then. "County Clare."

"That's the place," he said.

"You miss it?"

"There are times. But I didn't get to choose back then."

"So tell me, when did you see the Cliffs of Moher last?"

He took the unlit cigarette from his mouth.

"Years ago. I'm no tourist."

"Really?"

"That's how things have gone here," he said. "So I abstain."

"Fanore then? The beach?"

"Funny you mention it. I went in for a dip there only last July. Not an edifying sight, I should tell you."

"As cold as ever, was it?"

Her accent had slipped completely now.

"Cold as a landlord's heart. As cold as charity, my mother'd say."

"It has dangerous tides of course – they wouldn't change."

"You know Fanore then."

"We went in the summers," she said. "Before things went wrong."

He did not recognize the quiet sounds that were coming at intervals from her end.

"I want to ask you," he said. "But I don't think I should."

"There were always seals," she said. She was sobbing now. "And I thought, well this was some kind of magic, a sort of miracle even, how they'd come in to see us, and they'd look at us, as though they had something to tell us, or that I could tell them things and they wouldn't...they wouldn't tell others...."

He lighted his cigarette, and listened to her muffled sobs.

"They still come in," he said then. "I've seen dolphins there too."

"I'm glad to hear that. I am, really."

The sobs were being replaced by sniffs. He took a long pull from the cigarette.

"Yes, they're still there," he said. "Not the same ones maybe. But who's to know? Come on back and see for yourself. I'll drive you, if you like."

She spoke a stifled voice, pausing once to swallow.

"Tell them you did well. Tell your superiors, your boss."

He bit back hard on a curt retort.

"It doesn't sound like that to me," he managed. "Can we talk again maybe?"

"I don't know. If I have a choice, I won't."

"People are depending on you," he said.

She sighed. He could not tell if she was angry.

"Listen to me," she said. "The past? There's no 'past.' I understand that. I don't like it, in fact I hate it, but I accept it. It has taken me a long, long time. I am trained as a scientist, and that was my saving. Papa saw to that, he got me out. And I know it broke his heart. He had terrible things to do, and he deserved none of this any more than Mother did. If I had stayed, I would have been destroyed too, like Mother. Can you see that?"

"I'm working in the dark here," he said. "I'm only making guesses."

"You kept up your faith, did you? You're Catholic, I'm guessing."

"Well it's like they say about the Irish atheist, maybe. He doesn't believe in God, but he's still afraid of Him."

"Ah yes. The Devil then?"

"Not keen on him either. He gets the thumbs-down, during the daylight anyway."

"I don't believe in God either, but can you understand it if I say that I still believe in the Devil?"

"You could make a fierce good case for that lately, I'm thinking."

"My mother died of shame," she said flatly. "Do you understand that?"

"I'm not sure I do. For what happened with Padraig, you mean?"

"No, no. Something happened to her when she was young. She would never tell, and she refused to talk to anyone ever about it."

Minogue looked through the smoke settling in layers under the light.

"And over the years I have come to decide...to believe, I

suppose…that what happened to her, was the same as happened to Padraig. The same thing that almost happened to me."

Again he waited, fighting back hard against the surge of impatience. He sensed then that she was absenting herself from this, that it was over.

"Would you be willing to put a name on this? A term, I mean."

"There are no names that work," she said. "No terms. They can't describe it."

"Father Peter?"

In the quiet that was to follow her reply, he still held the mobile to his ear. The remorse came at him with unexpected force. He had brought it back to her. She had said it herself: made her live through it again. He swore quietly and squeezed the casing on his phone harder, half-hoping it would fly apart. Had the drink pushed words onto his tongue, made him dig in and push hard at her? It didn't matter now, did it.

So she had not been clearly angry then, when her hand had wandered over the button and she has pressed it. He thought of her sitting there, staring into space perhaps, replaying the past. She was an educated person, a woman who had carved out a decent life over there. Surely she had known this had to come about?

Her flat tone had signaled the end to the conversation even before he heard that last, short sentence from her, a sentence she repeated in a voice that he had been barely able to hear. He took a small mouthful of beer. It had a metallic taste now. He did not repeat her words again in his mind as he had done several times already. This time he murmured them aloud.

"'My brother wasn't the only one.'"

Chapter 32

Minogue was awake before the alarm. He had resigned himself to sleeplessness around three, when it seemed to him that any effort to still his thoughts would only backfire.

"Rough night? And you were late enough to bed too."

Kathleen's eyes caught light from the display, and glistened.

"I was awake anyway," she added.

"Was it the job?"

"No. I was worried before, but now I'm not. But Brídín? She needs it."

The returning quiet seemed deeper. He eyed the clock again, and then closed his eyes and curled up a little. Another fifteen minutes would do no harm. He had finally gotten through to Malone just after eleven last night, after leaving a text and a voice message. There had been that godawful easy-listening music in the background, the stuff that always played in the Chang family's restaurant. A good sign?

"Tell me something," Kathleen said. "What would you think now, if I were to say to you that I want to do something new. Even to *be* someone new."

He determined to keep his eyes shut, and not to stir.

"I'd say that seven in the morning isn't the best time to be asking hard – I mean important – questions."

The bed quivered and then shook as she rolled out.

"You're right, as usual," she said with a sigh. "So can we pick a time then? We'll call it a date? This weekend?"

He turned his face up from the pillow. She was already on the landing by now, and heading for the bathroom, humming.

After breakfast he checked the folder of photos that he had placed dead-centre on the Desktop. The battery was topped up. Immaculata would never be able to claim that she hadn't had a chance to go over the photos enough times to be certain of anything.

Kathleen was out the door ahead of him. The rain had died away sometime during the night, and dry patches were already appearing on the footpaths. An undecided breeze pushed back at the last of the leaves on the hedges. Kathleen was silent on the way up to the Luas. Absent was her usual survey of the roads and houses they passed, of laggard schoolkids and pensioners making their way home from the morning Mass. In its place was a contented expression, a gaze that didn't stray from the lower sky ahead.

Only when he pulled in at the Luas did she seem to wake up. She turned to him with bright, expectant eyes, and smiled.

A thudding text alert sounded from his mobile.

"Our minds are at work all the time," she said. "Aren't they?"

He could only nod and wait.

"So the answers arrive in their own good time, that's what I'm discovering. You know what I mean? Everything works out. God is good."

He blinked affably and came up with a half smile. She leaned in for a kiss.

The text was Malone: *m n dalkey U@*

"On time," he muttered. "As in: not early."

Minogue considered the N50 iffy, and he was willing to gamble on his own route through to Leopardstown Road. If there was any hold-up he'd improvise en route. He soon found himself slotted in a line of cars in the fast lane closing on the turn he wanted, in Cabinteely. Waiting at the light gave him a chance to rethink what he had brought with him, and what he hadn't.

Should he have printed off a copy of that map of Kenya, with those missions dotted around that Turkhana area? He imagined sliding it nonchalantly onto the table in that dinky little room, the 'office' that Immaculata would draw them to. He'd say nothing, just watch her reaction.

His was the last car to make the light. The road soon began its descent, and above the curve ahead that signalled the start of its climb back up toward Sallynoggin, the two hills, Dalkey and Killiney, slid up his windscreen. The obelisk that marked Killiney Hill was first to sink out of sight.

Most of the traffic seemed to be heading down toward the N11 for the rest of their commute into the city. He almost missed his turn off the roundabout: a gap behind let him space to wheel over in time. The road climbed again. He soon spotted the crest from where he'd begin the slow descent to the next roundabout, closer to Dalkey and the sea.

The minutes changed on the dashboard clock and he poked the radio on for the headlines. It was not what he wanted to hear. He poked the button again, catching the announcer in mid-syllable. It wasn't like he didn't already know the rest of the gobshite's name anyway, the one elected by bigger gobshites, to be leader of their political party.

Three schoolgirls plodded along the footpath, their gabardines tugged to their necks by heavy schoolbags. Right – there was a convent school nearby. He couldn't remember its name. He tried to estimate how long it had been since he had come along this road, but drew another blank. Shrubbery had grown to a decent height on both sides of the road. He caught glimpses of conservatories, stonework, serious landscaping. But there was a nowhere feel to the place. Unfair, yes, maybe even snobbish of him but what could he do? Even the occasional quick view of Dalkey Head between the houses was bland: all he could see was the headland that screened any view of the castle itself. No wonder he hadn't come this way for ages. It hadn't a patch on the coast road.

A trickle of cars came toward him over the rise ahead, and then he was cresting it himself. Brake lights glowed on the line of cars waiting their turn at the roundabout. So that's where the traffic had gone to. He touched the brakes, to wake up the phone-aholic in a new Passat who had come out of nowhere to within a couple of feet of his bumper. Soon he was stopped. He watched the steady stream of cars filtering through the roundabout from the very road where he was headed. He studied the scratches on the bumper of the Toyota ahead, the feeble attempts at touch-ups. Even inching ahead, the Passat crowded him again. A quick glare in the mirror had no effect.

His thoughts drifted to Mrs. McCarthy. What was she waking up to today? Did she imagine she was in the middle of a nightmare? Maybe she hadn't slept at all. Maybe she hadn't woken. He imagined McArdle shivering in some doorway near the DART station, or doing his begging openly at the entrance. And the hulking, explosive Walshe? Hardly much different. The pair could well be trudging toward the drop-in already, kept together by bonds that were stronger than Walshe's fits of rage, or McArdle's needling comments. For all their bickering, their fight-ing and even their routine betrayals, they were a pair by necessity, linked by their common cravings, and their fates.

What would fill the day for people like that? They had their rounds, no doubt. Cups of tea, a dinner; a couple hours of televi-sion. Scrounging smokes, scheming; maybe a scatty, grudging conversation with others at Disciples. Always on the make to work up any prospect of a bottle, or a high. But whatever today brought for them, it would likely be a day like any other, one more episode in a numbing succession.

He tried the radio again. They had moved on to something else. Some chirpy yo-yo firing out unfinished sentences about how the listeners could get control of their credit card debt. The driver behind had either lost it completely and was arguing with himself, or else he was having a highly animated Bluetooth con-versation. Minogue's mind slid by imagined lives: hedge fund dealer trying to cover a bad move. Philanderer trying to keep a lid on mistress issues. Early morning scam arranger. Or he could be just a well-groomed new breed of senior civil servant talking rugby.

He leaned his head against the window for a better view ahead. There was no let-up in the stream of cars pouring out on to the roundabout to his right. He began to tally the high-end makes. Audi TT, 7 series BMW right behind it. An AMG Merc, the eight cylinder. Another Audi.... Financial crisis? What financial crisis? He drummed his fingers on the wheel, and finished with a sharp, exasperated tap.

Somebody was beeping: the gobshite in the Passat. But still it did the trick, stampeding the clapped-out Fiat at the head of the line. The same Fiat got three separate beeps for its efforts. Minogue let his Peugeot roll ahead. A Renault bolted out in imitation of the former pack-leader Fiat. Across the roundabout, another line of cars wasn't doing much better, he saw. The one at the front was inching a little forward, only to stop abruptly when a lorry swung close – deliberately, Minogue guessed – and leaned on his horn. But then it was off, leaving the field to a black Range Rover.

The driver wore wrap-arounds, but the glare on the windscreen obscured the interior. Bono would hardly be driving something so crass. Another beep sounded from behind. He adjusted his mirror a little and gave the Passat driver a brief, cold scrutiny.

When he looked back, he saw that a gap had opened behind the Range Rover. The car behind made a shuddering start. Minogue's idle survey sharpened to a stare. It was an Escort all right, the same faded red as Malone's jalopy. All he could see of it now was a tight view down the driver's side. The line for the back edge of the door was heavier than it should be. The results of Malone's half-busted door mechanism on display? It made no sense.

The Toyota made its move ahead. Minogue ditched his confusion, let in the clutch and rolled forward, ready to pounce on a gap. He scanned the traffic coming his way, saw the Range Rover start but then suddenly dip at the front as it braked. No mercy here out here in Dalkey at rush hour: what we have, we hold. Yet another beep from the Passat behind. This time Minogue pressed the brakes three times, and turning slowly in his seat he planted a glare on the driver. Splayed fingers on the top of the steering wheel flexed open and went limp. Some over-the-top eye rolling came for the finale.

"Do that one more time," Minogue murmured. "And we'll see what kind of a diva you turn out to be. And what kind of a bollocks I can be."

Across the roundabout, the Range Rover was inching out again. A motorbike was now making its way by the line of cars behind it, crawling along cautiously, ready to tuck in for oncoming cars. Its front wheel wavered more as it slowed. From its dropped handlebars and low fairing, he recognized it as another of those overpowered rockets that shot by routinely on the motorway, filling the air with that exhaust note that sounded like a power saw meeting knotty wood.

A second helmet leaned out from behind. The driver responded to the shift by putting out his legs. Then, after making a short, staggered march on his heels, he brought the motorbike to a stop. The passenger slid off awkwardly, making a few hops to right himself. Novices, was Minogue's first thought. Flat tire? He couldn't see where the wheel met the asphalt. Engine trouble maybe. That Range Rover, the driver, what were those sunglasses called? Fly Shades? Was Bono actually a Range Rover type of guy? That would fit all right: Bono lived near here somwehere, and they had a gaggle of kids, didn't they? A celebrity making the school run then, he thought, and the two on the motorbike were doing a paparazzi gig.

He let down his window a little. The sound he had been hearing was indeed that motorbike, revving. The driver was back crouched over the tank, and his helmet was swiveling left and right. Those full-face helmets had always put Minogue in mind of an insect head. The passenger took a step in close to the cars, and began pointing and then jabbing the air. Minogue squinted, but he couldn't be sure he saw a camera. Maybe it was one of those new fancy shoot-on-the-go videocams. Or was this a row? Just what they needed: a bout of road-rage to gum up the damned traffic here entirely.

Something stirred in the back of his mind. He stopped

thinking, and just stared.

The Range Rover sank back hard as the driver hit the accelerator, and it lurched into traffic, swaying wildly. An instant after the squeal the horns came on. Traffic was suddenly at a standstill. Minogue looked back toward the red Escort and his blood froze.

The Escort's windscreen had turned white.

The motorbike passenger had one hand on the bonnet, but the other hand was still extended, pointing. Absurdly, it reminded Minogue of that children's game: Releevio, was it called, when a kid yelled 'safe'? Then, as though negotiating some awkward passage on a boat, the figure began skirting the bonnet of the car. When he reached the driver's window, he reached into the car's interior. His arm shook twice, and then he was running.

The motorbike was rolling forward now, and revving high. The passenger grabbed the driver's shoulder and stood on one footrest. Tearing and poking at his jacket still with his free hand, he swung his leg over the saddle. The motorbike wobbled as it made off, and then dipped, pitching the passenger forward. After a long, wavering yaw that took it close to the edge of the road, it straightened out. The passenger jerked backwards as the throttle opened. With a final weave around a car, the driver drew in his feet and changed gear again.

Minogue's legs were quivering as he got out of his car. He was aware of a car door opening nearby, sounds of leather soles on the asphalt.

"Jesus Christ. Did you see that? Can you believe it?"

The driver from the Passat was shorter than he had expected, and his face was drained of colour. He pointed toward the roadway where the motorbike had vanished, and he spoke slowly, little louder than a whisper.

"Did that actually happen?"

Minogue couldn't keep his arm steady. He pressed his knuckles onto the roof, tightening his grip on his mobile, and pushed the keypad hard each time. Jamming his mobile against his ear, he took a few steps back and let his door close. His knees were giving way. Two or three drivers were half-out of their cars now. Someone was shouting. A few of the cars made their way tentatively around the roundabout now.

"This is bad, isn't it?"

The driver of the Passat stood staring across at the Escort, shivering.

It was a man's voice answering in his ear now, a well-tamed country accent.

Minogue had to pry the words from his throat.

"A shooting," he repeated. "That's right, just now."

Everything seemed to pounce on him at once then: could a person actually forget to breathe? Was that drizzle he was feeling on his face? Who was that man who just flinched, and stepped back hurriedly from the side of the Escort as though he had put his hand on something hot? Was that a sign of the cross he was making?

The dispatcher asked again.

"My location?" Minogue repeated, his throat knotting again. The Passat driver was staring at him now.

"Do you know this area?"

"Well I go through here every day."

Minogue thrust the mobile at him.

"Tell them the name of this goddamned road here then. And tell them it's a Guard involved – a Guard! And tell them about the motorbike – headed toward town."

Even from his first step, Minogue's throat burned, and each grunting gulp of air only cut harder. He kept his eyes on the roof of the Escort, willing a figure to appear there climbing out the driver's side. He didn't care that there was a greasy feel to the asphalt, or that that traffic was beginning to move again. Panicked voices spilled out the open window of cars – *just happened, I don't know, I swear to God, Guards* – and thumped hard on the roof of a Fiat as he bounded by it, bringing it to a squealing stop beside him.

The man he'd seen crossing himself by the side of the Escort had stepped away from it, and was talking into a mobile. Behind rectangular glasses – the kind Kathleen liked so much and that he scorned – his eyes were clenched almost shut. Still talking, he took a few steps into Minogue's path, and breaking away from the conversation, he raised his arm.

"No," he said, hoarsely. "There's nothing we can do—"

Minogue brushed by, forearm up, and began to slow amid the first few particles of glass. He made a quick check of the pavement and saw one casing not more than a foot from the front tire on the passenger side. A sharp tang from the gunshots still hung in the air, sour enough to sting his nostrils yet. He crouched a yard from the car, and over the glass fragments sprinkled on the window seal he glimpsed a quick drip from the roof lining.

The driver's face was turned to the gap between seat and door, the seat belt flat and tight still over the chest. Minogue tried to ignore the wet gleam of blood oozing over the face, and stared hard at the neck, and then down at the chest. Nothing, nothing at all.

"Don't touch anything...."

The chill space in his chest had opened more, and in the heaving light, things were beginning to pulsate. Eyes scanning the pavement, he began to make his way around to the driver's side. Another casing had come to rest by a furrow in the asphalt.

"Look—"

"Shut up, will you," he heard himself say. "I'm a Guard."

A spreading delta of arterial blood had run down the driver's door, and was dripping on the fragments of glass. He forced himself to glance toward the face, and immediately recoiled, gasping. The pink and grey mass flowering above a bloodied forehead was bordered in places by small, pale shards that poked through the hair.

"Really, there's nothing we can do."

He had followed him over, and was keeping his distance. Shock had drained his face of colour, leaving only maroon patches by his nostrils. He swallowed nervously.

"I'm a doctor," he said, and pushed his glasses up on the bridge of his nose. The stems were thick, Minogue noticed, with that that weird, stripey wood look to them.

A car horn sounded. People's voices were nearby, men's. The light about him was beginning to lose its lurid cast, and return to the muted hues of an overcast November morning. His chest heaved slower, but the sharp stabbing in his throat was starting to throb. He began to draw in measured breaths through his nose. The weakness in his knees turned warmer.

"You need to sit down, I think."

The doctor poked at his glasses again. Minogue had to concentrate to keep his eyes back to focus now. He wanted to tell him to stop doing that thing with his glasses. To stop looking at him like he was a wild animal. To shut up, actually.

A bearded man with scaly, pockmarked skin came at a laboured jog from a van: J O'Neill plumber. He looked frightened, and resolute.

"I seen it all," he said. "Anybody doing CPR yet? I have it, but I might be a bit rusty. Is there…?"

Minogue wanted to answer, but weariness had crashed over him. The bearded man took a few steps toward the car, and stopped. He rose on tiptoe but then almost immediately he sagged and turned away, his hand over his eyes.

"Jesus!" he hissed, and shook his head violently, once. "Oh my Jesus."

Minogue had given up thinking. He was letting things come at him as they were. He glanced from the doctor's pinched face to the bearded man and back. He felt his legs begin to tremble slightly. A shiver ran up through him.

The doctor's face had a pained look.

"You really should sit down."

"Stop saying that will you, for Christ's sake."

"That's them, I think," the bearded man said. "Listen?"

Another man, twenties, with a rugby look to him, had come over. Minogue heard his sharp intake of breath, but he didn't catch the words he whispered.

The siren was constant now. Another one, quieter, joined it. Minogue looked around. Fifteen, maybe twenty people were standing by their cars now, mobiles glued to ears, darting glances about. Two more men had come over, and were making their way cautiously around to the passenger side of the car. Minogue turned to the bearded man.

"Tell them, will you? Get everybody back. Okay?"

"You're a Guard, you said," said the doctor.

Minogue had three cards left in his breast pocket. He held two out.

The Passat driver didn't seem to want to get any closer. He stood by the plumber's van, and catching Minogue's eye, he held out the mobile.

"They're on the way," he called out. "Okay?"

Minogue knew that it would be up to him to walk over. It angered him for a moment, but then a sudden calm swept over him. It was overwhelming relief he felt now, relief at the sight of this annoying bastard, a man now redeemed and onside just because he looked as ordinary and as scared as everyone else here.

"You're a detective," the doctor was murmuring. "An Inspector?"

Minogue felt no urge to answer. A woman with hennaed hair was scurrying over from the line of cars, clasping and unclasping her hands. There was a hem of some uniform under her coat. A nurse?

"Do you know the person in the...?"

The sirens had drifted into sync. The henna-haired woman arrived, to be met by the bearded man, his arms half raised, and Minogue's card still between his fingers.

"I do," he managed. "He's a Guard too."

He took his first step in what he felt sure would be a long, long trek where the Passat driver was holding out his phone. The shards of glass in that thick, curly hair flashed back to him.

"Garda Corcoran."

Chapter 33

It took Malone nearly an hour to show up. By then a more constant drizzle had started, and Minogue had been turning the key every minute or so to clear the windscreen. He was studying the display on his mobile when he saw the taxi draw up near the Garda cars.

Malone was kept waiting. Though Minogue could not see the Guard's face, he could tell by the slow movements as he lifted and lowered his mouthpiece for the walkie-talkie that word was out. Malone stood bareheaded, his hands in his pockets. He kept up his stare at some faroff place, while he waited for some other angry copper, the one at the far end of this walkie-talkie conversation, to deliberate on something.

The Guard slowly clipped his mouthpiece back on his lapel. Malone stooped to get under the tape, and he took his time walking over. He kept his eyes on the pavement not far ahead, his carefully neutral expression steady and unchanging. Minogue considered moving to the driver's seat, but he still felt pinned to where he now sat. Malone glanced at him and then altered his course to the passenger side, and sat into the back seat. He palmed his forehead and hair free of the drizzle.

"You came in a taxi," Minogue said.

"Yeah. No-one would take me. Then Fitz came after me. I had to get out."

"Came after you?"

"He was losing it," said Malone, quietly, and shrugged. He

wiped a clear spot on the rear window, and he looked across the roadway.

"This is our doing, according to Fitz."

Minogue examined his hands. It was useless trying keep them from trembling.

"You okay?" Malone asked.

Minogue said nothing.

Malone made to say something, but he hesitated and then sat back with a sigh.

"So he took that jalopy of yours out, to see if it was worth anything," Minogue heard himself say. Malone nodded.

"I told them," he said. "Fitz. I told him, there was no way I knew. No way."

Minogue opened the top of his cigarette packet, poked aside the two that had fallen, and made a count. Seven cigarettes in an hour, including the ten minutes giving the eyewitness to that bullet-headed copper from Dun Laoghaire, what was his name?

"Tommy, you need to know something. The word is already out about you."

"What word is that?"

"Don't treat me like an iijit. That you're an insider. That you're bent. "

"I know. I knew about that stuff a long time. Everybody did."

A glaze had come over Malone's eyes.

"That's why this happened," Minogue said. "Isn't it?"

Malone's eye drifted back to the space he had cleared on the glass.

"Are you armed?" Minogue asked.

Malone turned away from the window, and met Minogue's eye.

"You are," Minogue went on. "Yes?"

"Yeah, I am."

"Is it duty issued? Or the other?"

"Duty, of course. What do you think?"

"You're on case review, and you're carrying a firearm? On whose authority?"

"Boss, listen to me: I'm on loan. I been telling you that all along. Remember?"

"I don't believe you."

His words hung in the air. Malone's lips tightened and went slack again.

"Well I know that," he said. "Don't I."

Minogue closed his cigarette packet and slid it back into his jacket pocket.

"So you're ready then," he said. "That's why you're here. Am I right?"

Malone looked away.

"You have a conscience. You're going to turn yourself in. Right?"

"I told them this could happen," Malone said. "They'll probably deny it, of course. But I did tell them. And that's why I have what I have here. I told them I wouldn't do the job if I couldn't defend myself. See?"

"Told who?"

Malone made a long, slow blink.

"They don't want me telling you anything," he said. "They said to wait."

"Wait? Wait for what?"

Malone shifted a little.

"You mind opening the window here boss? The smoke?"

Minogue reached for the key again. Malone thumbed the window down halfway. The wipers came on once. The gait on the tall, flatfooted man coming his way had a familiar look. He had never seen Brendan O'Leary in a tweed cap and a raincoat before. It looked wrong, like golf clothes or something. O'Leary slowed a little when the wiper came to life, and he gave Minogue a blank look.

"I'll be waiting here," Malone muttered.

"What the hell does that mean?"

"It's you they'll be talking to."

Minogue stared at him.

"Just as well too," Malone added. "If I went over, I'd be pulling a Fitz on them."

Minogue's brain had locked up. He saw that O'Leary was waiting, keeping him in his peripheral vision while he watched the last of the site tent being settled around the Escort. The white nylon fabric seemed to glow under the pewter sky.

"Just go," Malone said. "Will you? I'm not going to rob your car."

The air was thick, more a fog than a drizzle, but it still seemed to fizz around him. His joints ached with each step. He sensed that O'Leary was aware of this, and measuring his own stride. Two Traffic Guards were routing the last of the cars up over the footpath and sending them back over the curb a couple of hundred yards off. He looked again for the mobile command post, but didn't spot it. Traffic, he supposed. He kept turning his mobile over in his hand, undecided yet about whether to phone Kathleen. They had the radio on most days in her office.

O'Leary gestured toward a gap between two of the squad cars. The Guard who had let Malone through the cordon maintained his heavy-lidded stare. Minogue looked for a face in the dark blue Nissan head.

"In the back, Matt," O'Leary said. "The far side."

Through the drizzle on the windows, Minogue saw outlines of two people.

"Who's the other one?"

O'Leary didn't answer, but waited by the driver's door.

Minogue got in the back seat, opposite the Commissioner. Tynan's face had an abstracted, preoccupied look. He shifted a little, picked up a folder that had been lying on the other seat. Carney was sitting almost sideways in the passenger seat, his back against the door. O'Leary answered a mobile phone halfway into the first ring. He listened briefly, said 'Five minutes, sorry,' and then he returned to his scrutiny of the water droplets forming on the glass.

"A terrible, terrible day, Matt."

Carney's voice was down to a whisper.

"But how are you doing, yourself?"

Minogue kept his eyes on the seatback, tried to breathe quietly through his nose.

"Garda Malone has begun the process with you," said Tynan. "Am I right?"

Minogue turned a little to meet Tynan's eye.

"He said he was going to," said Tynan.

"'And you're not gonna effin' stop me this time.'" Carney's version of a Dublin accent wasn't as bad as it could have been.

"Process," Minogue said. "What process?"

"Matt, you've had a shock. You know the score here now, better than many."

It was the first time that Minogue could remember that the Commissioner had used his Christian name.

"Garda Malone insisted," Tynan added. "We're going to respect his wishes on the matter."

Minogue let the silence drag.

"Do you want to talk to someone right now?" Carney asked him. "We have a counselling service lad here just in case. He's very good. Yes?"

"Tommy insisted on what?" Minogue said. "And what 'plan'?"

Carney shifted heavily in the seat again.

"Listen, Matt," he began. "Nobody expected this – nobody. This is not just about Irish gangs, or Dublin hoodlums. No. These people have no rules. They don't care."

Minogue kept up his stare at Carney.

"The gist of it is this: Malone is undercover—"

"—He's not undercover," said Minogue. Carney recoiled.

"He's a common-or-garden Garda detective," Minogue went on. "And he's working with me on a murder investigation. And that murder investigation got kicked up the line because someone decided that the publicity was too much to handle. And because in this country, apparently, you can pick up a phone, and use your connections to get what you want."

Carney rubbed at his forehead.

"I don't know the details there now, Matt, but you heard me say to you that— "

"Why is Tommy Malone sitting over there in my car, armed with a pistol, not under arrest, and I'm sitting here with you instead?"

Carney pursed his lips, and darted a glance in Tynan's direction.

"Can you do that later," Tynan said. "After Dan finishes what he needs to say?"

Carney leaned forward, his eyes bulging a little. "The answer to your question, Matt, is because the rumour mill works too well. Too well indeed."

There was an edge in his voice now, but what was getting to Minogue was the patronizing tone.

"So let me pose a question to you: what has you wanting Malone's arrest?"

"Things I heard," Minogue replied. "Tips. Bush telegraph."

"Was there any clear, credible evidence?"

"Well there is now, isn't there?"

"Like what, exactly?"

"They wanted to shut him up," Minogue said. "In case he tried to roll over."

"Who did?"

"I don't know who pulled the trigger, but I can guess. So can a lot of Guards."

Carney spread out his fingers. He grasped his thumb first.

"Dunne?" he asked. "One of the Egans maybe? The Connollys, is it, Black and Decker, now that Frank's gone? How about Limerick then – Dunphy, maybe one of the Shiels? Barry O, and his pack there in Meath, with his ponies and his golf course in Spain? Is it any of them you're thinking of now?"

Small rims of spittle had formed to the sides of his mouth.

"We knew there'd be talk," Carney went on. "That's built into the plan."

A wry and wholly insincere smile came to his face.

"And I'll bet I know who's been feeding you most," he said. "Starts with J? Second name a K...?"

Minogue said nothing. Carney sat back against the door.

"Things start and finish at my desk," Tynan said then. "So you can be sure you're getting the goods here. This operation of which he is a part has been going on for some time. His part winds down now – it has to. But we'll proceed with what we need to do."

Tynan was waiting for some acknowledgement.

"You have a right to be upset," Tynan added. "But the discussion about operational matters will not be going further here. It can't. Can't you see that?"

Minogue made a curt nod.

"By the way," Tynan said. "Do you speak any Chinese? Mandarin? Cantonese?"

Minogue shook his head.

"Me neither. But we do have three staff with the Garda Síochána who do. Two are Garda officers, and they can do both languages equally well. The third is a new employee, a civilian, who is the more expert of the three. So we're getting there."

He glanced over to Carney, who responded with a nod.

"Where's 'there,' you might ask," Carney said.

He waited for Minogue to show interest, but sensed it wasn't forthcoming.

"You deserve a snapshot at least," he said. "It'll help put things in perspective. Maybe you've heard bits of it one way or another already. You're up to speed on what Eastern Europe has come to mean for us here the past few years?"

"I am, I think."

"And we keep going East? Russians, Albanians, Ukrainian blags showing up? All the various affiliations and put-togethers from the Middle East and beyond, Afghanistan, Pakistan even? You've seen the traffic down in Liaison surely. Europol, the Americans?"

"But this has been going on awhile," Minogue said.

"Of course it has. And all this on top of our native species, and our neighbours from across the Channel there? My point here is that none of this is news to you, is it?"

"No."

"Good. So we had to look around. Do we have people who could make a difference in these situations? Languages, experience, connections. Drive."

Minogue looked from Tynan to Carney and back.

"You're telling me that Tommy's been choreographed? A copper gone bad?"

"It's not acting," said Carney.

"And the word went out that he was bent?"

"We didn't push that," said Carney, quickly sitting upright again. "We let people think what they wanted. We put out little signals a while back."

"What about Kelly, and the Ombudsman's inquiry? Was that staged?"

Carney's smile was full of grim satisfaction now.

"It came out of the blue. Like they say these days, why waste a crisis? So we ran with it. Nimble, adaptive, that's what's needed. We heaved Malone out of Drugs, and put him out here in purdah."

"Purdah. Working with me on case review you mean?"

"Purdah's the wrong word," Tynan interrupted. "It was cover, to make it credible that Garda Malone was being quarantined, because he was under suspicion. And it gave him a job where he could fester and build up resentment. To ripen, so to speak."

"This was all building up the role? A kind of PR?"

"That's right," said Tynan.

"We wanted him rolling in it," said Carney. His enthusiasm was unsettling to Minogue. "That was the plan. One step short of being sacked, or up on charges. God, we were ready to give him suspensions even – anything to rev up the situation."

Minogue's brain had stopped trying to think ahead.

"Willie Ryan's pub," he said. "The fight there?"

Carney rotated his shoulder, and massaged it. He gave Minogue a knowing grin.

"Matt," he said, drawing a breath between his teeth. "Do you think that he would have come out of it like he did after a go-round with two Guards?"

"Tommy's no pushover. He trains in the ring. When he gets going, he gets going."

"Those two actually volunteered," said Carney, and he winked.

"As long as they were given their anesthetic first."

"So the bruises are real," said Minogue.

"It'll go down in the annals," said Carney.

Minogue felt in his pocket for his cigarettes. He noticed O'Leary's eyes on him again in the mirror. They drifted away when he returned the look.

Carney's face turned grave.

"So what's the take-away from this, Matt? It's off, Malone's part – off. We can't do this. We just can't. This was never on the cards, what happened here."

Minogue's hand settled around the packet.

"Whoever did this – and we'll find them…whoever did this, had Malone as a big, big issue. It wasn't just revenge. They would-n't go after a Garda for someone like Kelly. They have Malone as a big liability. Whatever Kelly had on this Chinese fella – and we'll never know how much now – the thinking is with them that Kelly must have spilled it to Malone. And they see Malone getting this information and using it on them."

"'They.'"

Carney shook his head, and then glanced at Tynan again. Tynan nodded.

"They're sending a message," Carney said. "They've put down their marker, and it's a first for us: they're willing to murder a Garda officer in broad daylight. This is business on a global scale. All the others back along the chain can see this, all the way back to Shanghai or Macau or wherever, that this is how they respond to threats. Okay?"

Minogue considered saying it wasn't okay.

"And to those people," Carney went on, "not knowing something is a threat. They had doubts about Malone. Did he know, didn't he know; was he, wasn't he. So somebody made a decision, and that's what we see here today."

Minogue knew that he was being given time to absorb this. To come around, even. To calm him. But it was only making him angrier.

A mobile went off, muffled in a pocket. O'Leary thumbed his earpiece.

"No," he said, almost right away. "Maybe. I'm not sure."

His eyes sought Tynan's in the mirror.

"Can't hold them back?" Tynan asked. O'Leary's expression didn't change.

"All right," said Tynan then. "No desk, no podium. No studio. It'll have to be here now in a few minutes, or else they'll wait until this afternoon back at the media room. And absolutely no names."

O'Leary looked away.

"Did you get that?" he asked. "A few minutes, he'll be over. Who's doing it?"

O'Leary repeated the name of the station's Crime Correspondent. A faint hint of exasperation showed on Tynan's face. Minogue rubbed the fogged window. There was still only one Outside Broadcast Unit van in sight.

"Okay," O'Leary said, and ended the call. He turned in the seat.

"Live to air."

Tynan ran a finger across and then down a sheet of paper with handwritten notes, closed his eyes and then closed the folder cover over it. He turned to Minogue.

"How is that case coming along anyway?"

"We seem to have a move," Minogue said. "In a direction we hadn't anticipated."

Tynan began adjusting his tie, and then grasped his lapels and tugged at them.

"That person you referred me to," Minogue went on. "Moved up the list sharply."

Tynan fixed him with his trademark laboratory examination stare.

"You're serious, I take it. Walk over with me then."

O'Leary was first out of the car, and was scanning the faces around the cordon by the time Minogue stood upright. Tynan threw his coat back on the seat and pushed the door closed.

"Thanks, Dan," he said. "As always."

Tynan was in no hurry. He seemed to be trying to memorize what lay around the roadway here. Then he stopped, and waited for Minogue to turn.

"You were referring to Immaculata when you made that remark back there?"

"I was, yes."

"So have you got her figured out now?"

"I don't know about that, but I think I have her connected to Padraig Larkin – the victim – from a long time ago."

"But how long has that drop-in place been open – that Disciples place – four years?"

"I mean forty-something years ago."

Tynan frowned.

"You know she only helps out there? The 'Director' bit is more honorary than anything else. And do you know why?"

"Well I wondered, at her age."

"It's not her age. There are issues. Issues with memory and so forth."

For a moment, Minogue believed that Tynan was daring him to come up with a sharp comment.

"I have a fair number of questions to ask her," he said.

Tynan eyed the pack beginning to deploy themselves near the van. One of them was hoisting a camera.

"So is she proving helpful?"

"When it suits her."

Tynan seemed to be measuring distances on the pavement around him. His voice was toneless when he spoke.

"I see. So what's your next step?"

"I'm considering taking her in for questioning."

"Taking her in. Do you mean bringing her to the Garda station?"

"I do. It'll help, I think."

"How? Is it necessary?"

"I think it's important she know that she doesn't get to pick."

"Pick what?"

"What she'll tell us and what she won't."

"Do you mean 'won't' or 'can't'?"

"I don't know. But I wish I had known what you just told me about her earlier."

"So what have you got on her?"

"She's in snapshots with a relative of Padraig Larkin, pictures from way back."

Tynan's nostrils were showing signs of the chill air. Minogue pulled his own coat a little tighter. He wasn't sure whether it was skepticism he was seeing in Tynan's expression, or annoyance.

A flap on the nylon tarp over Malone's car stirred. One of the journos had had enough, and was calling out the Commissioner's name.

"Brendan," said Tynan, tugging on his cuffs again to settle his tunic better. "Remind me in an hour to resume this chat here by phone. It's a must-do."

He settled his laboratory specimen look on Minogue again.

"Immaculata is a very, very loyal person," he murmured. "You recall me trying to get that across to you? She'd go to the wall for people. That woman had carried I don't know how many people, for decades. The poorest people you can imagine. She's owed."

"But does she think she runs the Gardai?"

He was surprised at how little he felt when the words came out. Tynan merely shrugged.

"She may well know something," he said. "She may not even know that she knows it though. Remember the 'known knowns' and all that?"

"I never got that, I have to tell you."

Tynan looked from the lights over the cameras, and then at the tarp again. In those few moments Minogue glimpsed something he wouldn't easily forget, a look of pained helplessness. Tynan didn't look at him when he spoke now.

"We'll be talking. Give us an hour or so. Brendan?"

O'Leary hung back as Tynan began to make his way toward the cameras.

"Your number, Inspector," he murmured. "But more your firm commitment to keep the device turned on as well."

Chapter 34

It wasn't just surprise at seeing Immaculata in a nun's coif that made her look so different to Minogue. There was something distant, even listless, in her expression. He didn't ask her why she had chosen to wait on the footpath here for him. He eyed her coif, and tried to see how it was pinned back behind her ear.

"Yes I know," she said, as though hearing his unspoken question. "But this is a day for it."

She carried a small cloth bag with tassels across the bottom.

"You're not in some squad car, are you?"

"I'm not."

"I should tell you right now, that I was expecting that phone call," she said. "From your Commissioner. It was only a matter of time, I think."

Minogue unlocked the car doors with his remote.

"But I knew he'd find the right people, and we'd put things to rights...."

She was examining the car's interior, with no sign she was about to get in.

"Find who killed Padraig you mean, Sister."

"Yes. Mary, call me."

Minogue opened her door a bit wider.

"I'm going with Sister for now," he said.

An opening door behind made him turn. It was McArdle.

"You're coming back, aren't you, Sister?"

"Of course I am – go back inside, Davey."

"When? For dinner time?"

"Davey – inside. I've work to do. Close the door and don't be letting in the cold."

"Why are you dressed up?"

"Nuns don't dress up, Davey. I'm just paying a visit on an old friend."

McArdle squinted at Minogue.

"But he's Guard, you know, that fella with you. He's a Guard."

Minogue waited by the driver's side until she got in. Something about the sound of the car door closing, or the seat belt rolling up into its housing, or maybe just the leaden sky here again today, brought him back to yesterday's chaos. He closed his eyes a moment. He knew that he needed to think himself through it, or rather out of it, if he were to be able to get anything done here.

It had been after one o'clock when he had left the roundabout, and he and Malone had stopped at a dismal-enough pub in Cornelscourt. Fitz and Ledwidge had appeared at the roundabout while he had been working through the full statement with that McEvoy detective from Dun Laoghaire. They had spotted the van soon enough, and had stared coldly through the window at him until he looked away.

Stepping out of the van later, a sergeant had been waiting for him. He was told to give Dalkey a miss. They would receive instructions about when their files would be delivered to Harcourt Terrace. The sergeant's slow, toneless delivery of this message told Minogue that there was nothing to discuss. Nothing to ask, nothing to clarify.

"Are we waiting for someone?" Immaculata asked.

He turned the ignition and plotted the first part of the trip. To Monkstown, he figured, and then take the line of least resistance through Blackrock and to the N11. The nursing home was next door to the UCD campus in Belfield.

He waited for his break in the traffic.

"You're angry," she murmured. "I can tell. Like yesterday, on the phone."

He let the wipers cycle once. Did nobody here let you into traffic either?

"Yesterday was a long day. I wasn't the only one in bad humour, I can tell you."

He took his chance after a bike.

"Those photos you mentioned," she said. "Do you have them here with you?"

"I have copies with me."

He waited for her request then, the one he'd get considerable satisfaction in refusing. It did not come.

"Have you ever known Sister Albertina to communicate? Since she had her stroke, I mean? I was told that she opens her eyes sometimes."

Immaculata shook her head.

"I thought he told you about Albertina," she said. "John – your boss, I mean. He said he'd tell you."

"He told me she has been in a coma since, as far as he knew. Did he tell me right?"

"He did. Six years now, and I still can't believe it. As strong as an ox she was, Bertie – a farmer's daughter. It was a clot that went to her brain."

"So you haven't seen any sign she's trying to communicate, at all?"

"Not to us, at any rate," she replied.

"You lost me there."

"God has no trouble understanding her."

"Hasn't she been tested, or assessed recently?"

"Nobody can be sure what Bertie understands, or what she doesn't."

Her sudden testiness surprised him. He looked over.

"I feel that she hears me," Immaculata said then. "It's a strong feeling...."

He nodded. He didn't care much if she thought he was agreeing with her.

"Who are we to think we'll ever understand what God can do?" she added. "Or predict what He'll do for us? What we call miracles, that's just God working His own way."

"Miracles, Sister."

The flat skepticism in his tone didn't seem to register with her. Her face relaxed into a smile of deep contentment.

"That's right. And they happen every day. Every moment of every day."

Minogue felt none of the annoyance that he expected, and watching her gaze slip out of focus, he imagined her for a moment sitting by a lamp out in Africa, waiting out some dire, impossible situation with nothing but her faith.

"Every moment of every day," she repeated.

"And that's how you presented it to him when you phoned him last night," he said. "Albertina's brother, that he could expect a miracle today at the nursing home."

A look of pained uncertainty replaced her smile. She looked out the window.

"Yes I did," she replied. "Like you wanted, yes. But I don't know."

"You don't know what?"

"I didn't actually say that Albertina was able to talk now. I couldn't. That'd be a barefaced lie. But I told him the other stuff, the way you had it phrased. All that, what can I call it, all that *ambiguity*. It's the only polite word I can find to describe it."

"'Albertina has things to tell us.' Right?"

She nodded.

"'We seem to have a miracle on our hands'?"

"That too. I said I would, and I did. I can't blame you, you're only doing what you're trained to do."

Minogue let a few moments pass.

"I take it then you still regret telling me about how he talks to her all the time. Sergeant Twomey, I mean, talking to her every time he visits."

She seemed to consider his remark.

"I said it to you in all innocence," she said then. "That's what I realized after thinking about it. The nurses hear him, and they tell me. They see how devoted he is to her. He has someone come in and do her hair for her, her nails even. A nun, and a manicure!"

"But nodody has ever heard what he says to her, right?"

She shifted a little in the seat.

"He says prayers for her, he reads to her."

"And that's all?"

"You asked me that, I don't know, ten times last night."

"Reminiscing, and that sort of thing, you said."

She closed her eyes for several seconds. Summoning patience, or strength, he guessed.

"You have no idea the questions he started firing at me then when he heard that."

"But you were ready for him, right? You were able to head them off."

She took in a long breath, and soon let it out with a sigh.

"This is what spies do," she said. "In the films..."

She threw him a quick, anxious look.

"But he was a Guard all his life," she said. "Bertie's brother."

"He was – but so what?"

"I mean he'd be able to see through things quick enough."

"But he has a strong faith still, doesn't he? That hasn't changed."

She returned her gaze to the passing traffic.

He let her words replay in his head. 'Bertie's brother': she wouldn't even say the man's name. Maybe it was indeed fear, or something very close to it at least, that he sensed in her. For a long time after their phone conversation last night, he had believed it was resentment he had heard in her voice then, and doubt. Had she known how close he had been to putting the hard word on her then, as he paced the garage, his ear aching from pressing the phone so hard to his head?

It had taken a long time to persuade her last night. But whether it was the anger that he had thought he was holding back well enough from his voice, or the tension in him that she had picked up, she had finally agreed to make that phone call to Ferg Twomey. She had insisted on writing down each and every word of what he wanted her to say to him too, and then slowly reciting it all to Minogue. She had held out longest over using the word 'miracle' with Twomey. When she had finally phoned Minogue back later, she had sounded tired, regretful. Yes, Twomey had agreed to meet her at the nursing home in the morning.

"Look," he said. "I wish I could persuade you that you've done nothing wrong,"

Still she said nothing. He worked his way by a distracted van driver.

"We need to try this," he said to her. "It's the right thing to do."

Her voice had dropped back to a whisper.

"Is it," she said.

He settled on the slowest setting for the mist cycle. The roads were more damp than wet, but the traffic cast up a fine grey drizzle of its own. He stole a glance at her, and wondered if this warrior woman had somehow shrunken a little in the seat.

"I think Albertina would say it was okay, what we're doing," he said.

"Well I told you already" she whispered. "I feel that Bertie hears me."

She drew something out from a sleeve. He looked down, saw rosary beads.

"'Bertie,'" he said. "Is that what she prefers to be called?"

"She does."

Mention of the name had drawn that wistful smile he had seen earlier.

"Yes, that's what we call her, us sisters. Not the children, of course. Yes, she always liked that name. She used to say she should have picked 'Bertie' when she took her vows. That wasn't on, of course. But that was how she is, you see. How she was, I mean."

Minogue braked for a bus. From the corner of his eye he saw her thumb move up to the next bead. The bus driver changed his mind, and abruptly pulled in. Minogue managed to dart around him.

"Bertie was a hell of a driver too."

He looked over. She didn't acknowledge his surprise. Her smile had stayed, and even gained strength.

"Drove like a maniac sometimes, she did. She'd have that old Land Rover – and I mean *old*, it was given to them before independence even – flying over the road like nobody's business. A bat out of hell."

"Where was the bat from again?" he couldn't resist asking.

"The locals knew to keep well out of her way, even Jerome. Yes – Jerome Innocent Odinga. Constable Jerome. Jerome was one of our own, one of the first of the Luo to come through St. Brigid's."

"St. Brigid's," he said. "Now there's a name."

"Isn't it though? God but we were the proud Irishwomen when we opened that little school,—its corrugated roof and all. But Jerome would tell her to slow down, that it wasn't God's work she was about when she was driving, it was the devil's work."

She glanced over at Minogue.

"They're very superstitious in Kenya, you know."

"So I heard. Not like us, of course."

But again she seemed not to have heard him.

"I still have his letter," she said, and paused as though to search her memory for more details. "When I came back to Ireland for good, and I found out about Bertie, I wrote Jerome a little letter. Jerome went on to do big things. He ran some police department in Nairobi. Anyway, didn't he write me back a lovely long letter? He said the villages cried for Sister Albertina, but that God was by her side, and ready for her. Doesn't that tell you something, that after all those years, he would remember Bertie?"

Minogue offered a nod.

"He said that all that bouncing around Bertie had done on the back roads, down in the river beds in that old thing might have started the clots. He wasn't joking either. Did I tell you how superstitious they are still?"

"So she went to Kenya before she went to the Philippines. Right?"

Immaculata grabbed the next bead as though slowly devouring the rosary in her fist.

"She did," she said.

"Before she met him, like."

Immaculata made a single, thoughtful nod, and then she crossed herself, kissed the crucifix and tucked the beads back into her sleeve. From the other sleeve she drew out a hankie, its floral scent drifting by Minogue as she opened it. He heard her sniff once.

"How long were you working with her?"

"Four years. But it felt like a lifetime."

"You're very close to her, I'm thinking," he said after a pause.

She drew out the hankie again. Her breath caught as she spoke.

"If she hadn't come home for that visit... I used to think for many years."

The resolute tone swept back into her voice.

"But that was the decision. And she never went back. She stayed in the convent for six weeks, and then off she went to Manila, the far side of the world. That was that."

"And you learned of this when...?"

"Oh I was already back in Kenya, getting it in dribs and drabs. I remember the days being like weeks, or months even, while I waited to hear anything."

An uneven patch of road rattled through the car.

"You're in the snapshots too. On that trip over to the island."

Her nod did not suggest to him any agreement with anything he had said.

"I had to come back to Ireland that time. I had to have an operation done, you see. There's a thing in our family, to do with vertebrae. It got bad on me out there, it might have been an infection that put it into high gear. But at any rate, my mother and father, God rest them, they kicked up a fuss with the Mother Superior to get me back here for the operation. So I was back in Ireland the month before, and I was recuperating at home. Actually I was in fine fettle, rarin' to go, but my mother wanted me to stay."

"And Sister Albertina? Sister Bertie?"

"Well she was on leave. It wasn't easy back then, you have

to understand. We got trips home only every five years or so. It was all part of the calling. I'm not saying it was easy or anything. But she was home for a month. So like I said to you, I was confined to barracks up on the farm, doctor's orders and all that. But one day, didn't I get a phone call. A Monday, I well remember it, the month of Our Lady, and everything in bloom. It was Bertie: was I fit enough to come up to Dublin, and see her. And she sounded so cheerful! I don't know to this day if she was hiding it from herself as well as from me."

"You met her then, and Murphy."

"I did," she said, her voice trailing off. "Was I expecting him to be there? I certainly was not. You could have knocked me over with a feather when he shows up as we're getting off the train there out in Dalkey. I found out later on that she had met Father Murphy one evening over a dinner. Bertie's brother was a Guard, you see, and very well thought of. And didn't he bring her along with him on a visit to people he knew. Oh and they were fine people too, the father a judge and everything. And there was Father Murphy, the man's brother-in-law. The woman of the house, Mrs. Larkin, was his sister. All well-educated, accomplished people. Good-living people."

"Did you go to the house ever, the Larkins'?"

"I never did. I only found out all this later, much later. So there I was, walking down the road from the station and fetching up at a little harbour there. Bertie wanted to visit an old church out on an island. You know it?"

"Dalkey Island, I do, sort of."

"Right, so. This is sheer madness, I thought to myself, but it was a lovely, lovely day. Bertie told me about that saint to do with the place, and that she was the first missionary to leave Ireland all those years ago. So to me, everything looked normal."

Over the roofs of the car ahead, Minogue caught sight of a digger's arm rising and falling. The arm began to shudder and slowly descend out of sight. A man in a safety vest appeared out of the traffic ahead, twirling a sign. He planted it, Stop side toward Minogue, and with a contented look, that was little short of a smirk, he lit a cigarette.

"When exactly did you find out?" he asked her.

"I got a letter the day before I was headed back."

"A letter? She didn't phone you?"

"No. I don't think I slept a wink the whole night long. My mother was driven demented, because I wouldn't tell her. I must have fallen asleep eventually, or maybe I was so tired that I began to imagine things. She came to me, and spoke to me, but I couldn't tell what she was saying. It was the shock, maybe."

She looked over.

"I've never told that to anyone. You see that, in your line of work? Shock?"

Parts of his own scattered memory of yesterday afternoon came to him for a few moments, its events still as jumbled and accordioned. He still could not fathom how he had actually slept for long stretches last night, and had even woken up clear-headed too. He was still on guard, and jumpy, and still suspected that he was drifting in some kind of fake calm that could give away at any moment.

"At times," he said. "Anyway. You went back to Africa. Obviously."

"I did. And to this day, I think it was Bertie. It was her, her prayers, that visit. It was her way of telling me that they needed me back, and that she'd be okay. You see?"

Minogue imagined a young Immaculata reading a letter over and over again.

The Stop sign revolved around to Slow.

"So she was disciplined. Is that what it's called for nuns?"

"That's it all right."

"Do you know if she ever considered walking away?"

"Leaving the order? I doubt it. That sort of thing only began later on. But as for that man, may God forgive me, they should never have listened to him in the first place."

"Father Murphy you're talking about, I take it."

"I could never understand why he was sent out on the missions in the first place. But then, after how many years out there, that he would end up five or six hours away from me there? And that it would be me he'd call for at the end?"

The car ahead began to pull away at last.

"I never asked you," she said. "Where did you find those pictures?"

"Someone found them in a drawer, out in Dalkey Garda station, when it was being done up a few years ago."

She shook her head slowly, twice.

"Like I always say," she said. "'The Lord works in mysterious ways.' Doesn't He?"

"There are days, Sister, when that's not clear to me at all."

He didn't like the sound of gravel pinging off the underside of his Peugeot.

"I have to say," he began, not sure how he'd finish the sentence. "In these photos, you look pretty...content, the three of you."

She seemed to consider his choice of words for a moment.

"Funny you should say that. For me at the time, it was like, I don't know, a dream. So unexpected. And going in a boat like that, it was new for me, across to that church on the island. I can't believe I've forgotten the name of the saint there."

"Begnet," he said. "St. Begnet."

"That's it. Later on, it came together about why Bertie picked that place to go. That was after I got her letter of course. Do you know the stories about Begnet? This is not long after Christianity came. Instead of marrying a king's son, she took the green exile, across to England. She ended up an abbess, and there are miracles associated with her. I didn't know any of this at the time, of course. But I do remember thinking at the time that Bertie was asking me along that day because it was part of her plan. It was a fair journey down to Dublin from our farm. She knew I was after an operation. So it wasn't just a whim."

"But it was unusual for a nun and a priest to be together though, wasn't it?"

"It still is. But he didn't need me for chaperoning. She had taken care of that already, with her brother there. I think it was something else."

He waited. She began to study some part of the sky.

"It was so I could see how happy she was," she said. "And

that she knew it was ending. I think she was saying goodbye."

She was smiling when she caught his eye now.

"Ah, but see how God brought us back together after so many years?"

He tried to picture what awaited them at this nursing home. His favourite aunt had lain stricken for over a year, sunken-faced and helpless, only her eyes moving. A stretch of road had arrived. Soon he'd be at White's Cross and turning onto the N11.

"All I had was that one letter," she said. "That one letter, all the way from the Philippines. She said she was turning to God, looking for a life away from everything that had gone on. And she meant what she'd said too. She bore her burdens. She's still bearing them."

He was actually managing to get into top gear. Through the bare branches he caught a quick glimpse of Two Rock Mountain and the antennae on its crest.

"People don't believe in the Devil anymore," she said. "Do they."

"I'm not sure. Less so than before, I'd guess."

"Not the tail and the horns bit. I mean the Devil working through others."

She had returned to her study of the horizon.

"You were with him at the end, I heard," he said.

She turned suddenly, and for the first time he saw anger on her face.

"And that's when you knew for sure," he added. "Wasn't it?"

She turned back to the window. Long moments passed before she spoke.

"You're right," she said. "But don't think that I got the answers I wanted."

"But at least you knew why she had cut herself off, I meant."

She darted a quick, remonstrating look his way.

"He wasn't really a priest at the end. He was just another suffering human being. The Lord let it happen in this way, to show me what I should do."

349

She looked down at her cuffs and tugged each smartly in turn.

"He told me that he needed to tell someone, someone who'd understand. Later, afterwards, I realized that he had always meant to tell me. That was my role, my work."

"You said that he had tried, in his own way."

She looked baffled.

"You said it in that conversation with the Commissioner yesterday."

"God, that man forgets nothing! The Jesuits lost a good one in him, surely."

"How did Father Murphy try to make good?"

She seemed unsure how or even if she should answer.

"I heard things over the years," she said. "He was a good five or six hours away by road, over the far side of the valley. The Rift Valley? He got involved in land rights there, grazing rights. Government people were lining their pockets you see, and sticking to their tribal line in the allocations. He became a go-between, with the government and some locals, the tribes. An advocate. It was really social justice that he was working for."

"All his time there, he was doing that?"

She shook her head.

"He was getting himself into scrapes. I heard about him drinking, showing up in the stops. You know, the stops along the roads there, the lorries...? Sheebeens I call them. I didn't want to know about it. Let someone else handle this, was my approach."

"You stayed away from him."

"The local people liked him well enough. But I was ashamed that a priest would carry on this way, an Irishman too. So we had nothing to say to one another, nothing that was good, or Christian. I never even asked him if he was in touch with Bertie, or if he had tried to make amends for what he did to her."

"Doesn't it take two?"

Her eyes flashed, but she turned away, and she knit her hands together tight.

"You've no idea," she said. "A priest? A nun? Who has power there, you think?"

"But it was you he called on, in the end, wasn't it. You, he wanted to see."

"It was," she said, softly now. "Like I say, God works His wonders."

"Will you tell me about the arrangement? The pact, you called it, I believe."

Her eyes widened and she allowed a thin smile.

"I might as well have recorded the conversation, I suppose.... He told me that he needed a burden lifted off him, that his time was close."

"Was he ill then?"

"To my shame, I do not know. It was a man came to the school, a local man, someone who had become a friend of his, I suppose. And when I saw him, I knew he was sent. It was all part of the plan, God's plan."

"So you went to him."

"What else could I do? Of course when I got there, he wasn't at death's door, or anything like it. I knew the reputation he'd gotten over the years, with the drink and that. And that night, he showed it in spades, I can tell you. But to make a long story short, he asked me if he was to be called, would I help carry his burden afterwards."

"Burden?"

"Looking after her, after Bertie. Albertina. That was when I found out. How she'd had a stroke, and then another, and that she was paralyzed. I was completely...well I don't know what I was. I think I must have just sat there. I couldn't move."

She paused and swallowed.

"You know when someone says that their whole life flashes before them? Well, it's true. I thought, how is it that this man would know about Bertie before I would? The very man who had treated her like that? I was her friend, it was me who prayed every day beside her. We used to finish one another's sentences, we were so in tune. And now, to sit here, and be told this news? By this man...?"

"You got through it, though."

"Of course I did, but not under my own steam. True to His

ways, it happened: I wasn't angry, I didn't tear into him for ripping her from us, for endangering her soul. I just sat there in that room with him. He cried. He said it was his confession. Imagine that, a nun hearing confession. But I said nothing, I just listened and I prayed."

She was waiting for him to look over.

"You know what that was, don't you? You're Catholic, Christian at least?"

Minogue shook his head.

"That was grace," she said. "The Holy Spirit on the job. No wonder I couldn't open my mouth at the time. I accepted God's work. So when he told me about why he had been sent out on the missions in the first place, I knew that he had suffered too. And I knew that I had to help carry that burden. God fits the back to the burden, doesn't He?"

Slurs rose up suddenly in Minogue's mind. He waited for several moments.

"He told you about Padraig that day too? What had gone on between them?"

"He did," she said. "Yes."

"I suppose I was just paralyzed. I got a terrible feeling, so I did, that there was something there in that room besides us. It was only later on when I got my brain back working that I told him. Look, I had to say to him, telling me wasn't going to get him absolution. I wasn't a priest, was I? But by then, he was so, what would I call it, so exhausted maybe, I don't think he was taking anything in. So that's what I meant earlier, that by the end, I don't think he was a priest really. I even feared for his soul – but I don't want to think about that, even now."

"A fortnight later...?"

"That's right. He was gone. I suppose he must have had a premonition. I only hope – pray, actually – that he did what I told him, and made a proper confession."

She looked away again. The turn was coming up. A couple of minutes, he figured.

"Left at the lights here," he heard her say.

Chapter 35

Moss flourished at the margins of the driveway into *Áras Bhríde*: Brigid's Home.

"I never knew about this place," he said.

Immaculata said nothing.

He looked over at her.

"Was this place always here?" he asked.

She turned from the side window. Her voice had none of its usual vigor.

"As far as I remember, it was."

Minogue had a half-dozen freshly lined parking spots to pick from. He settled on one closest to the entrance, a glassed-in vestibule that had been added between columns by the doors. There were identical bumpers on two of the parked cars: Cut Hedge Funds, Not Hospital Funds!

"The grounds were bigger," she murmured, as though aware now that she had been too quiet earlier. "They had to be sold off, I daresay."

The overcast sky hadn't lightened a bit. Beyond the lawns and the cherry trees in front of a high wall, he saw the roof tiles of the homes that he supposed had been built on the former grounds. He tried again to fix what direction he was facing now. He had no clue really.

He checked his attaché case and phone while he waited for Immaculata. She was slow to get out, and he thought he saw her lips moving for several moments. Once out, she seemed to gain energy, and she passed him without a word.

Scents of floor wax and polish hung in the warm air, mingled with the astringent smell of disinfectants. A tall statue of Mary in a striking blues and whites presided over the foyer, smiling at the Toddler by her feet. There were two kneelers, and some soft chairs too. Beyond them was a small waiting room with the television off, and rows of books along one wall.

Behind the desk, and facing his way were some of the monitors and paraphernalia he associated with a nursing station. The woman writing on a clipboard there wore a nurse's uniform. Her head, a tightly managed mass of wiry hair, tilted up. Her name-tag was situated over her left breast, a location toward which that Minogue was not willing to let his eye drift. Her eye went to Immaculata.

"Well look," she said and rose, and on her way around the counter, her face broke out into a warm, toothy smile. She gave Immaculata a long embrace. Immaculata quietly repeated the nurse's words back to her, mixing it with English.

"*Jambo*, Eileen. *Habari*. How right you are. But we'll see it through, won't we."

Immaculata turned and nodded in Minogue's direction.

"This is the one I said," she said.

The nurse's thin smile quickly faded. Immaculata linked arms with her, and the pair set off toward a double-door.

On the far side of the doors, the flooring changed to polished cork. Minogue tried a few variations to quiet the squeak from his shoes. It was warmer here, and it felt airless. Care had been taken to mask smells here, but a stale rankness suffused the air.

Minogue followed them down a shorter hallway to the right. There were lots of pictures on the walls here, all of them watercolours. None were religious that he could see. Flame tree, Malawi 1962. Sister Mary Goretti—not the original, actual saint, it was clear—but wearer of a pair of those serious, and even severe glasses popular decades ago. Frangipani, Malawi, 1964. The same Sister Mary Goretti.

They passed a door half ajar. Minogue had no trouble

keeping his eyes from wandering there when his turn came to pass the same doorway. The last thing he wanted to catch sight of was an aged nun in some state of disorder. A radio was on in another room. He caught a bit of what sounded like a free-for-all bickering. Something about rewarding greed...? Ah: the bank crisis thing.

Immaculata slowed a little and moved to the side of the corridor. The nurse turned in also, and murmured something close to her ear, all the while keeping her eye on Minogue. Immaculata began fumbling in her sleeve again.

He turned aside to examine a watercolour of a village. Benin: where was Benin on the map of Africa again? Whispers and murmurs from up the corridor died down. Immaculata whispered something, and when Minogue looked over, he saw that she was near tears. The nurse drew her by the arm, and after a few steps, pushed open a door to her left.

The door swung shut with a soft click.

Minogue opened his mobile, and thumbed quickly to Malone's number.

"Where are you now?" he asked.

"I'm waiting here the over the far side of the car-park There's a side door to the place I'm keeping open. You're going in now?"

"In a minute," Minogue replied. "So start making your way over."

"Okay, on me way. He walked in, remember. No car. And that bag he's carrying, you're not forgetting that, are you?"

Minogue heard a door closing in the background at Malone's end.

"A gym bag, you said."

"Yeah, but what's in it, is what I keep on wondering. I tell you, he looks to be in damned good shape for an ould lad. You're sticking with your plan still?"

"It's a nursing home" was all Minogue could think to say.

"But look, boss, I'm saying it again. I don't like this. What's he carrying a bag for? And where's his car? Something weird's going on."

Another door was opening at Malone's end.

"I'm just coming around by the kitchen place now. Where's that Immaculata one, is she there beside you?"

"No. Immaculata's upset. The nurse here is having a few words with her I think."

"Nurse? Red hair? Laser eyes?"

"That sounds close enough."

"Your turn to remind her that this is a Garda operation. She gave me a going-over – fairly tore into me in actual fact. Wasn't she told about this?"

Minogue turned at the sound of the door opening. The nurse had locked her eyes on him before she had even begun to draw the door closed behind her. He turned aside.

"We're on," he said to Malone. "I'm waiting for you here by the door."

He closed the mobile, and steeling himself, turned.

"The other Guard?" she asked. "From earlier? Your 'side-kick'?"

There was a studied restraint in her stare, but it only made her seem more angry. The sound of a trolley filtered in from behind the doors at the end of the corridor.

"It's a police operation here," he said. "And he's part of it."

For a moment he thought she would actually laugh. She looked up toward a corner of the ceiling where her answers might be kept. Then her stare fixed on him again.

"I've never had a problem with the Guards," she said. "But this is something else."

"We do appreciate your keeping this low-key," he tried. "Nobody wants a commotion here."

"Is it a commotion you're planning?"

Minogue's response was a blank look. Her tongue moved around behind her cheek before she spoke again.

"Do you know how much this is taking out of her?"

He gave her a quick glance, but her stare only seemed to harden.

"It can't be easy," he said. "I suppose."

"Has she told you what to expect when you go in?"

"Not in so many words."

"Do you know what a coma is, or looks like, then?"

He had to meet her glare for a few moments at least.

"I think I get it," he said, evenly. "Thank you."

"Do you? I wonder. Do you have any idea of the good that people like Immaculata have done? And what's being said about them these days?"

Her eyes still bored into him, but he saw they had begun to moisten. She began to blink.

"I have no quarrel with that," he said. "None in the wide world."

Malone's arrival drew her glance over. She didn't return his perfunctory nod but turned her gaze back on Minogue instead. He saw something pass across her eyes then – frustration or anger, he couldn't be sure – before she turned away and yanked down the handle of the door to the room where Immaculata had gone.

Minogue waited for it to close completely, before catching Malone's eye and nodding toward the doorway to Albertina's room.

Minogue took a breath, and let it out slowly while he watched Malone take up his spot by the door. Then he stepped to the door and pulled down the handle. Just beyond the threshold, he paused and then came to a stop, and he took in the figure rising slowly from the chair.

"I'm afraid you have the wrong room," said Twomey.

Minogue quickly took in details: the Garda tie tight to Twomey's collar, an association badge pinned high on the lapel. The hair had faded to yellowy-white, but like in the snapshot, it had been brushed back with every strand in line. The eyes had taken on a more distant look of age.

He stepped into the room, and let the door hiss closed behind.

Sister Albertina did not look as frail or as wasted as he had expected. She looked like she was sleeping, or even napping. Her lightly furrowed forehead reminded Minogue for a moment of his own childrens' faces when they murmured through some troubling dream. The bedspread was a riot of bright, primary colours, and it made her skin look sallow. Her arms were to her sides, and he was somehow sure that they had been arranged like that only recently, along with the evened-out collars on her nightdress. Her nails were indeed manicured. Around one arm was a belt with wires, and nearer her wrist, a hospital-style plastic band with a label. On her other arm was a wide strap with rows of beads in pattern.

"No, Sergeant," he said. "This is the right room."

Twomey took Minogue's card down from where he had tilted it toward the window to read it.

"I know that name from somewhere," he said.

"So maybe you'll know why I'm here then."

Twomey's frown deepened.

"This is no place for you," he said. "You're intruding here."

There were flowers on the windowsill, and more on the bed-side table. There had to be two dozen or more photos round the room. No television.

"What are you looking at? I said you have no business being in here."

Minogue met his stare.

"I say that I have. And I say you know why too."

Twomey nodded toward the door.

"Did she put you up to this?"

"Let's talk."

Twomey shook his head.

"Some operator that woman. You haven't a clue, so you haven't. Not a clue."

"A clue about what?"

"You need to draw a line in the sand with that one. I learned that a long time ago. But I'd say it's too late for you to do that. You'll cop on eventually, I dare say. But for now, you need to get out of here. Right away."

Minogue cocked an eye at him.

"It's your sister I came to talk with," he said. "Or to listen to, I should say. Stay and listen if you like, though. I've heard you're very close, the two of you."

Twomey's eyes widened.

"You're a Guard," he said. "So start behaving like one."

"How would that be? You could give me advice in that regard maybe?"

"You're breaking the law. You're committing a trespass here. You're causing a disturbance. And you're going to be up on discreditable conduct before the day is out."

Minogue slid out his mobile and held it up.

"Go ahead," he said. "Phone me in. Meanwhile I'll get on with my work. I need Sister Albertina to verify those details for me here today."

"Verify details? Are you completely mental?"

Twomey brushed by him on his way to the door.

"Unless of course you'll do the decent thing here yourself," Minogue called out.

Twomey turned to face him, blinking as though shielding his eyes in a wind.

"Listen, whoever you are, whatever you are. This person here, my sister, is in a coma. Do you get that? A *coma*. Now get out."

"I didn't figure you for a runner, Sergeant."

"Nobody's running, and don't 'Sergeant' me, you. You don't even know me. Look at you, with your suit, and your business card rigamarole, and your little attaché case. You might have been a Garda once in your life, but by God you're no Garda now."

Minogue began to read the spines of the books arranged on the windowsill. *To School Through the Fields* had a bookmark halfway through.

"So your sister is in a coma," he said. "But she can read."

"I read to her," Twomey snapped.

"And she understands you?"

"It doesn't matter whether she does or not. You never give up."

"You're a wise man. It seems to have paid off."

"What paid off?"

Minogue settled a rueful stare on him.

"I don't actually believe in miracles myself. But things like this...?"

"Miracles? Wait – now I see it. Is she outside?"

"Is who outside?"

"You know who."

Minogue waited, said nothing.

"So that's the way with you," Twomey said then. "That tells me she's hereabouts somewhere. Tell me then, was she was raving on to you about some miracle too?"

"You mean Sister Immaculata, I take it, your sister's best friend."

"Best friend? Never. She's not in her right mind, that one. Never was, either."

Minogue took out the three snapshots that he had chosen, and he arranged them carefully along the foot of the bed. Then he stood back and eyed Twomey.

"Was she in her right mind back then, would you say?"

Twomey couldn't help himself. He picked one up, turned it toward the window.

"Where did you get these?"

"You remember that day, do you?"

Twomey put the photograph back down on the bed.

"None of this is any of your goddamned business."

Minogue flinched.

"The language," he said. "Aren't you, you know, concerned that she'll hear you?"

"Are you trying to be funny or something? Get the hell out of here this instant. Out."

"Why do you pray with her here every day if she can't understand you, or she can't even hear you?"

Twomey's voice came from low in his throat.

"She can't pray in words," he said. "But God hears her anyway."

"So you do believe in miracles then."

Twomey didn't speak for several moments.

"Miracles are one thing," he said. "Medicine's another. This is faith, plain and simple."

"Sister Immaculata phoned you last night with the news, didn't she?"

"She's worse than I thought."

"But still you came here, didn't you?"

"I'm here most every day. Not that I care for you or anyone else to know that. Especially that mad bitch outside."

"You're not concerned that she'll tell Immaculata what you called her?"

Twomey gave him a withering look. He shook his head, and looked away.

"I've heard enough of this," he said. "More than enough. You've been hoodwinked, and you don't even know it. Me, I was on to that Immaculata one from day one. Yes, even back then, before anyone was talking about things like that. You don't have to be a genius."

"On to what?"

"Figure it out yourself. I'll leave it at 'crush.' Just remember it was one-sided. Bertie did not feel the same way about her."

Minogue struggled to keep his look neutral.

"Never married yourself, did you, Sergeant?"

Instead of a reply, Twomey gave him a sullen smile. Shaking his head then, he looked away.

"Kind of ironic though, you have to admit," said Minogue. "You and your sister are so close, but she's still so afraid of you, that she won't say a word to you."

"You need a spell in a mental home, just like she does. A long spell."

Minogue's thoughts came in a clear, quiet voice: *This is it. It could go either way.*

"You know, and I know, that your sister doesn't suffer for no reason," he said.

Twomey's arm shot up. Behind the finger pointed steadily into his face, Minogue caught a glimpse of a younger man's vigour.

"Not another word," Twomey said. "Or I won't be responsible for what happens."

Five steps separated them, Minogue guessed. He made sure his back foot was firmly planted, and ready.

"But you know I'm right," he went on. "You said it yourself:

God listens to her. God hears her prayers. She can talk to God for you, can't she. On your behalf."

Twomey slowly lowered his arm, and his eyes slid out of focus.

"And you need that," Minogue went on. "That's why you talk to her. Why you confide. Because you know she'll intercede for you. God knows her suffering, her faith. All the good that she has done. If that's not believing a miracle, nothing is."

Twomey let out a long, measured breath through his nostrils. Minogue strained for any sound from the hallway outside.

"So who will she tell, your sister, after what she's been hearing from you here?"

"Be on your way, Guard."

"Inspector. It's on the card."

"I don't care what you call yourself. And you're no doctor either, no neurologist. I know what I'm talking about. I've read the reports."

"Some people would call it a miracle. I've read about things like this happening. Haven't you? People waking up, and then talking, and—"

"—Nothing happened!"

Twomey's words had come out in a hoarse, rushed whisper.

"Nothing *will* happen. It's *irreversible*. That's reality."

"But your faith says different. And what's more, I think that you know why this has happened too, don't you? You know it's not just 'medicine' or 'science.'"

"She's made you as cracked as she is," Twomey said.

"My question stands. Who would your sister tell about what you've talked to her about over the years here? All those evenings when you are finished reading, or you're tired of reading, and all you want is to have a chat with your own sister, your family? Who do you think she'd tell?"

Minogue saw no reaction beyond a slight narrowing of the eyes.

"Not you, she wouldn't," Minogue added. "And you know that. You know why too."

"You're only digging yourself in deeper," Twomey said.

"This'll earn you a lot more than a disciplinary review, I tell you. You won't know what hit you."

"How many times have you tried to explain yourself to her, to justify to her, what you've done? A hundred times? A thousand?"

"Justify what?"

"Everything, is what. All the way back to why you got her sent over the far side of the world. Your own sister. Your own flesh and blood."

"That's one thing you have right."

A tone of satisfaction crept into Twomey's voice.

"She isn't just some 'sister' in an order of nuns. She's my sister – a real, actual sister. And I'm her guardian what's more. Guardian, as in Garda Síochána, 'Guardians of the Peace.' Have you forgotten what that means?"

"Her guardian, is it? Is that why you took her out to the Larkins that day?"

Minogue let the pause linger.

"You're the one brought them together," he said finally. "You're the one responsible for what happened. And that's why you need to come here, and to talk to her. And to keep on telling her, to try to explain things."

Twomey's eyes found the window.

"You want something that she can't give," Minogue went on. "Something you can only hope she'll get for you. Because if anyone deserves to be listened to, it's her."

Twomey inspected the books along the windowsill.

"You want what everyone else wants eventually. Understanding. To be able to roll back the clock, to undo things. To explain you did everything for the right reasons."

Twomey began to rub his thumbs and forefingers together. Minogue felt prickling at the back of his neck.

"You're a man of faith," he went on. "You always knew your duty, and you did it. You say there are no miracles here, but a miracle is what you've been looking for."

Twomey reached for the door handle, and let his hand rest there. After a quick, baffled glance toward the window, he pulled hard at the door. It swung easily, hissing.

For a few moments, Minogue believed that Twomey would have a go at Malone. He watched Twomey's fingers twitching faster, Malone's slow pivot and his empty stare fixed on Twomey from across the hallway.

"I'm here to listen to you," Minogue said. "To hear your side. The truth."

Twomey's face had turned slack. He looked around the room.

"You always knew the right thing to do," Minogue said. "I think you still do."

Chapter 36

Twomey was staring at the photo nearest the window. It was one that Minogue had been drawn to right away, of a uniformed and much younger Twomey and his sister standing to either side of a small woman by a farm gate, their arms around her shoulder.

Minogue placed his pencil on the notebook, and he flexed his fingers. He had been trying to stop his eye drifting over to Albertina, to see the faint rising and falling of the bedspread.

"Mam, we called her," Twomey said. "If you're wondering."

The old woman had the same sharp eye of the younger Fergal Twomey. It wouldn't have surprised Minogue to see her face looking back at him from the first photographs of a shawled woman of the roads, her creel of turf heavy on her shoulder, her short-stemmed dudeen pipe clenched defiantly between her gums.

"She never went beyond the Primary. Nor did many of them, back in the wilds of Bruff. But she knew right from wrong. And she led a better life than the likes of him I can tell you, with all his holy orders and his years of theology and God-knows-what. A far better life entirely."

He let the snapshot he had been holding back onto the bed, and he turned to Minogue,

"Murphy I'm talking about," he said. "That excuse for a man. How he ever got to the priesthood, I'll never know. Never. Nobody will, I suppose."

He took another quick look aslant at the snapshot.

"He never even wanted to be a priest, I found out. Or so he said to me, and him bawling his eyes out in a chair not two feet from me. Thinking I'd feel sorry for him. I thought I knew human nature, I tell you, but I learned things that day."

"You didn't know any of this at the time, did you?"

"Do you think I would have let it happen if I did?"

He began massaging his chin and neck, slowly and thoughtfully.

"Bertie was home on leave," he went on. "She phoned me. She wanted me to come along that day, to the island there. Something about this saint. What would I know about saints? I thought she was just looking for a chaperone sort of, to keep things right. Or showing me off a bit, her brother, the new sergeant. But I often wondered later on, if some part of her was trying to stop the whole thing. At any rate I went along. I'm her brother after all, amn't I?"

"Maybe they were in love."

Twomey kept up his slow stroking of his Adam's apple.

"I see you're not disagreeing," Minogue said then.

"Tell me, what else did she tell you, and we'll compare."

"That after your sister was sent away, Murphy was sent out on the missions."

"Nobody is 'sent' on the missions. It's not a punishment. It's a calling. You think that the monks who left Ireland were being punished? Not a bit of it. An honour is what it is."

"Murphy went voluntarily then, is that what you're telling me?"

"No. He was persuaded."

"What does 'persuaded' mean?"

Twomey resumed his slow massage of his neck.

"Well who did this 'persuading' then?"

"His brother-in-law is who. Justice Larkin. He'd had enough of him."

"And why did he do that? Why would he be the one, I mean?"

Twomey patted smooth a small fold in the bedspread.

"So she kept things back," he said. "The most important things. I wondered about that."

"You've lost me. You're saying that it was Justice Larkin that got Murphy sent away?"

Twomey didn't reply right away.

"Now I see it," he murmured then. "If I don't tell you, then she will, herself. It's like she's given me a job. Like a child she'd pick to keep the blackboards clean."

"You ran Dalkey station for a long time. And you knew Sallynoggin too, up the road. Didn't you help out with the football clubs there? You'd have known plenty of people."

"It was my job to."

"So you knew Father Murphy too?"

Twomey took a long slow breath.

"I knew *of* him. I knew he was Peggy Larkin's brother. That he was new, and young. That he did youth club stuff, and the choir. That he was The Second Coming entirely, the cool priest, the one who'd get through to the young. They were already dropping off then. This is when things were going haywire over in the States, remember. Did you ever hear of a place back then called the Dandelion Market?"

"I did, yes."

"That's where you went if you wanted to pretend you were a hippie, or a drop-out, or whatever they called themselves. The young lad found his way there. Like a homing pigeon."

"Padraig."

"Yes. That was bad enough, but along came his uncle, the trendy new priest, the one who was so good with the youth. The one who hung out with the young people."

He paused and eyed Minogue.

"Can you guess where this is going to end up?"

Minogue shook his head.

"Come on now. You know a lot more than you let on. Give it a try, go on."

"Some out-of-the-way place some day, or one evening."

"See? I knew it. Now where might such a place be?"

"An old church, the ruin at Killiney. Over there near the coast road."

Twomey's face turned solemn. He seemed to be examining his sister's face.

"Not bad," he said. "Not bad at all."

"What happened there?"

"You're trying to let on you don't know already. Don't bother."

"I know that you took your duty seriously," Minogue said. "That's clear to me."

"My duty. There's a word you don't hear much these days." The irony in Twomey's voice had crossed into scorn.

"It wasn't just the law though," Minogue added. "You thought about more than laws, I'm thinking. More than the drugs or vandalism. More at the root of things—"

"—Sacrilege. Desecrate. They're the words you're looking for. But you don't even know that."

"Something far more important," Minogue went on. "Their souls, you were thinking about. Their immortal souls."

Twomey stared at him with narrow, glittering eyes.

"Wrong, Guard. You're wrong on that score. I was concerned for one only, the boy's. The other one? No. That one was already gone. Long gone."

"Gone."

"That's right – gone. You don't get it, do you?"

Twomey sat forward in the chair. Minogue watched his hands for signs he was going to push off from it.

"You're right," he replied. "I probably don't."

"You're not the only one. Nobody does anymore in this country. You think that all that's happened is bad luck or something? No. It was something else at work. And I knew right away what it was when I got into that room with Murphy. I knew it instinctively. I felt it in every fibre of my being. I was in the presence of something there, and I have never had one iota of doubt about it since. You know what it was?"

"I'm not sure."

"You're not sure. Are you not now."

The disdain was a glaze over Twomey's eyes. "You should be in politics, the way the words roll out of you. What

I'm talking about is nothing less than evil. Pure, unadulterated evil."

With that, he settled back in the chair. Minogue let the quiet last.

"Aren't you going to write that down?" Twomey asked finally. "What I said?"

"Later."

Something close to a smile came to Twomey's face then.

"For the history books at least," he said. "Right? Along with all the rest of it. Honesty. Responsibility. Sin. Even the church itself, it looks like. And people themselves too of course, Irish people. They're already gone. We don't have people here any more. We just have what everyone else has. Shoppers. Complainers. Liars. Thieves. Anything goes, these days."

Minogue shifted in his chair. Twomey closed his eyes and rubbed at them. His nostrils contracted and flared several times, and then he opened his eyes again.

"'Long gone,' you said. About Father Murphy."

"I knew right away. He tried everything on me that day, when I got to him. Lying came as natural to him as drawing a breath. He says to me, all he wanted to see was what the young people were going through with their experimenting. 'The drug experience,' he called it. It'd make him a better priest. He'd reach them better. That's the way his mind worked. And he kept piling it on. What would this do to the family if this came out? It'd be destroyed. People like the Larkins were the heart and soul of the parish. Charities, sodality members. Legion of Mary, Knights of Columbanus – you name it, they did it. On he went. 'What'd happen to Justice Larkin, all the good he does for the law?' He knew Tony had earned our respect, of course."

"The Guards' respect?"

"Who else? We steered cases to his court for many a year. Any decent state solicitor knew the job would get done right when Tony Larkin sat."

"You had met the Larkins, then, socialized with them."

"I wouldn't call it socializing. It was other things."

"Were you in The Knights?"

"I was. And I still am."

Minogue studied the beadwork on the band around Albertina's wrist.

"I thought I knew human nature," said Twomey then. "And of course, there was the respect bred into us for the clergy. But here was no end to how low he was willing to go to save his skin. He tried to put the blame on the young lad. His own nephew, I thought, a fifteen-year-old boy. Telling me that the young lad must be hallucinating, or he was having a breakdown."

"Because of the drugs?"

"Right. But then I put the other business to him, what the boy had told me. And I have to say, when I first heard it, I had my doubts. To me, that was impossible, just impossible. I couldn't conceive of something like that. But then, the moment I heard Murphy telling it was the boy who started it, that even his parents knew there was something wrong with him, that's when I knew. And that's when I walloped him – right then and there. My hand just flew out by itself."

Minogue drew a circle around 15. When he looked up again, he saw that Twomey had been eyeing his notes.

"How long after was this?" he asked him. "After that day out on Dalkey Island, I mean."

"It was three days. Yes, three days later I got that phone call from Tony Larkin. I was covered in paint, I remember. I had just bought a house out in Rathfarnham, and I was doing it up. Four minutes after ten o'clock that night, by the clock in the kitchen."

"Concerning Padraig? The incident with the neighbours?"

Twomey nodded slowly, twice.

"This little girl's parents had found out, and over they'd marched to the Larkins. They were out for blood. I don't know what the Justice told them exactly, but when I got there, he was very shook. He could barely talk."

"Padraig had a sister. Where was she?"

"She was at boarding school. She only found out later, years later actually."

"So you spoke to Padraig."

Twomey pursed his lips and studied the back of his hand.

"I did. I took him with me awhile. And I asked him what had gone on."

"And what did he tell you?"

"Oh he tried to wiggle around, all right. That it wasn't as bad as they were making it out to be. That it wasn't molesting – he had just wanted to look, he said. I told him it was serious, and that there were consequences. So then he tried to tell me it was drugs that made him do it, that he couldn't make his mind stop. But then, when he saw that I wasn't buying that, he starts telling me he couldn't help himself, because Murphy had gotten control of him, of his mind, or something. So that's when he told me what had gone on out at that old churchyard. 'A Black Mass' he called it. It was no such thing, but he'd been reading about the old Hellfire Club in the mountains. He was always interested in that stuff, I was told, the books, the history."

"There was more though, wasn't there?"

Twomey looked over at him.

"Just like his uncle," he said. "The same bad seed, turning everything bad. Getting inside something just to destroy it. Like a cancer. Tearing people down. Trying to tear God down too eventually."

"And Sister Albertina…?"

"Yes," said Twomey. "He told me about that then too. About Murphy and her."

"And did you believe him?"

"He said he'd seen them. But no, I didn't believe him. I didn't want to. But that's human nature, isn't it. It was only later on when I got Murphy talking, that I knew. That's when I had to believe that it really had happened between them, that so-called priest and her I had to face up to then, I just had to…"

His voice trailed off. He crossed his arms and studied the pattern on the bedspread.

"So yes," he murmured after several moments. "You're right. It was me who had brought my sister over to the Larkins' house in the first place. And it was me who introduced her to that family. Me who brought her, who delivered her, to Murphy."

Minogue resisted an impulse to ask another question.

"I remember thinking how considerate the Larkins were," Twomey went on. "I had let it slip one evening at a meeting that Bertie was home on leave. Nothing would do them then but to invite us around for a cup of tea. That's the kind of people they were. So they must have asked Murphy over as a sort of a balancing out, maybe. I knew that he was Peggy Larkin's brother, of course, but I had never met him in person by then. They were proud of him, of course. And why wouldn't they be? They had no inkling either. That's how it goes, I learned. That's how it goes."

"How did all this end up?"

A bewildered intensity had taken over Twomey's face.

"Don't you know all that already?"

"How would you describe it?"

"That family was shattered. That's the proper word. Tony Larkin? Dead by sixty-two. And poor Peggy? Ended up one of those behind-the-curtains drinkers. She blamed herself a lot, 'til her dying day actually."

"I meant how did it end up back at the time. From that time you found out."

"This is how: the Larkins got what they needed that day. That's what happened."

"And what was that?"

Minogue waited while Twomey seemed to weigh what he wanted to say.

"I knew that Tony worried about that boy. He knew the boy was a bit odd. There was no shame in him asking me to do what needed to be done. He knew that he himself couldn't do it, not to his own son. He trusted me to know the right thing."

"A favour, you're talking about. Are you?"

Twomey gave him a sudden, sharp glance.

"There was no 'favour.' I went to the neighbours, is what I did. They were nice people. They were upset, they wanted things done. But eventually I was able to calm them down. They knew me, or they knew of me at least. There was trust then. I explained to them what was at stake. The damage that could be done. So, after a long chat, they left the matter in my hands."

"This was before you went to see Father Murphy?"

"Nearly twelve o'clock at night? No, I went back to the house. I thought about the situation, about everything, and I prayed for guidance. There was no sleep that night, I can tell you, not a wink. But when the morning came, my mind was clear. First thing the next morning I went down to Sallynoggin parish church. It was right at the end of Mass. And in the door I go, and I say a prayer. Then I go around to the sacristy. He's there. And when he saw me, and sure enough, he folded."

"'Folded' in what way?"

"He bawled his eyes out, like the coward that he was. A great act, entirely. But he picked the wrong one to try and cod."

Minogue imagined a room, Twomey sitting in front to Murphy, staring at him.

"Nothing to the tears that the Larkin family cried," Twomey went on. "I told Murphy I knew about the session at the old church too. What he did with the young lad."

He paused and he eyed Minogue.

"That was when he tried the routine I was telling you about. All somebody else's doing, somebody else's fault."

"And did he say the same thing about Sister Albertina?"

Twomey stared at him. Slowly then, he raised his arm and made a circle with his forefinger and thumb. Looking through it at Minogue, he parted them slightly.

"That's how close I came. He got off easy, with the clout I gave him. It was only the grace of God held me back from worse."

He released the circle, but kept up his forefinger and slowly wagged it.

"I told him about the young lad molesting the girl, and that he was responsible for that too. I wanted him to know what he had done to that family, to his own people."

Minogue let his eyes roam toward Sister Albertina again.

"And even after all that," he resumed. "I can see in his eyes the hatred he has, the contempt. I mean, what am I to him? Nobody. I'm just a Guard – a gom. I don't have the seven years in the seminary, and all the finer points of things. And what's a mere nun to him either? Nothing. I can see he's thinking to himself there'll be a discreet little chat between the bishop and the

Commissioner. So I know what has to be done. And the man to do it is Tony Larkin."

Twomey let his forearms rest loosely on his lap.

"The rest doesn't matter. I just knew they'd come up with something. They had to. I told them that there was no way on God's earth that that man was going to stay in that parish, or any parish in this country. He could leave the priesthood, he could go to Tierra del Fuego, he could even throw himself under the train – I didn't care. I had gone out on a limb for Tony Larkin, and I wanted the ball coming back to my side now."

"Did you know he was sent on the missions?"

"I didn't, not at the time. But when I found out, I didn't care. And God as my judge, I don't care if he died roaring out there either."

The readout on the monitor flickered from one number to the next and back every now and then. Heart rate, pulse. Strong as an ox, Immaculata had said.

"But it wasn't over, that day, was it?" Minogue said. "You had to break the news to your sister, didn't you?"

Twomey's dull stare had come to rest on the foot of the bed. Minogue tried to make out anything clear from the muffled sounds in the hallway outside.

"My sister always liked to sing," said Twomey then. "And she had a good voice too. And that was the draw that evening, going out to the Larkins. It was the night of the Eurovision. They had a new telly, a colour telly, one of the first. That's what brought Murphy over too, and a few others. And when Dana took it, well the place went wild. It was Ireland's big day at last."

"'All Kinds of Everything.'"

Twomey scratched at his neck, and sat back more in his chair.

"She never had an easy mind after him. Betrayed, she was. I tried to explain it to her, but what good was that, coming from me? But I wasn't her baby brother anymore. No. I was the one who came to her with that news. From then on, things weren't good between us. She'd see me, or she'd get a letter, and it'd bring her back to that time. So I lost my sister because of that."

Minogue looked around the room again.

"But look," he said. "This is your doing here, isn't it? You're looking after her."

Twomey stared at him for several moments. Then, as though to discard some thought, he shrugged, and he looked away.

"So, you and Padraig Larkin," Minogue said. "You had dealings with Padraig, right?"

Focused and grave, Twomey's eyes had returned to lock onto Minogue's.

"I gave him a hiding, I told you, at the request of his father. He couldn't do it himself."

"I'm not talking about back then. I'm talking about now, or six months ago."

"If that's the answer, what was the question?"

"What do you know about the death of Padraig Brian Larkin?"

"Well, well, well," said Twomey, his face clouded in thought. "So full of yourself."

"What do you know of the death of John Joseph McCarthy?"

Twomey clasped his hands together.

"I'm not complaining," he said. "I've had my time."

"What do you mean by that?"

Twomey gave him a slow, sidelong glance, and then he leaned sideways in his chair. Minogue's back began to tingle.

"What are you doing," he said, rising. "What have you got there?"

Twomey hesitated and opened his hand to reveal a knit nylon strap.

"'We know not the day nor the hour,'" he said, with a faint smile. "You think I wasn't expecting you?"

From the corner of his eye, Minogue saw the door opening. Had he been shouting? Malone slid, more than stepped, into the room. Minogue saw now that Twomey was holding the straps of a bag, a worn-looking sports bag. Swimming, he thought, in the freezing sea out by the Forty Foot along with all the other fitness lunatics just like Pierce Condon has remembered him?

Twomey gave Minogue an almost kindly look. He shook but didn't flinch when Malone grabbed his arm, and his eyes did not leave Minogue's.

"He's the other one?" he asked.

"The other one of what?"

"Save your guff for someone who'll be taken in by it. You think I don't know what's going on?"

"Well tell me then," Minogue said. "Tell me what you know, or think you know. And we'll see, won't we?"

Twomey tossed his head, and Minogue heard a quiet snort.

"You and your 'miracle,'" said. "You have no idea. Not one of you."

Malone swung the bag across to Minogue. Twomey let himself back in the chair again.

The zipper slid back easily, and a scent of laundry detergent rose from within. Two well-thumbed books lay on top of a folded shirt. Wrapped in a plastic bag, a pair of shoes, polished. Shaving gear. A small pouch, 'My Rosary' from Knock shrine.

"Have you found what you were looking for?"

A trace of a smile remained on Twomey's face, but the eyes were cold and dull.

"What am I looking for? And where were you planning to go here?"

"Where do you think I was going?"

Minogue had no answer for him.

"I was right. You're no different from the rest of them these days."

Minogue pulled out one of the books. Thomas à Kempis *Imitation of Christ*. His own father had had one. He had found it after the funeral.

"Read it," Twomey said. "You're the kind that needs to."

Minogue gave him a slow, empty stare.

"If I do," he murmured. "Will I turn out like you?"

Chapter 37

Kilmartin had given up trying to guess what Malone had meant in his email yesterday. Minogue had been copied the same message, of course: yes, Malone would make it to the monthly meeting of Club Mad in Ryan's, the get-together for staff from the Murder Squad. The email also said that Malone might have 'some news for youse.'

Kilmartin had another hobby-horse to gallop on tonight, the court appearance and charges against Sergeant (Rtd.) Fergal Twomey. He took a sip of his whiskey, leaned back against the bar and repeated Minogue's words back to him.

"'She wouldn't stop talking afterwards.' Nuns talk – that's news to you?"

Minogue looked in his wallet for another twenty.

"This was different," he said. "This was about when they were starting out."

"Herself and the other nun, in Africa?"

"Albertina, that's right. They did everything. An orphanage, teacher training, getting a farm up and running even."

"My, my," Kilmartin said, with a trace of a sneer. "How the mighty have fallen."

"Who's the mighty?"

"You. I thought you were the antichrist entirely. At least you used to be. But now listen to you. Next thing we know, you'll be back in the pews again."

Minogue knew it wasn't worth arguing. Kilmartin would

find some way to needle him over this. He took the top off his pint with a half-delicate slurp.

"Look," Kilmartin said. "What I want to know is this. Forget for a minute whether she's gone a bit senile. Do you actually believe that she had no clue – no clue in the wide world – this would all lead back to you-know-who, to Twomey. Right to her best pal's brother?"

"I didn't ask her that."

"Are you ever going to?"

Minogue shook his head. Thwarting Kilmartin still gave him a kick.

"Some copper you are. You told me earlier that you figured she was always holding back something. Is it maybe because she played for the other team. Was that it?"

"Gay, you mean. A lesbian."

"Am I deaf? Why not buy a megaphone? She was holding *something* back though."

"She was. She was worried that somebody at Disciples had killed Padraig Larkin, that maybe an alibi wouldn't hold up."

"Doesn't she know right from wrong? I thought that was job one for the clergy."

"She was conflicted."

Kilmartin scratched the back of his neck, and gave a dry chuckle.

"'Conflicted.' Oh, I love it. You mean 'cracked' – okay: senile maybe. But still."

"But still what?"

"But still she went along with that low-down scheme of yours. 'The big lie' as I call it now. She set Twomey up for you, didn't she? The miracle talk?"

"No lies. There was suggestion at work there."

"Get serious, Matt. Dirty work is what it was! No need to feel bad about it. It was the lesser evil, and all that. It's the real world we have to live in after all."

Minogue wasn't going to let this one go.

"Immaculata didn't lie, and I didn't ask her to. She wouldn't have done it."

"What are you getting excited over? Don't get me wrong –
I'm only saying well done, bucko. Me, I'd have had a hard time
imagining the likes of Twomey still existed today in Ireland. As
bad as a Redemptorist in Lent, with the hell fire pouring down
from the pulpit. But fair play. You played him. You found his
weak spot, and you went straight for it and you dug in – and you
played her nicely too, after she sandbagged you. So me, I would-
n't lie awake worrying about it."

"I'm not."

Kilmartin studied the countertop, and then slowly rubbed at
it with his thumb.

"That said, you did use his faith on him. His beliefs."

Minogue should have known there was something rankling
with Kilmartin over it.

"But you got what you wanted," Kilmartin added quickly.
"Your own little miracle. Too bad you don't believe in them."

Liam laid out the change carefully in front of Kilmartin, and
he stood back.

"No bail-outs?" Kilmartin barked. "Loyal, long-suffering
customers like us?"

"Your rewards await you in the hereafter, gentlemen. Like
the rest of us."

With that, Liam lifted an evening paper and held it out. The
huge front-page photo was the archbishop in front of a nest of
microphones. He looked fit to vomit.

Kilmartin made a face, and he looked away. Liam moved
down the bar, wiping the counter and resettling beer mats.

"Twomey must have known what youse were doing from
earlier on though," he said then. "The crack team landing there
in his old haunt in Dalkey Station?"

"How would he know?"

Kilmartin's response was an arched eyebrow, and a rub of
his thumb down his nostril. "Go away out of that," he said. "You
take naiveté to a new height."

"How long is Twomey retired from the Guards?"

"There's that naiveté right there. A Guard never stops being
a Guard. You know that. There's always a connection, always a

foot in the door. Wait and you'll see, we'll find out sooner or later that he was getting the low-down from somebody about what you were doing."

He watched Kilmartin roll his whiskey around the bottom of his glass.

"Yes, Twomey knew something was up. And when that nun of yours phoned him the night before...? That put the tin hat on the situation for him, I reckon. Don't you think?"

"You're right about everything."

"Oh the circus is in town again," Kilmartin said, with the chill grin that Minogue had known for twenty and more years. "My point was, the psychology of the man. The way his mind worked. I have a word for it, are you ready?"

"Starts with an F?"

"I want my money back. No – it's that he had a mediaeval mind. You get that, the mediaeval bit?"

"Middle aged?"

"Don't make a fool of yourself. I'm saying that Twomey's a relic of another age. So knowing that, I believe that there's a man who actually wanted to get caught."

Minogue gave his friend the look of a farmer promised fine weather.

"If he did, it wasn't by the likes of me, I'm thinking."

Kilmartin screwed up his face. He spoke slowly then, as though to a child.

"What the hell does that mean? Could you be any more, I don't know – *cryptic*?"

Minogue remembered the long minutes in the lounge with Twomey sitting between him and Malone, waiting for the squad car from Donnybrook. Stealing glances at Twomey every now and then, he began to wonder if somehow the man's years had begun to show in his face. A Sergeant had shown up in the squad car along with the Garda driving, and it was to him that Twomey made the request to make a final visit to Albertina's room. Minogue watched from the doorway. Twomey didn't look at him as he made his way back with the Sergeant to the foyer, and to the waiting squad car.

"I don't understand people like him. That's all I can say."
Kilmartin recoiled in disbelief.

"And you're the one talked with him, interviewed him?"

"There's some part of him that nobody can reach. Not even his family."

"What, are you telling me that he just ignored you?"

"When it suited him, yes. I'd ask him to clarify something in his statement, to flesh it out a bit because we weren't clear on it. Nothing. Or he'd just say, 'read the statement.'"

"Seventy-something years old, but he went and did McCarthy. Talk about tough...!"

Minogue grasped his pint again.

"Not my idea of tough," he said.

"And he's not even trying any self-defence angle?"

Minogue shook his head. Kilmartin sighed.

"Well, whatever McCarthy said to him, it must have gotten his goat."

"That happens to be one of the few things he'd talk about. It was more than talk."

"Now you tell me. So? And?"

"He said McCarthy was out to get him. That he wanted a row. That he had a go at him."

"That day they met, you mean, or right from the start?"

"Both. McCarthy had a big chip on his shoulder, and it went back a long time. 'His mind was twisted.'"

Kilmartin scowled in mock confusion.

"Whose mind was the twisted one again?"

"You asked me what he said, and I'm telling you. 'He was out to destroy people.'"

"'People'? People like Twomey, and that sister of his, you mean? Just a wild guess now."

Minogue hesitated. Telling Kilmartin some of the words that he remembered from Twomey would only add fuel to the fire here: jackals, hyenas, parasites, perverts, agents of darkness.

"It was more than that," he said instead. "It was about tearing people down, ruining their lives. Destroying the good they'd done."

"'People'? What people?"

"The clergy, missionaries. I remember him saying 'desecrate.'"

"'Desecrate'? When's the last time you heard that word used? Desecrate what?"

"He didn't elaborate."

"And you didn't put him to the wall over it??"

Minogue evaded Kilmartin's challenging stare, and he counted to five.

"He saw McCarthy tearing down the legal system too," he said then. "The Guards, the judges. The courts. Society even, maybe."

Kilmartin whinnied softly and shook his head in pleased disbelief.

"Some speech, it sounds like. But do you think it was for real?"

Minogue remembered the sudden, raptor stares from Twomey. He nodded.

"I can sort of see it," said Kilmartin, the familiar cynical edge back in his voice. "Who better for slinging mud than a journo, right? Even a makey-uppey 'reporter' like McCarthy. Was he so addled that he woke up one fine day and said to himself, 'I'm a journalist now!'– along with soaking up all the usual 'social justice' whinge, of course."

Minogue shrugged. He felt an obscure urge to defend McCarthy.

"He'd been to Disciples before," he said. "He had talked to some of the regulars too. How much, it's hard to say. He was trying to do a piece on the drop-in for that newspaper. But it went nowhere. He didn't realize that one of the people using the place was Padraig Larkin, the same Padraig Larkin he'd played with when they were kids."

"But wasn't Larkin's family well-got, and McCarthy's ne'er do wells?"

"'Ne'er do wells'?"

Kilmartin waved away Minogue's rhetorical slap.

"Spare me the speeches here," he said. "I see what's on your mind. I'm only pointing out the obvious. One family's poor, the other one's rich. Is that better?"

"The parish helped the McCarthys a bit. They gave odd jobs to McCarthy's father. They got McCarthy's mother a bit of house-keeping work at the Larkins' house too."

Kilmartin had turned thoughtful.

"The Larkins sort of took young McCarthy under their wing a bit?"

"That's it, yes. But it was only for one summer though. They lost track of one another, after that. When McCarthy real-ized that it was Padraig Larkin who was murdered, he glommed on to it, and started digging up some stuff from the past."

A glint came to Kilmartin's eye.

"'Obsessed' is the word, pal. Like, aren't you forgetting something here?"

Minogue's answer was a frown.

"Come on. McCarthy was a junkie. What, you don't like to hear it said out loud?"

Minogue gave him a steady glare.

"*Extortion*. So Twomey didn't say it, but it doesn't mean McCarthy didn't *try* it."

Minogue turned to stare at the television.

"It's all there under your nose – McCarthy's work issues, getting the sack, going after Twomey. The aggression, the wild talk. Thinking he could run the frigging world. The mad ideas, and the delusions, trying to connect some of them poor divils out there at that drop-in place to it the big kerfuffle about the priests, and the abuse—"

"Are they delusions?"

Kilmartin waited for him to turn from the television, but before he could say something, the door opened. It wasn't Malone.

Kilmartin heaved a long sigh, his one of weary acceptance that he would always be misunderstood. His face slackened, and a thoughtful expression came over it. He looked reflectively at his glass.

"'Spin it and they'll buy it,'" he said. "Isn't that the way nowadays?"

"Spin what?"

Kilmartin gave him a quick, pitying smile.

"McCarthy wanted his big story, any big story. His Watergate moment. Right?"

Minogue elected a blank look for his response. Kilmartin gathered himself.

"Well you wouldn't want to be superstitious, would you?"

"Meaning what?"

"That there's got to be some kind of *mí-ádh*, some curse, on that family? Don't tell me you haven't thought about it. Human nature, man."

Minogue's reflexive decision to keep from Kilmartin parts of what Twomey had said in the interviews had proven itself to be sound. He'd never hear an end to it if he had let slip about Twomey's terse comments about 'evil.' By times, it had been like a bizarre soliloquy from the childhood catechism that Minogue thought he had long forgotten.

A florid-faced man with wet, baggy eyes made his way unsteadily by them. Minogue thought of Seán Brophy. So far, he had been able to avoid actually meeting him. The telephone conversations had been bad enough.

Kilmartin grimaced as he made several efforts to pluck something off his lips. When he had finished, he gave Minogue a knowing glance.

"I say Twomey knew his number was up, with you coming after him. You think?"

"I doubt it."

"Oh come on now. You would have gotten to him eventually, nailed him."

Minogue turned his glass on the counter. Liam tacked by, eyed their progress.

"The word is," Kilmartin said then. "No first-degree charge. Did I hear right?"

"You did."

"And you're okay with that?"

"Why ask me? Let the DPP worry about it. Or the Press Office."

Kilmartin climbed off his stool and reached into his pocket.

"Well bucko," he said. "This might be one of those rare occasions when I actually agree with you. So mark it down – I'm leaning your way on this. I know it's going to go mad, how it looks, a Guard, even a retired one, killing a tramp. Okay, okay 'homeless unfortunate.' But whatever about Larkin, this McCarthy was no saint. That's my point. And that word extortion is going to turn up, you can be sure. Forget any crusading journalist pain-in-the-arse stuff. Really."

He glanced over from his task of building up stacks of coins.

"Do you think Twomey went out that day to kill someone? Either time, I mean?"

"Well he told me that he didn't."

"'He told me' – and you believe him?"

"How would I know? He didn't budge on it. Make what you like of it."

"It was the same thing that put him over the top both times? 'Desecrating' was it?"

There wasn't much point hedging. Kilmartin would make something up anyway.

"More or less. They were very close, him and his sister."

Kilmartin reacted as though struck.

"Christ, there's the most sideways answer that's come out of you yet."

"It's all you're getting. It's all I've got."

Minogue began to study the nicks in edges of the countertop.

"All right, all right," Kilmartin said. "But I've got to say, Christ, this is too much, too much entirely. What century is this again? This is like some feud you'd read about in Sicily, or someplace. It's like this bloody country never changed a bit in the past while – what am I talking about, the past *hundred* years. Are you with me on that, at least?"

"Good for you. I hadn't seen the link – Sicily is an island too, am I right?"

Kilmartin groaned softly and he turned away, and drew out his mobile.

"Always the dig with you. Always the dig. And the dodge, of course."

Minogue had already decided to say no more on the topic. He raised his glass, gave Kilmartin the eye. The Guinness had a tart edge to it.

"All right," he said. "Enough of your fine mind there, before you go too deep for us all. Look, I have the maps up. I'll show you the route. They just call it 'the Camino.'"

"No."

"What do you mean 'no'?"

"No I don't want to know about some pilgrimage thing."

"It's not 'a pilgrimage.' It's a walk. You told me you were interested in doing it."

"Well I've gone off it."

"Christ, but you're fickle. Well I started my training the night before last. Five mile I did. I'm as a stiff as a board yet. I'll never be completely ready for it, but I don't care. I think I can do it, blisters and all."

"The blisters only add to it. A bit of good old Irish Catholic suffering."

"God, you're sour tonight. Too close to the subject of religion for you?"

Minogue checked his watch again. It wasn't like Malone to be late.

"The nuns got to you," Kilmartin goaded. "That must be it."

Minogue sized up the smirk. He doubted that he'd ever tell Kilmartin about the rest of his afternoon with Immaculata. They had driven back to her place in Merrion for a change into her 'civvies.' She emerged in wellies and an old coat, the farmer's daughter she had been so long ago, he thought, more than ready then for rain and gusts that would be scouring Dalkey Island.

It had taken them an hour and a half to raise a local who'd bring them over. He charged accordingly, and he had made them sign an indemnity that he then read aloud to them. Immaculata had been as limber getting in and out of the boat, and as handy too over the rocks, as he had been himself. She had said very little over there. He'd seen her lost in thought, making her way slowly over the sodden clumps of grass by the church.

Afterwards, they had had tea and a bun in Dun Laoghaire, in sight of the darkening water. She had come back into her talkativeness. She had never stopped being a countrywoman, he decided again, even an ageless country girl. Later, on the way back to the car, she had stopped to speak with a black man selling newspapers. Minogue hadn't asked her what language she had spoken, but he took away a lasting image of the astonishment that had lit up the man's face.

He took it easy going back along the coast road, and he slowed as he drove by Booterstown to catch a last glimpse of the bay. They said little in parting, but he was sure that she was about to cry. He felt unsettled, troubled even, when he got home. Later, after a mediocre pasta, he had fallen asleep in the chair reading, or trying to read, the book on the Caucasus that he'd gotten for his birthday. He had had that weird dream again before Kathleen's key in the door woke him, the one about the sea.

Kilmartin emitted a long, slow, plaintive fart.

"'Galway Bay'? Or was it 'The Mountains of Mourne'?"

Kilmartin made a wolfish smile, and raised his glass.

A couple arrived. It was not Tommy Malone and Sonia Chang. Kilmartin's eye lingered on the man's shoes, as though he was tabulating results of a test.

"I wonder," he said then, turning back to Minogue. "I wonder if we're going to hear more dirt now about the nuns, now that the priests are in the firing line."

"We did already. Magdalen laundries? Orphanages? Did you miss them?"

"Don't get het-up with me, mister. I'm an Irishman too, and I'm just as ashamed. It's other stuff I'm referring to – shacking up with priests, having a bit on the side. Yes, S-E-X. They're human, for God's sake. You think nuns are saints, or aliens or something?"

Minogue kept his eye on the mirror. Jackals, Twomey had said. Hyenas, jackals.

"There's people would like to drag them down, no doubt," he said.

Kilmartin's eyes opened wide, and he made a low, rumbling guffaw.

"Listen to you. Did I ever in all my life expect to hear you cheerleading for nuns?"

Minogue sought refuge in another sip from his stout. It was bitter enough. Immaculata had brought her own photos to the restaurant with her. She had been clearly pleased to trump his offer of copies of Twomey's photos. She didn't explain why she was declining his offer. She had carefully laid out her photos on the table between them, with an exacting order and position. He couldn't shake the feeling that this was the first time she had shown them to someone in a long time. After his question about the new building behind her and Sister Albertina, he had sensed that she didn't want questions, or even talk.

"It looks like you had one of those, ah, Damascene moments then?"

Kilmartin screened his pride in the esoteric phrase by feigning an interest in a group of office people. They had moved beyond the tipsy, to the loud-and-clumsy stage. A man slowly rose from the group, slack-faced and perspiring, to take a call on his mobile somewhere quieter. The wife, Minogue thought, as he watched him rub his forehead and hair: *where the hell are you*? He took in the tousled, thinning hair, the sideburns. He had not been able to get Garda Corcoran's face and Tom Jones' disentangled in his mind for days now. Yes, Corcoran's funeral was tomorrow, in Firhouse. Fitz had made it known again yesterday that there were two Guards whose presence anywhere near the funeral would be undesirable. To drive that home, he had even gotten Carney to deliver that message late yesterday to Minogue in a bogus happened-to-be-passing visit in Harcourt Terrace. Feelings were running high, was the expression that Carney had used. As if Minogue hadn't known already.

Nor could he purge from his thoughts the suspicion that what Kilmartin had said was true: Malone brought trouble with him, and it would only get worse. 'Some news for youse' indeed. Malone might have picked this evening to tell them that crunch time had come: for him, case review was over, dead in the water. At least in Drugs Central, he'd be around his kind and whatever happened, happened there.

Kilmartin made a display of consulting his watch.

"You're sure you told him half six here in Ryan's, this year too, as well...?"

"Where else is there?" Minogue said.

"No worries that some other posse is going to barrel in here guns blazing, looking to do the right Malone this time?"

"How is that funny? You big Mayo mullocker."

"You just don't appreciate wit. I know the hammer came down the other day."

There had been over two hundred Guards involved in Monday's raids. Minogue's contact in Serious Crimes had told him the interviews were coming up with unsettling similarities: those who admitted to even hearing about Corcoran's murder were all swearing holes in pots that the shooters were hires over from England. Someone there had decided that they couldn't wait to find out what Malone did, or didn't know. 'Someone...?' Shrugs, pretend guesses: 'Chinese.' 'The Turks.' 'The Russians.' Snow White – or one of her fecking Dwarfs, maybe.

"Oh I get it now," Kilmartin added. "He invites us here, lets us think he's going to actually apologize for all that undercover trick-acting. But really, what he's going to do is start another row in the jacks here and get us barred out of here. His idea of fun."

Minogue eyed the television again. Kilmartin leaned in, whispering.

"Or he's finally to turn himself in, admit he's been dirty for years."

Minogue refused to take his eye off the screen.

"It's getting too hot for him is why," he heard Kilmartin say. "The new crowd doesn't care, they'll do whatever they want, see? Twenty-something examples of that in Dublin this year so far. Malone sees the writing on the wall."

Minogue let his mind take him to Glencree, and the long climb up over the waterfall. A flailing wind, the stand of old oaks with their stoic, orchestral groaning.

"Ah what the hell," said Kilmartin, shifting gears back into that fake heartiness that had been his default mode. "What's your hurry home? Let Kathleen have her bit of peace and quiet."

The forest and racing clouds vanished from his mind's eye in an instant, and Minogue now saw of the paraphernalia that Kathleen took to leaving in open view. Candles, Bridget's crosses, copies of the prayers. Yes, the same Kathleen had probably mentioned their row to Maura Kilmartin. He had become a little remorseful at his rant about her wanting to turn the clock back to some Golden Age, when everything in Ireland had been pure as a mountain stream, when there were holy women everywhere and other 'Celtic' fantasies.

Stills of priests from older snapshots began appearing on the screen. Many wore glasses, he noticed, and most were smiling: avuncular, learned, charming, respected. Desecrate, he suddenly thought: couldn't it be used for what they'd done to kids?

"Jesus holy God in Heaven above. I can't believe what I'm hearing – seeing."

The terse words, more grunt than whisper, had come from Kilmartin. His eyes were locked on the screen, an angry bewilderment clouding his face. His lips barely moved when he spoke.

"How the hell could this happen? In Ireland? I don't get it. I just don't get it."

He seemed to be waiting for a remark from Minogue, some signal.

"Maybe they're right," he said then. "Just string 'em up..."

A familiar urge to mischief rushed to Minogue, a desire to prod Kilmartin back.

"String who up?" he asked.

Kilmartin's elbow was sharp.

"No jokes about this bucko," he said, between his teeth. "Ever. It's beyond—"

Malone was holding the door open. Sonia Chang's face showed the same tentative self-assurance that had always baffled Minogue. Working their way around customers toward them, Malone reached for her arm, and Minogue caught sight of the ring.